I0686078

THE
WATCHERS

THE
WATCHERS

A NOVEL

AZ ZEHAVA

Copyright © 2020 by New Earth Publishing

All rights reserved. This book or any portion thereof
may not be reproduced or used in any manner whatsoever
without the express written permission of the publisher
except for the use of brief quotations in a book review.

Printed in the United States of America

First Printing, 2020

ISBN 978-1-5136-6438-5

Behold, I shew you a mystery;
We shall not all sleep, but we shall all be [C]hanged,
In a moment, in the twinkling of an eye, at the last trump:
for the trumpet will sound...and we shall be [C]hanged.

1 CORINTHIANS 15:51-52

KJV

1

the tree

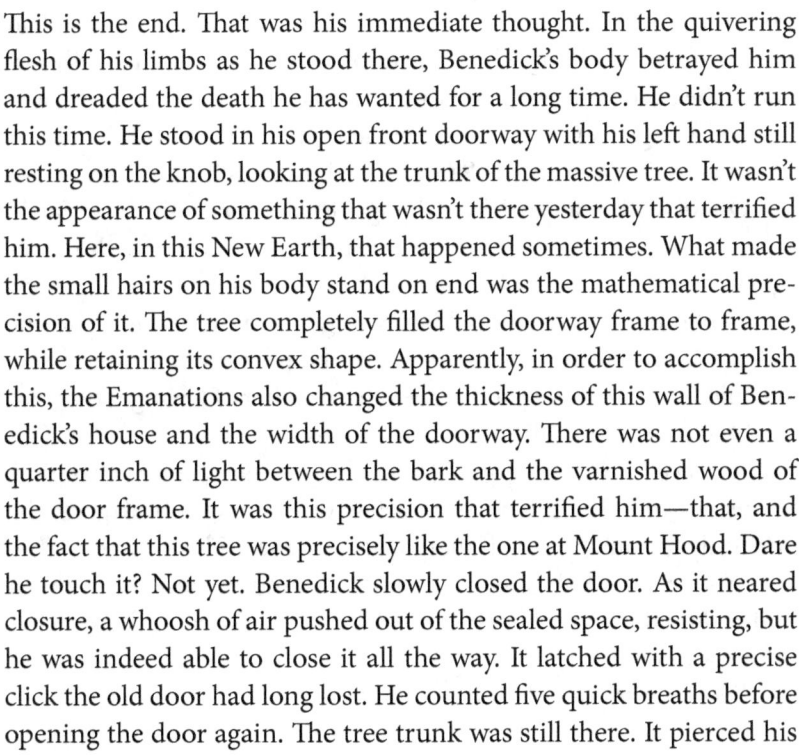

This is the end. That was his immediate thought. In the quivering flesh of his limbs as he stood there, Benedick's body betrayed him and dreaded the death he has wanted for a long time. He didn't run this time. He stood in his open front doorway with his left hand still resting on the knob, looking at the trunk of the massive tree. It wasn't the appearance of something that wasn't there yesterday that terrified him. Here, in this New Earth, that happened sometimes. What made the small hairs on his body stand on end was the mathematical precision of it. The tree completely filled the doorway frame to frame, while retaining its convex shape. Apparently, in order to accomplish this, the Emanations also changed the thickness of this wall of Benedick's house and the width of the doorway. There was not even a quarter inch of light between the bark and the varnished wood of the door frame. It was this precision that terrified him—that, and the fact that this tree was precisely like the one at Mount Hood. Dare he touch it? Not yet. Benedick slowly closed the door. As it neared closure, a whoosh of air pushed out of the sealed space, resisting, but he was indeed able to close it all the way. It latched with a precise click the old door had long lost. He counted five quick breaths before opening the door again. The tree trunk was still there. It pierced his front porch and reached to such great height that he couldn't even see the top of it from the front window. Yes. This tree was exactly like the one at Mount Hood.

He spun in a slow circle. Everything else in the front room looked the same as it did yesterday: the polished wood and upholstered furniture, the stuffed full bookshelves lining the walls, and even the volume he had been reading last night sitting next to his reading chair, exactly where he had placed it. The sun was streaming in the three East windows, creating puddles of light on the red Persian rug. He examined the windows and discovered that the wood had exactly the same scars, the windows still needed cleaning, and the latch on the second window was still broken. To calm himself, Benedick decided to look at it from outside. He hurried through the house to the back door, but stopped in the middle of the kitchen, stunned. The back door was gone.

Seamlessly, the butter yellow painted sheetrock wall stretched from the end of the cabinetry to the window, and a painting he had never before seen hung where the door used to be. Did he really not notice the back door was gone when he made his coffee, prepared and ate half a bagel? Or had that happened only just now while he was standing in the front room? Panic buzzed through him.

Out of all the categories of Changes that occur on the New Earth, Benedick was now convinced this one belonged to the rare third category, subtitled catastrophe. Benedick scrolled through the contacts on his phone with a tremored index finger until he reached the one called WI. The woman who answered the phone wasn't impressed. She told him that there had been quite a number of Changes that day.

"Anything unusual?"

"Oh no, Sir, just mountains here, flowers there, colors changing, the usual stuff. There have been a few of the new subcategory, the ones only for one person, if that's what you mean?"

"You're sure?" He was trying not to sound impatient. He didn't understand the logic of having non-Watchers answering the Watcher Information line.

"Nothing anyone should be concerned about," she insisted.

This woman was either ignorant, or she was very cheerfully lying to him. Fee had been emailing him about a tremendous uptick in Changes worldwide—more than officially reported—and out there in Las Vegas, they were very concerned. If he thought he could reach her, he would have called her directly. But no, he must deal with the WI.

"What is it, exactly, you are reporting?"

"I don't feel qualified to say for sure," he said carefully, "but I think I'm looking at a third order Change here." He heard her intake of breath, but then she said in a politely patronizing tone, "Sometimes people think an unusual Change is a third order Change, but it's just a different sort of first order. Don't be alarmed. Are you the only one who has seen it?"

"I rather doubt it. I live on a busy street."

"It's visible outdoors, then?"

"It's a very large tree in front of my door." He paused, trying to find the words for what he sensed was true. "Tell them I was at Mt. Hood and that this tree is exactly the same, they will know what I mean."

"Yes, Sir." Her voice still carried that polite, placating tone.

"And all the doors of my house are blocked."

"You cannot leave your house?" Her throat tightened to a squeak.

"Perhaps by a window. I'm not even sure about that."

"One minute," she said, and placed him on hold. Everyone pronounced WI as "wee," but Benedick often thought it should be pronounced "why," because that is the question he had on his mind every time he has had occasion to call them. This is the first time they had no ready answer.

Benedick stood in his kitchen doorway, where he could see the stretch of wall where his back door should be, and in the other direction, down the hall and through the front room, his open front door. On the phone, the WI was playing soothing, instrumental versions of hits from the 1980s. So many things were different on what only Watchers called the "New Earth," but it was just these sorts of small things, like ridiculous hold music, that remained ever the same. It was a species of divine, dark humor.

Benedick was not a very good Watcher. He had no interest in conducting research, and only glanced at the condensed research reports sent out to all the Watchers on a weekly basis. He had retired from his University job already on the Old Earth, even before the transition, and was content to continue his retirement on the New. Of course, he was obliged to write down everything he remembered from his life prior to the transition to the New Earth, for that was a duty all Watchers shared, and that was quite enough for him. Two years ago, however, the Watcher Council approached him with a request to teach the Born, the children who were born to this world, and he agreed.

Benedick laid down the phone and put it on speaker.

It was true Benedick had felt something was coming. He had been aware that he was thinking about Bea with a sense of loss that was almost fresh, that he had felt he could not continue living as he was. He had come to the vague conclusion that retirement from teaching the Born was the change he needed. He looked at the tree trunk standing in his doorway. This was something else entirely.

Everyone who sees a Change is supposed to report it to the WI. They were infrequent enough that apparently the regular people maintained a website where one could post a selfie with a Change. Because they most often happened at night, he had heard about regular people who contribute at night or go driving every night hoping for a first order Change, but it was an aphorism that the Unity never grants a Change to the one who seeks it.

Benedick walked away from his vigil next to the phone, and sat down at the kitchen table next to his lukewarm coffee. He couldn't drink it. Indeed, he felt he might have to surrender what he had already consumed. Breathing deeply in an effort to quell the cramp in his stomach, Benedick listened to the reedy and wordless strains of *Papa Don't Preach* from the phone on the countertop, and watched the wind blow soundlessly outside.

As ignorant as Benedick was, he couldn't help but be aware that Watcher researchers who studied such things had recently decided there were now two subcategories of first order Changes. The first, and most commonly experienced type were changes in the landscape, both natural and human made. They included everything from a field becoming a forest, or a river changing its course, or a mountain pushing up or disappearing, to changes to cities and buildings in cities, both small, and not commonly, dramatic. The researchers now called these Changes "balancing," because after a number of years of study, they have concluded the purpose of these are to balance the whole of the planetary body. An Egyptian Watcher named Layla made herself quite famous by discovering that balancing Changes happened along magnetic leylines on the Earth and corresponded to changes made by humans. Some of the balancing Changes are durable, what passes for permanent on the New Earth, while others are very temporary, like applying a planetary poultice for a few days in the form of a tree here, a field of flowers there.

Benedick leaped up and walked briskly to lean over the kitchen sink as his mouth filled with saliva. No vomit came, but a headache formed in the center of his head and pushed forward to his eyebrows. He leaned on the sink supported by his elbows. He could feel the planetary spin, the friction of it against the field, and here in this house, something was off, disconsonant. The worst of the nausea passed and he drank a glass of water before returning to his chair at the kitchen table.

Although these Changes are regarded by the regular people as reflecting a nature intelligence incomprehensible and awesome in the minds of humans, a cause for celebration, Benedick had always been frightened by them. He just never got used to the idea of a world so nakedly impermanent.

And the Changes aren't always positive. Some of the durable changes can sometimes be rather unwelcome, for instance, a popular lake removing itself from the landscape. Watchers have written many, many articles about the initiation of human activity on the land that results in a balancing Change, sometimes very far away, along the same leyline. Mine something here, you might lose a lake two hundred miles away. That's where the Watchers in charge of second order changes come in. Benedick didn't know much about that.

Watchers learned about the Unity from the regular people in the same way they learned about everything new. The regular people knew all about it and the Watchers just listened and learned, without betraying they were learning. It was a strange game they all, universally, knew how to play from the beginning. Watchers have gathered that the Unity is sort of what Old Earth people called God, but its not personal, not a person that lived in the sky or anywhere separate from humans. It's everything, and everything is part of it, including humans. Its doings are called Emanations, for instance, the regular people say the Emanations make the Changes. But, the Emanations are part of the Unity, too, or so they say. Benedick preferred old time religion. He never really believed it, but he understood it, or thought he did.

He heard the woman return to the phone. "Mr. Benedick? Mr. Benedick?" He leaped across the room to answer.

"I'll need to call you back," she informed him. "Apparently...this is being sent to the Council and it might be some hours before we can advise you."

It still bothered Benedick when regular people formally addressed him as "Mr. Benedick." It sounded oddly antebellum, as if he were a relic of Southern plantation life. But these innocents knew nothing about any of that, and Benedick was the only name he had now.

"I'll wait for your call," he said.

"Ah, Mr. Benedick? I don't know how to say this, but the Watcher I spoke with doesn't want, well, he asked that you...."

"Stay inside my house."

"Yes," she said with relief.

That was Benedick's instinct from the first.

He hung up and gazed out of the back window that used to be next to the back door and tried to organize his thoughts, but couldn't. He now wished he had paid more attention to the research the various Watchers have been eagerly engaged in since they found themselves on the New Earth fifteen years ago. Benedick watched the leaves of the maples fluttering in the silently gusting breeze outside. He wanted to go outside and feel that breeze, ground himself in the world, but could not.

Benedick recalled the time that Watchers called Changes "Aberrations." How deeply shocking to them all were those very first

Changes after the transition. The Watchers would have gone mad indeed, had not the regular people taught them by example to look upon them with appreciative wonder. As their understanding grew, only the temporary Changes were called Aberrations. It was about five years ago that Watchers dropped the term entirely as being too pejorative, and developed the orders. The regular people didn't talk about different kinds of Changes. Studying and classifying them didn't interest them at all.

Benedick turned around and looked through the house at the tree. It had been over an hour since he had opened the front door and saw it. Watchers have not found any purpose attached to what they called "gratuitous" Changes. They are always ephemeral, sometimes lasting only a few minutes, definitely an hour at most. It was because gratuitous Changes were always witnessed by only one person that the woman asked Benedick if anyone else had seen it. A tree appearing for an hour for one person would be exactly that kind of Change. But no. This tree, on the front porch and visible to the entire street for over an hour, is clearly not gratuitous.

Actually, it felt quite durable. It pulsed with presence; it bent spacetime. Even in the kitchen, he felt it, another being, in his house. A tree appearing in a house is not something Benedick had ever heard of, but by itself, would not be inconsistent with a balancing Change. That's not what made the woman put Benedick on hold. What made the woman put Benedick on hold is that, whatever form they take, first order Changes of either type, or second order Changes for that matter, never interfere with any human being, *ever*. A human is not moved where he didn't want to go nor prevented from doing something she wanted to do. The world just Changed, and people continued with complete free will, even during the Change itself, continuing to drive on a Changing road, or stopping on the side of such a road. The Emanations held every molecule perfectly suspended and aligned so that anything a human decided to do during a Change would be accounted for. First order Changes were gentle, kind, and for the most part, generous. This Change took Benedick *prisoner*. Nothing like that had ever happened before, so far as he knew.

Benedick turned his eyes and looked at the unwelcome painting on the kitchen wall where his back door should be. God only knows when the Watchers would call or show up. If he were waiting for regular people, he would feel secure he would not be waiting long. Regular people are an exquisitely gentle breed. But no. He was waiting for his own kind, and they would do what they needed to do and he would be expected to bear it.

The painting looked vaguely familiar. Benedick drew closer. Maybe the Emanations painted something from his own past? It was a landscape, and it had an odd shape, much taller than wide, like a miniature door. The entire top half of the scene was nothing but heavy, architectural clouds, dark with a coming storm. The bottom third was water, with a narrow wedge of empty beach on the bottom edge. Underneath the storm clouds was a town, reflected in the water. Benedick peered more closely, for the painting was not large. This was not a town he recognized: buildings, two shadowy boats on the water's edge, the low arc of a stone bridge. He almost missed the second boat, the mast of which was on the very left edge of the frame. The bridge, in the center right of the painting seemed significant to Benedick. On the left of it, a small collection of red tiled stone buildings, and to the right of the bridge, on the right edge of the painting, a tall, pale tower, perhaps a clock tower. It looked like a university, but no university Benedick has ever known. The general feeling the painting gave him was foreboding.

He looked out the window again at the gusting trees. He could log in and pour through the WI for research relating to Changes, run searches for paintings and trees and so forth, but he didn't want to. That wasn't it, exactly. He felt, quite certainly, the answer was not to be found in the WI. The Watchers would come to that conclusion. They would have to come here.

Benedick turned and walked to the front of the house. There was a straight backed wood chair that stood next to the hall table. He and Bea had scattered such chairs around the small house to be used for extra seating when their friends came over. Benedick picked up the chair and moved it to face the front door and sat down to wait.

He felt the pulsing presence of the tree as a force acting on his body. It was almost like an insistent knock on his internal door. It disturbed him, because he felt it was a message he was not receiving, could not receive. He was a bad Watcher, indeed.

Benedick hadn't thought about Mount Hood in a long time—the groundbreaking and the strange rain that put a stop to it. He had met Vinamrata almost fifteen years ago at a coffee shop here in Portland right after the transition. Benedick was dutifully logging his memories into the WI and Vin was on his way somewhere, but in those days, there was always time to talk to another Watcher. Benedick liked him and frequently had coffee with him there. Vin told him all about the yoga and meditation studio he had had in the Old Earth, and his lifelong dream of creating a mountaintop retreat, never realized. How wonderful it would be to live in a mountaintop retreat and get paid for it!

Once Vin realized that, as a Watcher, he was trusted to "spend" as much carbon as he required, he saw this as his big opportunity to "create his own reality" and live his dream. Immediately, he stared getting pushback from other Watchers who tried to point out to him that a mountaintop retreat was unnecessarily destructive to what was now virgin forest on the North face of the mountain all the way to the Columbia. Not only that, but the center would only be accessible via a long journey by car, which was wasteful, and there didn't seem to be a demand for such a thing—these people were healthy. In that first year, however, there wasn't any process by which Watchers could resolve disputes, so Vin pressed ahead with two others who also found the idea of living in a luxury retreat inviting.

Benedick counted himself more curious than partisan, and readily accepted Vin's invitation to the groundbreaking. There arrived, however, an uninvited guest, an unwelcome messenger in the form of a 450 foot tall Doug Fir tree that appeared in the center of the clearing where the groundbreaking was to take place. It was a giant, perhaps the tallest of its kind, and one of the tallest trees on Earth, surely.

Vinamrata declared himself unimpressed and called a lunch hour. He figured it was one of those first order Changes he had heard about and expected it to be gone by the time he had finished his sandwich. The regular people were spooked from the beginning. Benedick is no sensitive, but even he could feel the pulsing presence of the tree and tried to convince Vin to at least call the WI. He refused. He joked about the superstitious locals and complained that if he called the Council, they would decide that the tree "meant something," and it would be forever before he was cleared for construction. He wanted to break ground today. He had waited his whole life for this and he wasn't going to allow a bunch of nerds in Las Vegas to muck it up for him. He was full of energy, Vin, and he was impulsive, that was part of his exuberant charm, but he was also afflicted with a surfeit of self-certainty that sometimes made him deaf to any voice outside his own head. When an hour had passed and the tree was still there, he ordered the construction crew to remove it. They refused. They tried to explain that it could be dangerous, but Vin just threw his hands up, saying, "It's a tree!" Benedick heard one of the other two Watchers say, "How hard can it be? Everything drives itself around here." When Vin climbed up onto the construction machinery himself, the regular people started running, and trusting them, Benedick ran with them. Looking back to see Vin motoring confidently toward the tree, Benedick stopped to yell one last time, across the clearing, pleading with him.

"It'll be fine!" Vin called and gave Benedick a thumbs up as the machinery lurched into the trunk of the tree.

Benedick was insensible to anything else until, ears ringing, he found himself horizontal, on his elbows, looking at clods of dirt in front of his eyes, and clods of dirt raining down all around him. As he pushed himself upright he saw Vinamrata's fist on the ground in front of him, his thumb still pointing up.

There were many pieces of those three Watchers that were never found at all. It was after this lesson in humility that Watchers got serious about studying the Changes. But Benedick wasn't engaged in any personal, vanity projects! Far from it! What was it doing here? He was still sitting in the chair, just feet from the tree but still not touching it. He reached out with his mind and was surprised when his attention was immediately seized and moved into it. Then, like a wave, his attention was back inside himself. He rode the presence of the tree, pulsing outward into the tree, and then inward into himself, back and forth for some minutes. It struck him that it were as if he and the tree were two organs in the circulatory system of a larger being—a being that would have its way.

He was interrupted by voices outside his front door. It was probably his neighbors looking at the tree. He heard the voices circle around under the three East side windows and then to the back of his house. Benedick didn't bother to move. They would figure it out. Then he heard the voices again in front of him and some bumping against the front of the house. The face of his next door neighbor, Ronald, rose up unsteadily in the front window. Ronald cupped his hands around his round eyes and long nose and peered in. When he saw Benedick sitting in the wood chair in front of him, wearing a bathrobe, he removed his hands. He knocked on the window and then yelled through it. "Are you alright, Mr. Benedick?"

Benedick rose and walked to the window.

"Yes, thank you. I am well. I have already called the WI." That he had to raise his voice to be heard through the glass irritated him.

"Oh, the Watchers are coming then? Is there any indication when they can relieve your situation?"

"God only knows." Benedick said it as an expletive, and then cringed when Ronald's face screwed up in an affectionately indulgent smile. Dotty old Watcher. "The Watchers do things in their own way," Benedick added quickly, jerking an arm towards Ronald, "I'm fine, thank you." Benedick retreated several steps.

"Let me know if you need anything, alright? We could break the window."

Benedick quickly raised his hand in a forbearing gesture, and Ronald, with the impeccable grace common to his kind, climbed down from his perch and disappeared. Relieved, Benedick went to dress himself before he returned to the wood chair.

As the sun fell and then slanted in the Western windows, orange on the pale wood floors, Benedick stirred. He had completely lost track of time. His thoughts had spun great complicated skeins of past, present, and possible futures. He had not come to any grand conclusions, but he had a settled feeling, as if he had, at least, untangled the various categories in his mind.

Benedick realized that he didn't believe in gratuitous Changes. Benedick didn't pretend to be an expert, but, even before he had spent an entire day with this tree, he had always regarded the Unity as purposeful. Changes don't happen every day. Presumably, this world sometimes goes weeks without any Change at all, anywhere. That the Unity would cause a Change of any sort to happen without purpose didn't make sense. Third order Changes are messages from the Unity to humanity, and they are exceedingly rare. In the fifteen years since they have been on the New Earth there has been only one, the tree on Mount Hood. Of course, the regular people have tall tales of third order Changes "throughout history," but those tales are nothing but false memory and can't be counted.

What if "gratuitous" Changes are, in fact, third order Changes? Each one a message, but delivered to only one person? Some so called gratuitous Changes are quite dramatic, like one would expect for a third order Change. For instance, a lonely driver on a desert road at night might be treated to the spectacle of a waterfall cascading down a wooded mountainside. The driver can get out of her car and even hike up the rocky face, but in less than an hour, it will vanish and the driver will find herself standing next to her car on the side of the road again. Without exception, no one else ever comes upon the scene before it is finished. For awhile, it was a focus of intense study to determine if people who are chosen to see these displays are special, or go on to make a special contribution, but no correlation has ever been found. But, what if our definition of "special" is too restrictive? What if the purpose of the message is to write upon the spirit of the person? Is not our spiritual evolution the most important contribution of all? If the transition to the New Earth had taught Benedick anything, it was that.

This train of thought was interrupted by bumping noises on the front of the house under the front windows. Benedick summoned his patience for the reappearance of Ronald. However, it was not Ronald's face that rose up in front of the window, but instead the face of a man he didn't recognize. The man rose effortlessly into view on a ladder that preceded him. Brown skinned and muscular, his long, straight hair in a ponytail, the visitor wore the clothes of a Watcher and carried a clipboard. He cupped his hands around his face, and upon spotting Benedick, motioned him over. He scrawled on the clipboard and then turned it around. It said: My name is Orion. We have just come from Las Vegas. Will you please check all of the windows to see if any are unlocked? Root cellar door? Basement window? Benedick looked out the window, beyond the man. Down on the ground there were four people standing around the base of the ladder. Benedick saw her immediately. She was standing apart, farthest away, gazing up at the man in front of Benedick, her cream colored wool shawl resting on her shoulders. She had the same straight posture, same lifted chin, ethereal calm. She turned her head and Benedick felt her eyes on him.

Benedick walked to his desk for a piece of paper and scrawled: The lock on the middle East window has been broken for a long time. He held it up to the window. Orion scrawled again: We think if a window is unlocked it's okay for us to come in. Benedick scrawled back: Are you sure? Orion scrawled quickly and turned the clipboard around. It said: NO.

2

transition day

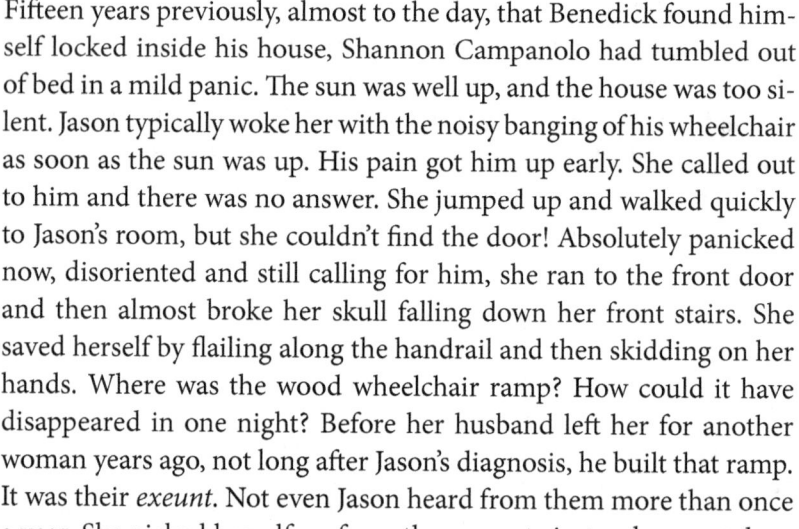

Fifteen years previously, almost to the day, that Benedick found himself locked inside his house, Shannon Campanolo had tumbled out of bed in a mild panic. The sun was well up, and the house was too silent. Jason typically woke her with the noisy banging of his wheelchair as soon as the sun was up. His pain got him up early. She called out to him and there was no answer. She jumped up and walked quickly to Jason's room, but she couldn't find the door! Absolutely panicked now, disoriented and still calling for him, she ran to the front door and then almost broke her skull falling down her front stairs. She saved herself by flailing along the handrail and then skidding on her hands. Where was the wood wheelchair ramp? How could it have disappeared in one night? Before her husband left her for another woman years ago, not long after Jason's diagnosis, he built that ramp. It was their *exeunt*. Not even Jason heard from them more than once a year. She picked herself up from the concrete just as her next door neighbor popped his head above the rose hedge, concern on his face.

"Have you seen my son?" she asked him, trying to keep her voice even.

The man cocked his head to one side. "Are you alright?" he asked, "You don't have a son. None of you have any family."

"So, you don't know anyone named Jason Campanolo?" she asked, now terrified she had lost her mind.

"Of course I know Jason Campanolo. You know very well the Campanolo Barrientos live just down the street," he pointed to the right, "Should I call the WI for you? At the very least, perhaps I'll bring a first aid kit."

She had no idea what a WI was, but she didn't want him calling anyone for her right now. "No, I'm alright."

"You're bleeding," he said.

She looked first toward her throbbing right knee. It was bleeding, but not a great deal. There was a small hole in the right knee of the light trousers she wore. That's when she noticed she was wearing someone else's clothes. She rubbed the grit out of her abraded palms, which were not bleeding, and decided that, physically, she was fine.

"No, no thank you. These are just some scrapes. I had a bad night. I'm alright." She was obliged to limp for several steps before her knee would loosen sufficiently for a normal gait. She raised her hand toward the concerned stare of her neighbor and hurried down the sidewalk, now realizing that she had flown out of bed fully dressed... including sensible shoes. Then she saw him. Her son, Jason, who had been crippled by disease, was *running* after two other kids she didn't recognize in the front yard of a house two down from her own. It was he who named her.

"Good Morning Sunrise!" he called, and then the other two kids said the same thing to her. Jason jogged over and stood expectantly in front of her. He didn't say anything, but somehow the fingers of her trembling right hand closed around two wrapped chocolates in her pocket and she handed them to him. He smiled and then ran away. Somehow she knew not to run to him crying, throw her arms around him, ask how it happened that his diseased body was well. Instead, she smiled at them and kept walking down the sidewalk on shaking legs. She was going to loop around the backside of the neighborhood and go back into her house and hyperventilate there, but when she turned the corner, instead of a residential street, there was a forest with a well beaten path through it where people were walking their dogs. There had never been a forest anywhere around here. A Home Depot and a Walmart were here, but no forest. She chose this neighborhood not because it was a particularly nice one, but because it was near the University where she worked as a secretary in the Admissions office. Not having a choice, she walked into the forest until she found a place she could pull herself together. Once out of sight, she began to feel calmer. She sat down with her head between her knees and breathed deeply.

These were the facts: her name was Sunrise, she had no family, she belonged to a group who, none of them, had family. Her son was well! Her son had no knowledge he was her son; he belonged to another family that bore her name. And there was a forest where the markets and a lot of other things used to be. Two things convinced her she was not insane. She *felt* it, the truth of all of these things, and the name Jason gave her: Sunrise, like, Son Rise up out of his wheelchair. Her name was her dearest wish. There was purpose in this.

As soon as Sunrise was back at the house, she searched for her cellphone and found it on her bedside table, unchanged. The contact list was full of names she didn't recognize, but the one she wanted was there. She wasn't sure what she would say to Jack, but she just wanted to hear the voice of her oldest friend. Jack picked up on the first ring and didn't even say hello.

"What the hell is going on? I thought I was the only one until I saw you were calling."

"Jason is well!" she said.

"That's fabulous!"

"But he's not my son anymore!"

"Oh my God! I don't have parents, or a brother. Their names aren't even on my phone. Bruce is gone."

"We both knew that Bruce was going to be gone," she said. It felt good to joke about Bruce.

"Okay, yeah, he was way too young for me, but I mean *gone*."

"I know. There's a forest at the end of my block."

They both sat on the line in silence for several moments.

"Do you know what your name is? Have you been outside yet?"

she asked him.

"What do you mean? I just woke up."

"Go outside and talk to someone who knows you. They'll tell you what your name is."

Jack dropped his phone on the table. She heard the noise of his exit, and then, "Holy Fuck!" Shannon listened through the phone for clues, but then he yelled back at the phone, "My apartment isn't an apartment anymore! It's a row house!" She heard the door bang closed, then there was silence for ten minutes before she heard him come back in and pick up the phone.

"Diego."

"As in Rivera?"

"I guess. I did study him in Mexico for my dissertation…and I'm also something called a Watcher and, by the way, I'm wearing weird clothes. Apparently, I was wearing them in bed. I didn't notice until you called and told me to go outside. I was about to say I have to get dressed first, but then I noticed I was already dressed."

"And wearing shoes…in bed."

"Yes! This is seriously fucked up."

"Do we look the same?" There was a dreadful silence on the line before they agreed to each go to a mirror and look at themselves at the same time. Shannon went to a hall mirror hanging next to her front door, Jack to his bathroom.

"I've still got my rugged good looks," Jack said, "at least from the waist up."

Shannon's body had one foot in the unknown soils of West Africa by way of Macon, Georgia, and the other foot in Genoa, Italy, by way of Brooklyn, New York. Perhaps once it had the best of both worlds, but her third decade proved brutal. She had the same body as yesterday, including the ten pounds of winter weight she carried right on through to summer.

"I don't know why I'm so relieved that I look the same."

"Stop," Jack said, "I'm relieved to know the big hair and the big tits are still there."

She had said it to be funny, but she realized after she said it that it wasn't quite true. There was something different about her other than the odd clothes—a split tunic over a shirt and loose pants. She had grown accustomed, and then indifferent to the beaten down look she had acquired: the sloping shoulders, the disappointed jawline, the sad anxiety in the outer corner of each eye. She had just let it happen, but now, in the image of herself in this mirror, all of that was gone.

"Do you think there are still airplanes? I really need to see you."

Jack, now "Diego," agreed to find out what kind of transportation exists so he could come to Flagstaff at the first opportunity. Sunrise walked out her front door and walked around the hedge to find the neighbor still in his garden, now watering a lush bed of dahlias next to his front door. He was the same neighbor who lived there yesterday, but perhaps because he seemed so eerily *different*, she couldn't remember his name. It was a bit tricky to start up a conversation.

"The dahlias are growing strong, aren't they?" she said. The man looked up and smiled at her.

"Would you like a few stems?" After being assured that she did, he went inside the house for some clippers. Sunrise was so impatient for knowledge, the skin of her arms was tingling with agitation. His was an unusual name, she recalled, old fashioned. He had been a barber before he retired. *Cleon*, that was it. Cleon returned and cut an enormous bouquet and put it into her arms. She made a mental note: it is late summer, same as yesterday.

Thinking of the forest that replaced part of the neighborhood, she asked, "So, how many people do you suppose live in Flagstaff?"

He chuckled, "About 500 thousand, I suppose. But I would have thought that number would be the sort of thing *you* would know more exactly already."

Sunrise made another mental note: the population is about half what it was, and she should know that.

Cleon's round and friendly wife came out of the front door carrying a tray of iced tea and glasses, and the name came to Sunrise easily this time.

"Good morning, Mabel."

"Good morning, Sunrise."

After declining a glass of iced tea, Sunrise spoke in a tone she hoped was casual. "I saw the Campanolo boy playing in the front yard with his friends this morning."

"Which one?" Mabel said, "There are four of them."

"Jason, for sure, I recognized."

"The Mister was saying that you were concerned about the boy this morning," Mabel said.

"I had a dream, but I'm now sure it was nothing. He is well, Jason Campanolo?"

"Oh yes, he is well. All four of them have energy to spare. What is it do you suppose, if you don't mind me asking, that connects you and the oldest one, Jason? I've always wondered."

"What do you mean?" Sunrise modulated her voice into perfect, mild surprise.

"Well, they all know that Jason has always been your favorite. It's interesting that it doesn't bother any of the other ones, even when you slip Jason candy and none of them."

At her expression of surprise, the two laughed and Mabel added, "Don't deny it!"

They both looked at her, waiting for her to confess the solution to this mystery.

"I guess I didn't realize I was treating him differently," she stammered, "I will try to be more conscious of that in the future."

Her phone vibrated. "Excuse me," she said to them as she picked up and turned away.

"There are still planes," Jack said, "and I'll be coming in before dinner. I sent you a text with the information. That all works the same too."

"Alright, we'll catch up then. We'll have a lot to talk about…Diego."

"That's going to take some getting used to Ms.…."

"Sunrise. Can't talk any more right now."

There were about one hundred questions Sunrise wanted to ask her neighbors about Jason, and what they "remembered" about him and her, but she felt quite clearly it wouldn't be appropriate. She was also struggling with an increasing agitation that she was finally able to decipher when she turned around to see Cleon still spraying water everywhere. He was hand watering! Gallons and gallons.

"I guess we aren't worried about having enough water in Arizona this year," she fished vaguely. They were on severe rationing yesterday.

"What do you mean?" he asked, and he and Mabel looked at each other.

There is enough water here now. An abundance. Sunrise recovered quickly.

"Water is something we should all be grateful for," she said.

"That's so strange," Cleon said. He and Mabel looked at her wonderingly.

"So strange," Mabel echoed, "That's exactly what you said to us yesterday morning as you walked by."

Sunrise could only blink for several moments.

"We are strange," she stammered finally.

"I think it has something to do with your focus on the Emanations. You people think too much about them, if you ask me," Mabel said.

Once back inside her house, Sunrise began taking notes on all the new things she was learning. She couldn't possibly remember it all. She wrote, "Emanations?" on a new line, by itself. She couldn't very well ask what they were when, supposedly, she focused on them all the time. When she had written down everything, she searched the whole house. There was absolutely nothing belonging to Jason, not to mention her ex-husband. Not even one photograph. There were photos in frames of Jack and herself with people she didn't recognize, all of them wearing the weird clothes. Other "Watchers."

Then she remembered that Jack said the internet worked. She found her laptop in a desk. It was not the same, but it had the same password: It'saNewDay. It was a password she chose in a moment of despair, but it came into its own now. As soon as it booted, a screen popped up that said, "Watcher Information." The words had a red capital W, and a red capital I. Ah, the WI. They were going to call the WI. There was a phone number there and Sunrise called it.

"Good Morning, how may I help you?" a cheerful woman asked.

"I'm not sure, yet," Sunrise stammered.

The woman didn't seem fazed, "We're getting a lot of that this morning. Are you a Watcher?"

"Yes," Sunrise said uncertainly, not knowing what the consequences of that admission were.

"Name, city, and state?" the woman asked. Sunrise could hear her fingers tapping on a computer keyboard.

"Sunrise," she said. Her last name couldn't be Campanolo, so she left it at that. "Flagstaff, Arizona."

"There's a message here on our home screen that there's sunspot activity today that might affect Watchers. So, please be aware. I've made a note that you've checked in with some minor difficulty."

"Alright."

"Anything else?"

"I guess not," Sunrise said helplessly.

She clicked around on the WI, but there wasn't anything there she could see. It seemed to be a new website, but the woman on the phone had some kind of home screen and separate area that apparently carried information. Nothing else on the web made sense. There weren't any websites she was used to using. Then she typed in, "Wikipedia." It was there. Her fingers paused over the keys before typing, "Emanations." Her eyes stopped blinking. It was all there.

Hours later, when it was time to pick up Jack, she looked outside for her midnight blue car. She had learned on the internet about the blue cars—they were all the same, but came in different sizes from two to eight seat vehicles. No one owned one, they were a service you used. You kept one as long as you needed it, and if it broke down or you needed a different size, you traded it for another. They ran on something besides gas, some kind of electronic energy that ran under the roads. On main roads and highways, they connected together via magnetic knobs front and back, like the little wood train cars Jason had played with as a toddler.

Each of these houses once had had a garage and driveway, now gone. There were only a couple of these cars parked on the street, but there was no way to tell if or how she could use either of them.

According to the internet, most people used transit. She would have to learn how to use that another time. She had always biked to work, and Jason had used a special bus for school. Typically when Jack came to visit, he took a cab to her house. She looked up cab service. It still existed, and when it arrived, it was a blue car too.

On the way to the airport, the cabbie kept calling her Ms. Sunrise the whole time, as if it were completely normal. They talked about the sorts of things one talks about with cabbies, but for Sunrise, much of it was new information: weather patterns, traffic patterns, local news. On the highway, the car drove itself.

When they stopped in front of the arrivals concourse, Sunrise made the panicked realization that she had completely forgotten her purse. Or, rather, she had never found her purse in the house, and forgot to find it strange. Keys, phone…but no wallet!

"I'm so sorry," she said, her face hot, "I don't know what's wrong with me. I just realized I didn't bring my purse. I don't have anything to pay you." She desperately turned in her seat, looking around her, as if she would somehow, magically, find her forgotten purse. Tears of humiliation started in her eyes.

"You people really do live in your own world, poor Dear," the avuncular cabbie said as he unbuckled his seat belt and got out of the car. Sunrise waited nervously as he walked around the car and opened her door. He reached his hand out to her and Sunrise didn't know what to do so he slid it under her shoulder and helped her out of the car. She stood next to him, staring into his face, looking for clues as to what she needs to do next. He put a hand on each of her shoulders and looked into her eyes.

"I know how to pay attention, but I don't know anything about paying a person."

Sunrise knew she would have to think about that later. For now, the relevant information was that she didn't have to pay him. He was already walking away from her.

"Thank you, Sir, truly," she said to his back.

He looked back at her as he opened his door, "Maybe paying is something you do only with each other?"

"Are there many things we do only with each other?" she asked beseechingly.

The man laughed a genuinely hearty laugh, "Oh, yes!"

The airport was essentially the same, only nicer, like everything else. It smelled better. It was full of public art. The odor of damp, molding carpet, cleaning chemicals and diesel fuel wasn't there. It had only the faint odor of humanity common to all large, empty gathering places. The arrivals board was in the same place and she walked past it toward the concourse where he was to arrive. She couldn't sit, but stood impatiently.

The first thing she noticed about all the people walking by was how robustly healthy they all looked. Of course there were old people and children in strollers, but she didn't see walkers, wheelchairs, or obese people wheezing along. In short, everyone here seemed to enjoy a decent quality of life that kept them healthy. Also, the airport lacked that frantic energy she was used to. Everyone seemed to move with ease, whether they were hurrying or strolling, they didn't move holding fear in their bodies. They weren't afraid of being late, losing their jobs, being mistreated by their fellows, but moved gracefully, confidently, and with a friendly expression, even if walking alone. She turned her eyes to the security gate for an explanation only to discover that security looked more like hospitality. There were people in airport uniforms there, but they were checking tickets, giving directions, solving problems. No security. Sunrise let that sink in. This world is safe.

Then she saw him, tall, sandy haired, handsome Jack striding toward her about fifty yards away. It was true that Jack looked the same, but there was something else. It wasn't just the clothes he would never choose to wear. Jack loved dressing well and now he wore plain brown trousers and a neutral toned tunic with those same soft loafers she was wearing. Jack had always been tall, but he seemed taller now because of the way he held his body very upright, his shoulders squared, and as he came closer, she saw that his handsome face was not younger, but the muscles of his face were more relaxed, more smooth; he was more handsome than before. He picked her up in a hug.

"Thank God you are here!" she said.

"You look great! The uniform suits you!" he said.

"That's good because my closet is full of this stuff," she laughed.

As Jack set her down she noticed, just past Jack's left shoulder, a tall, dark skinned man wearing the clothes of a Watcher staring right at her. He looked strangely familiar, but she was sure she didn't know him. Their eyes locked and he began walking quickly toward them. When she pointed him out to Jack, he pointed out another one, a very young, willowy, platinum blonde who turned at that moment and saw them. And still another man emerged from an elevator wearing the clothes of a Watcher. In moments, there were five of them standing together in the concourse, none of them knowing what to say first.

"I'm Sunrise," she said, "and this is my best friend…Diego." They looked at each other with bemused smiles.

"Those aren't your real names, right?" the blonde asked.

"They are now, I guess," Sunrise replied, "Yours?"

"Mandrake," the dark skinned man interrupted in a deep voice thick with a French accent. "What kind of name is that?"

"Isn't a mandrake some kind of herb or root from children's books?" Diego asked.

Mandrake took out his phone and typed into it. "Ah," he said, "*Mondragore* in French. *Mondragore*," he mused, "It makes some sense."

"You're French?" the blonde asked.

"Rwandan," he said, "From Kilgare. That's where I was headed, Ms.…."

"My papers say Crystal."

"You have papers?" They all crowded next to her.

"Yeah. I woke up in my hotel and the desk clerk was calling me Ms. Crystal and when I checked out, he gave me this." She held up two sheets stapled together, a registration and hotel receipt. The only name was Crystal, no last name. "My address is right, but the name different. Oh, and I didn't have to pay for anything." The other four all nodded. "What about the date? It's the same for all of us? It's still August, but the year is 1015 instead of 2020, right?

"Whatever that means," Diego said. "Why were you in Flagstaff, if I may ask?"

"I wasn't in Flagstaff, actually. I'm a bodyworker in Boulder, and I was in Sedona for a women's healing gathering. That's where I woke up this morning, sort of. My direct flight home rerouted here." Crystal said.

"Did they give a reason for the redirection?" Sunrise asked.

"Something about technical difficulty."

"Can I ask you a personal question?" Sunrise asked, and Crystal shrugged. "Is the name Crystal significant to you?"

"Hmm," she said, wrinkling her small, pierced nose, "A lot of us in my crowd believe we are Crystal children…kind of like Indigo, you know, but one level up." The others looked at her uncomprehendingly.

"It's New Age. And I work a lot with crystals, so yeah."

"What do you mean, you *sort of* woke up in Sedona?" Diego asked her.

"Well, Sedona isn't a city anymore," she said. "My hotel and everything else that still exists was moved outside the city limits….Sedona is some kind of spiritual center now, and that's it. Everything revolves around something called the Lotus Temple there, or at least that's what my cab driver said."

"Why does that sound familiar? Lotus Temple…." Sunrise began tapping into her phone.

The other man, who had been silent, interrupted. "I didn't wake up in this world, I was *awake* when it happened, when everything changed."

Sunrise stopped tapping and looked at him, a young, muscular man, whose forebears perhaps hailed from Mexico. "What?" is all she could say.

"I was awake. Last night I was in Kansas City, and I had just witnessed the autopsy of a murder victim. I'm a crime scene investigator, I do that all the time. Completely normal night. We finish up and I leave the building around midnight. There were some other people who walked out in front of me and another guy walking out behind me, some of them I knew. As soon as I got out of the building, I was blinded by the headlights of a car coming in. I brought my hand up to my eyes, and when the car passed…." He seemed overcome with an emotion Sunrise couldn't read. She looked at Diego, who prompted him, "What?"

"The cars," he said, "they were the first thing I noticed."

"What about the cars?" Diego asked him.

"Well, you know by now. They were all blue, all the same." The others nodded. "The parking lot was tiny and there were trees everywhere. This coroner's office used to be out in an ugly area of town, you know strip malls, big box stores, run down buildings. All of that was gone. I thought I was going effing nuts, pardon my language. The people who had walked out in front of me were gone, as in completely disappeared. I look back at the guy behind me, and he doesn't skip a beat, he says, 'Are you having a problem, Mr. Orion?' Inside, I'm thinking, Mr. Who? But, somehow I knew not to…." The others started laughing. "Yeah, like not to start jumping up and down going, 'Hey, this is crazy!' I just said, 'I can't find my car,' and the dude reaches into my pocket—that's when I noticed I'm dressed like this—and he takes out my phone and helps me call the car, just like that. I don't say anything to the guy, but he says, 'Congratulations,' to me and sends me off as if I had just come from a goodbye party. I don't know what to say except goodbye, and I just get in the car and close the door."

"Orion?" Diego asked.

"It does make sense. I'm Oneida. My Indian name is Teha-luhuakanlati, which means 'he is watching the skies.' The others nod their heads.

"Yeah, so I catch my breath for a few minutes sitting there alone, but I've got to move, right? I figure the car out right away—it's still a car—but when I program my address into it, it doesn't exist. So I programed it for my street and a cross street, because I just couldn't believe it. I'm sure I don't need to tell you that everything in my neighborhood was completely different. I have no family contacts on my phone. I am, essentially, homeless. In an hour, I have a connection to Madison, Wisconsin. I have to see it for myself, that my parents are really gone."

They were all silent for a few moments.

"It's too bad there wasn't a way to ask the guy…congratulations for what? Then, at least, you would know where to go," Diego said.

"Neither of us has any family left either," Sunrise said. "The man who lives next door to me told me that Watchers don't have any family."

"What is astonishing is that the guy, right away, knew you and addressed you as a Watcher, just like that," Diego said.

"I don't know anything about any Watchers," Orion replied, "He didn't say that. But yeah, he was exactly the same guy I've known five years, but he knew me as someone else."

"Wow," Crystal said, "that's the trippiest story ever."

"Well, I guess that's one answer," Mandrake said gravely, "I won't find my family at home." Crystal laid a hand on his shoulder.

"Where were you when it happened?" Crystal asked him.

"I'm a Ph.D. student at UNLV—environmental studies," he said, "I was here in Flagstaff visiting a friend. Now the friend is gone. When I got to the airport to go back to Las Vegas, my ticket was gone. Then it gets even more strange. When I asked for a ticket to Las Vegas, the woman at the counter and the one next to her laughed like I had made an incredible joke! When I insisted they said, 'Enough of that, where do you really want to go?'"

"Las Vegas doesn't exist," Diego said.

"No, they know it, they just think it's funny and you can't get there—at least not on a plane. So, I get on my phone and realize my family is gone."

"Wait," Sunrise interrupted him, "Your friend was gone, but you woke up in his apartment?"

"Her apartment," Mandrake flushed, "Yes. She was gone, and all her things were gone."

"But there were other things there?"

"I didn't snoop!" Mandrake said, "That wouldn't be polite. I just got out of there. I ate and came to the airport. When they wouldn't let me go back to Las Vegas, I got on my phone and found only one friend I knew and he told me crazy things. I need to go home."

"Crazy bad or crazy good?" Sunrise asked.

"Both. So many people completely gone. But, no one there knows the word "genocide." There are no statues, no memorials, our history is gone. They think war is a vague conflict of some kind that happened in times past and is no more. Most incredibly, there is no more poverty. I simply must go home."

"Are you sure?" Sunrise asked, "I mean, yeah, go home and visit. But I think if you belonged at home, your name would have been... *Mondragore*, isn't it? But, it's Mandrake. No offense, but I think you're an American now. Your friend's apartment? I bet it's yours. You probably have the key to it on your key ring right now."

"What do you mean, 'belonged'?" Mandrake asked.

"I think we'd better find a place to sit down and compare notes," Diego said.

"Although we think we have just arrived, it's clear to me that this Earth knows us well," Sunrise said. "I can give you proof of it, if you like." Sunrise held up one index finger and then touched her phone. Immediately, Mandrake's phone began to ring. Instead of answering it, he turned it around so everyone could see: Sunrise was calling.

3

the ladder

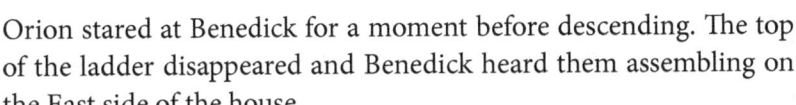

Orion stared at Benedick for a moment before descending. The top of the ladder disappeared and Benedick heard them assembling on the East side of the house.

Benedick gazed down at them. He had intended to fix that lock for a long time, but for one reason or another, had never completed the task. Some people didn't bother to lock up, but Benedick did, more out of habit than fear. What if it hadn't been unlocked?

It wasn't Orion who rose into view behind the middle window on the East side of the room, but rather a dark skinned woman with an impressive mass of long, natural hair. She turned her sympathetic eyes to him as she ascended into the slanting rays of the setting sun, which turned them amber. They regarded each other through the glass, her black curling hair blowing fitfully around her face, so that she seemed to him a rather kindly Medusa. Benedick was hardly breathing as she placed her hands on the sash. She looked behind her once before she lifted the window all the way up, paused for a moment, waiting for disaster, and when none came, she smiled.

"Good evening, Benedick," she said, "I'm Sunrise."

She accepted Benedick's hand through the window, before hoisting herself through. Immediately behind Sunrise, a very tall, slim

African man wedged himself through the opening with difficulty, his eyes meeting Benedick's apologetically when Benedick lunged to help him.

"Thank you, Sir. I am pleased to meet you. My name is Mandrake." His voice was slow and warmly resonant, the voice of a man who has been loved his whole life. Indeed, Benedick liked him immediately.

Mandrake made way for Orion, and then Fee pulled her tiny body onto the sill, and carefully turned her legs into the room. As soon as she saw Benedick, her face colored with pleasure and she reached for his hand with both of hers. In the fifteen years since he had last seen her, she had not aged at all. If anything, she looked more delicate. But for her grave carriage, and serious expression, she would look like a bubblegum popping Chinese teenager. He instantly felt the same intensely protective impulse as when he had first met her.

"Benedick, so good to see you again."

"You look more fully like yourself, if you know what I mean by that."

She laughed lightly, "I do."

"That's good, because I only sort of know what I mean," he said, smiling back at her. Although everyone called her Fee, Benedick called her Phoenix. He remained on formal terms with her, no doubt owing to the remarkable circumstances of their first meeting.

The other three were watching this exchange with something just short of amazement, which Benedick supposed was due to the fact that she touched him, and also due to the relative difference in status between himself and Phoenix. Although there were no formal differences in status amongst the Watchers, everyone present knew that Benedick was the least of them, and she the best.

It was obvious right away she was the best because for one, she was the first in Las Vegas, she was ordained, so to speak, by the gift of the shawl, and the regular people knew her as "the one with the shawl." They knew she was the best. But, most importantly, she had an interpretive skill, a connection to the Unity that was unparalleled, plus she voraciously read the database and the research maintained by the WI and understood the big picture better than anyone.

"Did you not know? It was Benedick who gave me this shawl," Fee told the other three.

Benedick ignored them. He was unaccountably joyful to see the child again.

"It was a gift from the Unity. I just found it," he said, only to her.

"But the two are linked, are they not?" she said slowly, "the gift, and the finding?" She paused, looking out the front windows of the house. "I didn't see it, even though I was there a whole half day before you arrived. Sunrise said on the way here that it was curious this strange event should happen to the least of us. In a way, Sunrise is correct that you're the least of us, but the Unity has a certain affinity for you," she looked at the tree trunk filling his doorway.

A man struggled noisily through the window carrying a large bag.

"Through the back of the house, I think," Fee said to him. "The kitchen is in the back?" she asked Benedick.

"Yes," he said, "I'll show you."

"We brought provisions since we weren't sure how long this confinement might last," she called after Benedick. The men bringing in the bags were not Watchers, and didn't seem particularly interested in anything other than making several efficient trips up and down the ladder.

"Benedick," Fee said, "Sunrise was in Las Vegas with me when your call came in. She and I meet regularly, and this time she had brought her friends, Mandrake and Orion. Apparently, they had never seen Las Vegas.."

"Actually," Mandrake said, "I used to live there, as a student at UNLV, but I hadn't been back since the transition."

"Ah. Well, I felt it significant that they arrived just as your call came, so I brought them. Sunrise is an expert on the Lost and the Misplaced, Mandrake specializes in Naturework, and Orion tracks Changes in star patterns. You haven't yet met Dougfir, who is a local tree expert. It's he you hear outside climbing the tree."

Indeed, Benedick could hear the clacking of heavy metal cleats on the other side of the wall and a thick, red rope spun into view through the window at regular intervals, distracting him.

"I've been afraid to touch it," he confessed.

"Completely understandable," Fee said, "but the neighborhood children have had no such qualms. The regular people seem to have a native instinct about these things that we lack."

"Your wife, Beatrice, was Lost, isn't that right?" Sunrise interjected. "Do you mind if I ask you about her?" Lost family members were a delicate subject amongst the Watchers. There were unsubstantiated beliefs that those not present on the NE somehow "didn't make it." It was an unspoken pejorative.

"I understand." Benedick winced, "but her name was pronounced Bay-ah-*treece,* like the French. Yes, Bea was Lost, although I had hoped for a long time that she was only Misplaced and maybe I could find her." Benedick still struggled with the sense of fresh loss that had haunted him in these last weeks before he opened the door and saw the tree.

"I'm sorry to have to ask," Sunrise said, "I'm just trying to figure out why I'm here. We spent a long time on the way here trying to figure out the connections. One thing I'm noticing right away is that chair." Sunrise pointed to Bea's chair, on the other side of the little table next to his. "That's not just a chair. It was chosen to fit one small person. It looks worn, and if you don't mind me saying so, that bright floral upholstery doesn't really match the rather academic decor of this room."

"That was Bea's," Benedick confirmed. That's how it was all over the house, two of everything, hers and his.

Sunrise and Fee stared at each other.

"Are there any other traces of her?"

"Not really," said Benedick, "unless you count her empty room, her pillow, her...indentation on her side of our bed." He smiled.

"I do count *all* of those things, actually," Sunrise said. "She had a *room?*"

"Yes, you may see it, if you like. It's entirely empty. She used it as a painting studio, it gets lovely morning sun."

Benedick led them to the room adjacent to his own bedroom. It was four bare walls and a bare wood floor, nothing else.

"So, all of her paintings, her belongings, everything, are gone except that chair, her pillow, and this room. Is that correct?"

"Well, the garden she planted is still there. She planted all the Japanese maples out back, a nature garden. Oh, and her empty bedside table is still there. It doesn't have any of her things in it, but it's on her side of the bed." That was the first thing Benedick saw on First Day, the bare surface of Bea's bedside table, all the orange plastic pill bottles gone.

"This is extraordinary," Sunrise said. "I'm not sure how to explain it to you in less than several hours." She and Fee glanced at each other again. "For instance, my son is one of the Misplaced. He was a child at the time of the transition and he showed up First Day as one of the neighbor's sons. His room and all of his things were entirely gone. I didn't even have one photograph of him. I haven't seen a *single* case of a Lost person leaving any trace whatsoever in this world. If a Lost person had a room, the room either vanished entirely, or it became someone else's room. That's why it was so common for apartment complexes to become row houses. Apartments belonging to the Lost just disappeared. And you have a chair, for crying out loud, and her own pillow. It's disturbing, to be honest."

"We've solved the mystery of why you're here," Fee said drily.

"Are you saying she's not Lost?" Benedick asked.

"No," Fee interjected.

"That's what's so perplexing," Sunrise said.

Fee shuddered and her pale complexion became white.

"What is it?" Orion, Sunrise and Mandrake made a quick circle around her, but they didn't touch her. Everyone knew that Fee didn't like to be touched.

"I don't know yet," she replied, "something came over me for a moment, but it's gone now."

"Came over you?" Benedick asked.

Fee sighed and her eyes became unfocused. "A passing shadow. A resistance. It touched me for just a moment."

"But this Earth doesn't have shadows," Sunrise said.

"As you say, disturbing," Fee replied, "but I'm fine now."

Their eyes landed on Bea's chair. Benedick was standing next to it, one hand resting on the back.

"Something I've always wondered," Benedick asked Fee, "about how the regular people always say that we are loners. The kids...."

"That stupid song...." Sunrise rolled her eyes.

The children of the New Earth had a teasing song they sang to any child who said they wanted to become a Watcher, the gist of which is that Watchers chose their careers because they were never chosen by mates.

"Am I the only Watcher who was married in the OE?" he asked.

"So far as I know," Sunrise said, "but I can't say for sure."

"I don't know of any other Watcher who had been married." Fee said.

"Perhaps because it was our destiny to become Watchers, we formed few connections," Mandrake said.

"I don't believe in destiny," Orion said.

"Interesting theory," Fee said, "if you conceive of destiny as a choice previously made."

"Previous to this life or an unconscious choice previous to the transition?" Mandrake asked.

"Either is possible," Fee said, turning her misting eyes to gaze out the front windows. She wasn't herself, Benedick thought. In her every missive to him over the years, every call, he was always surprised by the juxtaposition of her youth and calm authority. She seemed always to know the answer, or how it could be found. Benedick anxiously watched her until Fee turned back to them, her calm detachment restored.

"Benedick didn't have children." Fee told Sunrise.

"She couldn't," Benedick said.

She filled her life with other people's children. She taught generations of children art at the Community Center in their neighborhood. She rode there on an old purple bike with a child's plastic wicker basket and artificial flowers tied to the handlebars that she wedged into the rack out front. She, who made so little money, would have loved this world much more than he. Why not her?

They heard the noise of someone coming up the ladder. Benedick strode to the window and held out a hand to Dougfir, but the fit, young man who had just climbed a giant tree didn't need it.

"It's a normal, healthy *Abies douglasii* all the way up," he said.

"Commonly called Doug Fir, for short," Fee finished. "So, it's a normal tree, and there's nothing else you can tell us?"

"It's a common tree in this area. This one is quite tall. I would estimate at least 300 years old, at least it appears so. Other than the strange coincidence with my name that you remarked on when you arrived, there isn't anything unusual about it. I took photos of it all the way up and sent them to you."

"Thank you. I'll call you if we need to follow up."

After Dougfir had climbed out of the window again, Mandrake wondered aloud, "What do you think the coincidence of the name means?"

"It seems to me, that there are layers and layers of coincidence here. Most obviously, we are to understand this is very significant. I feel it's life and death."

"Foreboding. That's what I felt when I saw the painting," Benedick said.

"What painting?" Fee asked.

"It's in the kitchen," Benedick said sheepishly, leading the way.

"Why didn't you tell us there was a painting?" Sunrise huffed, "We called a tree expert, but we didn't know to bring someone who knows art!"

"Sorry, I was a bit unnerved. I wasn't thinking."

"It's alright," Fee said. "Sunrise, just take a digital image of it and send it to an expert. You brought a high res camera, didn't you?"

"It's not the same as seeing it in person, but okay. Perhaps if the painting sticks around for a couple of days we could come back with an expert, if they feel it would be helpful."

"You don't think this is durable?" Benedick asked her.

"No," Fee interjected. "We can't know for sure, but we don't think so."

"This painting appeared where my back door should be," Benedick said. The others looked out the window to see the back stairs still propped against the house. Sunrise took numerous pictures of the painting, the shutter whirring, and then photographed the back stairs through the window.

"I'll find an art expert on the WI," Fee said.

"That won't be necessary, actually, " Sunrise said, "My best friend, Diego, is an art expert. He specializes in Lost and Found art. I can send these pictures to him now with an explanation. He'll call us when he gets the message."

A kettle whistled and Benedick handed around mugs of tea until he realized he had one left over.

"What are you doing, Mandrake?" Sunrise asked. Mandrake was sitting in Benedick's wood chair in front of the tree. He had a pad of paper in his lap covered with writing.

"It was an instinct," he said. "I don't know anything about paintings, but here was something I could perhaps help with."

"How so?" Fee asked.

"Well, even though this is a Change, it's Nature. Everyone thinks of Changes as coming from the Unity, but those of us who are Natureworkers believe….No. I will say we *understand* that Changes are mediated through Nature. Everything is the Unity, the intent, if you will, is the Unity, but the execution on this planet is through Nature. The Emanations are Nature, they are two words for the same thing."

"How is that relevant here?" Fee asked.

"Instead of viewing this as a Change, and merely symbolic, I choose to view this tree as if it were durable, indeed, in this moment we know nothing else. It exists *now* as a part of Nature. Nature is just the materialist word to describe the continuous energetic creation of the illusion of materiality."

"What?" Benedick said.

"If you ask Natureworker, we would tell you that the Emanations, as we understand them, are waves of energy made of sound, or I should say, structured by sound. All of this we perceive as solid is an illusion created by the Emanations. Obviously, right? When a Change happens, something appears from nothing. The converse *must* be true, that everything that appears is, in fact, nothing."

Sunrise and Orion looked at Fee. "Continue," she said.

"What most Watchers do when they speak of this non-materialist New Earth is mere translation, like from French to English: the Unity equals God, contribution equals job, distribution equals money, Diego equals Jack. Even though the two things aren't the same in any case, it's easier to manage the transition to think of it that way. But Watchers don't have a category for the Emanations to translate to. Even though we don't *say* it anymore, Watchers still *think* of Changes in the Emanations as aberrations. Don't you see? They can't be aberrations because they are everything, both here *and* in the Old Earth. We just didn't know it. We thought of the Emanations as Nature, a material, durable, thing, because we couldn't conceive of anything else."

"And we are stupid monkeys still, I'm afraid," Benedick said.

"Less stupid now," Mandrake replied, "and the regular people are smarter than we are because their understanding of these things is complete. It's their normal. We think of them as ignorant children because of their false memories, but they understand this world in a way we Watchers do not."

"Can we please track back to the original question?" Fee asked, "How is Naturework relevant here? Aren't you people concerned only with second order Changes?"

"Well, that's just it. I think this *is* a second order Change," Mandrake said.

For the first time since Fee arrived, Benedick saw genuine surprise in her eyes.

"Explain?"

"I can see why you think this is third order, of course. It's obviously not first order because it has locked Benedick inside. That's unusual."

"To say the least," Sunrise said.

"And we think of second order Changes as those *we* have specifically asked for. But I've been treating this tree as if it were a natural phenomenon, because from my point of view, it's *all* natural phenomena...."

"Interesting perspective," Fee said.

"And," he continued, "the message I'm getting loud and clear is that this is not a purely symbolic message. This tree belongs here, or more precisely, it was *placed* here."

"Placed?" Benedick asked, "Like the regular people place a lake?"

The most famous example of a human caused second order Change was from Salt Lake City, which on the NE lacked its lake.

"Exactly like that," Mandrake said. "The false memory story of Salt Lake was that it dried up hundreds of years ago during a climate change event. After the regular people of Salt Lake cooperated with a Natureworker, a lake did manifest roughly in the same area. It isn't at all like the original Salt Lake that we Watchers remember, and when the lake reappeared, a mountain range pushed up behind it, but it worked."

"Why in the world would someone place a tree *here*?" Orion asked.

"That makes no sense," Sunrise said.

"My information is that it was not someone, but many someones," Mandrake said.

Fee seemed to be only half listening, her eyes were again gazing out the front windows, and she started when Sunrise's phone rang. Sunrise put Diego on speaker.

"I can't believe you don't recognize it," he said.

"The painting…it's famous?" Sunrise replied, "You know, not everyone had rich parents who sent us on an European tour…."

"I was an art student!" he protested. "*Anyway*, it's a *very* famous painting that has also been very *Lost*." The intake of breath in the room was audible. "But this isn't all of it. This painting represents only the middle section of the original, and it's smaller, presumably to fit into the space. The original occupied a much more significant section of museum wall space. The name of the painting is *View of Delft*, by Vermeer, a Dutch painter. It was one of the most popular paintings in the OE. Many of us in the Lost art world have wondered why this painting would be Lost, because it doesn't fit the pattern."

"What do you mean, it doesn't fit the pattern?" Benedick asked.

"Well, as you know, most of what we know from the OE is gone: books, movies and so on. It's obvious why a lot of it is gone, right? It doesn't fit in this world, it would be corrupting."

"Not just corrupting," Fee corrected him, "The conclusion is that these people would reject it pre-consciously because it wouldn't comport with their version of reality. War makes no sense to them at all, slavery is equally incomprehensible, categorical inequality wouldn't occur to them. They can't conceive of someone killing someone else for money. They have a hard time with the concept of *money*, as it is, isn't that right, Benedick?"

Benedick nodded, "The Born reject my stories of the OE as not making any sense at all. They think I'm making it up. I have to bring them along very slowly, using analogies."

"In the same way that Changes weren't possible in the OE because people didn't believe in them, OE concepts *can't* exist here because the belief systems of the NE people reject them," Fee concluded.

"This painting," Diego continued, "doesn't have any themes that are nonsensical in this world. It's just a landscape of Delft, a city which still exists pretty much the same as it ever was in the old center. There's a church steeple there on the right side of the painting, but on the NE we still have overtly religious art that still exists and is exhibited in museums. The meanings of them are Lost to the regular people. When you see them, the docent explains the spiritual meaning of them in a way consistent with their own spirituality, rather than the original. And as you know, churches still exist in many cities and are put to community uses consistent with this world....although what you might *not* know if you haven't been inside one is that the stained glass in them is Changed."

"No saints with severed body parts?" Sunrise smirked.

"Definitely not. And no murdered gods on a cross, of course, which was very shocking to the Christians amongst us."

"People do still wear crosses, though," Mandrake said.

"Yes, and the other symbols from the OE, but they do it consistent with their belief system. According to them, all of these symbols refer to the intersection between spirit and matter."

"What do they think the churches are?" Sunrise asked.

"The regular people believe that humans have been seeking communion with the Unity for thousands of years, and that other religious buildings are just inferior versions of the Lotus Temples."

"Interesting," Sunrise said, "Do we think it's significant that there's a church here, in this painting?"

"We think it's *all* significant," Fee interjected.

"Any other thoughts, Diego?" Sunrise asked him.

"There's no reason why this painting would have been Lost in the first place. There's absolutely nothing in the original that's inconsistent with this world."

"Can you venture an explanation as to why it would be Found here, in the context of this tree?" Fee asked him.

"I wish I could, but I really can't imagine. It's just a landscape. Obviously, I would begin my analysis with why the middle section and not the sides? It has to be more than just size. The entire painting could have fit here in miniature."

"Yes," Fee said, "Please continue to think about it, if you will, and let us know if you come up with anything new. This is very important."

"Will do," Diego said.

"Before we sign off," Sunrise interrupted, "you might like to know I have Orion and Mandrake here with me." The two men leaned in next to Sunrise to say hello to Diego.

"Oh my!" Diego said, "I'm jealous!" Orion and Mandrake laughed.

"Wait a minute," Fee said, "You all know each other?" There was a stern concern in her face.

The smile faded from Sunrise's face, "We were all together First Day. First Day anniversary is coming up next week, so we were all getting together. Diego was supposed to fly in this weekend. Is that a problem?"

"A problem? No. But, is it significant that on First Day you were together with people who would become experts on every topic necessary to solving *this* mystery, *this* day…."

"Except me," Orion said.

"I'm not so sure," Fee said.

"And one other, as well," he said. "There were five of us. Unaccounted for is Crystal. She's a healer for Watchers."

"It's a Chinese box," Fee said, "but I feel we don't have much time."

"I feel it too," Mandrake said, and the others nodded. The exuberance of reunion evaporated.

"I'll get right back to the observatory tonight," Orion said.

"No holiday for you, I guess," Sunrise said, "or any of us."

"And I'm here with the person I spent First Day with, as well," Fee said. She lifted her eyes to Benedick's and in them he saw no self-assured calm, no answers, only questions, and concern.

Sunrise ended the call with Diego. Fee walked back into the living room, with the others following.

"Make sure you get pictures of the tree, the door," Fee said to Sunrise.

"And that chair, if you don't mind, Benedick."

Benedick walked over to the bookshelves and pulled out a tall, glossy art book. "Bea and I loved Amsterdam. We visited the Netherlands several times." He flipped through the pages and then held the book open for them. "This is it. That's why the painting looked familiar." They all studied the photo of *View of Delft,* spread across two pages.

"All of these are scanned and uploaded on the WI, right?" Fee asked, indicating Benedick's extensive library. All Watchers came into the NE with their books intact. It was a vast store of secret knowledge shared amongst the Watchers on the WI.

"Yes, of course," he said.

"You said the painting gave you a feeling of foreboding. Anything else?"

"The bridge. It seemed significant to me. I thought it connected a town and a University, but it's just a church. I know that church, it's on the square."

"But you *thought* it was a University," Fee said, "and in the original, the tower and the entire right side of the painting is bathed in light." Almost to herself, Fee said, "In a way, the community of Watchers is like a world wide University, collecting and sharing information, is it not?"

"A bridge between us and...?" Sunrise said to no one in particular.

"May I receive copies of all the pictures?" Mandrake asked.

"I will send a copy of them to all of you," Sunrise said.

"I don't know about your schedules, but I would appreciate it if you could clear as much time as you can," Fee said. "Ordinarily, I would rely on the core group in Las Vegas, but it's clear to me that it's you assembled here who are attached to this event."

"I have to remain near the observatory, in order to contribute, but I'll send a report to you all if I see or learn of any unusual patterns," Orion said.

"Benedick, please keep in touch with us all about how it's going here. Obviously, even with the open window, I don't think it's recommended that you leave just yet."

"I think that's right," he replied. "And, one more thing?" He cleared his throat. "I know most Watchers aren't interested in the beliefs and false memories of regular people, but I did read a number of books when we first arrived. Don't they have an origin story that involves a World Tree, or somesuch? That a World Tree brought the first peoples to this Earth, and that it's supposed to return?"

"That does sound familiar, Benedick. I will look into that," Fee said.

As they all prepared to leave, Benedick willed her to leave last. He wanted to talk to her alone.

When the others had climbed out the window, she gathered her shawl in preparation for the climb down, and before he could stop himself, he reached out a hand and touched her shoulder. She turned around quickly, but her face betrayed no alarm.

"I wanted to ask you something without them here."

She watched his face.

"Is it not true that you—the best of us—and I also—the least of us, and the first two in Las Vegas...." he paused and she watched his face. "Isn't it true that we are the only Watchers that no one else remembers?"

"Why do you ask?"

"I had a feeling about it. I don't know why, but in the first year after the transition, I searched and researched other Watchers. It was curious," he wiped the side of his nose nervously, "you know, that the profiles of Watchers, the private ones only for other Watchers, don't have this information on them...who knew whom. You can't run a search for it. You can search a particular person by their Old Earth name, which Watchers knew them on the OE, but there's no aggregated information about it. You'd have to run millions of searches to figure it out."

"But you asked around, discreetly."

"Yes."

"You felt you needed to be discreet."

"Yes."

"Continue."

"I didn't find anyone *I* knew on the WI, that was easy. But, you don't even have an Old Earth name. More interestingly, I've never met anyone who had known you, or who had heard of anyone who knew you. Naturally, I couldn't talk to all of the Watchers on the planet, but enough people that it was odd." She watched his face, waiting. "Is this something that is known? It is, isn't it?"

"Yes, it's known, but only by me. No one else has thought to look into it, except you. You're correct. All of the other Watchers are remembered by one or more Watchers who knew them on the OE, except us two."

"Do you think," he started quickly, and then stopped because she was watching his face so intently, "Do you think it's possible we aren't real?"

"No one is real," she said quickly, but then seemed to regret it. "In the philosophical sense."

"I mean, we might not have existed on the Old Earth at all. Or, if we did, all of our memories—my ailing wife, your trafficking, all of it—might just be like the regular people, equally false."

"This is a thought that has occurred to me." The way she said it and the carefully curated expression on her face told him that her statement was a dramatic understatement.

"What would it mean if you and I are just created things, Aberrations?"

"In this world," she began and then stopped. "Everyone is a created thing, including the regular people, don't you think so? Are there *any* memories we can rely on? So what if Diego and Sunrise remember each other? Couldn't that memory be false? It's interesting that we two have no such memories. That's all that can be said with any certainty at this point."

"I'll just say it," Benedick said, "Maybe we are all just Aberrations put here to aid in the transition, and when we are no longer needed, we will just disappear like this tree."

She shivered, and the shiver transferred to his body. He couldn't tell if it were fear, horror, excitement, or the vibrating string of truth recognition.

"Is that all?" she asked him.

No, that wasn't all! He spread his hands.

"Try not to worry," she said.

4

las vegas

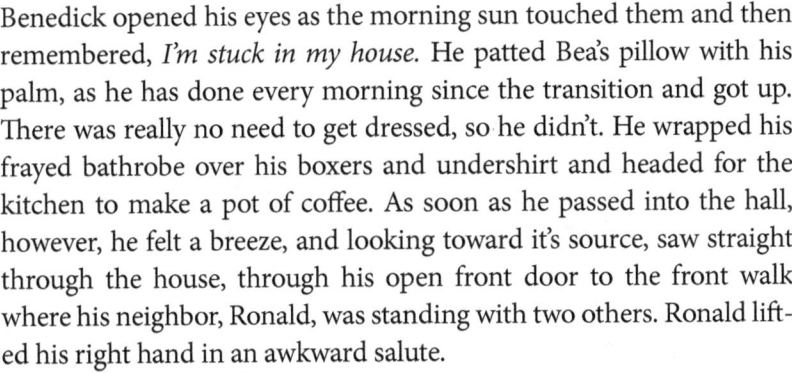

Benedick opened his eyes as the morning sun touched them and then remembered, *I'm stuck in my house.* He patted Bea's pillow with his palm, as he has done every morning since the transition and got up. There was really no need to get dressed, so he didn't. He wrapped his frayed bathrobe over his boxers and undershirt and headed for the kitchen to make a pot of coffee. As soon as he passed into the hall, however, he felt a breeze, and looking toward it's source, saw straight through the house, through his open front door to the front walk where his neighbor, Ronald, was standing with two others. Ronald lifted his right hand in an awkward salute.

"I guess it's gone," he said.

Benedick walked through the house to the front door and looked at the jamb, at the walls. It was all as it had been before the tree.

"Indeed," he said, and closed the door. He turned around and walked back down the hallway to the kitchen. No painting. The back door had returned.

Benedick picked up his cell phone to call the WI. "This is Benedick, Portland, Oregon."

"Yes?"

"Please forward a message to Fee that the tree is gone. She asked me to send this message. She'll know what it means."

"Yes, Mr. Benedick, I know. There's a pending message waiting for you and I quote: When Benedick calls to report the tree is gone, tell him to come to Las Vegas. Send to him the longitude and latitude.

"Sir, I have just sent those coordinates to you. You can program them into a car in the same place you would put an address."

"Longitude and latitude?" Benedick asked.

"That's what they said. I guess addresses don't work in nowhere." Benedick detected a bit of a smirk in her voice.

He immediately opened the back door. He half expected to see a wormhole to another universe there, but there was only the same decaying porch of wood nailed down, a pair of dusty rain galoshes, and an abandoned coffee cup on the railing half full of rainwater. He closed his eyes as the breeze shuddered the leaves of the maples and quaking aspens and the sun slanted down upon the side of his face. He opened his eyes and sat down on the stairs. Everything was as it had always been. The sun was shining upon a lovely summer day, the aspens were whispering their very own music that Bea had loved so much when she sat here next to him on the porch. She was simple like that. It was good enough for her to just sit here with him on the stairs with her coffee and listen to the trees. The sun, the breeze, the crystal memory of Bea sitting next to him should have warmed him, but he felt nothing but cold in the pit of his stomach.

A tiny bird darted into the branch tips of the tree directly in front of him, followed quickly by two others, and then ten more, peeping to one another in their tiny cipher. They gathered about the thistle feeder hanging there, alighting, and darting back into the branches in charming arcs for fifteen minutes. Then, as suddenly as they came, they departed, flying West.

Benedick returned to the kitchen, leaving the back door open and started a pot of coffee. While he waited for it, he sent a message to the school where he taught the Born that, once again, he would not be teaching today, nor likely for several days. He told them he was ill, and he didn't even feel it was a lie.

His illness was one of spirit, rather than of body. The event of the tree felt like an infection of sorts that shadowed his thoughts. He couldn't shake it. Although he was unlike other Watchers in that he was not particularly grateful to find himself on the NE, his life for the last fifteen years had not been without a certain contentment. He lived, until very recently, the life of a retired widower in the same Craftsman cottage he had shared with Bea before the transition. He drank coffee, sat in his yard, reread the books in his library, walked in his neighborhood. His only obligation, prior to the last two years had been to set down all of his memories. It was a strange life, to spend several hours a day reliving a lost world—setting down the names and details of everyone he knew, the songs he knew, the places he had been and what he had seen there—but not an altogether unpleasant one. All Watchers were obligated to do this as a check on their own memories, to cross reference each other, and also to support the contributions of researchers, many of whom studied what and who had been Lost. He was happy to help out.

Although the loss of Bea was terrible to bear, it had carried little sting because it was as if she were merely away. There had been no final illness nor accident, no foul play nor suffering, no goodbye, no funeral, no memorial. He didn't have to sift through her things and part with them. She was away, and he missed her. He never grieved for her, not even in the beginning, and never really accepted that she was truly gone. He had just gotten used to coping without her. But now, her loss felt fresh, and it caused him pain so profound he felt it in his body. He was truly, permanently alone and at the end of his life in this unfamiliar place where Bea had never existed, except in his own memory.

Sometimes, he questioned his own memory of her, because he had no one else to check it against. Was it strawberries she hated? Or raspberries? Which beach did she always go to when she was a child? He did remember how she smelled and felt in their bed. He had always fallen asleep before she did to the sound of turning pages, the light of her reading lamp in his eyes. Her nightstand used to be covered with a tower of books stacked like balancing memory stones, until they were pushed aside by pill bottles. In those days, right before the transition, he would lie awake staring at her face silhouetted by lamplight as she slept with an open book in her hands, willing strength into her. He had strong feelings attached to all of these memories, so they couldn't be false. Could they?

Most Watchers—apart from the loss of friends and family who were either Lost entirely or Misplaced and therefore no longer knew them—were overjoyed to be in the NE. There was no want, indeed, there was no money at all, for in the NE the primary value was the Unity. People lived for each other. If anyone in this world would ever try to dominate others, that person would be judged rather than admired. The natural human desire for progress and improvement was channeled to the common project of improving the lived environment for everyone, not just themselves. The implications and consequences of this value were what made the NE different in every way. No want, little serious crime, no war. Although Benedick recognized the obvious benefit of these things, from a purely personal standpoint his life was not much changed. To him and Bea, war was a rumor, a story lived in far off places, they had retired comfortably within their means, and their neighborhood was safe. He would much rather have had Bea in the OE than be without her here. But no one had asked him.

It was strawberries! He remembered now. She hated them all her life, but when she was young, her hatred of strawberries was such that he was not allowed to eat them himself. In high school, she learned that human skin renews itself every twenty-eight days, and if she caught him eating strawberries, she would not allow him to kiss her for three weeks. He had forgotten that. Benedick rushed to his computer and typed into the memory log he kept in the WI: *It was strawberries she hated.* He would come back to it later and finish the entire memory.

Since he was already at his computer, he navigated to the car service site and reserved the smallest car, and asked that it be delivered, a benefit of his age. He could have taken a train. They are fast and comfortable, he could walk from car to car, have a civilized dinner, and be there in half the time, but his desire for corporeal comfort was overwhelmed by his desire for spiritual solitude. He wanted to be utterly alone, not obliged to speak to anyone.

The other advantage of taking a car was that the trains don't go to Las Vegas; it was nowhere, a rumor, a joke. He would have to get off somewhere in Nevada and take a car from there. This was simpler. It was a beautiful summer morning, and having had enough of the inside of his house, Benedick packed a small valise, locked the door and sat down on his front porch stairs to await the car. He felt strangely happy to be going on this trip, like a child going away to summer camp. This was odd because since the transition, he had come to dislike travel. He and Bea had traveled a great deal. She had written out a bucket list when she retired and they spent many happy years traveling to Europe and Asia and South America. The thousands of photos he had taken came with him to the NE, and were uploaded to the WI. However, the photos he had taken of Bea—standing in front of things—did not survive. There was *one* the Unity overlooked, or allowed him, he knew not which. He had been taking a photo of a mountain vista and her pointing hand came into the frame from the left. That was his computer home screen, Bea's index finger in front of the Swiss Alps. Although everyone in this world had a recreational travel allowance, Benedick had never bothered to use his at all. It just wasn't the same without her.

It was pleasant sitting out front. He usually avoided the front yard because the regular people who were his neighbors were so friendly, they would insist on talking to him. He really didn't have anything to say to them. He had spent his entire career teaching history at Lewis and Clark University, which still existed even though history no longer did. He and they had no common history whatsoever, and although he had a small collection of New Earth history books on his shelves—they were separated from the rest in a vertical stack— and he had read them all right after the transition, he wasn't interested in their false version. It was a novel without dialogue and it bored him. There was nothing that he wanted to talk about that he was able to say to them or that they could even comprehend. Today, however, it was a contribution day with the ten o'clock rush hour already past and thus adults and children alike were away upon their own errands and pursuits. He must admit to himself that he did like his neighborhood better now than in the OE. This street used to be wide enough to accommodate two parked cars, and a car and a bicycle as well, passing each other between. It was a wide expanse of concrete that most often served as a vast parking lot. Impatient people crowded their too wide cars quickly and loudly down the center, and when they parked, they became angry if there were even one bending curve of nature that touched them when they abandoned their vehicle. Bea had tried to plant a nature garden out front, but the drivers parking on their street angrily broke any branch that dared touch them, and trampled everything else, so she gave up.

The street was narrow now. Most people didn't use a car and had no need to park them everywhere. His neighborhood was well served by friendly public transit of several types, and these people enjoyed walking together. The houses were also smaller after the empty rooms disappeared, and the garages and driveways were gone, as well. Thus, the houses were closer together, and more alike in size. To the extent that people did drive on these streets, the silent cars waited, and then passed each other in a careful swerving ballet. Life was more slow and the people moved more slowly. These would appreciate a nature garden, if Benedick cared to plant one.

In the beginning he used to wonder where the extra space went. Were the blocks shorter and backyards larger or the neighborhood, in its entirety, smaller? He wished he had known more of his neighbors in the old world. It would be interesting to know how many of these were here before and how many were brought in, so to speak, from outlying areas of the city that had disappeared. He never discovered the answers to any of these questions. The overall effect of these differences were that his neighborhood felt more like a village unto itself, rather than a suburb. The neighbors socialized with each other a great deal and invited him to their frequent parties. Although he didn't enjoy them himself, and rarely accepted their invitations, it made him happy that they enjoyed them. The sound of friendly laughter floating in his windows on a summer evening cheered his solitude.

A car silently picked its way along Benedick's street, slowed and parked in front of his house. He walked down to the curb as a young woman closed the door.

"Would you like a ride somewhere?" he asked her as she handed him the fob.

"No, that's alright, Mr. Benedick, I'll stay for a coffee and take transit back."

Benedick navigated South, out of town, and merged onto the Interstate. As his car came down the onramp, two cars driving parallel to him parted. A message appeared on the dashboard screen that said *Entraining,* followed by dots that blinked in sequence. When Benedick saw the message, he let go of the steering wheel and the car positioned itself between the two other cars. Once between, there was a small jolt as it electrostatically connected with the car in front of it, and a second small jolt as the car behind him engaged. *Entrainment Mode Engaged* appeared on the screen. Benedick touched the screen again to program the destination. His fingers hesitated before typing *Las Vegas.* The screen displayed a map with the preferred route to Las Vegas, and at the top it said *Las Vegas (Nowhere).* The purported destination was an exit branching off the freeway. The red line trailed down the exit and then stopped with a dot at the edge of a large, empty section of map without roads. Benedick stared at the dot, wondering how in the world he would find her. The last time he made this drive, on First Day, he did this very thing, but on that occasion he was not looking for an exact location.

There were many miles between here and a place where it would start to matter, so Benedick allowed his eyes to wander to the window. The Interstate was in the same location it was before the transition, but it was now a narrow dark ribbon of road two lanes wide, unmarred by painted lines. The road South and the road North were separated by a wide median planted thickly with trees. Only when the car was at the top of a rise could one see the road going North at all, visible over the tops of the trees. Parallel to the road to Benedick's right, a train speeded past him, and the wind of its superior velocity buffeted the side of the car as it whooshed past. Then he remembered what the WI operator had told him, that she had sent him coordinates, a longitude and latitude. He found the message and programmed the coordinates in place of the destination city. He didn't know what to expect, but he certainly didn't expect what appeared on the screen. The map disappeared and a new one took its place. This map showed the red line reaching down to Arizona, then tracking East, but instead of terminating in a red dot, a new screen appeared. The red line terminated at the freeway exit without a dot, and then a red dot appeared in the middle of the empty map area. Between the terminated line and the dot was a swirling symbol with the word, *pending*, that appeared superimposed upon it. The swirl rotated in cycles, and at the end of each cycle the word reappeared. *Pending.* As in, the computer doesn't know how the car will get from one place to the other just yet.

Benedick pushed the button that released his seat, and it glided free of the console, moving backward and swiveling to the right. He folded away the passenger seat and stretched out his legs. He had brought a book to read, but he found himself just staring at the passing landscape. He had made this drive many times with Bea, not to Las Vegas, but to San Francisco, where her best friend lived. On the Old Earth, Benedick and Bea shared a beat up, brown Mercedes. They got rid of his VW Golf commuter car when he retired from his University job. Although the Golf was more economical, Bea loved the gas guzzling Mercedes.

These NE cars ran on two kinds of energy, neither of which Benedick understood. It was the electrostatic type that kept the car glued to the invisible track under the freeway and to the other cars, which at the same time, powered the cars. Then there was another type, stored in the car, like gasoline, but it was some kind of particle, another version of the electrostatic type. The regular people claimed to have invented it, their "history" books talk about the four scientists who discovered and developed it. Of course, none of these four people ever existed, but the engineers among the regular people knew how to make it, and repair it, a feat that impressed him.

There used to be an olive place where they would stop in Northern California, and a candy shop a couple of hours prior, on their side of the Oregon border. Both were gone now. In this New Earth, the highway system was organized around the system needs of the cars, but otherwise there was nothing between one city and another,

other than regular exits, each with a rest stop and a service station, should a malfunction occur. The rest stops were all different, with different restaurants and shops, but made according to the same plan. In between these, nothing but forest and field. It was a more beautiful and functional system, but Benedick missed the sense of adventure he and Bea had when, next to an ugly strip mall, or decaying roadside town, they found a store crammed with antique knick knacks or a forty year old roadside restaurant with peeling paint they told everyone about after. Everything passes away, he thought, as he glided quickly past miles of natural landscape.

He didn't remember falling asleep, nor did he remember laying down his seat and pulling a coverlet over himself, but his sleep fuddled mind became aware that his prone body was speeding up, jolting, and then slowing down several times such that his stomach lurched. At first, he incorporated these sensations into the dream he was having. He was in Delft. The city was much more vivid in his dream than in his memory, though perhaps this was only his dream version of it. He was leaning on the stone bridge in the painting, looking out over the water, talking to someone he couldn't see. The man was talking a great deal, his mouth very near Benedick's ear. Benedick strained to hear him over the roar of the rushing water in his ears, but the man's words carried no sound at all. Water was moving very rapidly under the bridge to the horizon, with all manner of boats upon it, as somehow, the water was a large river that ran to the horizon and then dropped off into a starry void. As an aircraft carrier moved under the bridge, it knocked against it. Benedick was afraid the bridge would be broken, but his unseen companion laid a hand on his shoulder reassuringly, laughing gently. There was a tremendous vibration, and then it was a cruise ship smacking into the bridge. He felt that jolt in his body, and he became conscious he was dreaming. As he opened his eyes and remembered where he was, he tried to remember what his friend on the dream bridge had told him. He was not to worry, but he couldn't remember what it was he shouldn't worry about.

He returned his seat to an upright position and squinted at the screen as the car continued to jolt in semi-regular iterations. The map showed he was near Ashland, Oregon, where he had grown up. He had been asleep several hours. At the top of the screen, there scrolled a message, *Malfunction. Please leave highway.* Benedick touched the screen. He knew he was annoying everyone entraining with him. They were all looking at their screens and muttering, well it isn't *us*. His car was not working anymore for some reason, and the other cars were pulling him along, but the energy distribution wasn't even, so they all jolted. His car disengaged from the cars in front and behind and putted off the highway at the next exit and rolled to a stop. He waited. After about fifteen minutes, a small midnight blue towing vehicle came into view, stopped and then backed into the front of his car. Then, jolting all the way, towed him to the rest stop.

When he got out, he was assured that a new car was already on the way to him, that it would be only thirty minutes or so, and would he like some lunch perhaps? Benedick wasn't hungry, but a cup of coffee to pass the time sounded inviting. This particular rest stop had an Olde English theme, a sanitized version of it anyway, which was not a surprise given its proximity to Ashland, still famous for its many sanitized Shakespeare productions, at least those that were amenable to New Earth retrofitting. Macbeth, of course, is no more. He stood outside the rest stop, a two storey building straight out of a Dickens novel, squinting into the middle distance, trying to see the town. He hadn't been back since the transition, there wasn't anyone he knew there, but now he wished he had time to stop. He would look at the University, his old house, the theatres, see what was the same and what had Changed. It felt unreal. His former life there, his parents, Bea, a dream, in this moment only as real as the unseen companion on the bridge from whom he had just parted. No…less real than the man on the bridge, who seemed to be standing next to him still. A drift of smoke trailed into the air from a field in the town below, three hawks flew over, and then Benedick went inside.

The space was dark and heavy beams crossed the low ceiling. There was a long counter of dark wood, a large fireplace, now in August cold, and a number of small wood tables surrounded by chairs. There were about ten people sitting down. He was the only Watcher, and everyone looked at him when he walked in. A woman in seventeenth century clothing greeted him, and he opted for the counter, where another man not much younger than himself sat. It was indeed possible to get coffee here instead of ale, and Benedick gratefully curled his fingers around the mug.

The garrulous man one seat away from him was talking non-stop to the woman behind the counter, and now included Benedick in the conversation. He should get the bangers and mash, he was advised, as it was as good as one could find in London. The man was visiting Ashland, but always stopped here for a meal first. The woman was tapping on her phone.

"Here it is," she said, handing the phone to the man.

"How old were you?" he asked her.

"Twelve. This was in my back yard."

"It's beautiful," the man said, and handed the phone to Benedick, who accepted it to be polite. On the screen was a photograph of a child version of this woman taken at her own arm's length. Above her, a glowing orange flower, lotusform, supported on a delicate, green stem that must have been at least five feet tall. At the top of the webpage were the words, *UnitySelfie*. A documentation of a gratuitous Change, though the regular people didn't think of them like that. To them it was a spiritual event. Benedick handed the phone back to her.

"Lovely," he said.

"I don't have a picture of it," the old man said, "we didn't have those back then, or the web, but me, my brother, and my friend were blessed once when we were kids."

"The three of you!" she breathed excitedly.

"Yes. We were walking a path through a forest that we walked nearly every day. We were talking like little boys do, nothing at all special. But then, all of a sudden, we all stopped. We all felt it, the sense of awe. We looked around and then, on our right side, the trees disappeared, and the ground split, starting from where the path was, off to the right, it split and fell, and new trees and plants covered the ground. Flat ground became a ravine."

"As you watched!"

"Yes. We watched the whole thing. I don't have the words for it, except to say that every time we passed the ravine from that day forward, we always stopped, as if it were a temple."

Benedick couldn't help but be caught up in the man's story even though he knew it was false. The Unity made it up for him.

"This ravine still exists there?" he asked, to make conversation.

"Oh, yes. I was back in my hometown just recently and I saw my boyhood friend, Jerome. We walked through there for the first time in years. Tragically," he said, frowning, "my brother, Trayvon, died in a terrible car accident before the SafeCar was invented. He was only twenty-four."

Benedick didn't know this man's history, or whether a Watcher had confirmed that he had existed on the OE, or had a brother. But Benedick knew this much: it was impossible that this man had a brother who died forty or so years ago *here,* and impossible that anyone experienced a balancing Change fifty or sixty years ago in a world only fifteen years old. In short, it never happened.

"I'm sorry for your loss," Benedick said.

"Have you ever been blessed by the Unity?" the woman asked, gazing warmly at him. They were now intimates, the three of them.

"No," he lied. She laughed, and he could swear it was a laugh of disbelief.

She blinked slowly at him and left her eyelids just grazing her large pupils as she smiled. Why this woman would decide to flirt with a man his age mystified Benedick, but he couldn't help but be cheered by it, this flow of energy. Perhaps she was one of those who were attracted to the mystique of the Watcher. She didn't know, but suspected he held secrets and that excited her. The type was well known, among both men and women. Alas, there never had been nor ever would be a basis of relationship between a Watcher and a regular person. There was simply nothing whatever to talk about.

Benedick heard a low whistle from the doorway. His new car was ready. This one was indeed brand new and was somewhat more elegantly appointed than the older model that had broken down. He stowed the passenger seat and his valise, and settled in for the six remaining hours of travel.

As he was about to engage the car, he was startled to see the young woman in her seventeenth century dress run in front of him. He brought down the glass of his window.

"Please take this," she said, pushing a lidded ceramic coffee cup full of coffee through the window. "It's not much, but it comes from the heart. Keep the cup." Her eyes were still heavy lidded, but now they were lined with tears. "The Unity bid me do it, don't ask." It was then Benedick noticed she was wearing a small gold Unity symbol on a necklace. As she brought her palms together in front of her and then turned away, Benedick realized that what he had taken for sexual interest was instead simple connection, or perhaps love, of the general type common amongst them. The deep spirituality of the regular people mystified him, he couldn't share in it, but he respected it. He watched her walk away and disappear into the building before he left.

Once again entraining on the highway, speeding towards Sacramento where he would track East, Benedick sipped the blessed coffee and wondered what the gift meant.

He looked out of the window at the endless passing trees, delighting in the occasional view from a rise. The car passed where highway 66 should have been. Klamath Falls is no more. He remembered how in High School, he and his friends would pack into someone's father's car and go watch their football team play in the superior stadium there. One of his friends liked a girl from Klamath, and they must have burned a tanker full of gas going back and forth between those towns for him, but it never worked out. All of those little towns cut out of the forest are gone, and the forest primeval stands as if from the beginning of time. At the transition, nature was an excellent negotiator and claimed its half of the Earth. What happened to that Klamath girl and her family when the town was Lost? He had never cared to investigate such things.

As the time passed, he couldn't help but be affected by the devotion of the young woman from Ashland, her pressed palms bowing to him, and Ashland itself in the distance, a shadowy clutch of buildings visible but separate from him, like the silently gusting trees outside his window. It was a strange mood that seized him. He felt, he knew not what. Unstable, possessed by the past, concerned about the third order Change or whatever it was, nervous about returning to Las Vegas. A different thought bubbled through him every minute. He was not himself. He made an effort to read, to entertain himself, but to no avail.

Meditation was a skill he learned from the regular people after the transition. They practiced many forms of it, depending on their tradition. He didn't visit their temples, or interest himself in their beliefs, but the Watcher Council encouraged spiritual practice as a coping mechanism for Watchers. He had not meditated since the Watchers visited him, closed up in his house, but now he felt almost compelled to do so. He let his eyelids fall down his eyes so that the passing trees became a blur of unfocused green and then he let it all go. It wasn't his, it didn't belong to him. Ah, he had forgotten that.

At the end of several hours of meditation, Benedick felt calm. He was not himself still, but he was calmer and more grounded than himself, and that was good enough. The last time he made this drive in a midnight blue New Earth car was on First Day. He had awoken in his bed and discovered Bea gone and all the rest of it, and for some reason he still did not understand, he felt compelled to go to Las Vegas. It was an idea that possessed him. He was absolutely convinced he would find Bea there, and so he figured out how to get a car and he went. That drive was just like this. He was unstable, not himself.

On that day, he had programmed no coordinates. He had been to Las Vegas a number of times, though not with Bea, she hated the very idea of it. He had no idea why he thought he would find her there of all places, but he was absolutely seized by the certainty that she was there. Of course, he didn't find her there or anywhere else, but nothing could have prepared him for what he did find.

On First Day the car took the exit where the red dot blinked, which was nothing but a concrete path through the gritty, red hardpan common to the area. The car continued on the exit, where there were no buildings, no gas stations. It continued until it crossed another concrete street in the middle of a desert wasteland. Still, Benedick didn't think anything of it. It wasn't until he had driven down this second street for some time, a drive devoid of any building, any car, any human presence whatsoever that he began to feel a cramp in his stomach. He passed empty intersections, one after another. He looked at his navigation screen and saw all the streets laid out, but the map indicated no buildings. He pushed his finger across the screen to gain a bird's eye view of where he was in relation to the downtown grid and saw that he was in it, on The Strip, at least as he remembered it, for there were no street signs. He stopped the car. He looked at the screen and then at the endless vista of barren hardpan. He couldn't believe it. He left the car in the middle of the road, and started walking. The Venetian Hotel should be there, all the casinos, traffic, noise, people. There was absolutely nothing but concrete streets and wasteland. Then, he saw something that looked like a person sitting next to the road. *Bea!* Although his mind formed the thought, his heart didn't believe it. Nevertheless, he ran toward the little heap, and soon he could see that it was indeed a person, sitting very upright, perfectly still. A person who was much smaller than Bea ever was in her life. Maybe dead, maybe a mannequin, or a mirage, he couldn't say, but he needed to find out. As he approached at a cautious walk, he could see that it was a very young woman, living, and quite naked. She sat erect with her back against the left curb of the street gazing in front of her with open, unblinking eyes. He could see her long, black hair hanging smoothly brushed down her back, her profile, her bent right knee and right arm that rested on her thigh, her hands in her lap. She didn't look at him but continued to stare straight ahead. He was embarrassed by her nakedness and cleared his throat. Still she didn't look at him. She was wafer thin, anemically pale, and her breasts were flat against her fragile, birdlike chest, the overall effect of her body was a being that was both tiny and unsexed. He was relieved to see that she was sitting with her ankles crossed over her pubic bone. He cleared his throat again as he moved within view. Her unlined, double lidded, Asiatic eyes turned slowly to include him in their compass.

"Are you alright?" He spoke to her as to a child. He assumed she was mentally ill, likely malnourished and dehydrated, and he didn't want to frighten her away.

Instead of answering the question, she said, "I am Phoenix." Her childlike voice had a hoarse and strangled quality, but the words were delivered with a measured, calm authority that steadied him. She gazed at him, awaiting his response.

"I am…," he stammered.

"Your new name," she said.

"Benedick," he said. How she, sitting here alone knew anything drove all previous thoughts from his mind. One thing was for sure, he simply must provide clothing for her. He was increasingly terrified that she would stand. He was old fashioned in that he always wore a button front shirt over a singlet every day, but on this morning— what Watchers would henceforth call First Day—he had awoken wearing a tunic over his singlet. He quickly pulled the tunic over his head, but then he saw something move on the ground in the direction she had been gazing.

"What was that?"

She returned her eyes to their former direction, but she said nothing.

"There it is again. It's flapping or waving, like in a breeze."

"There is no breeze," she said.

Still holding the forgotten tunic in his hand he crossed the pavement, stepped over the curb and walked quickly toward the movement. The hardpan gave way to sand. He didn't remember Las Vegas having sand. His sand filled shoes threw up a spray of it with every stumbling step, but still he kept his eyes on the moving thing. Every purpose that crossed his mind became his singular resolve in this place. He simply must see what that moving thing was. The clothes of a dead body? Someone alive, signaling for help? He hurried towards it.

Finally, he saw a piece of neatly folded fabric lying on the sand. He looked around as far as he could see. No sign of any person or body of a person anywhere. One corner of the fabric lifted again with a small gust of breeze close to the ground that traced the sand beyond it, then disappeared. He picked it up, looked under it, and finding nothing, shook it out. It was a cream colored, rectangular, fringed shawl of fine wool, with a narrow charcoal border. It was the perfect thing to cover the young woman.

"I found this," he said to her as he held it up for her inspection, "Perhaps you can put it on." She didn't object, so Benedick carefully draped it around her shoulders, careful not to touch her. She took the edges in her hands and wrapped it tightly around her and stood. The edges of the shawl reached her knees.

"Thank you, it's perfect," she said, but then wrinkled her brow. "Look, it's stained."

Her fingers were pressed against a corner of the shawl where there was a small, round, red spot.

"We'll wash it out later," he told her. He put his own shirt back on. "I have a car here. Would you like me to take you home?"

"I slept there last night," she said, indicating the bare expanse across the street.

As Benedick struggled to formulate his next question, she continued, "Across the street was where Caesar's Palace used to stand. Had you ever been there?"

"Yes," he said. "Once I saw Tony Bennet when I was here for a conference."

"This body came here every year at this time, where it was sold to men. Had you ever bought a person's body when you were here?"

Benedick finally choked out, "No, I…it never would have occurred to me. I married very young."

"Yes, well, when this body was a child, it was taken from its home by a particular man, who photographed it and made money from it. And after it had become an adult woman, it had to continue to dress as a child. I have no idea how old it is, or what it was called."

"How came you by Phoenix? And how did you get here?"

"I woke up here, dressed just as you saw me. The memory attached to this body is that I figured out long ago how to focus my mind on nothing, to retreat from my physicality, away from this world. It was natural for me to retreat into this state when I woke here. In that state, as I was questioning my own memories of what happened, that name came to me.

"You might have died, exposed out here for much longer," he said.

"I had come to some conclusions before you arrived," she said, looking away from him, "and I would like to see what you think of them." She lifted her eyes to his face, "This world is no longer the same world we were living in."

"It is quite changed...." Benedick responded.

"You don't have to tell me now," she interrupted him. "This is the place where Las Vegas stood, but is no more." He nodded. "There is purpose in this, but I don't know what it is. Am I to assume many people are missing? Do you know?"

"Yes, many people are missing. I came here in search of my wife."

"Ah. Interesting. You have a home?"

"Yes, the same as before."

"I must have a home also, a cottage. We should look for it. The cottage will have everything I need."

At this point, obeying her was all he could do. Not having found Bea, he had no other purpose. He wanted to put his arms around this small person and protect her. He wished he could protect her, retroactively, against the horrors to which she had already been subjected. Not able to accomplish that, he felt an intense desire to care for her as if she were his own child. He resolved that nothing terrible would ever happen to her again, so long as he lived.

He drove the winding streets, as they both watched the navigation screen, panning out and then back in. After about an hour, a low building came into view.

"Ah. There," she said.

It was an adobe building sprawled on the empty expanse. It had small windows in the front, and only one door, which made it looked institutional, like an office building or a research station. It bristled with antennae and a dish. Benedick insisted on preceding her to the door, which was unlocked.

"Hello?" he called. The hallway was sparsely furnished, and a jacket hung on a hook by the door.

"It's alright," she said, "This is my home." She pushed past him and began quickly exploring the various rooms, of which there were many. "Others will be arriving, I suppose. You can stay in this room," she said pointing to the one directly off the front hall. She disappeared into another room, while he stood anxiously in the hallway, alert and listening.

"I will bathe and dress," she called to him, "do make yourself at home."

Inside, the house was enormous, and opened up to the back, where the desert could be appreciated through many large windows. Benedick thoroughly searched all the other rooms. There were thirteen furnished bedrooms in all, including the one Phoenix had occupied, two large common rooms, and a fully stocked kitchen, with cabinets and a refrigerator full of unopened food packages. Exhausted, Benedick decided to nap while she showered. He didn't wake until the next morning. It was eerily similar to the previous day in that he woke in his bed alone, fully dressed, though this time he was not wearing shoes. It took him a moment to remember that he was in the husk of Las Vegas with a woman he had just met. He stumbled into the common room to find her sitting behind a computer, typing into it, completely absorbed. She was wearing the clothes of a Watcher, which fitted her narrow body as if tailored for her, and she had the shawl draped loosely over her shoulders. She had bobbed her long hair, and had it tucked behind each ear as she leaned forward into the screen. There was a cup of coffee at her elbow. Benedick would never forget the contented pleasure in her eyes when she looked up and said, "Welcome to our New Earth."

Benedick was alerted that he was nearing his destination. He packed up his valise and the remains of the lunch he had eaten enroute. The map showed the car nearing the exit and then driving down it.

Off to Las Vegas with you! That's what someone is likely to say if you tell a tall tale and they don't believe you. You laugh at that one. *Go to Las Vegas!* An angry person might damn you there. Benedick arrived at the spot where the first map terminated in a red dot. Nowadays, the road was a dead end without a curb to mark it. It just ran into the red dirt and stopped, nothing but empty expanse ahead of it. He remembered that a Watcher once told him it was a favorite make out spot for local teens. *I ended up in effing Las Vegas…*that's what someone says when they had gotten lost.

He watched the spiral on the screen cycling. The word, *Pending* didn't come. After a few moments, a digital road stretched out in front of his avatar on the screen. Amazed, Benedick looked up and indeed, the dead end stretched into a road that led into the desert. As the car drove forward, he pinched the screen to obtain a bird's eye map of his path, and his eyes opened wide. The formerly empty desert on the car's screen was now full of streets. These were not the streets of old Las Vegas. They looked like a creature, an octopus, then a tree with roots, then a fractal, it's arms bending, reaching out, touching like synapses, then retreating. The streets were not only moving, they were *writhing*. As he moved along, the street behind him disappeared. In the review mirror, only trackless red dirt. This was no longer his journey, one of his own making. Perhaps it never was. He felt drawn forward, into the implacable eye of the place. He felt nauseous, as the streets curved into view and connected with the car, which drove itself forward, unexpectedly turning with the road that moved under it. After an hour, the car stopped. On the screen, the red dot blinked. He squinted into the sun and saw Fee, it was unmistakably her, walking toward him down the road, and he got out to meet her. Behind his car there was no road, and he could see that behind Fee and the car she drove only red, hardpan dirt. They walked toward one another on a stationary rectangle of concrete centered in an empty desert. He was still nauseous and disoriented, but this empty place struck him as familiar.

"Benedick," she said with pleasure.

"This is familiar," he said and she smiled. "Is this…where we met?"

She nodded. "Caesar's Palace, if it ever existed, was there…I think," She looked at the expanse of sand across the street. "Or near. You probably remember that when you arrived here First Day, you could find your way around the streets of old Las Vegas. It was just the buildings that were missing, everything material."

"Yes. When did it become like this?"

"The writhing has been going on for several months. It started Changing two years ago, more or less, but it's only been a couple of months that it's been like this. We've been monitoring it from above, trying to figure out if it is some kind of message."

Benedick shuddered. "No wonder you came to Portland."

"Exactly."

"In those first years after the transition," she continued, "we at the cottage agreed that Las Vegas disappeared because it was the ultimate symbol of materialism. That city was all about what men could build, the money they could hoard, and the bodies they could control and use, through one mechanism or another. It was all about what could be bought or sold; nothing was sacred. And we decided that the streets were left there as a sculpturescape, a monument, for the same reason…so we would never forget."

"But the regular people don't even remember it. For them, it means nowhere."

"Right. So, clearly it was a message for Watchers, yes? And my cottage was here, remember? With room for more?"

"But?" he asked, hearing it in her voice.

"We're getting the feeling that we don't belong here anymore. I won't bore you with the details, but we're getting the message over and over that this is coming to an end."

"And you think the tree is part of it?" he asked.

"Absolutely. It's all happening at the same time. For one thing, you probably don't know that the painting that appeared in your kitchen…."

"*View of Delft.*"

"This morning it was Found. Ordinarily that would be considered a gift. It would be reassuring. But that painting had hung for centuries at the Maurithuis Museum in The Hague, and it reappeared in the Rijks. The curator reported the Change. What that means, I can't tell you. Furthermore, I did look up the origin mythology of the regular people. There is a World Tree. It's a long story with Gods and Goddesses and grand happenings, but the point of the Tree is that it's a conduit *between worlds.*"

"As in, the Old Earth?"

She gazed at him steadily.

"You came here for me First Day," she said, "and found the shawl. I wish I could tell you that we've discovered the answer to this mystery, but alas, I cannot. I brought you here to this place in hopes that we might stimulate a response, discover a clue."

"I'll do my best," he said, looking away from her face to the waiting desert.

"So all of the Watchers you work with are here?" he asked.

"Watchers from all over the world."

"The best of us," he said, with mild surprise.

"Yes. It is popularly believed that the best of us are on the Council, but that's just an organizational body. It is a clearinghouse of information, it manages all the research, the WI, and relays information. It's those of us here who are responsible," she spread her hands, "for better or worse, for the interpretation of the information."

Benedick couldn't imagine how they might go about that, on a day to day basis.

Seeming to read his mind, Fee smiled and continued, "We spend a lot of time in…esoteric spiritual practices known to the Old Earth and also those which we have discovered ourselves." Benedick's eyes ran to the horizon.

The small hairs on his body stood up, and a shiver ran from his heels to the back of his head. This place was not just an empty Las Vegas. He realized that it was not a normal place at all. For one thing, it was silent. There wasn't a single fly or gnat, no breeze blew against his face. It was utterly still. And although the unobstructed sun blazing down upon them would have meant oppressive heat over one hundred degrees on the Old Earth, Benedick felt neither heat nor cold. It was a strangely cool desert sunshine, suffocatingly close. The stillness, the emptiness, and the odd body temperature hanging air should have made it feel dead, but it wasn't dead. That was the thing. It was the most alive place Benedick had ever been, Old Earth or New. The aliveness was everywhere. They were not alone. She watched him realize all of this before she spoke.

"We've come to believe that this is, or has become, some kind of ground zero of the Changes, or of the Unity on planet Earth, or the place where the spirit of nature, the Emanations, and the human spirit come together…it depends on which of us you ask."

He waited for her to tell him why he was here.

"Are you tired? Hungry?" He denied he was either. "If you don't mind, what I would really like is for us to just stand here for a little while, to see if something happens."

"Alright," Benedick said.

"Keep those eagle eyes of yours sharp," she laughed.

Benedick looked carefully at the ground, the sky, the horizon, turning methodically around the clock of the compass. He saw nothing, not even a flying insect or skittering creature. They stood there quietly next to each other for he knew not how long before she spoke.

"I guess that's it," she said, shrugging. "Let's go have some dinner, shall we?"

5

the cottage

Benedick was curious to see Fee's "cottage" again, and it did not disappoint. The front was still low and plain, but outside, there were all manner of projects in varying degrees of completion, and new structures dotting the curtilage. Inside, instead of one jacket hanging in the foyer, there were piles of them hanging on top of each other on many hooks, and the floor was littered with shoes. He took off his and placed them with the toes lined up in an empty space by the wall. People were everywhere: on computers, reading books and papers, cooking, sitting together, but wherever they were and whatever they were doing, they stopped and looked up at Fee when she walked in. As an answer to an unasked question, she shook her head no.

All eyes turned to him, and though the expressions were kind, he felt like a criminal. He had failed to bring needed help. Fee introduced him around to everyone there, and walked him through the house. The two enormous common rooms were connected by sliding pocket doors and the back wall running behind both rooms was formed by a marching succession of plate glass windows that looked out over the desert, now bathed in the bending sunset colors of end of day.

Every person was very friendly to him, and whatever was cooking, something with tomato and a great deal of garlic, revived his appetite. Fee tracked back to the same room he had occupied First Day. Someone who lived there had cleared away their personal belongings and stacked them in the closet, and the bed was freshly made. So accustomed to solitude, Benedick stalled in the privacy of his room for an hour before he gathered the courage to emerge into the noisy common rooms.

He chose a chair out of the way, backed up against the wall. All of these people had introduced themselves and kept reminding him of their names when they spoke to him, but he just couldn't keep them straight. There were thirteen bedrooms, so there must be that many who lived in the house, plus some extras who were staying in the outbuildings, probably another seven or so. They sat on each other, teased each other, jostled one another in the kitchen, in motion even while at work. They were like puppies, with the youngest, smallest of them, Fee, their dam. She brought him a cup of tea.

"Don't worry," she said, "it's not like this all day. We get up very early and the entire morning is silent until lunch." She laughed as a blonde woman triumphantly grabbed something from a short, round woman with long, dark braids, and the latter ran after her.

"How, exactly, did all of these people end up here?" Benedick asked.

"More or less as you did," she said, "one by one, they showed up. When the house was full, they stopped coming. The others who are staying in the buildings outside are guests invited here for a particular purpose."

"Such as?"

"Well, in the same way that we asked a tree expert and an art expert help us at your house, sometimes here at the cottage we ask experts on various subjects to help us. Sunrise is a leading expert on the Misplaced, for instance, and she has been here many times."

"What is my area of expertise?" He spoke the words in a self deprecating tone, in irony, but her brows drew together and her lips became a thin line across her face.

"I think, after lunch tomorrow, everyone will want to go through the details of your experience. Once we establish all the details, perhaps you can help us deconstruct them, for instance, I think it was significant that you felt the tower in the painting was a university clock tower. Things like that."

When they were called to dinner, Benedick was shown to a place at the large kitchen table, where a dozen or so people had crammed themselves around its periphery. The others sat at the kitchen counter, or on folding chairs, with their plates in their laps. The energy was more subdued, more polite, whether from hunger or an attempt to make Benedick comfortable he couldn't say. He was served a steaming bowl of black beans and brown rice, avocado and cilantro and a garlic seasoned tomato relish. It was delicious.

"When we came in, I saw a lot of things growing outside. How does that work here? Isn't this a desert?"

Several people looked at a red haired woman who sat at the end of the table.

"When we first got here, we drove to the nearest town for everything. When we became a huge crowd, that got old really fast." Several people chuckled. "So, I knew that, even in the OE, there was a place where people grew vegetables in beach sand. It was called Findhorn. I had never been there, even though I'm Scottish, but I had heard of it. So, a lot of it out there is perennial food plants." Benedick remembered that people were calling this woman Fend. It must be short for Findhorn, a less pretty name for a woman.

"But surely those plots I saw don't feed all of you, year round?" he asked. Several people exchanged glances. He felt like a regular person in the company of Watchers.

"The very thing occurred to us," a man named Sangoma said, "We couldn't grow enough to feed us, without dedicating ourselves to it full time. We're not here for that. So, we extrapolated out a solution." He glanced at Fend.

"You met Mandrake. He's a Natureworker. He did a little at your house. At Findhorn they used Naturework in the OE. They communicated directly with nature to grow vegetables in sand, among other things."

"Mandrake said that nature was the Emanations," Benedick said.

"We think so. At first, we worked in partnership with the Emanations to grow the food, and then…we just started manifesting it, without growing it," Fend said.

All eyes turned to Benedick. *Manifesting?*

"You mean, you ask the Emanations to…."

"Create a sack of beans, for instance."

They continued to watch him. He blinked a couple of times. "Like Salt Lake City?"

"But everyday. Whatever it is we need."

"Wow," was all he could say. They laughed, apparently satisfied that he understood.

His mind was full of questions and it took him a long time to formulate them as he let the conversation flow past him.

"Can I ask?" he interrupted, "I can't help but wonder why, if it's possible to manifest food, why other Watchers don't do this, or regular people?"

Fee spoke. "We wondered the same thing. To do Naturework has been within the Watcher bailiwick for a thousand years, according to the regular peoples' false history. We think they don't believe they *can* do it, so it doesn't occur to them. We actually have experience with Watchers outside Las Vegas. A number of times visitors here who have seen what we do have gone home and attempted to do it themselves without success."

"So, it's not a secret ability?"

"Oh no. We don't really have secrets. We think the reason it works for us has something to do with the special energy here."

"But you said yesterday, when you met me in the desert…." He wasn't sure if he should complete the sentence.

"That we think we don't belong here any more."

"Right. Surely that's not true if you're still…provided for."

"On that we all agree. When the day comes that Nature no longer provides, that's a clear message. Until then, we soldier on."

At the end of the second day, Benedick felt as if he had aged ten years. These people still worked like Old Earth people, long, demanding days. They seemed to enjoy it, but Benedick didn't have the stamina to keep up. Just one afternoon of going over, in painstaking detail, what happened at his house was enough to convince him that the cottage work was for the young. At dinner he was the informal guest of honor again, and he was asked to tell the story of meeting Fee, starting from when he woke up First Day. All of this was on the WI, if they wanted to read it, but they wanted to hear the story. It was common for newly acquainted Watchers to get to know each other through an exchange of First Day stories. It's a summary, a capsule, of your Old Earth existence and your New Earth place all in one.

"Something I've always wondered," Benedick said to Fee, "is why were we all dressed and wearing shoes, but you…nothing?"

"Presumably so that I would need the shawl."

"Perhaps also to symbolize the complete obliteration of your former identity," said Benares. "To distinguish you, give you a special tale," said Sangoma, "a mythology."

"You're very mythological," Sundancer said.

"Right down to the name," said Benares.

They cleared the table and washed the dishes before retiring to the common rooms where everyone flopped onto a chair or an oversized pillow. Candles were lit, and music began playing over speakers tucked into an alcove. *The Girl From Ipanema*. Bea had loved that song.

"Is this what you do every night?" Benedick asked to general laughter.

"There's nothing we do every night," Yiri said. He was a dark skinned man with an Australian accent. "We play games a lot. We're fiercely competitive."

"How not very New Earth of you," Benedick said, causing another round of laughter.

"We go on long walks." "Read." "Howl at the moon." "Dance party night is my favorite."

"So Benedick," Fend asked him, "What do you think of the cottage?"

He had to sort his thoughts for a moment before answering. He both liked and disliked it, but he knew that wasn't what she was asking.

"It's probably the least New Earth place in the NE, but at the same time, the most intensely NE," he said. No one laughed.

"No one has said that before. Can you explain?"

"Well, because of your isolation, everything here is Old Earth, you don't have to interface with regular people, you haven't been changed by them, you don't have a story. Everything here, the games, the music, the food, the furniture, is a time capsule. It's been strange for me. I can almost believe the transition never happened. And yet, this is, to borrow a phrase from Fee, a kind of ground zero of the New Earth. The energy is palpable. I feel that almost anything could happen in this place."

"You aren't the least of us, after all," Fend said laughing.

"If you don't mind," Benedick said, "I can't help but notice that I'm in a room with a group of people tasked with interpreting the phenomena of the NE world wide, for all Watchers. That doesn't happen every day." All eyes were upon him; they were attentive and engaged. These people were inexhaustible.

"Have you, collectively, come to any conclusions about what happened to us?"

They laughed again. Perhaps it was all the laughter and joking around that kept them young and energetic.

"In a word…no," Fee said, "Are there theories?"

"So many theories!" Yiri said.

A woman named Manat held out her hands, and Yiri threw at her a fabric ball that had been resting on the floor next to him.

"I've heard a lot of theories, some of them quite nutty," Benedick said.

"We're all deaaaaad!" Yiri interjected.

"But I figure the best theories are here," Benedick finished.

"The best theories are here," Fee agreed.

"To outline it broadly," Sangoma said, "there are several camps, with a million sub-theories within those camps, some of which have been abandoned, some not. The main camps are, one, this *is* the OE, just Changed; two, this is the NE and the OE no longer exists, those theories presuppose some kind of progression or era theory; the OE never existed and it is we who are afflicted with false memory; four, there was a split, the NE was created as a split off from the OE."

"A split?" Benedick asked.

"That's a sexy one," Yiri said, "It has a lot of currency right now."

"You kind of have to start with the beginning of the Universe," Sundancer said.

"It's a long story," Sangoma said, "which splits off, pun intended, into more sub-theories than anyone can count."

"Sangoma is right, but the basic premise is common to almost all of them," Fee said, "which starts with there is no beginning to the Universe, actually."

"No beginning?"

"I meant that metaphorically," Sundancer told him. "A lot of the split theories presuppose that there is no such thing as linear time. You know…the regular people have that saying, 'When we choose, the Unity Changes'? That's basically it, but we expand it out."

"What Sundancer means," Sangoma said, "is that the regular people say that each person is part of the Unity and every choice affects the whole…a butterfly's wing, etcetera, but they mean it changes *going forward*. They believe in linear time. None of *us* in this camp believe in going forward."

"Or going backward," Mathilde said.

"That's why you guys can never get anywhere," Yiri quipped and threw the stuffed fabric ball against the wall, which Sundancer intercepted.

"If it's true that the Unity is everything," Fee began.

"And *we* think it's true," Sundancer interjected, and threw the ball against the wall toward Yiri.

"Then, linear time doesn't really make sense. If you, Benedick, were all there is, everywhere, there is no Other to mark anything like Time against. You just are. And you don't experience anything because, again, there is no Experiencer and Experience. Everything is just you, and you *are* it *all* at the same time."

They all watched his face. "Okay, where do *you* come in, and me?"

Fee smiled. "Clearly, at some point, the Unity formed the desire to experience, and split itself."

"The Big Bang," Sangoma said, "or something like it."

"This is where it gets tricky, because I said 'at some point' which commonly indicates a time before now. But I mean just that, a point. It's a location on the body of the Unity. The Unity encompasses the Big Bang, ancient Greece, 1969, and Las Vegas circa wherever this is and beyond."

"Not to mention the probable, innumerable, alien worlds and their so called histories," Sundancer said, "and futures."

"We can't help but talk in terms of linear time," Fee said, "because we experience the illusion of it. We are stuck inside it, like a bug in a terrarium. But the advantage of living out here is that one day melts into another, we spend a large portion of our days in altered states. The illusion is less compelling for us."

"After a particularly long session in practices," Manat said, "I feel that this house is an island floating in a starry abyss, completely outside of time. I have no past at all."

"But," Benedick objected, "What I don't understand is how it would work. Say, for example, there was one world I didn't marry Bea, or another when I had children with her, or died young. How could I be experiencing all of these things, these trajectories?"

"Exactly," Yiri said.

"Inside your own head you have an unconscious and a conscious mind. Each of them are right now having completely different experiences in tandem," Benares said.

"But what would rise to the level of a split, if you will? Cornflakes or eggs for breakfast?"

That started an argument that went on for some time. Some argued that there were a set number of parallel universes, based on OE physics theories. Others argued for an unlimited number, which is why the Universe was expanding, and was missing so much mass. Others argued that perhaps the Universe constantly remade itself, it was always only a moment old; conscious beings were *all* subject to false memories—the NE was proof of that possibility.

"If that were true, then it's possible that something we did out here Changed ancient Greece," Benares said, "All of those history books in your house, Benedick, might in fact be different from what you read and taught out of in another place in spacetime. We chose and Changed the Unity, and far away, along some inconceivable ley-line, ancient Greece Changed and everything else Changed as a result. That might be happening all the time, the Unity rewriting existence upon itself. It's a story written on the body of the Unity."

"But that would violate the law that energy can't be created nor destroyed. If the Unity rewrites, overwrites, then data is being lost." This was a very tall, black skinned woman, who spoke quietly.

"It could still save the data, Mathilde, even though that timeline ends. It picks up in a new spot, with everything Changed. That obeys the law, and also quite neatly conforms to the observed reality of a Universe that is expanding at an increasing rate," Benares offered. "There's a mythological repository called the Ashkashic Records...."

"It *all* might really be just data...," Kali suggested.

"Not that again!"

"...if we are just a sim," she continued doggedly, "We might, in fact, be a sim run by a sim. You have to admit, that would explain a lot."

"A sim?" Benedick asked.

"A computer simulation, which is being run perhaps by another simulation, perhaps layers of them. In the OE, we didn't have the technology to run a sim of that complexity, so it would have been the end of the line, but this world is capable of it."

"But you have to presuppose that *consciousness* is cramming itself into a computer," Yiri objected.

"What's the difference between consciousness cramming itself into a biological computer, a brain, or an electronic computer, a hard drive? At high technological levels, the difference between the two becomes increasingly small." They began to argue about this and also about whether they should even be arguing about this, if it were even relevant to Benedick.

Benedick blinked. There is no ground to hold onto at all, if any of this were true. He would surely go mad if he lived in this house. When that argument died down, Fee continued to skip along the trajectory of her thoughts, unaware that Benedick could no longer listen.

"Presumably, to the Unity, nothing is good or bad, because it is all itself. That's why I don't agree with the progression theories, that everything is evolving to some better state, like a growing child. If anything appears to be progressing, it's only because individual humans desire it and judge it so, not because the Unity creates it." Fee said. "For the most part, what most humans desire is an end to suffering. Unfortunately, different people have very different ideas about what suffering is, and what ending it would look like."

"Hence, the split, the transition," Sundancer insisted emphatically. "The idea is that Earth reached a point in which there were large numbers of people sorting themselves into two groups, more or less, and these groups became increasingly incompatible. Both groups formed a strong enough desire to live separate from each other that the Unity split the Earth in two."

Benedick thought of himself and Bea and decided that he did not agree with this theory. Why would they decide to split from one another?

"Now, whether there has always been two with a separate history…."

"In which case, the regular people are right about their thousand years of New Earth following a Dark Age….we just weren't experiencing it."

"Or, this world really is new."

"Maybe all of us have another version of us in the OE."

"But there are missing people here, they aren't replicated here."

"Maybe there are multiple universes in which we have other selves, but we choose which one to experience consciously."

"But if that were true, then many people you interact with, say on a street car, are just zombies, unattended vehicles with no driver, their preferred existence being somewhere else."

"That would explain a lot," Sangoma said. This comment was met with laughter.

They were all talking at once, rehashing what to them were old arguments.

"How would you characterize the two groups, exactly? If there are two groups, I mean?" Benedick asked.

"Well, if you think back to the Old Earth right after 2012, the so called end of the world...," Sundancer said, "There were basically two groups fighting, and I don't mean the American political parties. It was all over the world, and cut across all demographics, namely people who believed in dominance and those who desired partnership. That was the fundamental disagreement. If someone is trying to dominate you, force you to do what they want, they are, *ipso facto*, not your partner. Conversely, the dominance model really depends on a respect for hierarchy. A dominant person is concerned primarily for themselves. He wants privilege, genuflection, even if it's metaphorical. Someone who sees themselves as your equal will never accept any dominance you manage to exert, and they will view your attempt to dominate him as a character defect that disqualifies you as someone worthy of respect."

"But then, there's the other axis," Benares said, "Materialist and non-materialist, and they don't line up. Not only is this world egalitarian, but it's also non-materialist. There were plenty of people in the OE who were, for instance, materialist and egalitarian...they were called Communists."

"And intensely spiritual, non-materialist people who wanted to force everyone to live by their law," Kali said.

"They were called Republicans...," Yiri quipped.

"Republicans loved money," Sundancer objected, "and so did the Taliban and all the rest of them."

"It's not correct to call those people spiritual, much less intensely spiritual," Benares objected. "Those people were religious...there's a big difference between spiritual and religious. I don't know of any intensely spiritual people who were materialist...think Buddhist monks, or the yogis...."

"Priests and nuns," Fend offered.

"I guess," Benares granted, "some of them. Status, institution building, and dogma enforcement are all materialist projects."

"Well, if you're going to open up the definition of materialist that wide, then we can't say this world isn't materialist. The regular people build institutions and enforce social norms. They are just different institutions and norms."

"But they're non-materialist norms…and they don't have religious dogma."

"I'm not saying the theory is wrong, but I think we can all agree that it's messy. There isn't a neat axis," Yiri said.

"Axis or no, there are some facts to back it up," Sundancer insisted. "For instance, who in the OE would you say were infamous *kumba-ya* types? Quick, the first group you can think of who believed in peace and love and all that?"

"Hippies in the '60s?" Benedick ventured.

"Yes, precisely. Well, I actually spent several years tracking hippies from the OE to the NE via the WI. I interviewed thousands of Watchers and compiled a list of names of hippies still alive at the transition. There are an inordinate number of hippies from that list here in the regular population. Other people have looked for dictators, warlords, and haven't found any."

"But my kind hearted, community oriented parents aren't here," Fend said.

"And that I have no explanation for," Sundancer admitted.

There was a man with waving, shoulder length silver hair and a square jaw who, throughout this argument, laid on his back near to Benedick, never saying a word. He just stared at the ceiling while he listened. Fee noticed Benedick looking at him.

"Marco, tell Benedick what *you* think," she said.

"Oh…alright," the man turned his eyes to Benedick without otherwise moving, and spoke with a pleasant accent Benedick couldn't place, "I don't exist, neither do you. None of this is real. Only our experience of it is real, but when we merge with the Unity, experience stops. I find I am happiest when I'm seeking Unity. Someday perhaps I will attain it permanently. Until then, I try to make myself useful."

"He's a great DJ," Sundancer said, and that was the signal the dialectic was done. "Is anyone up for Tango?" she asked. The man lying on his back agreed, and, reluctantly, or so Benedick thought, brought himself upright.

The group enthusiastically started moving back the furniture for an impromptu milonga, and Benedick excused himself to go to bed. Fee had seen on their infrequent calls that he had grown a beard, and now wore glasses, but she was unprepared for how aged he was. His shoulders curled forward, he walked carefully, he held a cane in a hand that shook. What was she thinking asking him to teach the Born? Fee accompanied him to his room, and then continued out the front door, the gritty soil audible beneath her feet. She kept walking straight ahead until she could no longer hear the music bleeding into the dark night. When the cottage disappeared into the dark as well, she stopped, winded. She stood there for a long time seeing but not seeing, thinking but not thinking, and then she saw a street come skidding across the hardpan in the moonlight. It was moving very fast in a curving line, a bulb, a cul-de-sac, a node on its end. It speed-ed towards her and stopped abruptly in front of her toes. She almost stepped over its curb, but instantly, it was gone, skidding away away swiftly. Trembling, breathing quickly, she threw her arms upwards.

"What?" she yelled. There was no answer.

Three months ago, Fee had become ill in a world where virtually all ills were curable. Her body wasted and she remained in bed all day, every day. The only thought in her mind was that she wanted to go home. She was deeply homesick, which was odd because the cottage was the only real home she had ever known. The New Earth was fine, the Watcher machinery hummed along without a great deal of intervention. She wasn't needed and she was ready to go. Not even the writhing streets could rouse her. They would figure it out. It was Benedick's tree that got her out of bed. Like an aged warrior leaning on her staff, she stood, ready to do what she had to do. Home would wait a while longer.

Having Benedick here brought her right back to First Day, when she entered the empty cottage almost naked. On that day, she was unmoored. In her mind there was the identity of a girl

who had been sitting naked on the windowsill of a hotel room, her knees drawn up, guarded by the man who called himself her father, but wasn't. The life experiences of this young woman stacked themselves into a file folder in her mind. Fee could read them, like a deposition, or an insurance claim, but she didn't feel any of it. It wasn't an identity she could attach to, even if she wanted to.

When she read that file folder, this is what it told her: that the man and his wife kept her locked in her room with nothing but a tall stack of books, for as far back as her memory stretched. Supposedly, she was homeschooled, but to this day, Fee had no understanding of mathematics beyond arithmetic. Books, but no t.v. Even as he forced her to make movies that no one should watch, she was not allowed a tv in her room lest she watch something unseemly. They were very strict, and gave her a proper Christian education. Honor thy mother and father, ask for forgiveness of your sins. These funhouse mirrors of morality structured her days.

No men came to the house. The girl had the man's terror of prison to thank for that, but he couldn't resist the once a year payday offered by high season in Las Vegas. Every year they made a pilgrimage there. The man was always happy in Las Vegas, but it was there, every year, that the girl thought of nothing but suicide. As if he knew her thoughts, the man taunted her, saying that if she left, he would just get another one, and it would be her fault. Getting you, that was my sin, he would say, but if you left, the second one wouldn't even be my sin. It would be yours. He would grab another little girl.

Alone in her room at home, overlooking the green square of grass edged in wood fencing, the girl would often think of this other girl, the one he would get if she found a way to throw herself in front of a car. She would have to be Chinese-American, to pass for his daughter. She would be much younger. She still lived with her parents, went to school, wrote down the name of a cute boy in the margin of her notebook. Over the years, locked in that room, she dreamed up enough of this girl's life to fill ten novels.

Was any of that real? It seemed to her a book she read long ago. It was entirely possible that the man didn't exist and that none of it ever happened. Nevertheless, when she met a Chinese-American woman, a regular person younger than herself, sometimes she would wonder: is this the lucky version of me, the one I saved?

She trusted Benedick right away. That was the strange thing. He was there for her, and she knew it. She was beaten for it, but she never would call that man by his name. But that man's first, middle, and last name were the first words she spoke to the WI operator upon arriving at the cottage, while Benedick slept in the first bedroom. She ran a search on him. He wasn't here. Although she has never said so, Benedick is the only father she's ever known.

And now, it was her turn to take care of him. He was there First Day, he was there at Mount Hood, and now this. None of them could make the connection. She understood well what it was to be locked in. But was Benedick grabbed to get his attention, or hers? Was it a threat?

What about Mandrake's idea that it was a second order Change requested by many beings? Many on this planet, or many beings somewhere else, perhaps on the still existing Old Earth? She shuddered. Even after fifteen years, the Old Earth and its violence terrified her. She felt danger, and not just to Benedick. This beautiful planet that had become what so many hoped it could be had millions of lucky versions of us, delicate creatures who deserved her protection. She felt personally responsible for every single one of them.

When she returned to the cottage, she checked on Benedick, who slept insensible to the tango music and the light from the hallway that now fell across him. One way or another, Fee would find a way to preserve them all.

Benedick slept deep and long. He found himself again on the bridge, but there was no companion. After standing there for some time watching so many things of the world pass, caught in the cataract beneath him and then fall down into the void, he saw a man approaching. He was walking from the tower side of the bridge, and wore the clothes of a Watcher. When he reached Benedick, he extended an arm toward the red roofed buildings at the other end of the bridge.

"It's time for you to go," he said.

"It's time for you to go," the man repeated. When he said it a third time, Benedick realized that these words were spoken by a woman into his bodily ears.

When he opened his eyes, Fee told him he was oversleeping.

"We made your breakfast to go, or should I say, brunch, and packed your valise for you. You were sleeping so soundly, we didn't have the heart to wake you."

As Benedick stowed his valise in the car, he had the uncanny feeling that Bea would be waiting for him at home. This place was deeply affecting. He could almost believe it, that she would be there.

"So, you'll take a plane from Los Angeles going back?" Fee asked him.

"I'm ready to be home. This has been a rather exhausting vacation."

She laughed, but it was a staccato laugh without mirth. Although they were not touching, he felt her clinging to him. She studied him with haunted eyes, looking older than he had ever before seen her.

"What's going on?"

"It's nothing I know for sure. I can't even articulate it, to be honest."

"You're driving yourself too hard. You should take care of yourself."

"I'm missing something, but I don't even know what it is. All of the other lessons we have learned here, how to manage the WI, how to interact with the regular people, how to live out here, and so forth, all of these things were like Easter Egg hunts. There was an answer, and we had to work to figure it out. This...."

Thinking of Bea, Benedick said, "Sometimes there just isn't an answer, or at least, not one knowable right now. Maybe the lesson is to be comfortable with that."

She looked up into his face. "Would it make sense if I addressed and sent to you a letter, and then when you opened it, it was blank?" She looked out at the desert, where beyond their view, the avenues of Las Vegas writhed. "There is meaning in the message, but we can't figure it out. It scares me."

Benedick didn't recognize the fear in her face until that moment. He had never known her to be afraid before.

"Remember when I told you that the first time I saw the painting, I felt foreboding?"

"Of course."

"I had a dream on the way here that I was inside the painting." Her eyes opened wider. "I had forgotten about that until this morning. I was standing on that bridge with someone I couldn't see. That person told me it was going to be alright."

He could see it was the right thing to say, for her eyes filled with tears. She reached out for his hands.

"Stay in touch," she said.

"It will be alright!" he called to her before he slammed the car door. She waved and stood outside watching him drive away until there was nothing visible but a cloud of dust between them.

6

the prisoner

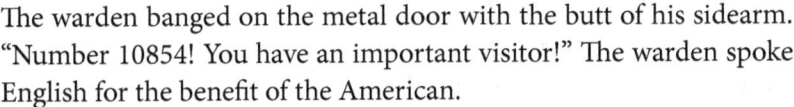

The warden banged on the metal door with the butt of his sidearm. "Number 10854! You have an important visitor!" The warden spoke English for the benefit of the American.

The American leaned forward and looked through the barred window at the top of the door, but immediately stepped back, a hand over his nose. He coughed. He didn't need to place his face so near the stench of that room to see a shirtless, emaciated youth, hardly more than a boy, with matted coils of black hair kneeling alone in the back corner of a concrete cell filled with other men. The other men were healthier than the youth, muscled and tattooed, wrists to chin. They argued and jostled in the small space. They regarded the visitors with a momentary, dull aggression, then resumed their former activities. The youth in the corner was still, except that he was rocking himself back and forth and mumbling some kind of mantra in Portuguese too softly to be heard. He didn't react at all to the noise or to the presence of the visitors.

"This is the one?"

"Yes, sir," the warden said proudly. "He will never trouble you or your associates again."

"Are you sure this is the one? I imagined someone…more tough."

"No one stays tough here, Senhor. These," he waved a hand at the other men, "will be as he is before long."

"What is he saying?"

"He…," the warden raised a finger to his skull, "you know…he has lost himself. He repeats his name, he loves the forest and justice, blah blah blah."

The youth hummed a few bars of a song, and then added in a sing-song voice, "They are listening to different music and that's okay."

The American looked at the warden, who smiled. "Don't trouble yourself. It's nonsense."

"I don't want to seem callous, but why do you bother keeping him alive here? If he hasn't given you anything, he probably won't."

"It's his father. His mother died, and now all his father does is demand he be released."

"How does the father know he's here?"

"He doesn't…or maybe he does, I don't know. The guards are local and this man's family has been in this area a long time." He shrugged. "Don't trouble yourself, Senhor. It doesn't matter. It's not like the U.S. The old man can sit outside all he wants."

The American looked back at the kneeling youth, who was now holding his dirty, bent and broken fingers in front of him, each of them moving up and down to the melody of music only the prisoner could hear. His vacant eyes stared through his visitors. The American looked away. "He's better off dead," he said to the warden. From behind him, he heard the youth say something in Portuguese; he said it to them, his voice clear and strong. When the American looked back at the prisoner, he was still moving his fingers, each broken fingertip pointing every which way, conducting its own orchestra, but his eyes were upon the American and his host. The American involuntarily shivered, despite the stifling heat.

"What did he say?"

"He says in the future I won't be there." The warden smiled and shrugged again.

"*Nenhum de vocês estará aqui.*"

"He says none of us will be there."

The eyes of the prisoner left them again. They were focused elsewhere, where a shaft of sunlight was falling on piano keys and the dark, curling hair of a small girl, aged eight or nine. She was resting her head on her arms on the edge of the piano bench while he played, her legs bent beneath her on the floor. When his fingers stopped at the end of the song, she lifted her head to look up at him.

"That's Maē's song, isn't it?"

"That's one of her favorites," he said, as he leafed through the creased and buckled song book.

"Tell me again," she said.

"Again?" Her large brown eyes stared up at him. She didn't inherit her mother's extraordinary beauty, but he didn't mind. The child's eyes were copies of those of his own Maē, now long dead. "Alright. I was a musician, I graduated from music school, you know this. And I was wild then." They both laughed. She knew this story already. "My hair was crazy, long to here," he touched his bicep.

"She says you weren't even wearing a shirt."

"Probably not. I was playing at a node, in São Paulo. We were there before you were born. It was hot, it was our summertime."

"In December!"

"Yes. It's opposites there. I was playing with my whole heart, I didn't even see the people. They came and they went. We didn't have the app for the phone back then. People had to sign up on a sheet of paper if they wanted to follow you. The people came and went and I played."

"Then she came."

"Yes, she came."

"And she was so beautiful."

"It wasn't just that. Our eyes met, and I knew right then. She was there right in front of me signing up on the paper, and I lost my place in the music. She was staring at me, and everyone was staring at me, so I said, 'You don't have to sign up to see me play again. I will play for you anywhere.' And everyone laughed, and she ran away."

"She was so embarrassed."

"I saw her name on the sheet, and then I finished playing. I wasn't very good after that. All I could think about was what I was going to do after I was finished. I was a bit wild, yes? And so I just sent a text to her number on the sheet. It said two words: where? when? And she was bold enough to send back to me a place and a time. Do you remember the park next to the water, the place we showed you?"

"Under the big tree."

"Yes. I arrived early and I set out a blanket and chilled wine, and I set myself on a little folding stool in front of the blanket like a little stage, with my guitar."

"And she fell in love with you."

"Is that what she says?"

"Yes. She told me you weren't the best, but you played like your life depended on it. She said it was impossible to walk away when you played."

"And now?"

"Now, I want to hear *my* favorite." She placed her chin on her forearm, her eyes gazing upward at his face.

The laughter of the men, the warden and the American, intruded into this scene. They were going away. They had said something in parting the youth didn't hear. They were laughing at him, but the prisoner didn't care.

"They will be named in honor of the dead, so we will always remember them even after we forget," the prisoner mumbled.

The warden and the American walked away.

"Don't kill the old man!" the prisoner yelled after them, as he rocked back and forth.

"*Não mate o velho…Não mate…o velho. Lembre…Não mate….*" The prisoner continued to rock himself and repeat this phrase—don't kill the old man—until the two men slammed the big door of the dark corridor behind them.

7

the born

Benedick curled his fingers around his warm coffee mug and gazed out of the open back door, listening to the birdsong produced mainly by chickadees and warblers flitting about, but his patience was several times rewarded by the more distant, plaintive call of a varied thrush, its one note vibrato carrying its question through the trees. Another thrush, perhaps the mate to the faraway caller, floated down to the ground in front of Benedick and began sifting through the leaf litter, pausing to descend upon an unlucky beetle. It was making a scratch scratch rustle sound that Benedick found pleasant and though he only caught glimpses of the bird in the undergrowth, he marked its progress by the dry debris the creature tossed into the air as it went. The early morning sun streamed sideways through the leaves of the trees that suddenly kept themselves absolutely still, and indeed Benedick stopped his coffee cup at his lips. The trees were holding their breath as the gray neighbor cat, his head thrust forward, stalked the ground feeding bird, which, oblivious to the danger continued to scratch scratch rustle. When the animal leaped, and missed, Benedick returned to his coffee.

It had only been a week since the tree appeared in Benedick's front doorway, but, between the drama of the tree, and the trip to and from Las Vegas, it seemed like an eternity since he had been to the school to teach the Born. He missed them and he was sorry, after all, that he would stop teaching. He and Fee agreed that this semester would be his last.

To Benedick, the Born were still miracle. They resonated with the miraculous, for when they began to arrive, their arrival was both surprising and also world creating, in that they put an end to a lot of fraught, and sometimes strident speculation amongst Watchers. Prior to the first birth after First Day, there were some fairly outlandish theories about what had just happened. Some Watchers argued that they were all dead, and that the New Earth was heaven, or purgatory. Others claimed that the NE was a static place, still others that none of it existed at all and that they were all insane. There were many theories back then, but Benedick didn't follow them. He was completely preoccupied with finding Bea.

When the first babies were born, many of those arguments died. In no tradition claiming a heaven was there reproduction, and the obvious continuation of family life and social relations made the NE a very odd sort of insanity, if it were that. The eldest of the Born were now not quite fifteen years old, though the regular people didn't call them the Born, of course. They believed they were all born to this world, and they have very old, detailed and false historical records to prove it. The term, Born, was unique to the Watchers' own private vocabulary, along with Lost, Misplaced, Tracked and Untracked, all the categories in which they placed the New Earth "regular," or non-Watcher, peoples.

Because no records followed the Watchers to the NE and all of the regular records were false, Watchers had to rely on their own collective memories logged into the WI. Given that, it was impossible to track even a fraction of the regular population from the Old Earth to the New, thus most of the regular people were "untracked," not verifiably a member of the population who made the transition. This was as true for children as adults, and Watchers all assumed that children who were present on First Day had the same false histories. Thus, it is this generation of the Born who are the only verifiably genuine, integral human beings on this Earth, and as such, these unique beings hold a special fascination for Watchers.

In truth, Benedick rather enjoyed teaching the Born, which was a surprise to himself. He had been a lot less sorry than Bea that they couldn't have children. However, the Born were pleasant human beings, each of them deeply wanted and carefully raised. They were kind and innocent, funny and respectful. They were all healthy and cooperative. Benedick enjoyed their youthful enthusiasm. In his mind, he compared these youth with those he knew in his neighborhood in the OE, afflicted with every type of blight. New Earth children were never "accidents," and they were fully provided for, every one. They had a family life that followed a gentle rhythm and relational ties were strong and included a community beyond the nuclear family. In the OE, such care in the production and raising of children would have been economically impossible. There's no profit in it. There *was* profit in prisons, war, pollution, prostitution, and illness, both of mind and body. The wealthy profited off of all these things while protecting themselves from them with their money. That's just the way the world was, and it didn't seem possible that it could ever change.

The one thing that made *this* world possible—to raise healthy children and to heal the adults of their unremembered traumas—was the complete absence of money motive. They've never even heard of profit, or money, for that matter. They didn't use it at all. Theirs was a resource sharing economy, in which the twin values of unity and living in balance with nature were the fulcrum of social life.

Benedick taught the Born with grave misgiving. He didn't think anything of it, at first. As it was explained to him, it sounded perfectly reasonable. Once the first babies were born, the idea that they might all be immortal in some heaven was dealt a blow, and the obvious aging of Watchers over the last decade and a half, made the wound mortal. No one now believed that Watchers would have anything other than a normal, human lifespan. Eventually, they would begin to die. Obviously, they had to find a way to create a renewable Watcher class, who could manage the information they would be privy to. The

New Earth would need a new generation of Watchers numbering in the millions to manage the WI, to research new topics that arise, to carry out Naturework projects. Benedick didn't receive a satisfactory answer when he objected that he had no experience with children whatsoever, that perhaps another Watcher might be a better choice. It was just an experiment, he was told. It was one of those recommendations that came out of Las Vegas, and he agreed.

Having taught the Born for a year, he wasn't so sure the decision was a good one. The idea was that if the Born were taught when they were young enough, then they would acquire the Old Earth information as a second language, become bilingual in a process that was the reverse of what Benedick and the other Watchers experienced. But, it's one thing to go from being wounded, frightened, jaded, and defended and learn that you can leave all of that behind. It's another thing entirely to teach someone who is an innocent that the world can be, and was, an ugly devolution that produced horrors beyond their ken. Even the eldest amongst the regular people were as innocent as a sheltered pre-school child in the OE. Was it even moral to do that to someone? Benedick wasn't sure. And consent? Neither the children, nor their parents could even understand what they were consenting to.

His conscience was allayed when the vast majority of his students dropped out of the program in the first year. They simply rejected the information he gave them, which was hardly anything at all. Last year, the class met only once a week for an hour. They engaged in thought experiments. They played Monopoly, and other OE games preserved in the homes of Watchers. He merely tried to introduce them to the idea that—a thousand years ago—the world used to be a materialist place: no Unity, no Changes, run by money.

He had suggested that the project be terminated when so many of the students quit, but the word from Las Vegas was that they wanted him to persist with the small number who wanted to continue. And would he be willing to teach the class every day before school? Benedick just couldn't see how it would work, given the secrecy of the WI. When would they be given access to it? Wouldn't the kids want to tell other kids? Secrecy wasn't compatible with this society; these people were open, undefended. It seemed completely impossible. Fee and her team had thought of all that, he supposed. Maybe they had ideas he hadn't thought of. They asked him for another year and he agreed.

He was down to twenty-two freshmen at the local high school, a mile from his house, an easy commute on the streetcar. He always stopped for a second cup of coffee on the way. It reminded him of his old University days. The morning routine was pleasant and the kids a pleasure, but it bothered him. On this first day after the tree, and Las Vegas, as he watched the kids file into the room, he felt the same creeping dread he felt when he first looked at the painting. This wasn't right. He would send a message to Fee on the WI as soon as he got home.

He had planned a lecture about money. Trying to teach them that all value was measured with money on this Earth was like trying to explain that people used to like to drive nails into their feet and walk on their hands. Why would anyone do that to themselves? It was an undertaking.

Benedick tried to use analogies to explain the OE to the Born in the same way Watchers used analogies to orient themselves to the NE after the transition. For instance, the Born were familiar with the system their parents used by which all the resources on the planet were accounted for on a massive AI computer system and allocated by necessity. People kept themselves in constant awareness of this resource management via a feedback system in which your own use was tracked. You could see your use of various resources on a daily, weekly, monthly and yearly basis, compare months, or years to each other, and also find out how your use compares to the average use per person in your area or any other area of the world. Each person's goal was, ultimately, to conserve. It was like a video game to them, and making your very own contribution to the health of the whole was "winning."

This was nothing like the OE, indeed this system was pretty much contrary to the encouraged excess of the capitalistic extraction, exploitation and profit machine. However, the system they used to manage vacation allocation was something like money in the form of a grant they called "credits." Each person received a certain number of them yearly for leisure travel. The amount of credits each person received, worldwide, was related to how well resources had been managed the previous year, combined with the birthrate in each location, fed into an algorithm. If the world were doing well, you got more vacation, while after a high consumption year, everyone had to tighten their leisure belts, more so in high birthrate and high consumption areas. You could use, give, or save them, as you wished. It was an excellent analogy. Once the kids were settled, Benedick started class with confidence. The topic of money, if anything, would convince them of the superiority of their system. It was no threat to their innocence.

"We have touched on the idea of money before…," he began.

"You could get stuff with it," Wangari Maathai offered brightly.

"Almost, Wangari. You *had* to have it to get stuff, so to speak. But we're going to talk about how money was related to work, which was similar to your concept of contribution, but not the same. Work was not necessarily something you wanted to do, or that did any good, but something you had to do because someone told you to do it in order to get the money. Okay?" Twenty-two blank stares.

"Money was like the credits you get for going on vacation, but they had to do work in exchange for their credits. People typically received something called a "check" with their credits on it every week, two weeks or monthly."

"But how did they know how many credits they got *before* the year was out?"

This student was not the brightest among them. Before Benedick could remind him, the other students were correcting him, "They didn't *have* central computer systems!" "We covered that, remember?"

Benedick tried to blunt the force of their corrections, "I know it's hard to believe that people wouldn't have thought of that, but you have to remember this was a long time ago—he had to lie about that for now—and people were more primitive. They just cut trees or dug up whatever they wanted without thinking about it first, or planning ahead."

"That's one of the reasons the Dark Age happened in the first place," said a boy with an impossibly long name—José Cláudio Ribeiro da Silva—called Cláudio, one of Benedick's favorite students. The boy was so relentlessly good, Benedick could almost believe he was incorruptible, and perhaps could become a Watcher, somehow.

"Not only did they not award credits based on environmental balance," Benedick continued, "but the credits you received were not equal to everyone else's. If somebody wanted more credits, they just took more out of nature."

The da Silva boy looked physically pained by this information.

"It was very sad," Benedick found himself saying.

"Not equal?" Thuli Ndlovu asked.

Benedick didn't want to get into income *inequality*, when they didn't yet understand *income*. He would have to explain for weeks. He just wanted to cement what they've learned about exchange value of work, but this always happened. Every time he tried to teach them something simple they would ask so many questions and get him so turned around that he would lose track of what they were supposed to cover. Before the tree happened, they had spent a half hour on sports competitions, specifically basketball and how it was different, which was entirely irrelevant to the lesson. Everything was connected to everything else, work, exchange, value, environmental balance, competition and cooperation, sports, culture…and he found these young, nimble minds moved too fast for him. It was easy for them to drag him off track, to talk about things not on his syllabus.

"No, it wasn't equal, but we won't get into that right now," he said.

"But why did they get credits for…their contribution?" Thuli persisted.

"They didn't have the concept of contribution. Try to imagine a life in which every single person is completely alone." A girl opened her mouth to say something, but Benedick held up a finger. "Imagine that you are an adult living alone in an apartment—or raising children completely alone—and no one helps you with anything, ever. You have to do everything for yourself, and the way you take care of yourself is by using credits, called money. The way you got the money was called work, or commonly, a 'job.' Everyone had to have a job."

The children blinked at him.

"A job was a set of tasks someone else makes you do in order to get the money credits. That someone was called a boss."

"I don't understand…," This was Berta Cáceres, a quiet, thoughtful girl. "First, why would someone force someone else? How could they? And why would someone have to be forced to contribute? That's why we are all here, because we *want* to contribute. Everyone does."

The other kids nodded agreement. "Everyone does."

Benedick took a deep breath, "It's not contribution. People didn't contribute back then. That's not how it was. It was called work for a reason. A lot of the work people had to do wasn't a contribution, it wasn't good for anyone. A lot of the work was destructive or harmful or wasteful or unhealthy."

"*Wasteful?*" That was anathema to them, they with their conservation video game system.

"Then why would they do it?" Berta asked, "It makes no sense."

This was complicated.

"People had to have credits for everything, and they only got them from the job," he repeated. Benedick was still trying to avoid talking about inequality and power. "So, they had to use their credits in order to, for instance, get on the transit. People would run out of credits all the time and then they couldn't ride the transit any more." Benedick used the simple example of the transit because if he had said that people had to buy food or a doctor visit, these students would find it just too incredible, and the room would blow up in arguments.

"So, you couldn't just get on, you had to wait in line for people to give their credits?"

"Yes, and also, if you didn't have exactly the right number, you had to do a mathematical exchange while other people waited for you."

"It sounds like a test," Trulia said and the others laughed.

"Yes, it was like a test, now that I think of it, but they didn't think of it that way." Benedick was careful not to say "we," for he wasn't supposed to have been alive at that time. "It was like facing a series of tests, all day, every day."

"And you could run out and so you couldn't go anywhere?" She was incredulous.

"Yes."

"But that's dumb! You can't go to school or contribute or anything?" Benedick had hit the wall of incredulity early.

"And then you would lose your job." Benedick couldn't help himself. He knew that it would set them off, but he was enjoying talking about how nonsensical the OE system had been. As a young man, he had known it was inefficient, wasteful, brutal, but he had accepted it. He had pushed all of these thoughts away in order to make a living. It was fun talking about how stupid it was. He almost wanted to laugh, but they would not understand such dark humor, so he contented himself with rocking on his heels.

The room erupted, as expected.

"And the bosses could take away the job anytime they wanted, so people were forced to do things that were unhealthy, or stupid, or wrong."

"I would just refuse," Berta said.

"But then you wouldn't be able to ride the transit," Cláudio said.

"Or get stuff," Wangari said.

"That's exactly right," Benedick said. "If your shoes and clothes were worn out and needed to be recycled, you couldn't get new ones."

"You had to be naked?" Berta raised a skeptical eyebrow.

"Not naked, but you had to wear them as they were, or try to fix them yourself. If it snowed, you couldn't get a coat, you went without. You had to have a job for everything."

"Let me get this straight," Julia Hill said, "You get your credits from your job. If you run out, you can't ride to your job and then you lose your job, and you can't get any more credits."

"Exactly." Benedick rocked on his heels again.

"And then you can't get transit or clothes or anything," she said.

"Yes. That's why people didn't refuse jobs that were stupid or unhealthy or wrong."

He explained how jobs weren't awarded based on necessity or contribution, but on the basis of making more credits. A lot of people with incredible talents weren't allowed to contribute, and a lot of people had to sit at home and do nothing." In the privacy of his own mind, he placed "home" in quotes. A cardboard box, or under a porch, like a dog, a sagging tent and faded blue tarps against a cyclone fence, these were homes. Unbidden, the image of a schizophrenic homeless woman wandering frozen streets barefoot holding her dead newborn in her arms rose in his mind's eye. That happened not at all far from where Benedick was at this moment standing, in this city, though now it seemed to him a distant, Dickensian fever dream.

"How did your contribution *make* credits?" Julia asked. The analogy was imperfect. They didn't understand.

"This is what I'm trying to get to, exactly. Each person with a job had a boss. This boss was the person who made you do the work. Every hour of work made credits because you were either taking something from nature that gave your boss credits, providing a service that gave your boss credits, or you were selling something that gave your boss credits. It was the goal of the boss to get more credits out of you than he was giving you. That is called 'profit.' Whoever made the boss more credits, more profit, got better jobs with more credits."

"Another test," Tsuli said.

"Yes, everything was a test, and the only way to do well on the test was to make a lot of credits. Your worth was measured by how many credits you had. Some people had few and a small group had millions more." There he did it. It was out of his mouth before he could stop himself.

"How many vacations can one person take?" "Millions?" The room erupted.

"But, how did they get so many credits?" Gifford Pinchot asked. He had a look on his face that asserted a certainty he could pass all the tests and amass the millions.

"One very common way was to force many other people to spend long hours performing hard, dangerous work for you in exchange for few credits, or none, and you keep all of the credits they produced for yourself." Gifford's face fell. "Or, you could go out and grab a forest and cut down all the trees and exchange them for credits you keep for yourself. Or you could make lots and lots of toxic and completely unnecessary chemicals and spread them on the ground or on things people use or eat."

"These people got *more* credits, not less?" Julia asked incredulously.

The room erupted again. The kids objected that people would never allow any of this, that a person who wanted to do something like that would get mental health care. "The people with many credits arranged and maintained the system such that they could do these things. Remember that I explained the political system was controlled by a small number of people? Those people relied on credits from the ones with many to keep their positions as the ones who got to control everything."

"I don't get why people allowed these people to make all the decisions?" a boy named David Brower demanded.

"Why would some people *want* to make all the decisions? Collective wisdom is always better!" Cláudio said.

"But the Changes must have been constant!"

"The cities must have boiled with them!"

The comments came fast and the students began arguing with each other again. Class time was almost over, and they had only covered half of the material he had planned. It wasn't usually this hard. The tree had put him off balance. He couldn't remember the practiced order in the syllabus, he couldn't remember the soothing tone of voice he used, or the particular words. It was a damn good thing the Watchers decided long ago to keep secret unnecessary truths, like genocide, or human trafficking. These things remained a grim, dead language only Watchers knew. Regular people couldn't handle it.

"Well, here's the thing," he interrupted, "there weren't any Changes in the OE."

The students stared at him, uncomprehending. He might as well have told them that in the OE, air was solid. The Unity, Gaia, the Emanations were all eternal facts of life to them, like gravity.

"OE people couldn't even imagine such a thing could happen.

OE people viewed Gaia as a dead rock. Or, rather not dead…" *Damn!* he thought to himself, *I'm blithering!* "because to be dead, something would have had to be alive in the first place," he corrected himself. "They thought of Gaia as "The Earth" which was a material rock not capable of change, except through mechanical causation. They didn't have Emanations at all."

The students continued to stare. They didn't understand the concept of something that didn't have life in it, something "material." Even a chair was an Emanation with the Unity in it, *duh*, everyone knew that.

"Now, Gaia really did Change, but only in ways comprehensible to OE people." This was not the common understanding among Watchers at all—in fact, it was a point of contention—but he was struggling to put it into terms the students would understand. For some reason, it was so much more difficult today.

"For the materialists of the old world, these changes had to be material, the result of cause and effect. For instance, they had waves ninety feet tall come out of the ocean called tsunamis that took away a city, or a big fire that would remove a forest, but in the OE, the Emanations couldn't *give* anything. The people didn't consider that possible, so it never happened."

"But what happened to the people when a wave would take away a city?"

Natural disasters weren't on the syllabus. He was turned around again. He had to pull himself together and choose his words carefully. "Well, because people couldn't conceive of Changes in which the Emanations kept track of everyone, sometimes people would, accidentally, get caught up in a wave or a fire and die."

"A whole city?"

"Sometimes, yes."

The room erupted again. It's not that they didn't know about death. In their collective false memories, they knew of many deaths resulting from accident, age and illness, mostly. They didn't know about personal violence, however, except by mentally ill people, nor famine, nor large numbers of dead from any cause. Even accidents were rare.

Death from anything other than old age was something they had, in their version of history, largely "engineered out" through a clean, balanced environment, universally good nutrition, education, safe travel, mental health care, improved medicine, and so forth long ago.

"You see," he began again, "they didn't have the concept of Gaia, and so how could Gaia Change? We are a part of Gaia...." Benedick trailed off because he realized something that was perhaps connected with the tree. "In a sense, if we are part of Gaia and our understanding can limit Changes, then, in a certain way, *every* Change is a second order partnership Change." The kids didn't understand the significance of what he was saying, but the ten o'clock bell had already rung minutes ago. He had to promise them they would start tomorrow exactly where they left off before he could get them to leave for their regular school day.

Mandrake had said he thought the tree was a second order Change, but Benedick didn't really believe him until now. Benedick texted Fee. He asked her to call him, nothing more. To lecture her on the education of the Born, and the categories of Changes would be presumptuous. He would sound her out, suggest she gather perspectives, when she called. When he looked up he saw Cláudio waiting for him.

"You're going to be late for school, Cláudio, what is it?"

"I just wanted to ask...I want to be a Watcher, but why do Watchers have to know this stuff? What good does it do?"

Benedick was on firm ground with this question. "Watchers are responsible for keeping track of Dark Age history. If we don't know our bad history, we might repeat it."

"But...if you *do* know about bad stuff, doing it becomes possible, don't you think?"

He gazed at the boy's face, his smooth forehead knitted between the eyebrows.

"You would make an excellent Watcher," Benedick said.

The boy left rather unsatisfied it seemed to Benedick, but what more could he say? It was a philosophical question to which there was no settled answer. Benedick thought to himself that *remembering* evil was not so much the danger as *feeling* it. The boy would know nothing about that, of course. But, Benedick himself had been less terrorized by, say, the history of the Holocaust than the bullies who beat him in grade school and the adults who let them. He had no feeling connection to the Holocaust himself, he could *think* upon those horrors with remove, but he had *felt* a life long hatred for living bullies in any form. And what about people trained to hold racial hatred? Few of them had ever been personally wronged by the targets of their hatred at all. Yet, they were trained to hold strong feelings of hatred for them through repeated, embellished, emotionally evocative stories, that themselves were very much like the false memories of the regular people. The human brain can be wired to feel anything.

It was because these people did not remember being imprisoned, hunted, starved, harassed, struck or violated that the wounds and the terrors caused by those memories disappeared with them. The shadows of those wounds were more than adequately treated by the health and healing services and their low stress lifestyle. And the Born! The Born were magnificent, the first Earth generation raised by parents who were whole. The Born were the one thing that made Benedick glad to be in the New World.

Cláudio and his younger sister, María do Espirito Santo, sat in the sunny kitchen of their family home. María was sketching Cláudio on a pad and he was holding his body still while his eyes followed his mother, Alondre do Espíritu Santo, as she moved about the room. The home vibrated with the chords of Bossa Nova played on a piano in the living room by their father, Alexandre.

"Tomorrow is Automation Day," Alondre said. "Of course there wasn't just one day that everything became automated, but on Automation Day, a lot of machines all over the world that had been developed were put into service on the same day."

"We know," María said, without raising her head.

"In my day, it was a no school day, a big holiday. I don't know why we don't celebrate it anymore. Automation has liberated your generation as well." María continued to sketch and Cláudio sneaked a look at his device.

"Don't look down," María admonished him.

"My mother would make those special sticky buns on Automation Day. Would you like me to make you some sticky buns?"

"They give us a cinnamon roll at school for it," María replied.

"It's not the same! When I was small, they shut down all the factories and, first thing in the morning, all the people came to the factories and dressed up the machines like people…isn't that funny?"

"You told us."

"And sometimes, one of the elderly people would go to the place where they used to stand on the line, and they would put their own clothes or a silly hat on the machine that replaced them. People sang sentimental songs, and there would be a long table with those sticky buns and coffee and the manager of the factory would give a speech about progress and freedom that I found very boring as a child…but the old people would become quite emotional. It was a lovely day. Too bad we don't do it anymore."

"Is it true that they retired, no matter how old they were?"

"Almost true. The youngest of them found something else to contribute, but they received extra credits for a long vacation. A factory contribution was hard. When the machine made the contribution for them, they were able to rest. Most people felt those people deserved a rest."

María put down her pencil and touched a device at her elbow. A pop music station for teenagers broadcast through the kitchen speakers.

Alondra insistently whispered at them to turn it down. "You will upset him. Our people have been listening to Bossa Nova since before the Dark Age."

"Exactly," María said and both kids laughed. They turned it down, and María resumed sketching. The kids had never seen their father depressed, but the spectre of it was something that was omnipresent. He was finely tuned, their father, a sensitive man, and they had to be careful. Most especially, they had to be careful about music, which in their household was a family member with its own history, idiosyncrasies, politics, passions, grudges. What they listened to was important.

What they were listening to now on the radio was a song about a girl whose love decided to become a Watcher. In the catchy refrain she begged him to come back and watch over her instead. María sang along under her breath as she sketched.

"That song is dumb. Watchers don't actually *watch* anything," Cláudio said.

"Then why are they called Watchers?" María asked.

"Yeah, that's a good question," their Mama said, "Why is it?"

The boy's confidence dimmed. "I haven't asked him that yet."

The piano stopped abruptly.

"Turn it off! Turn it off!" Alondra hissed at her children.

"It's alright!" Alexandre said as he came into the kitchen, "You don't have to force them." His handsome face smiled.

"We like it," Cláudio lied, "We are just mixing them."

"Wait," Alexandre held up a hand excitedly, "I will not resist the greater force of teeny bop, I will submit!" He bounded out of the room, and soon they heard the piano again, at first haltingly, and then with more confidence. It was a jazz riff over the top of *Watch over Me*, as it played on the radio. It was quite good, and the children and their mother raised their eyebrows at each other, incredulous. When the song ended, he called to them to turn the radio up. When the next song came on, this one about a boy who nurtured an unrequited love for his sister's lover, Alexandre elevated it on a swell of jazz improvisation. Alondra almost joked that this talent could make him famous, but stopped herself. That was nothing to joke about.

They all knew that, when young, Alexandre had wanted to become a famous jazz musician. In his native Brazil, his generation was one in which there was a great resurgence of the old Bossa Nova, Samba. The streets and clubs were packed with musicians who were playing on the three year apprentice contribution, playing the nodes, trying to become professional. He thought he might have a better chance of attracting a following if he moved to the U.S. So he and Alondra went north and eventually landed in Portland. Perhaps because his native chords sounded best floating out of open doors into warm air and the North is too cold, or perhaps because the people are too cold themselves, he eventually had to accept that he was talented, but not enough.

Alexandre became inconsolable. He had been sure that he had a great contribution to make to the world rather than an ordinary one. There were several sad, hard years for them both before he was able to restart his life. He joked that his sole contribution to society for several years was as a volunteer subject for the Health and Healing Services.

He tried giving music lessons for awhile, but it bored him. Eventually, he got a degree in computer science. As it turned out, he was quite good at it. His ability to hold the musical structure of notes in his head, which was a kind of code, easily translated into skill with computer code, which contained its own silent music. In his exile, he had become a cheerful man who liked to joke around, but his handsome eyes turned down at their outer edges as if to say, É lamentável, but one might as well laugh.

Warm, moist air scented with cheese, garlic and starch rolled over the two children as their mother removed a large pan of *pão de queijo* from the oven. As she commonly did, she pulled one steaming hot cheese bun from the pan, tossing it between her burning fingers and dropped it in front of Cláudio.

"Why him first?" María protested.

"You can have it," Cláudio said and rolled it to her and waited for the second bun to drop on the table in front of him. They both pulled them apart immediately. Singeing their fingers and lips had always been a part of this ritual. Their mother said it was their punishment for impatience, but in some part of their shared childmind, it was a form of gratitude.

The piano ceased once more, and Alexandre reappeared in the kitchen to lift the lid on a simmering pot of black beans and stir them. He added more cumin.

"Why don't you go outside and play before dinner?" he said.

Cláudio grabbed a basketball on the way out and bounced it down the sidewalk to the street, and María followed. There was a basketball hoop set up there on the curb and he began to shoot the ball into the hoop. When she held out her hands, he passed it to her. She backed up into her favorite spot and threw the ball. It dropped into the hoop.

"Up two," Cláudio said.

"Okay," María said, and shot again. The ball dropped into the hoop again.

"That's only one, ball hog," Cláudio said.

She frowned and bounced it to him. He dribbled to a new spot and tossed the ball, which missed.

"We're down one now, so maybe ball hogging is better," she teased. He tossed it to her, she shot and missed.

"What's the score again?" she asked.

"Let's see, passed shot up two, you shot without a pass for one, then two misses which brought us down two. We're at one now. You want to start a timed game?" He fingered the device in his pocket, the one that once attached to the post counted their shots against a timer.

"Not really," she said, and his fingers released the device. She passed the ball to him.

"We'll never beat our all time record anyway."

"That was amazing," she agreed. They dribbled and shot in silence for several minutes.

"My Watcher teacher told me that a thousand years ago they played this same game."

"Yeah?"

"But instead of one team, you had two teams and they tried to prevent each other from scoring."

"That's dumb. You end up with less."

"Like, I would be raising my hands and bumping into you to try to prevent you from getting the two points."

"But why?" She aimed and sank the ball. When it came back to her, she tossed it at her brother.

"Well, it's because my score would be separate from your score. I would get more points and you would get less. It's to see who's best."

"Best at what, exactly? Being a jerk?"

He shrugged. "You want to try it that way?"

"Fine, I guess. What do I do?"

"You dribble around and try to shoot while I try to take the ball away from you." He bounced the ball to her. She caught it, but wouldn't dribble it.

"That's not very nice!"

"That's what they did."

"They were stupid barbarians. I don't want to play that way." She bounced the ball back to him.

"Well, let's do it the hard way then."

The hard way was harder because there were specific spots on the court that you had to shoot from, in order. It was timed, like the casual game, and you had to dribble in between the spots, which were not next to each other. It was necessary to be strategic about who made the shot from where because each of you had to do half. You had to play to your strengths.

"That's fine. I'll take one, five, seven and thirteen, I always hit those. You can decide the others, if you want." Cláudio attached the device in his pocket to the post and pushed start. They had an efficient run in the beginning, but the ball got away from them on a rebound, and then María dribbled on her foot and they lost their confidence. They didn't even finish, the time had run so long it was laughable. Dinner would be ready soon. Cláudio pocketed the device.

"My teacher told me a secret that I'm not supposed to tell anyone else," he said.

"What?" Her eyes brightened. Cláudio walked in a circle dribbling, not meeting her eyes. He knew it wasn't a nice thing to say, but he just couldn't hold it inside himself, alone, any longer.

"Before the old basketball game, a thousand years before *that*, they *still* played the same game," he paused, "and if you got fewer points at the end they *cut off your head*."

"Liar! They did not!"

"That's what he said."

He could have told a comforting lie, or at least, stop arguing, but he couldn't. He wanted someone else to know, to validate to him that it was a horrible thing to know. That this knowledge would cause a person to lose sleep, have nightmares. So, when she argued that no one would ever do such a thing, he insisted that their forebears *did* do it, and she became so upset that she ran into the house before him vowing to tell their parents the secret. Cláudio felt so sick to his stomach, he didn't even care.

Before they even sat down to dinner, Cláudio found himself opposite his father's kind, sad eyes in a pool of lamplight next to his father's chair. All important conversations took place here. He told Cláudio why they were there, explained how he injured his sister with his words.

"Did your sister misunderstand you?" he asked.

"I'm not supposed to talk to people about it," Cláudio objected weakly.

Alexandre Ribeiro da Silva was ever a gentle man, but he was tall, powerfully built, and possessed a strong magnetism that now gathered into his eyes as he lowered his gaze, "This is very serious. It is not a burden a child should carry. You are going to tell me everything."

8

the dead

Benedick was lying on his back in the dark. It was uncomfortably hot and his skin was sticky under the cotton sheet that covered him. He laid wide awake, sweating and longing for Bea. She liked a night like this, a little too hot, with the window open. He got up in the dark and opened the window and was surprised to hear the trees shuddering in a gusty breeze. The moving air gave him unexpected relief. He unplugged his lamp and walked around the bed with it and set it on Bea's nightstand and clicked it on. He laid back down, turned towards her side of the bed and closed his eyes. He could almost imagine that she were there, reading very quietly.

It wasn't the regular people that gave Benedick his name. He had possessed that name for almost a half century before the transition. Born John David Eggleston in Belfast to Scottish Presbyterians in 1945, he moved with his family to Ashland, Oregon as a teen when his father got a job teaching Shakespeare at the University there. Ashland was a kind of heaven for John's family. It was a tiny, quiet place set like a cubic zirconia next to the greater jewels of mountain and stream. Although it was a small town, it wasn't small minded, but literate. Shakespeare plays were staged all the year long in its several theatres and tourists came in their multitudes to see them. It was a girl in that little town who gave Benedick his name, a girl named Beatrice.

Beatrice moved to Ashland from Medford a year after John had arrived. His too long, wheat colored hair and foreign accent, round in the back of his throat, which he often exaggerated for effect, proved irresistible to the local schoolgirls. Also, he knew many sections of the plays by heart, so he naturally became a star in the Ashland High School production of *Much Ado About Nothing*. It was the week of the last show of this play that Beatrice showed up in the lunch room, sitting with the Juniors. All of the Senior boys were talking about her right away, having concluded that she was now the most beautiful girl in school. She pronounced her name like the French do, a two syllable Bea that sounded to John David like the prettier, more petite cousin of Beauty.

He asked her to come to his house that day, not only because she was lovely to look at, but also because he wanted to see the look on every boy's face as they passed together down the front walk of the school and beyond. John David was indeed a teenaged boy and such miscarriages of character were not yet smoothed away. Bea agreed and they did walk down the front walk of the school, and all the way to his house eight blocks away. She was talkative and friendly, honest and kind. She was smart, which surprised the boy schooled from infancy in the words of great *men*, and she already knew a great deal about literature from her own reading in the Medford Public Library. Her favorites, however, were Virginia Wolfe, Georges Sand and Zora Neale Hurston. By the time they reached the window seat in John's family living room, he had lost the desire to exaggerate his accent, and in fact couldn't think of anything to say at all. As he looked at the long dark fringe of her eyelashes lying on her cheeks against the sun, her smile that laughed at its persistent glare, he was forever hers.

"It's so bright here! I can hardly see," she said, and turned her back to the window.

"I'm going to have to change my name to Benedick," he said.

"Benedick and Beatrice!" she said laughing, thinking he was joking.

"Yes," he said, without any smile at all and he kissed her.

Bea called him Benedick from that day to their last together, that hot, summer night fifteen years ago, when she said, "Good night Bene," and he never saw her again.

Benedick didn't know how long he had been asleep when he woke quite suddenly on Bea's side of the bed, with the light of the lamp still in his face. He turned it off and rolled over to his side of the bed. He was beginning to drift again when he heard a distinct thump in the next room, like wood striking wood. He exhaled. Surely not still another Change? He swung his feet to the floor and heard another sound, identifiable as the heel of a shoe upon wood, then another. His hand reached out for his lamp but touched only air. His panicked mind remembered that he had moved it.

"Who's there?" he asked, frantically reminding himself that this world is safe.

There was no response other than the continued progress of the heel strikes toward him. He stood up and quickly walked toward the light switch next to the door, but as he reached it, he was struck on the side of his head and could no longer think of anything for several seconds. He was vaguely aware of resolute hands closing around his shoulders and turning him, and then pushing him down to his knees. As his blinkered mind began to reboot with a surge of pain above his ear, a large, warm hand closed itself across his forehead. For a moment, it seemed to Benedick a soothing gesture, a parent checking a child for fever. Then the hand tilted his head back in one smooth motion and he felt a blade on the left side of his neck, a bee sting that sprinted across his throat. He began to struggle, but already he felt a warmth spreading down his chest that was also strangely soothing, and then nothing.

9

blood

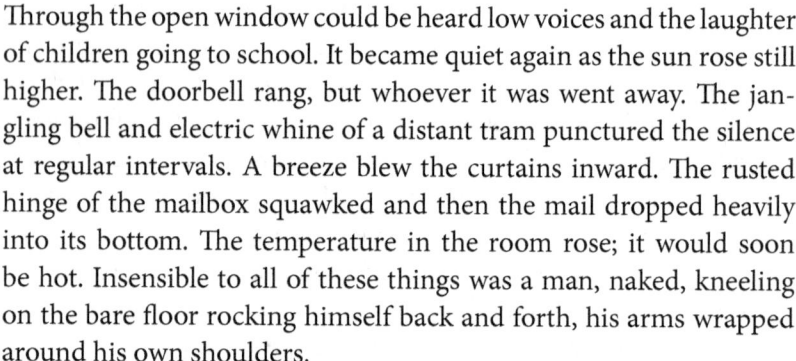

Through the open window could be heard low voices and the laughter of children going to school. It became quiet again as the sun rose still higher. The doorbell rang, but whoever it was went away. The jangling bell and electric whine of a distant tram punctured the silence at regular intervals. A breeze blew the curtains inward. The rusted hinge of the mailbox squawked and then the mail dropped heavily into its bottom. The temperature in the room rose; it would soon be hot. Insensible to all of these things was a man, naked, kneeling on the bare floor rocking himself back and forth, his arms wrapped around his own shoulders.

He whispered to himself quietly, almost too quietly to be heard, *"Lembre não mate, não mate o velho, Não mate."* In this whispered perseveration, he was reminding himself: Don't kill the old man. He ceased rocking. His body was perfectly still, his arms still held his own shoulders, but his downturned face was taut with agitation. Very slowly the man lifted his chin, even more slowly he lifted his eyes. He knew what he would see, and didn't want to see it.

"No! No! No! No!" he wailed, "They are gone! They are all gone!"

The man cried bent over, his saliva pooling in the front of his mouth and dropping from his bottom lip in a long string. With a loud cry, he unwound his arms, laying his hands on his legs. In his right hand, there was a knife, red with blood.

"*Não mate o velho!*" He lifted this hand and brought it down on his thigh, the knife burying itself in the flesh of it. Seemingly without even feeling it, the man lifted the knife again, "*Lembre! Não mate!*" and brought it down again. "Gone! Gone!" He struck again. His blood ran down his thigh and made a small puddle next to the larger pool of blood surrounding the old man's head.

1 0

the visitor

Cláudio was very deeply asleep, dreaming about his parents' home town in Brasilia. He and his father were there together, having a long conversation at a wood table underneath the great spreading Jambo tree behind his grandfather's apartment building. His grandfather had allowed him and María to build a rude platform in the heights of that tree last summer. His father was drinking a cold beer and he was drinking a soda. It was a clear vision that caused him a great deal of surprise when he awoke from it.

His sleep fogged mind remembered that what woke him was a banging noise, though once awake, he wasn't entirely sure he had heard it. Then it started again, an insistent banging on the front door, and then a man yelling. Before he could figure out what the man was saying, his mother was next to him, just visible in the first light of dawn.

"Cláudio, quickly up, come with me." His sister was huddled behind his mother, who pulled them both into her bedroom in the back of the house. "I have called emergency and they will be here soon. The man is sick and they will take care of him." She wrapped each of them in a blanket, patting their shoulders.

"What if he breaks in the door?" María asked.

"That's why we are here. If he breaks in the front door, we will flee out the back. Okay? It will be alright. They will be here soon."

"I wish Daddy were here," María whined, but Alondra shushed her.

A loud bang sounded on the wall next to them and they all screamed. Alondra put her hand over her own mouth and she held up the other in front of her children's' faces. They could see him in the windows, a shadow backlit by the first glimmering of the rising sun. He tested the sashes of each window, as the children breathed quickly into the hands they pressed against their mouths, María quietly whimpering. He came nearer, bending back and forth in the nearest window, trying to peer around the white shade that shielded them.

"I know you're there! Open the door!" Bang! again sounded on the other side of the wall, on the back side of the house. They jumped, but kept their hands over their mouths. The banging continued for several minutes then stopped. The back door shook, and then was still.

"Is he gone?" María asked hopefully.

The banging on the front door resumed with more violence. Then the man began to launch his body against the door to break the lock. Alondra grabbed both children and took them to the back door where they crouched together.

"They will be here soon," she repeated, beating in time with the shaking concussions of the front door, "They will be here soon."

The sturdy door finally splintered, and Alondra pushed the kids out the back door. Thinking quickly, Cláudio pulled the blanket off his shoulders and flung it on the ground to the right as he, his sister and mother ducked left into overgrown camellias next to the house. They were crouched together in the middle of the largest shrub when a Watcher burst out of the back door. The Watcher saw the blanket and sprinted past it around the side of the house, just as Cláudio had hoped he would.

"That was brilliant," María said. Her smile faded as the Watcher reappeared around the corner, and Cláudio saw for the first time that he was covered in blood. His hands were bloody, and his pants red with blood to the knees. It had to be the most intense mania that allowed this man to batter down a door and then run with wounds such as those.

"What happened to him?" María whispered, but Alondra shushed her.

The Watcher ran past them to the center of the yard and turned in a circle, looking for them. "Why do you hide from me?" he called. Then answering his own question he said, "This blood, don't worry about this. It was an accident. I won't hurt you!" As he turned toward them and looked at the camellias behind which they were hiding, the Watcher smiled. "Oh! I know where you are!" he said and then he laughed.

As he took a step toward them, a pack of Health and Healing Services helpers burst from the back door. The Watcher yelled at them and backed away. "Stay away from me!" When they continued to advance, he pulled a knife from his pocket and pointed it at them. The three largest helpers, men who were tall, muscled and clad in heavy vests for protection, advanced ahead of the others. Two of them had in their hands heavy looking white balls connected by a strip of heavy white fabric a foot wide.

Cláudio had heard of this, but had never seen it before. They were going to wrap him like a spider, swaddle him, and then calm him. The largest men sprang forward, and like well trained athletes, positioned themselves quickly on either side of the hand with the knife, the fabric spooling out of the balls as they moved apart. They each pressed a button on the balls to stop the spooling and then advanced very close, watching for an opportunity. Cláudio could hear the voices of the men, low and reassuring, talking to the Watcher the whole time but Cláudio couldn't hear what they were saying. A fourth helper leapt suddenly from behind the Watcher and distracted him for a moment. The three large men, strong and nimble threw the balls very quickly back and forth to one another so that the fabric wrapped the hand, the knife and the man's arm. The Watcher yelled, "No!" and began to frantically pull the fabric away with his free hand, but it was spread in the middle with a sticky substance that stuck tight. All of the helpers then quickly swaddled his two arms tight against his chest and immobilized his neck with a whiplash cuff. Cláudio could only see the backs of the HHS helpers as they retrieved the knife, still wrapped in a section of fabric.

They were still talking to the wrapped Watcher and he to them, saying a great deal that Cláudio could not hear. They were holding him tightly on either side of his body, rocking him and he did seem to give up the struggle. He began to sob, tears running freely down his face, and as a needle was withdrawn from the Watcher's arm his face relaxed, and the men released him.

"That man is really suffering," Alondra said, tears running down her own cheeks.

"They will take care of him, won't they?" María asked.

The Watcher fell forward onto his knees in the scrubby grass, and even though Cláudio knew the man could not see him, it seemed as if he were looking right at him, his eyes meeting Cláudio's eyes. The Watcher cried out, and then his eyes, wet with tears, rolled upwards and he would have fallen forward had not the helpers caught him as he fell and carried him away.

11

the bridge

Benedick had wanted to talk to her about something important, and now he was unreachable. When the WI operator told Fee that Benedick didn't make an appearance at the school for his class two days in a row, she boarded a plane for Portland.

The face of the house, its inscrutable high windows, small porch, implacable door shut tight stared at her mutely. The mail box lid was propped with uncollected mail. She knew the door would be locked, but she tried it anyway. She knew that no one would answer her knock, but she knocked just the same. Wrapping her shawl around her, though the evening was warm, she circled around a thick planting of bamboo to the privacy of the side yard and was surprised to see the ladder already leaning against the side of the house. Her eyes followed it upwards to find the middle window wide open. An old fear, long forgotten, the fear of what men could do to other men, began to circulate in her midsection. She glanced around before ascending the ladder.

The interior of the house was just as she saw it last, though silent. She called through the window and received no response. Deciding at once that she herself would find whatever it was, she climbed through and turned immediately down the hall. Bea's room was empty, but as she passed it she could see into the door of Benedick's bedroom and dared go no further. Visible was the top of his head on the floor, his face turned away from her, spread around it a pool of blood. A hot breeze coming from an open window inside the room brought to her face the heavy, wet, acridsweet odor of blood and thoroughly dead human flesh. Fee brought her shawl to her mouth and nose as her stomach squeezed. She dropped to her knees, still staring at the top of his head.

"Benedick, what happened to you?" Immediately, she felt this was the product of her own failure. Failure to read the signs, predict. Failure perhaps to keep him in Las Vegas until the mystery of the tree was solved. Rising to her feet, she walked around the pool of blood and kneeled in front of his face. His eyes and lips were open, surprised, and flies crawled across his cheeks, his head, his neck. Furiously she waved them away, but they were persistent and she couldn't stop them. Bringing her hands to her eyes, her throat gave voice to the frustration and grief she had held in abeyance since she stood on the sidewalk in front of the house and knew he was dead.

She had known he was dead. But this. This was a jagged double border of ashy skin that stood dry on either side of a meaty wound that ran across his neck. *This* she did *not* expect, nor even thought possible. Wiping her face, logic told her that this was not merely a personal tragedy. This is something that needed to be dealt with, quickly. She needed help.

Ordinarily, she would call Las Vegas, but she remembered herself saying that Sunrise and the other four were connected to Benedick and the event of the tree. Sunrise answered after only two rings. Her voice sounded like she had just been laughing.

"Happy First Day!" she said.

"Oh, of course. I don't celebrate that," Fee said. "You have guests? Can you step into another room?" Fee told her about Benedick.

"That's impossible."

"My thoughts exactly, but I'm standing in the presence of his dead body. Can you contact the other four for me? The Watchers you were with First Day? Could you all fly here?"

"*Fly?* Fee, Orion lives in Portland and we are all *here*, at his apartment, all five of us. And, I don't know if you know this, but Orion is an expert investigator."

"I thought he was…something to do with stars?" Fee felt a dull throbbing in her head that slowed her thoughts.

"Now he is. In the OE, he was a murder investigator." Fee heard the phone drop on a surface. Distant music ceased and was replaced by the low vibration of human speech. Fee was standing in Benedick's kitchen. His coffee cup, printed with a bamboo pattern all around sat on the counter. Next to it was a matching plate with crumbs on it. She found she needed the reassurance of the floor. Sliding down the wall into a crouch, with her knees up against her chest, she stared at the back door, where the painting had hung the last time she was here. *Foreboding indeed.*

"Fee? Orion says to stay out of that room. Don't touch anything. He's going to make some calls and try to find equipment and supplies that he can use for this. We'll be there as soon as we can."

"Tell absolutely no one else," Fee said. She was sure that it would be disastrous if this became known to the regular people. She wasn't even sure if it were a good idea for the Watcher community to know about it just yet.

Fee didn't know how long she sat on Benedick's kitchen floor, but the room was completely dark before she heard a knock on the front door. She rose on cramped legs and turned on the light. When she opened the front door, all five of them, Sunrise, Diego, Mandrake, Crystal, and Orion filed into the living room.

"It's a terrible thing," Crystal said.

"And how much worse for you who found him," Mandrake said.

"Where is he?" Sunrise asked. Fee wordlessly turned and looked at Benedick's bedroom door.

"Was this window open?" Orion asked. He put down the large duffle he was carrying and walked over to the middle window.

"Yes, that's how I came in and found him. I haven't moved anything."

As Orion methodically removed the contents of his duffle and examined the window, and took fingerprints, the rest of them huddled in the living room chairs. For a long time, they did nothing but watch Orion work, that half of the room and the hall illuminated by bright lights, and the living room where they sat, in shadow.

"And I told you to look at stars," Fee mumbled. "Do you remember? The last time you were here?"

"You don't know how obsessively I've been looking," Orion said and then disappeared into Benedick's room.

"We need to figure out who did this and why, obviously, but what do we do now, tonight?" Diego said. "We can't just call the coroner, and let him see…."

"No," Fee said. "We have to prepare him ourselves."

"Weren't there religions that said you had to be buried within twenty-four hours?" Sunrise asked.

"Muslims," Mandrake said.

"And Jews, I think," Crystal said.

"We can say that it's a Watcher belief. We prepare our own and then we cremate them right away."

"I never thought I would become such an excellent liar," Mandrake said.

"It's hard to keep track of what's actually true, at this point," Crystal said.

"Has anyone checked the WI yet? What did Benedick write today?" Sunrise asked.

"Nothing," Fee said. "His last entry was before he left for Las Vegas. He had been home only a day before this happened."

"He wasn't the most diligent diarist," Sunrise said.

"No." A ghost of a smile.

Fee got up and turned off the floodlight aimed at the window. Only the light from Benedick's room down the hall now outlined her silhouette. "We don't want to alarm the neighbors," she said. Diego turned on the small reading lamp next to Benedick's chair.

"All of these books will need to be packed up and sent to the Council. I guess as Watchers die, they will have to create a Watcher library," Fee said.

"What do you mean, as Watchers die?" Mandrake asked.

"He's the first to die." Fee waited out the uncomprehending stares.

"In fifteen years?" Crystal asked. Fee nodded.

"On the entire planet? Not one Watcher has died?" Mandrake asked. "There must be millions."

"Out of roughly four billion people in the NE, there are exactly four million of us."

"It's true, I've never heard of anyone dying. It never occurred to me to find it strange," Mandrake said.

"We've been too busy to think outside of our own box, I guess," Diego said.

Camera flashes illuminated the room in quick succession. Mutely, they all looked down the hall toward the source, and another succession of flashes burst from the hall. They looked at each other in the whining strobe of the camera.

"He is the eldest of us…Benedick was," Fee told them.

"In the world?" Diego exhaled.

Fee nodded. Mandrake stood in the front window looking out at the streetlights and passing pedestrians, and Sunrise got up to look at Benedick's books. Diego and Crystal sat looking at their hands. Several hours later, Sunrise was half finished with one of Benedick's books, Diego and Crystal were dozing, and Mandrake was still moving from one part of the room to another.

"I need to tell you all something," Fee said, causing them all to turn to her, "It's not something I'm proud of. We in the core group decided some time ago to try an experiment." Fee stopped speaking. She kept her eyes on her folded hands for several moments. When she looked up, her eyes were brimming with tears. "We thought it strange that no one had died. But we were also concerned with the certain eventuality that we would start to die. We thought it poetic or symmetrical that the eldest of us begin this experiment, and he was someone I felt I could trust with such a delicate task." Fee paused again, unable to continue.

"Benedick. What was he doing?" Orion asked, "This is probably the key." He pulled over a wood chair.

"Well, imagine for a moment if all the Watchers died today. Who would maintain the WI? Who would perform Naturework for second order Changes? Who would provide a link to our history and make sure that it doesn't repeat itself?" Fee asked. "This is what we were thinking when we decided to choose a small group of the Born and begin teaching them a little bit about the OE in a way consistent with their beliefs."

"How consistent?" Sunrise asked.

"For instance, we don't tell them about the transition or First Day. We teach them about the OE as if it happened here, long ago, which is what they think anyway. Their false history is that a thousand years ago we came out of a Dark Age about which they know little, very little information survived. The world at that time was a physically challenging place, but with the help of the Unity, they survived and built this." Fee raised her hands.

"Physically challenging?"

"The usual mythology…dark lords seeking power working against the Unity destroyed the material economy and the Earth. The people of the Earth were afflicted with famine and disease and so forth. A savior figure—a young student—lead a rebellion against them and saved humanity."

"Star Wars," Orion said.

"And every other movie," Sunrise said.

"We hadn't gotten very far, with the Born," Fee said. "We hadn't really worked out the details of how they were supposed to graduate, if you will, into becoming someone who could believe the story we would tell them. We were just experimenting with a small group to find out if we could teach them anything at all. We chose them from among a very large group of local youth who said that they wanted to become Watchers. Kids all over the world believe that it's a normal career choice, contribution, whatever."

"Perhaps the person who did this doesn't like the idea of this class," Orion said.

"A regular person?" Sunrise said incredulously. "Surely this is some kind of Watcher malfunction? It *couldn't* be a regular person."

"A mentally ill Watcher, maybe," Crystal volunteered.

"Let's not get ahead of ourselves," Fee said, "Orion, what did you learn?"

"Benedick has been dead two days, give or take. The person who committed this crime was very precise, premeditated. Benedick was hit on the head and his throat cut, probably in that order. He's wearing pajamas, I'm guessing two nights ago. There was no struggle. Nothing appears taken nor disturbed. It's been a dry summer, so the ground is firm. The assailant appears to have left the same way he came. This was a personal crime committed by a relatively large person, I'm guessing male. Whether he wanted Benedick dead, or just a Watcher, I can't say. I don't think the results of any lab work will bring any surprises. There is a small pool of blood from the assailant, which is odd because the method of injury is not at all obvious. Benedick died quickly. So we have the killer's DNA, if its possible to match it to someone. Maybe we will have his fingerprint amongst those that I have taken." Fee bowed her head.

"Can we see him now?" Crystal asked.

They all filed into the bedroom, Orion last, and stood in a circle around the body. Fee was the first to kneel next to Benedick's head, then Crystal knelt beside her and laid a hand on Benedick's shoulder.

"I'm sorry," Crystal said, gazing at Benedick's face. The others knelt next to them.

"The Unity allowed this?" Mandrake asked.

"I can't count how many questions I have," Sunrise said.

"This doesn't feel random," Crystal said. "If it's illness, there is some kind of purpose in it, at least according to that person's way of thinking. What was it?"

"Regular person or Watcher?" Orion said.

"Will that person kill again?" Diego said, "and if so, why?"

"What kind of story are we going to have to make up to ask so many experts these questions and *not* tell them that a Watcher has been murdered?" Mandrake asked.

All of them were kneeling in a circle around Benedick's body in shock. Crystal reached for Fee, but was waved away. Sunrise exchanged with Crystal a glance of silent sympathy and opened her mouth to say something, but was stopped by Fee's intake of breath. Without looking up from her hands, which were now resting on Benedick's left shoulder, she spoke.

"I didn't know him well, the way a person knows another person. We didn't spend time together. However…," her chest moved quickly, like a tiny bird's, in and out, "I don't have the words for it. It was only the two of us there on First Day and we understood each other. He was like a father to me." Crystal carefully laid her fingers on Fee's shoulder, then her head. Tears slipped down Fee's cheeks.

"We are agreed to keep this between us. We will prepare his body ourselves. Fee wiped her face. We will manufacture a Watcher burial tradition to explain it. The coroner will come and pick up Benedick's body and cremate it. I will take the ashes back with me to Las Vegas. We will have to make this house very clean. It will likely go right back into the housing stock database, the same as if a regular person died. We can't have regular people finding blood in here, even between the floor boards." She delivered this set of conclusions without lifting her eyes.

"Let's move him into the kitchen and wash him there," Sunrise said.

"I'll work on this room," Orion said, and Mandrake offered to help him.

When Sunrise saw Fee staring at a coffee cup and plate on the counter in the kitchen, she moved them out of sight into the sink. "We'll take care of Benedick, Fee. Why don't you just sit down." She didn't even demur, but sank into the nearest kitchen chair as Sunrise, Diego and Crystal pulled off Benedick's clothes and prepared a basin. Mandrake brought two clean bedsheets and laid them on the table.

"These will do for winding sheets. It will be part of our tradition that we are never autopsied. We bind our dead and tie them securely ourselves," he said, and then returned to the bedroom.

After an hour, Benedick was clean, his neck was bandaged with gauze, and the body was dressed in winter wear so that he would have a beige turtleneck beneath a woolen tunic. They had closed his eyes and mouth.

Orion and Mandrake came and stood next to Fee. "The bedroom is clean," Orion said to the others in a low voice. "We put everything into a cardboard box that I'll take with me."

Crystal came in through the open back door with a bowl full of lawn daisies and dandelion flowers that she placed in Benedick's hair and down the center of his body. Then they lifted him onto one of the sheets.

"We don't have a liturgy," Sunrise said.

"Sure we do," Crystal said and in a clear voice began it.

"Here lies our friend. A mote of the Unity made conscious was he and we were glad of his presence. We are grateful for the opportunity to be here with him a short while. While his transition is difficult for us who feel his absence, for him it is a day of celebration for his journey here is complete and he sets out upon a new road. Through our tears, we say Congratulations, Benedick, and godspeed. We are all one in Unity and thus he will forever be with us and we with him."

After she spoke, Crystal reached into the bowl she was holding and threw handfuls of rose petals on the body and the sheet and then nodded at Diego and Sunrise who wrapped him. Once he was wrapped in both sheets, he was tied head and foot with jute twine, into which they placed the stems of flowers.

"Let's carry him to the front room."

They laid him out on the carpet in front of the door, and then arranged themselves in chairs around him. No one spoke for a long time, but instead looked away from each other and listened to the clock ticking silence and their own thoughts.

"When are the people from the Council going to come for the books?" Sunrise asked Fee quietly.

"They were asked to wait until we were finished here. I messaged them, so they should be here soon. They will take his books and all of his devices. The rest will stay and be processed the same as a regular person without family. The coroner should be here a bit after."

The mention of his books reminded Fee of the World Tree mythology. Like many human mythologies, there is a sacrificial God. The male God is sacrificed, and the Female God walks across him to the New Earth. But Benedick is no God, and they were already on the New Earth! Fee felt overcome by fatigue and helplessness.

Within an hour, four efficiently working Watchers pushed them and their chairs out of the way and began stacking the books into boxes and taping them securely. Fee wandered over to where a woman was standing at Benedick's desk peering down at his computer, which was booted. Seeing Fee standing behind her, she said, "We're uploading the entire contents into the WI to be sorted later. We'll wipe this machine and reuse it."

But Fee wasn't wondering what the woman was doing. She was staring at Benedick's home screen. She knew at once that the finger coming into the frame from the left was Bea's. She looked at Sunrise, who looked at the screen, and back at Fee. She didn't understand. Bea was pointing the way. Her finger ostensibly pointed at some mountains in the background of the photograph, but the angle of Bea's finger combined with the angle of the laptop screen on Benedick's desk suggested something entirely different. When Fee followed the trajectory of Bea's finger with her eyes, it led straight to Benedick's back door, where the painting had hung.

"It was strawberries she hated," Fee murmured to herself.

"What?" Sunrise moved closer, alarmed by the faraway look in Fee's eyes.

"That was Benedick's last entry into the WI. Apparently Bea hated strawberries."

Sunrise opened her mouth, but couldn't think of a question to pose. She looked at Diego instead, who rose from where he was sitting.

"Oh good," Fee murmured, "Diego, is that painting that was here still at the Rijks?"

"*View of Delft?* Yes, so far as I know it's still there."

"Why do you ask?" Sunrise bent down to her, as with a child.

"That is where Benedick will be," Fee replied.

At once Sunrise and Diego drew closer to each other, and to Fee, but were afraid to touch her.

"You haven't had much sleep," Sunrise said to her, "Perhaps you should let the rest of us handle this for the next day or so."

"Yes, that will be necessary." Her agreement did not relax them. Her absent eyes, and the assured, but unattached tone of her voice did not match her words, which themselves implied more than they communicated. She was in her own world and they didn't know how to reach her.

A man in a coroner's uniform let himself in through the front door, with three other people. The large room was suddenly crowded and noisy. Fee motioned for the first coroner to come into the kitchen, and Sunrise followed.

"A Watcher's body requires special care," Fee began, speaking to him with authority.

The man stood up straighter and lifted his chin. "We know very well what to do with Watchers. We take great pride in our ability to handle Watchers with the greatest delicacy."

Fee and Sunrise exchanged a surprised glance.

"I'm very sorry if I have offended you, I am not from Portland," Fee said, and the man visibly relaxed. "Please, if you will have patience with us strangers and confirm how you handle the bodies of Watchers here?"

"Of course. We touch them as little as possible. It is required that they be cremated within twenty four hours, but our service takes pride in completing the cremation of a Watcher immediately. You may even ride with me and Mr. Benedick, and watch the process, if you like. In the alternative, we can send the ashes, packed carefully in a red box wrapped in brown paper so that it, also, is not touched, to any address you like."

"Thank you very much, sir, for your patience. I should not have doubted your correctness." Fee and Sunrise followed the man into the front room where the other three had taken up positions on either side of Benedick's body. The man took up his position at Benedick's feet and removed two very long and wide satin ribbons from his jacket. He kept one and handed the other one to the men standing on either side of Benedick's head. Each of the four men grasped one end of a ribbon and knelt on the floor. It wasn't until the men at Benedick's feet began to work the ribbon underneath him, and the men at his head did the same, that their purpose could be deciphered. Once the ribbons were in place, the four lifted him together and set him down into an open body bag. The first man slipped out the two ribbons and pocketed them while another zipped the white shrouded body out of sight.

"Will you come with us?" the man asked.

"Yes," Fee replied.

"Excuse me," one of the Watchers packing books asked, "Shall we take that box, as well?" She pointed to the cardboard box underneath Orion's duffel.

"Oh, no," Orion said, moving in front of it, "That one is mine. Thank you."

Sunrise walked through the house with Orion, closed the windows and doors as the movers took out the last boxes.

"I'll take Benedick's ashes back to Las Vegas with me," Fee said. "We have to find this person quickly."

"Agreed," Orion said. "I would suggest that we all meet in a secure online workspace tomorrow to plan our next steps. I'll send you all a link."

"Will you be alright?" Crystal asked. The five of them formed a concerned circle around Fee.

"Yes," she said, "but perhaps not in the way you think. It's clear to me now that Old Earth and New Earth are in symbiosis. As Old Earth devolves, Las Vegas writhes. Benedick is the bridge. I must walk across it."

"Is that possible?" Sunrise cast an alarmed glance at Diego.

"It must be."

"With respect, Ms. Fee? We're ready to go." The coroner stood on the porch, a polite distance from the open front door.

"I'm ready."

1 2

the investigation

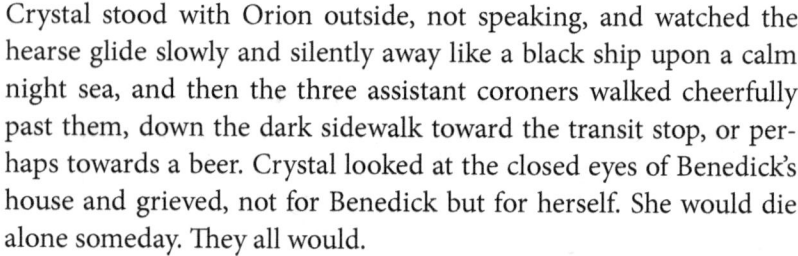

Crystal stood with Orion outside, not speaking, and watched the hearse glide slowly and silently away like a black ship upon a calm night sea, and then the three assistant coroners walked cheerfully past them, down the dark sidewalk toward the transit stop, or perhaps towards a beer. Crystal looked at the closed eyes of Benedick's house and grieved, not for Benedick but for herself. She would die alone someday. They all would.

"It's almost midnight," Sunrise said, walking down the walk toward them with Diego and Mandrake, "if we walk quickly, we can make the next tram to the hotel." Crystal didn't have to look at him to know that Orion's eyes were on her. She didn't move.

"I don't think I can sleep yet," Crystal said.

"I'm not sure it's safe for us to walk around alone until this is…. He might be watching us right now."

Orion said, "I'll stay with her." Crystal turned toward him, and reluctantly raised her eyes to his as the others walked away from them. He reached for her, but she stepped away, "They can still see us," she said. They watched together until the others were swallowed by the dark.

"You can stay with me," he said, his eyes soft and warm in the moonlight.

"It can't be the way it was before," she said.

Orion wrapped his arms around her and pulled her body close. She had kept herself separate from him all day, had felt herself master of her feelings for him, but at this moment his muscled chest and shoulders were primal comfort. She had forgotten how good it felt to be held by him. She pressed her face against his neck and breathed in his skin scent. Orion, yes, were the utterances of her heart. He remained silent as he moved his hands over her head, down her silky hair, her shoulders, then around to her face as she pulled away from him.

"I can't do that again," she said. "It's too painful. I can't tell you how much I would love to take the blue pill and forget about all of this. We would sign up for a house with a garden and I would have a baby, and you would drag a telescope into the backyard and tell her the names of the stars." Still he remained silent, as she swallowed her tears. "There's no blue pill for us and there never will be, especially now."

"It's okay for us to find a little happiness here, yes even now. This world doesn't need Watchers to be miserable," he said gently.

"Yes, but find happiness how?" she said. "We would have to be strangers to our own children. We would have a million secrets from them. I don't even think that's possible. Children find out everything. And if we raised them to know our secrets, they could never play with other children. We would have to live in a Watcher commune. Have you ever heard of a Watcher commune?"

"Maybe there is one somewhere in the world."

"Maybe it's because I'm watching the last of my thirties slip away, but I'm tired of being needed by this world. I'm tired of work. I don't want casual liaisons with Watchers. I miss my Mama. I miss Thanksgiving. It's not something I'm proud of, but I think, to hell with the regular people. I would give almost anything to forget it all and have a baby with you." Orion kissed her and she wound her arms around his neck.

"When I'm not with you I can just focus on work, and let time pass," she murmured.

"But that's not enough," he said. "Come home with me, Crystal. Forget about everything for a few hours at least. We'll forget together."

When Crystal woke in Orion's bed the room was still dark, but he was gone. She wrapped the sheet around her and found him in the living room. Through the plate glass windows of his high rise apartment she could see a faint orange aurora radiating over the Willamette river that did not yet reach into the dark room. Instead, Orion was bathed in the glow of a computer screen, his broad shoulders and back bare, his hair hanging forward as he bent over the mouse, scrolling. She moved forward, dragging the sheet over the floor, and he turned.

"Hey, lovely. A goddess has come from my bed." His hands sought the bare skin of her belly, which he kissed.

"Couldn't sleep?" she asked softly, and then, hopelessly, as an afterthought, "Did you find anything?"

"I did," he said with his face pressed against her. She drew back.

"We won't be able to confirm anything for several hours," he said, keeping his hands on her bare hips under the sheet, drawing her to him.

"What? What did you find?"

"Well, yesterday, when you suggested that Benedick's murder was the work of a mentally ill person, I looked into it right away, even before I examined the scene. There weren't any local Watcher issues, obviously, we would have known about that right away. So, the first thing I did was look through the logs of the local police and Health and Healing Services that are automatically forwarded to the WI, to see if any regular people had lost it in the previous twenty four to forty eight hours." She raised her eyebrows.

"The Resolutions Corps are not police, you know. They don't have that."

"At the *RC*, Nothing jumped out at me, but I did make a list of possibles, of people who had been admitted to the HHC. And I made a note to also check in with the doctors there. There might be people who were not admitted, but who were in outpatient crisis, or people receiving ongoing care."

"There are serious privacy issues with the outpatient people, and they won't understand why we are prying."

"We'll have to brainstorm a story."

"Another story! I was raised to be honest and truthful always. Now, lying is practically a part of my job description."

"Adaptable to new situations," Orion said, and Crystal giggled. "Long hours," she said laughing…no chance for advancement!"

"And no pay at all!" Orion joked. "I don't remember applying for this position…you?" Crystal made no response. She was looking down, and he couldn't see her eyes through her hair.

"Hey?"

Very quietly he heard her say, "Must be willing to give up everything and everyone you ever loved."

"We agreed…." he said.

"I can't help it. It's really bothering me, even worse than the first year, I don't know why."

"We have to remain relentlessly positive. Remember? That was what we agreed last night…right there in that room."

"I was under the influence of Orion," she said, and allowed a small smile to ghost across her lips. "I think for a long time I honestly believed…," she looked up at him, "I really did believe that this was temporary. Some kind of weird side trip. I think I'm finally realizing that this is it. This is where I will die."

"We are young…."

"That's the problem!"

"Okay…maybe you need to spend time at the HHC as a patient."

"And somehow that will magically change the situation? We will magically have a big group of friends we can tell anything to? We will magically grow a family to spend all these many holidays with? Good God! I saw my family only three times a year: Fourth of July, Thanksgiving and Christmas. Now these people have a dozen holidays, which is great for them! But for us, it's twelve opportunities to feel alone. And I hate it when the regular people invite me for the holiday. I can't talk about anything I want to talk about, and so I just listen to them talk about how wonderful every aspect of their lives are. They rub my nose in it. And don't tell me that we can have each other. It's not the same. Our table set for two. Might as well move into a trailer with twenty cats."

"They don't have trailers here." When she rolled her eyes at him he pulled her closer, "Come on! This does no good! Does it? There's no point in going on about this. We have to accept what is and make the best of it. I do know some Watchers in this town, and they are good people. We can make an effort to connect more with them. Maybe they're as lonely as you are?"

"I don't understand why it doesn't seem to bother you at all?"

"I grew up on the Rez. Lots of empty, wide open space. The land was lonely, and it taught me how not to be."

He pulled away from her.

"That's not all, Crystal. There was one strange lead. There was a log from both the RC and HHS about a man who was reported missing, *possibly* with a mental health issue, the report was flagged for that because he had had a history of depression." He looked down at a paper in front of him, "That was Wednesday morning at 11:10. His wife reported that he was agitated the night before and never came to bed. He stayed up all night on his computer, which is *very* odd behavior for a people who only contribute twenty-five hours a week. In the morning, he was nowhere to be found, but she figured that he had gone to his office early for some reason. It was after someone from his office called and told her he never showed that she became concerned and reported it."

"That's not very persuasive, missing depressed person."

"No, but here's the strange part: when I woke up a couple of hours ago and went to the RC department records to see if there were any new developments on the depressed guy not forwarded yet, that report was *gone*, scrubbed."

"Like some old style cover up type thing?"

"Or a Change. The report is scrubbed from the regular records, but preserved in the WI."

"What the hell is this? Either the regular people have conspired to kill and then cover it up, which seems completely impossible, or the Unity has done it, which seems equally crazy."

"Except that the Unity does everything, right? We *are* the Unity. Every time we choose, the Unity Changes."

"That's what they say, anyway."

"And that's not the last of it. Just to be sure, I checked the WI for reports related to Watchers, not expecting anything, and there's *now* a Watcher in the local mental institution…."

"Healing Pod," she corrected him.

"Get this: he was picked up *yesterday* in mental health crisis, and they don't know his name."

"*Yesterday*? But there was nothing yesterday!"

"Exactly. I say we go over right after shift change at seven this morning and see what's up with this guy."

1 3

brasília

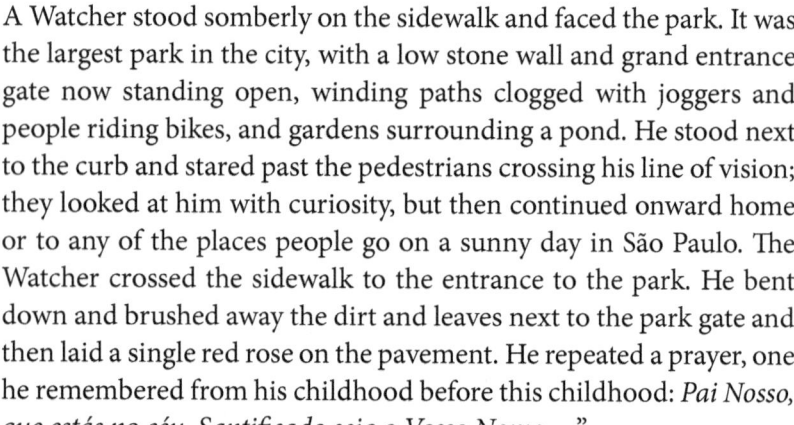

A Watcher stood somberly on the sidewalk and faced the park. It was the largest park in the city, with a low stone wall and grand entrance gate now standing open, winding paths clogged with joggers and people riding bikes, and gardens surrounding a pond. He stood next to the curb and stared past the pedestrians crossing his line of vision; they looked at him with curiosity, but then continued onward home or to any of the places people go on a sunny day in São Paulo. The Watcher crossed the sidewalk to the entrance to the park. He bent down and brushed away the dirt and leaves next to the park gate and then laid a single red rose on the pavement. He repeated a prayer, one he remembered from his childhood before this childhood: *Pai Nosso, que estás no céu, Santificado seja o Vosso Nome....*"

"What are you doing?" This spoken by the boy, who unexpectedly appeared next to him.

Still overcome by the emotions and memories of another time and place, but also overjoyed to see this boy, he told the truth, "I put this here to honor a man who saved my life." He looked over the low wall into the vast park beyond.

"You almost died in this spot?" the boy asked.

"Not at this spot. This was the place where the man put himself to save me from that place there, where I spent much of my youth."

"The park?"

"This park wasn't always a park, but that's no story for you. I wouldn't even know about the story of the man who saved me had I not overheard it."

The man said all of this while looking into the park, away from the boy. He turned back toward him, not so much boy, actually, as an almost man. He could stand here with him all day.

"I saw you standing outside my grandfather's house," the boy said.

"Did you tell your mother and sister?"

The boy looked away, "No."

"Do I scare you?"

The man looked so miserable as he asked this, the boy lied, "No."

"You are from Brazil," the boy said, "It didn't occur to me until the next day that you were talking to us in Portuguese the whole time." The boy looked the man bravely in the face. "Is *your* life so terrible that you must claim my father's life?"

"Is that what happened?" the man asked quietly. His eyes rolled up as if he asked the question of himself. "I have endured terrible things," the man replied finally, "Things that you are not capable of imagining, *gratidão à Unidade*. Did I claim your father's life? Yes, certainly, and what of it? He is dead and has no use for it now. Was your father's life taken from me? Yes, certainly. I am here in the park, and not in the house with you. So you see, your father and I, we are even."

"That you are here at the same time we are here, it's not a coincidence, is it?"

"No." The man looked miserable again. "I wanted to see you, and tell you that I was sorry for scaring you. I wanted to make sure you are okay, but I didn't want to scare you again, so…." he shrugged and smiled sadly. "Are you all right? How is your mother?"

"She is mostly happy, but she cries sometimes…."

"She cries? That makes me both unhappy and happy too. I'm ashamed to admit it."

"Why happy?" The boy drew back from him.

"Tears are flattering to the dead. I am a dead man also, and we dead must stick together." The man looked into the middle distance of the park opposite.

"If I promise not to tell, will you tell me the story of what happened here?"

"You want to know things that are not good for you to know. Try to be like everyone else. It's better." The man looked at the boy and smiled. "You will never be a Watcher and that is a good thing."

This upset the boy. "The other Watchers told me that I might or might not. It's not up to them."

"Surely the old man explained…." The Watcher began to rub his forehead back and forth, "The old man…." *Não mate…*

"Are you alright?" The Watcher was breathing hard, in and out.

"The old man, the Watcher,…what was…*is* his name?"

"Mr. Benedick."

"Yes, yes, Mr. Benedick." He continued to rub his forehead and spoke with closed eyes. "Mr. Benedick surely explained to you that only the Unity decides who becomes a Watcher, and unfortunately there is no choice."

"Does your head hurt so much? Do you need a doctor?"

The man opened his eyes and jammed his hands into his pockets. "I'm fine. It's only that I am remembering something I didn't want to do. It's easy for me to lose track of where I am in time…Am I remembering this before I did it…or after? We are in Brasilia, it must be after…or I could be…in the park still?" A panic overtook his face and his terrified eyes stared past the boy. The man's hands itched to rub the headache that was throbbing behind his left temple, but he resisted the urge. It always upset people when he rubbed his head. He clenched and unclenched his fists inside his pockets.

"Maybe you should go back into a pod," the boy suggested uncertainly. The man smiled reassuringly, but the smile was anything but. His lips were pulled tight around his teeth, and the many horizontal lines from nose to eyebrows made liars of his eyes. "We could call them?"

"No," the man said, breathing hard to quell the throbbing. He cocked his head and his eyes rolled up to one side. "Wait. I don't hear anything."

The boy listened too. He heard birdsong, some children squealing. Some people who were passing them were talking.

"That's good, that makes me feel better," the man said. "When I was…in the park…it was never quiet. Not in the morning, not in the day not in the middle of the night, never. Always someone yelling or banging. No one is interrupting us, no one is yelling." He put a hand on the boy's shoulder. "You are really here. It's after the park. Please don't call them. I'm okay. I'm not in the park. It's after. I remember everything in order now. I don't want to go back. It wasn't easy to escape from the HHC. It took a long time to get them to let me out of the pod and walk around. And then figure out how to escape. And then I had to avoid every place they would look for me. But they didn't know what I know…that you come here every year at the holiday."

"How did you know that?" The boy's face betrayed a return of his fear.

"I…I know it from your grandfather."

"You know my *vô*? How do you know him?" The boy was happy now. He had wanted to trust the Watcher from the beginning, and anyone who knew his grandfather must be okay.

"I'm from this town. I don't know him well. He may not remember me. But, he told me all about you." The Watcher smiled broadly this time.

1 4

the pod

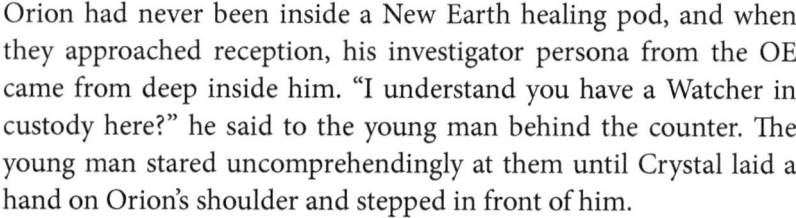

Orion had never been inside a New Earth healing pod, and when they approached reception, his investigator persona from the OE came from deep inside him. "I understand you have a Watcher in custody here?" he said to the young man behind the counter. The young man stared uncomprehendingly at them until Crystal laid a hand on Orion's shoulder and stepped in front of him.

"Good afternoon. We have heard that there is a Watcher in one of the healing pods? We are here to help him," she said.

"Oh! Sorry, I didn't understand. Yes. Do you know him? We can't find out his name and he won't tell us."

"Unfortunately, we don't think we know him, but we will be able to find out for you. I'm a healer in an HHC in Boulder, and I have helped people in the pods there. If I may, I would like to talk to the healer who is helping him before I talk to the man himself?"

"Of course! I'll page the healer."

The healer was a regular person, a young man who had a number of degrees and certificates, as do most healers in this world. This particular man, in addition to having a Ph.D. in psychology and the usual esoteric healing modalities, focused on sound healing.

"So, we have him in a padded pod right now. In ours, the wounded person has control over the environment. Although he knows that there is one person who is monitoring his condition and safety through a camera, he can turn the healing tones off or on, close off the pod for privacy and so forth. He has chosen to keep the pod private, and he has kept on the healing tones most of the day. I think it's really helping because he is much improved."

"Can you tell us how you came to have him here, from the beginning?"

The man began scrolling on a device with a finger. "We responded to an emergency distress call yesterday morning at approximately six thirty a.m. We found the man, a Watcher, in the back yard of a home, in a disoriented, psychotic state, bloody and raving."

Orion and Crystal looked at each other.

"Oh, don't worry. The blood was his. He had stab wounds down the front of both thighs. Luckily, the wounds were shallow and he managed to avoid major arteries. He didn't even lose that much blood, so he should recover quickly and completely."

"May we ask, what was he raving about?" Crystal asked.

The healer scrolled, "Ah, he was convinced that Watchers were bad people, even though he is one, I guess, and he said they were going to destroy the world. He insisted that he is not a Watcher and the family, the one who lived at the home he broke into, was his family."

"Sorry to interrupt. Perhaps you should just continue from where you left off? He broke into a house?"

"Okay. So, we responded to this back yard. The Watcher had broken into the house and the family was hiding from him in the back yard and he was attempting to find them. He insisted that he just wanted to talk to them because they are his family and he wanted them to explain everything to us."

"Hmmm," Crystal said, "Interesting."

"He threatened the helpers with a knife and so they wrapped him and brought him here, completely sedated. We cleaned him up, dressed his wounds, put him on an IV with heavy sedation in a hospital bed. Over the course of the day, yesterday, we managed to calm him down. By the end of the day, he was still lightly sedated, but fully conscious, eating and drinking, so I made the decision to take him off the IV and move him to a pod in an attempt to wean him from the sedatives." A look of insecurity crossed the man's face. "He can't process what is bothering him until he is off the sedatives," he said.

"Of course," Crystal said, "And?"

"At first, the pod seemed to make him much worse. He retreated to the back wall and knelt there repeating this set of four phrases." The man again referred to his notes on the device. "His name…."

"He has a name? I thought…."

"It's not his name. It's the name of a dead man. He says his name, he says that he loves the forest and its peoples, he is a musician, and that he loves justice. We couldn't figure out why he was saying these things, and so we increased his sedative and tried to engage him, draw him away from that activity…."

"Hmmm," Crystal said, "It almost sounds like something a person would do if they were losing themselves, you know, repeating the essentials of his identity so he doesn't forget them."

"But, he doesn't *have* any confusion about who he is. The issue is that he's sure that he's someone he is not."

"Alright. Go on, please."

"Well, this morning he awoke in the pod and, for want of a better term, went berserk. We didn't really foresee that. His clothes seem to be the problem. I was just conferencing with other healers to figure out what to try next when you arrived."

"His clothes are a problem?" Crystal said.

"We put him to bed with a heavier dose, so that he could sleep. We turned on the healing tones, and an aromatherapy mist. He slept well all night. However, apparently, at some point in the night he got up and put his street clothes on. I mean, *his own* clothes were bloody, but we obtained new ones for him and put them in the pod, just in case he wanted to dress in the morning. The pod monitor didn't see him get dressed, but he awoke fully dressed, and this was very upsetting to him."

"Was he wearing his shoes in bed?" Orion asked.

"How in the world did you know that?" the healer asked.

"It's something that Watchers do sometimes," Orion said, and

Crystal nodded.

"He now refuses to wear any clothes at all. He ripped off his clothes and threw them around the pod, and he is raving again. He insists that he is not a Watcher, he insists that he is a dead man and demands to talk to his wife, you know, the woman at the house he broke into. We would rather not put him through another wrapping. We are trying everything we know to calm him, but nothing is working. I hope you can help."

Standing in front of the pod door, Orion strained to listen through it, but could hear nothing. The healer knocked on the door, and turned on a two way speaker.

"Excuse me, Sir, there are two visitors here for you."

The shade on the small, rectangular window banged open, and Orion saw a handsome man, about forty, his eyes narrowed, pupils darting. As soon as the man saw them, the shade banged closed again, and he yelled through the speaker, "No Watchers! I am *not* a Watcher!" He kept yelling this assertion tirelessly. His English was heavily accented, but Orion couldn't identify what type of accent. Orion said to the healer, "Let me try."

Orion leaned down to the speaker, "We can help you. We can arrange to have you speak to your wife." The healer's mouth dropped open, "I don't think it's a good idea to lie…."

Orion lifted a finger to still him. The shade on the window opened.

"You can get my wife to speak with me?"

"I think so," Orion said, "but not as you are."

"I'm not going to put on those clothes!" the man yelled and walked away from the door. They could see that he was completely nude except for white bandages encasing both thighs, the left one having a small oblong of pinkish red stain on it. He was walking in circles in the center of the padded, egg shaped room. Orion leaned down again.

"We can get others for you. Would you like some pajamas?"

"Do Watchers wear special pyjamas?" He said pee-yammas. South American, Orion concluded.

"No, nothing special," Orion said.

"Alright then." Helpers brought a pair of pyjamas and opened the pod door. Orion and Crystal moved aside and watched through the open door as the man put them on. The helpers turned on the healing tones, pressed acupressure points. They gave him a glass of juice and a small capsule.

"Thank you so much," the healer said to them. "I think you can visit with him now, if you like."

The man was wearing a pair of blue print flannel pajama pants with a softly draping, white pullover shirt, and sitting in a bean bag chair in the pod, now calm. The helpers brought two more beanbag chairs and stood behind them.

"You can leave us now," Orion said to them, "Isn't that right, Mr...."

"Silva," he said.

"Yes, Mr. Silva is calm now," Orion said and the helpers left the pod and closed the door. Orion walked over to the intercom and turned it off. He and Crystal both sat opposite him.

"We are here to help you," Crystal said, and Orion nodded.

"You said you can help me talk to my wife."

"We will, but first we all need to understand what has happened," Orion said.

"Alright. I don't know what happened, so you explain it and then we can call my wife."

"We will take it step by step," Crystal said. "What is your wife's name? We are asking just to confirm."

"Alondra do Espírito Santo."

"The woman who lives in the home where you broke down the door? Do you remember that you broke down the door?"

"I didn't have my keys! They wouldn't open the door for me."

"Okay. Let's back up. It's good that you remember that, but I would like to start with the last time you spoke to your wife, before you broke down the door. When did you last have a normal conversation with her?" Crystal asked.

The man's eyes rolled to the ceiling, and then returned. "She was going to bed, and I was staying up. We said goodnight."

"I don't suppose you remember what day that was?" He shook his head sadly.

"Do you commonly stay awake late, or was there a special reason you were staying up late?"

He stared blankly and then rubbed his forehead back and forth with the heel of his hand. "Take your time," Crystal said, "No pressure."

"I usually go to bed with her, at the same time, but I was upset."

"You don't remember what upset you?"

"No. I was going to find out about it, though. I was sitting at my computer when she went upstairs."

"Were you working on your contribution? Did something happen at your office perhaps?"

"I contribute by computer programming. I help maintain the computer systems in this city."

"Very good. What else do you like to do?"

"I play guitar and piano. I cook. I play with my kids."

"Excellent. I will let your healer know that you like to play music. They can get you a guitar and I'm sure there's a piano in the building somewhere you can use." The man stared at his own hands and said nothing.

"Did something happen at your office that upset you? Something to do with computers?"

"I don't think so." Crystal was distracted by Orion, who was staring at the man's hands. She followed his eyes and noticed for the first time that the man had dried blood under his nails. Orion looked up at her, and then asked, "What do you remember next? She went upstairs, and you were sitting, upset, at your computer."

"I stayed up all night. I remember drinking coffee all night."

"Did you go to your office?

"No. I'm sure of that."

"Okay, very good. So, do you contribute a typical week? Monday through Thursday? Or an end week, Friday through Sunday?"

"Typical week."

"That's helpful. What did you do instead of going to your office?"

The heel of the man's hand again pressed against his forehead. He rubbed it back and forth, his face pained.

"When you do that," Crystal asked, "with your hand on your

forehead, what is happening? Is your mind blank or...."

"I see pictures. Flashes like snapshots."

"What are the pictures of?"

"Terrible things."

"Such as?"

"Dead people, for instance. I've never seen a dead person like this."

"An older man?"

He looked at her and cocked his head, "No. Not old, mostly young. Young men wearing dark clothes and helmets dead in the mud, with their body parts off, like animals came and pulled them apart. Piles of dead people that don't even *look* like dead people," his palm began rubbing again, and he was breathing hard, "there are so many there, piled like sticks. A young man with some kind of device on one side of his head and the other...it's as if parts of his head are blowing out the other side. Pictures like this. Many, many pictures. I can't make them stop."

"Okay, let's stop thinking about the pictures. We will breathe together for a few minutes," Crystal said.

While Crystal breathed with the man, Orion jumped up and knocked on the door and then disappeared behind it.

"Let's try something else. Do you remember coming here to the HHC?" Crystal asked him.

"No. Apparently, I was sedated when I arrived here."

"Ah. Moving backward from that, what is the next thing you remember?"

"Falling down in my own backyard, with the HHC people holding me."

"Before that? You said you remembered battering down the door. Before that?"

"Wanting to go home, and realizing that I had lost my keys."

"Okay. Where were you going home from?"

"I was...I don't remember. My legs hurt and that's when I noticed they were bloody."

"Bloody at that point? Okay."

Orion returned and sat down. Mr. Silva continued, "I got on the transit and no one would come near me."

"Pardon me," Orion said, "I brought some nail scissors, so we can get that blood off your hands."

"Oh, thank you very much," the man said and allowed Orion to take one of his hands and shave off the nails into a small plastic bag.

"So, you got on the tram all bloody?" Crystal asked.

"I know it's strange, but I just wanted to get home. I felt that if I could just get home, everything would return to normal. It would all be okay again."

"There's no going back," Orion said softly, and put the plastic bag and scissors in his pocket.

"Excuse me?"

"Nothing. Continue. People were frightened of you. They were probably messaging the HHS and the RC."

"Yes, they probably were."

"You got home. You couldn't get in. That's it? You just wanted to get in, take a shower and go to bed?"

"Yes, exactly. It was all a bad dream that I wanted to go away. And then when the HHC people showed up, I just wanted Alondra to tell them who I am, explain everything, but she wouldn't!"

"Okay, Mr. Silva, you told me a story. Now I'm going to tell you a story," Orion said, "a story about me."

"I don't think that's wise," Crystal said.

"All of us, we were just thrown into the deep end fully dressed," Orion said to her, and then glanced at the man, "with our shoes on. It's gotta be that way for him too. There's no way to dip a toe into this."

"But he has *three* worlds to deal with, not two," Crystal whispered. "His life in the OE, his false memory life in the NE and now *this*. I think we should talk about this outside."

"He may never know the first one, depending on whether he can even be tracked back to it. There's no way to do it slowly. Can you think of a way to do it slowly?" Crystal was silent for a moment. "And meanwhile, we have a certain…*mystery* to solve."

"I want to hear his story," Mr. Silva said. "If he thinks it will help explain this, I want to hear it."

"Oh, I think my story will explain a lot," Orion said.

Once again standing on the other side of the pod door, Orion and Crystal looked in at the new Watcher with concern. He was still sitting where they left him, staring straight ahead, unblinking.

"He didn't throw off his clothes," Orion said.

"He seems to be processing it."

"I know you didn't want to, but I think it was really helpful that you told him your First Day story too. To know that this is a common thing among us both supports him, and breaks down his resistance to his new reality. Nothing can happen until he accepts that he's a Watcher now."

"So, you think he murdered Benedick?" Crystal asked.

"Those nail clippings will likely tell us for sure. I'll have that blood sequenced right away. Meanwhile we should see if our new Watcher can be tracked back to the OE. The more information we have, the better."

"There's a Watcher who is a healer here. Maybe he looked into tracking him already."

"Speaking of Watchers here," Orion said, taking both of her hands into his. "The people in Las Vegas know how connected you are to this event. Our suspect, if you will, now resides in a pod in Portland. Bringing him along and healing whatever break he has experienced will take some time. We need you here," Orion leaned down to meet her eyes, which fled from his. "I need you here."

"He could be transferred to the facility in Boulder."

"There's no blue pill. You're right. But maybe there's a purple pill. Transfer here, live with me, just the two of us. It's better than nothing. Hey, that's all Benedick ever had, even in the OE, and he was happy. He was very happily married."

Crystal was still looking away from his face, staring into a future that concealed itself from her, that Changed and couldn't be relied upon.

"We can ask Las Vegas to ask for your immediate transfer, for this special case…or if you prefer, we can wait and go through normal channels, though I think a delay would make our work more difficult. Everything is here."

When still she remained silent, Orion placed his palms on both sides of her face to bring her eyes to his. "Just give it a try. We can never go back. We can't get our families back. But, I think you will see that an untraditional happiness is better than the unhappiness we have now." He kissed her, but she didn't return it. He kissed her cheeks. "I love you. That should matter."

"It matters," she said. "It does." Her eyes met his, and she smiled, a small insecure smile. "Alright. I will put my heart at risk again. For you." Orion wrapped her in both of his arms.

"We can be happy. You'll see."

The healer in charge of Mr. Silva approached them, "I really appreciate all you've done for him today. I want to tell you that the family, the one who lives in the home the wounded man broke into, they are here if you want to speak to them."

"Oh, are they receiving healing services then?" Orion asked.

"After such a terrible shock, HHC helpers insisted that they take a day or two off and come here for an assessment and healing. I am told that all three are doing well and will not need intensive therapies, which is a miracle after what they went through."

"Oh, that is good to hear," Crystal said. "I imagine we will want to talk to them, but I think it will be better to wait until after their healing. We'll visit them at home."

"My thoughts exactly, but I wanted to give you the option since you do seem to do things differently for your people sometimes. Speaking of which, I noticed that you turned off the intercom in the room? May I ask what transpired, so that I can make a report?"

"Oh, of course," Crystal said. "I want to say first that it's no slight to yourself that we turned off the intercom. We Watchers have our own methods and culture, as you have said, and it's customary for us to speak to each other in private, which is why I'm very surprised the system assigned you to this wounded person, instead of a Watcher?"

"I didn't think about that," the man returned, "That *is* interesting, isn't it? I can't say why, to be honest. Usually, that would indeed be the case, Watcher healing Watcher."

"For that reason," Orion interjected, "No slight to yourself, of course, we will ask that this man be transferred into the care of a Watcher?" He tried to use his gentle NE voice, but failed somewhat. The man's eyelids twitched once in confusion before he agreed.

"Of course, that makes perfect sense. And for my report today?"

"He objects to clothes that are particular to Watchers, and so, as you know, we obtained clothes for him that are not particular. He still insists that he is not a Watcher, and we talked to him about that. He doesn't remember much about the events that lead to his stay here. We intend to, over time, encourage him to remember as much as he can. Even though he claims to detest Watchers, speaking with us calmed him a great deal."

"Very good. Excellent. Thank you. I will see you here again?"

Orion looked at Crystal who said, "Yes. Yes you will."

When the man walked away, Orion said, "Fee should be home by now. I'd like to fill her in on what's going on, and ask her to help us expedite your transfer."

"Alright. While you're doing that, I'll find that Watcher healer and talk to him. Just so you know, Sunrise says that the people at Las Vegas never answer their phones until after lunch."

Orion decided that he would leave a message for Fee and then email them all with a time and a link to meet in the secure online workspace. He was surprised when she answered instead.

"Fee, I have news. We, Crystal and I, think we have found Benedick's murderer."

"Of course you have."

"I thought you would be more surprised. We can tell you all about it at the meeting."

"You wouldn't be surprised if you were looking at what's in front of me now. I won't be able to make the meeting, Orion....my ride is here." Fee switched the call to videocall. Orion first saw a number of people standing around her as the phone camera panned around and then in front of her. He wasn't sure what he was looking at, it was something brown, until she panned the camera up. It was an enormous tree, just like the one at Benedick's, standing in the sand of the desert. What the camera didn't show, but Fee saw, was a glowing umbilicus of light bursting from the top of the tree and rising into the clear sky and beyond. She turned the camera to her face. Her eyes were gleaming, her expression calm, her gaze transcendent.

"Say goodbye to everyone for me please Orion? I don't know when I will be back or if."

Orion didn't know how to respond to this. "I will," was all he said before the call terminated.

Fee looked at the weeping faces around her. "I didn't say goodbye to anyone the first time, and I'm not going to say goodbye now. We know none of this is real. We are all one in Unity. There are no goodbyes."

One by one, each of her dearest friends embraced her and she let them. Then she wrapped her shawl tighter, tucked it into her waistband and climbed the tree. It was easy. Once she got on top of the lowest, broad arm with a boost from below, there was a branch every step of the way up. She climbed quickly until the branches were so weak and close together, she could go no further. Looking down, she could see only layers and layers of fir needles spreading out beneath her. Looking out, with the sun in her eyes, she saw only sky and miles of sand and the writhing streets of Las Vegas. Sitting down in a nest of crossing twigs growing from the very top of the tree, she closed her eyes, which drew together to stare at the darkness between them. In a moment, a tunnel of light opened in front of her closed eyes, it stretched for miles it seemed. In this tunnel, she saw a miniature room, like that in a doll's house, turning, traveling down the tunnel towards her and then into her forehead. Once the doll's room entered her mind's eye, it opened like a present and revealed itself to be a room in the Rijksmuseum. She took one step forward and then she was gone.

15

the misplaced

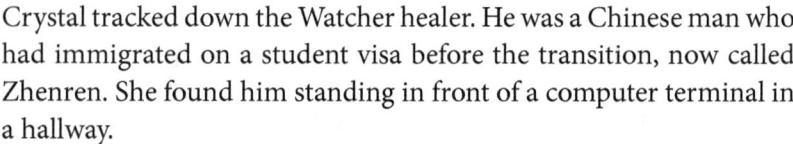

Crystal tracked down the Watcher healer. He was a Chinese man who had immigrated on a student visa before the transition, now called Zhenren. She found him standing in front of a computer terminal in a hallway.

"I just spent several hours with the Watcher in the healing pod," she told him. "His care will be transferred to me, I believe, in the next day or so. I was wondering if anyone has tried to track him yet?"

"Did they tell you that he woke up with his shoes on this morning?" He bounced on his toes, grinning at her.

"Yes, they did. So, I just wanted to know, before I spend a lot of time reaching out to everyone on the WI, if you had already done that? Has he been tracked?"

"Oh yes, I did that as soon as they brought him in wearing Watcher's clothes. I sent emails to all the Watchers from Brazil, with his claimed OE name and photograph. He says he's from Brazil. That and his name was all I got out of him yesterday, he was pretty out of it."

"And did you get any responses?"

"As a matter of fact I did, from two Watchers who didn't know him well, but knew of him because he was active in the resistance movement in São Paulo. Apparently, he is an accomplished musician.

He played Bossa Nova. Supposedly, his father lives in São Paulo still, but his mother, so far as we can tell, didn't make the jump."

The use of the word "jump" told Crystal something about Zhenren. Watchers who believed the NE was some kind of "upper level" existence that was somehow earned used the word, jump. They assumed that those who didn't make the jump were somehow unworthy and perished, or lived on in an OE purgatory, perhaps waiting to graduate to the NE. Crystal thought this belief system too self-congratulatory.

In fact, few Watchers had much patience for this, which is why most Jumpers kept their opinions to themselves. There was a second camp called "Splitters," who believed that the other half of humanity still existed in an Old Earth world somewhere else, and that those people had no memory of NE peoples, or perhaps, they had a false memory that all the NE people had perished in some kind of plague. Splitters used the words, "moved" and "remained," as in, "His parents didn't move to the NE, they remained in the OE." Watchers who weren't sure just used the official term, "Lost," and avoided the topic as impolite. Crystal counted herself in this last category. The only thing of which she was sure is that her Mama was one of the worthiest beings she had ever known, more worthy than herself, certainly, and Mama was Lost to her forever. Crystal kept her expression neutral.

"Any other family?" she asked.

"A wife, who we could not track, and two Born children, that's it."

"We knew about them."

"Yeah, but here's the interesting thing: in the OE, this guy was a saint. No one knew him well, but he was an activist who was disappeared during a time of land conflicts. You know, gave up everything in college to fight logging, mining, support indigenous rights, that sort of thing. He was presumed dead, but I guess he was only in prison. Would have been in there a long time."

"Interesting." *That would explain a lot*, she thought.

"Do you really think he's a new Watcher?" Not knowing the exact circumstances of this particular replacement, the idea clearly excited him.

"Yes, we think so. Our difficulty is that we still don't know his name, his Watcher name, due to the nature of his necessary confinement. Even if he weren't in an HHC pod, there's no one here who can tell it to him, a regular person who knew him in the OE. I guess we'll have to fly him to Brazil after he's better and try to find a regular person who knows him. Once he has a name, we can set him up in the WI and begin to integrate him."

"Oh yeah, I forgot about the name issue….Hey, I have an idea." Zhenren jogged down the hall and then returned with his personal laptop that he propped next to the HHC terminal." Crystal watched his face as he navigated to the WI. "My idea is that I will enter all the information we know about him into the WI on a search form. If it's the same for him as it was for us, he should be in there already, right? Here it is." Reading from a creased paper, his fingers flew over the keys. He looked at Crystal and then hit "Enter." Their mouths dropped open as the page minimized onto a single line in the index: Novo. He clicked on it and there it was, OE name: Alexandre Ribeiro da Silva." It was exactly as it was for each of them on First Day. There was a page with his basic information, but the rest was blank.

"Wow. He has a name now."

"Novo as in new. Obvious, I guess," she said.

"A reference to Bossa Nova too, that's his music. I find Watcher names so interesting. My name in Mandarin means heart. I was a heart surgeon in the OE. The technology the regular people have is way beyond me, though. It's amazing really, what they can do." He was smiling at her again.

Crystal wasn't in a chatty mood. She had a dozen thoughts running through her mind, and she hardly knew where to begin.

"So, has he told you about the OE?" Zhenren asked her. "Has he said what the OE purgatory is like? Has it moved on fifteen years too, or maybe time doesn't exist there? I tried to talk to him yesterday but he was too out of it." His unblinking eyes searched her face.

"He doesn't know about any of that," she snapped. "And you should *not* be talking to him about the OE. He isn't ready to know about that." She would have to talk to someone about this guy. His ideology made him a threat to Novo's recovery.

"He doesn't remember the OE at all?"

"He didn't *come* from the OE! He was a regular person. The people he…attacked, for want of a better word, really were his family members. They don't remember him. This situation is particularly delicate because he is dealing with three worlds, rather than just two, and unlike us, he remembers nothing of the OE prior to the transition."

Zhenren's face fell, "Oh, so his family history is *real*? He was already here? Are you absolutely sure he didn't move up?"

"No, nothing like that. We are sure." She had dealt this Watcher's belief system a blow, and she left it to him to figure it out. She took out her phone to call Sunrise.

"Perhaps his former presence here is just false memory?" Zhenren said to her back, "Maybe *Watchers* can have false memories *too*."

"Anything is possible," Crystal said as she brought the phone to her ear and walked away from him.

"Sunrise…Have you received Orion's message?"

"Message? No."

"Something must have happened. We believe we have found Benedick's murderer. Orion is going to send everyone a link to meet."

"That's good news. There's a reason you're calling me now, I suppose?"

"Well, the interesting thing is that the murderer is a deranged regular person who has become a Watcher."

"*Become?*"

"Just last night. He woke up in his shoes this morning, I kid you not. I'm guessing that he didn't sleep after the murder, he came in quite manic. He had a family, who are now Misplaced to him."

"Holy crap… I'm speechless. They now have some misplaced substitute father and husband? How did that happen with everyone already here?"

"No substitute. He is believed dead. Orion and I are going to talk with them and I wanted your advice first."

"Find a place to sit down. This might take awhile to unpack."

María do Espírito Santo walked out through the lobby of the Health and Healing Center with her mother and brother in search of their Care Coordinator. María had just had her first massage and Reiki session, and was feeling very relaxed and happy. She had been very worried about the injured Watcher, but the woman who talked to her in the counseling session assured her that he was receiving care in this very facility and was doing well. María wasn't upset with him, it was only their door that was injured, after all, and that could easily be repaired. Her brother and mother weren't so sure that the man wouldn't have hurt them if Cláudio had not been so quick thinking and thrown the blanket. If he had found them, what would he have done? María, being the youngest and thus, closest to the Unity, felt certain that they would have been held safe. There was something in his face that she sympathized with, loved even, and she had seen that her mother and brother had felt it too, even though they denied it now.

They found their Care Coordinator, a skinny, sharp nosed man with a name tag that said, Sukhsimran. It had been a busy morning, so they had to wait behind someone else checking out, a hugely pregnant woman who must have been six feet tall without accounting for her tall Afro hairstyle.

"She's carrying low," María's mother whispered with a wistful smile, "it's almost time."

The woman's skin was glowing and fragrant from the massage oils and her hair was a perfectly formed halo around her head, such that María was dying to ask her if she used hairspray or what. Her mother nudged her to make her stop staring. The woman noticed and gave María a smile wide enough to show all of her large, white teeth.

"Now Darling," Sukhsimran said to the pregnant woman, "I'm supposed to *again* remind you that you really should take some time off from your contribution…."

"It's a busy time of year," the woman said.

"I know your contribution is important to you, but it's important to keep your stress level low. At least keep the hours as low as you can, no more than four hours per day…and I don't mean seven days a week!" He was teasing her and she laughed.

"Don't worry, my office mates are annoyingly insistent on getting me out of there."

"And don't forget your massage next week."

"No one has to remind me about that!" She laughed again.

"You look fabulous darling. See you Tuesday."

After the woman had glided away, surprisingly light on her feet considering the load she was carrying, María's family found themselves in front of Sukhsimran's kiosk.

"So, are you the only representative of the Silva side of the family here?" Sukhsimran asked Cláudio. He asked the question in a friendly, teasing tone that sought to draw Cláudio out.

"My husband is deceased," Alondra told him.

"Oh!" Sukhsimran was surprised, then pained, "I'm so sorry for your loss. I don't know why I didn't know that. I'll make a note on the main page here....So, you are the man of the house." Cláudio stood up straighter. Sukhsimran clicked pages on his computer. "I'm showing that you don't need follow up appointments. While you all were in the counseling session, I called the contractor who was repairing the damage to your door and he said they would be finished by three. They were painting when I called."

"Painting?"

"They are painting the door to match the old one. It might even look better than it was before. Okay, José Cláudio Ribeiro da Silva, Alondra and María do Espírito Santo," he handed Alondra a small sheaf of papers, "you are officially checked out of the HHC. If you need to excuse any absences, those releases will do. By the way, don't forget that school aged children are entitled to have one HHC session per semester. So many kids don't use it."

"Is that true?" María asked. "I will definitely be back!"

"Thank you," Alondra smiled.

As they turned to leave, María saw a Watcher sitting on one of the firm, gem colored couches that lined the vast reception space. The afternoon sun was slanting in the wall of glass at the front of the building and made a large rectangle that illuminated the floor at the Watcher's feet, the couch she was sitting on, and projected a giant screen of light on the two storey tall wall behind her. It was as if there were a movie projected on the wall behind her, but the film had broken. It was as much blank enigma to María as the Watcher herself. María saw her in three quarters profile, her silky white gold hair tucked behind her ear. Full lips, eyelashes lowered in focused concentration as she listened to whomever it was talking to her on the phone. Watchers weren't known for their beauty, at least not in María's experience, but this woman was that, and María didn't even know she was staring until the woman raised her sky blue eyes to hers. María looked away when the woman smiled at her.

"Let's go," Alondra said.

"Did you *see* her?" María asked Cláudio.

"I saw," Cláudio said with a detached air, his eyes straight ahead, and his hands in his pockets.

"I want to be like her when I grow up."

"A Watcher?"

"No, I want to be beautiful," María said.

"Beauty inside is what is important, you know that," Alondra said.

"I want to be beautiful inside and outside!"

Alondra laughed. "Every girl of fourteen does. When you are older you realize that it's much better to become beautiful to those who love you than to be beautiful to the whole world. When everyone thinks you are beautiful, it's a false and lonely love."

"You were beautiful when you were young, weren't you?" Cláudio asked.

"Cláudio!" María hissed. Alondra laughed again.

"Yes. I can remember almost to the day when I stopped being a person, and became a creature that people looked at. It's a strange thing, not altogether pleasant. Be your own beautiful self, María." Alondra put an arm around the waist of each of her children, nearly grown, as they swept through the double doors that opened for them. It was noon and it was easy to decide to go out for lunch, rather than go home, because their visit to the HHC didn't count toward their consumption tally at all. So, even though they three had spent the entire previous day in massage, sound baths, counseling and other pleasant relaxing activities, they were still at zero for consumption from the time they left home for the HHC. It felt like a holiday.

They decided to go to the Hawthorne neighborhood, which María called, "music street," because it had the greatest concentration of musician nodes in the city. María wasn't a very good musician, but she loved music, and especially new music. She spent hours every day on *Nieuwe*, an app originally developed in the Netherlands to discover and promote new musical talent.

Riding the aerial tram down from the HHC, which sat on the top of a high hill overlooking a forest that separated it from the city proper, to the bottom of the hill, next to the river, was a benefit of a healing visit that enticed more than one youngster to arrive at an appointment on time. Riding down, one could see up and down the river, and the neighborhoods that nestled against it. On a day like today, sunny and warm, it was as pleasant as a carnival ride. At the bottom, they would catch a street car to the Hawthorne.

Most of the people waiting for the next aerial tram were contributors, for lunch time was also shift change. Indeed, in an HHC, there was a constant flow of people in and out of the offices, for healers were not allowed to contribute more than four hours per day, in order to conserve the vital energy they needed for such an important contribution. Open all hours with six shifts per day, HHCs were always one of the busiest places in every city, and one of the most cheerful. Several nurses in front of them were eating warm popcorn out of brown paper bags, and when the one nearest them saw María watching them hungrily, she poured some out into her palms.

The closed tram car swung gently back and forth on its suspended cable as it lowered them quickly down the hill. The river sparkled in the sun, and in the distance the kids counted ten kayakers, like a pod of whales, moving down the current. The kids pushed their way to the other side of the car to see in the other direction a launch and two college crew team boats, beating their way toward them, against the current. María chose one boat and Cláudio the other, to see which would reach them first, but they were lowered behind the trees and buildings before the race was finished.

There were streetcars circulating constantly at this hour, so it wasn't long at all before they landed on Hawthorne Street. It was the perfect place to go on a free afternoon, for what made Hawthorne special is that all the shops and restaurants on the first floors of the buildings had folding doors that opened during the good weather months. The wide street, that supposedly in old times used to have room on each side for people to park cars, had instead long patios on each side of the street, so that the coffee shops and restaurants spilled out of their open doors on both sides of the sidewalk. It was like a street fair.

What began as hunger on the aerial tram, now became an ache in Cláudio's stomach as he smelled garlic, then french fries, then pizza from the open doors. However, their mother's favorite restaurant was yet five or six blocks away, and each one of those blocks would have a musician's node. He cut his eyes to his sister's face as she bounced along ahead of him. Her eyes were wide as she scrolled her finger across the Nieuwe app. She was walking quickly on her toes, pulling them along, down the block to the end, where on the corner there would be a large circle of concrete topped by an artist designed mosaic and a small round roof. At her insistence, Cláudio opened Nieuwe on his phone. He couldn't see the node from where he was because the crowd extended backward down the sidewalk in all directions, but as they came within ten feet of the little roof, the artist popped up on his screen. He was a Spanish guitarist and composer. From where they were standing, the music could be heard indistinctly, so they kept pressing forward every time people left, scrolling their phones. Eventually, they found themselves pressed against one of the wrought iron pillars of the metal roofed shelter, and Cláudio, at least, had a good view. The pillar had a robust set of electrical plugs, but the man wasn't using any of them. He had a plain black acoustic guitar and a matching plain black outfit, nothing else. The simplicity of his presentation was appealing. Cláudio didn't listen to this type of music, but he couldn't help but be impressed by the man's skill. It was truly phenomenal, and he wasn't the only one to notice. Ordinarily at a node, people might stop for a minute or two and fill out the questionnaire and move on, perhaps a small knot of friends or followers would camp out there, but here people packed the street side benches with their lunches in their laps, and a standing crowd smashed themselves into the neighboring patio, annoying the people seated there trying to eat their lunch. Cláudio eyed both the people eating, and the tiny rivulet of humanity one person wide who were squeezing themselves past the crowd to continue down the sidewalk. Cláudio's stomach squeezed with hunger nausea, as the unhappily idle bile in his stomach threatened to vault out of it.

He should have eaten at the HHC. Both his mother and his sister had. However, the morning nurse was very young and pretty and he didn't want her to serve him breakfast like a child. Instead, when she had offered to get him a tray, he had said something that he hoped would sound nonchalant about how he would catch lunch later. He was quite hungry already then, he didn't remember why he didn't eat the night before, and now he was truly suffering.

His mother loved the guitarist, and asked María to follow him for her, to which María objected that if she did that, the app would think *she* liked Spanish guitar. Cláudio listened to their negotiations impatiently.

"I don't know how to use it," Alondra begged, "you do it for me."

Cláudio took his mother's phone from her hands and downloaded the app. "See, it's automatic. He has some kind of beacon set on his page on the app. Because you're standing here, he pops right up. You answer the questions and click right here to follow him. The app will save the artist, the songs you heard, and when and where you heard them. It couldn't be easier."

She took the phone back from him and squinted at the screen.

"All the downloads are digital, so they don't count, right?" Alondra asked.

Ever the conservator, he thought. A bit too resource conscious, in his view. "Yes, you can download his recordings a hundred times if you want, just like images and books and whatever. Digital doesn't count toward consumption." Cláudio and his friends had vast libraries of digital books, music, films, and art stored on their devices. It used to be quite limited only a few years ago until a group of scientists developed a way to dramatically multiply server storage and efficiency. Cláudio and his friends went a little crazy after that. None of them actually read or listened to everything they downloaded. Someday he was going to go through it all and clean it out.

Although the temperature was only in the upper eighties and they were standing within the compass of shade provided by the round roof, the press of the crowd was making Cláudio sweat. Finally, the man finished his set, and as a body, the crowd moved down the sidewalk.

"What did you give him?" María asked. He had felt so sick while he was standing there, Cláudio had forgotten to answer the questions. He was going to give him a ten out of ten for skill, but already they were out of range. She pulled him backwards, lecturing him on how important the nodes were to new musicians. This is how they developed a following and earned better gigs! Cláudio didn't argue, and scrolled through the app as soon as they were close enough. No, he didn't listen to this type of music generally, or this artist specifically, no he didn't want to follow him. Ten for skill. There. He didn't answer any of the other questions. Alondra waited for them across the street.

María was excited that her mother had the app, for now they could discover new music together. María talked quickly, showing her mother the features, one after the other, her albums, her playlists, and how her mother could build them, as well. Cláudio smiled and focused on putting one foot in front of the other. He would probably never again see that HHC nurse in his life, not to mention that she was too old for him anyway, but now he suffered and cursed himself. For all he knew about women, he might have made himself ridiculous.

Hooray, they arrived at another node, and Cláudio sweated patiently in the heat and listened as María told him all about the musicians on this one—the Unity love them—who were making full use of the electric plugs. Ordinarily, Cláudio loved noisy music, but in his weakened state it felt like an assault. What was worse, this node sat right in front of a busy pizzeria, and enormous, steaming pizzas were traveling past him to the patio at face level on a near constant basis. He wanted to cry.

Four more blocks, four more nodes, he repeated in his head. María was lobbying him to support these musicians, explaining their lyrics, why their music was so much better than certain more established bands. His head swam as he scrolled through the questions, and then everything slowed down, he stumbled forward and fell. When he again opened his eyes, he was lying on a bench in the shade of the circular roof, this one he noticed was of thatch. The music had stopped, whether only in his head or for everyone, he didn't yet know. Then, the face of the pretty HHC nurse appeared above his own. She was saying something to him but he couldn't understand it. Then he heard his mother say, "He's smiling. That's good, right?" His cheeks were slapped, and he opened his eyes again to see the pretty HHC nurse's face transform into another face entirely, one decidedly more maternal.

"Do you know where you are?" the woman asked him. Another HHC nurse placed a small device on his finger, which began to blink with red numbers.

"Pizza," was all he said.

Once the nurse with the device reported that his vitals were all normal except his blood sugar, which was terribly low, he was put into a chair with an entire pizza before him. Cláudio had never been so happy in his life. His mother and sister sat down next to him, relieved at how quickly he became himself again, and he sheepishly admitted that he had been too proud to eat. The story of Cláudio and the pretty HHC nurse made the rounds of the pizzeria, the staccato bursts of laughter traveling across the room, and then outdoors to the patio. The band started up again, and this time, Cláudio didn't think them half bad.

In all the confusion, Alondra almost forgot to give the waiter her bar code, so their lunch could be quantified by the district computers and noted. Although Cláudio was eating enough for two or three people by himself, Alondra wasn't worried. She was conservative by nature, and never consumed too much. Alexandre had been the exuberant one. When the kids wanted something they always asked him. Since his death, she has tried to loosen up, to say yes, even though it meant that she was consuming more than she usually would. They were only children for a short time, after all.

Most people didn't worry so much about consumption, there was enough for everyone to live a comfortable life in balance with nature. However, there was a certain mental illness that drove people to want more than they could enjoy, and this mental illness brought one to the attention of the district people. Alondra's conservatism was partly her nature, but also partly her terror at becoming the focus of a district person's attention. This fear was a result of what happened with her friend, Elizabeth.

This friend couldn't stop getting herself new shoes, so many in fact she couldn't even wear them all. At first it was something Alondra and her friends teased Elizabeth about, and then it wasn't funny anymore. Clearly, there was something wrong, but Alondra didn't know how to broach the subject with her. Finally, Elizabeth received a formal call to have a resource management meeting with a district official to talk about her overconsumption. They referred her to the HHC, and for a time, she wasn't able to get new things, other than groceries. Her friends supported her by getting little presents for her while she received treatment; it was not at all uncommon for some people to try to fill a gap in themselves with unnecessary things. It passes. A different kind of person might have laughed it off, but Elizabeth was sensitive, and deeply embarrassed. She had been selfish and caused waste. Although Alondra begged her to stay, Elizabeth left for another city as soon as she recovered, and Alondra missed her.

"What are you thinking about?" María asked her.

"I was just thinking about Elizabeth, I don't know why."

"I just talked to Amanda yesterday," María offered, "they are doing really good."

"Doing well, María. I'm glad to hear they are doing well. I've sent Elizabeth messages, but she hasn't returned them yet. She must be very busy." Alondra said it even though she had no illusions that she would not be soon hearing from Elizabeth. Already there was another family in Elizabeth's old house, but Alondra couldn't yet bring herself to meet them. There were still too many memories stacked in that house, and she didn't want to see it with new colors and different furniture. She was sure that she would hate the people there for not being Elizabeth and then be ashamed of herself for hating them. She hoped that in time Elizabeth would come around.

"Amanda says her mom really likes the contribution she is making in Anacortes. It's a smaller place, and she's already getting to know a lot of people. And the houses they got to choose from were all cooler than the one they had here, at least that's what Amanda says, and in the one they got her room is bigger."

"In smaller towns, they let you go over your square feet per person, especially if there are a lot of houses available. Maybe she feels more secure in a small place. If so, I'm glad for her."

"Maybe we should move to a smaller town. You can be an artist anywhere."

"I have a following here, María, and what do you need with a bigger bedroom?"

As they left, Alondra pointed out to the kids the patio outside the pizza restaurant. Her friend, Said, had designed it. Said was a bird fanatic and the metal railing had flying birds all along it, and the patio tile was covered with an abstract feather pattern in fused glass. Of all the patios on Hawthorne, it was one of her favorites. She told the kids about how she and Alexandre would ride their bikes here, cram them into the overstuffed bike rack in between this patio and the next and have a drink. There was always live music, of course, with the node right next to the restaurant. Sometimes, Alexandre would play the keyboard or guitar for a song or two, if the band playing were game. She stopped talking, because she felt tears swelling in her throat and she didn't want to upset the kids.

Those were the best nights. They would stay out too late and then fly home on their bikes through the empty quiet moonlit streets, the only sounds the whirring of their wheels, their own low voices, and an occasional tram skimming by them, on those nights that he played.

Having eaten, Cláudio didn't object at all to María's suggestion that they visit a few more nodes. Perhaps by the time they reached the end of the street, the kids would be ready for an ice cream before they headed home. As they moved down the sidewalk, Alondra broached a sensitive topic with María.

"Going to the HHC today reminded me that you *still* haven't had your appointment."

"They asked me about that in the physical today. I wasn't going to tell you."

"You've been bleeding for a year almost. You're in your first year of high school already. Surely, you are the only girl who hasn't done it yet?"

"I'm afraid. I don't want someone cutting into me."

"It's a tiny incision. Cláudio did it."

"And he said that his penis swelled up like a squashed game ball."

"Only two days," Cláudio said, "it wasn't that bad. I took a lot of baths."

"I don't see why I have to have it *now*. I don't even have a boyfriend."

"Look, the reason why we do it is because our biology and our spirits are out of sync. The body is still an animal's body. It just wants to make babies, lots of them, as soon as possible. You don't know it, but your body wants to be pregnant right now."

"Ew."

"And during the Dark Ages, overpopulation almost killed this planet. They didn't have the valve at all. People had lots of babies whether they were ready or not. The body doesn't know about emotional maturity, or love, or university education or resource management. It's an animal that just wants to procreate as much as possible, starting at age 14 or so. Meanwhile, the average person isn't ready to have a baby until ten years after that, and most people don't want to have more than one or two."

"Or zero," Cláudio said.

"Even at my age, I could probably turn on my valve and have another baby. Without the valve, Daddy and I would have had many more babies. That's why, as soon as this animal reproduction machinery turns on, we block it."

"But if all the boys have already had it done, I don't have to." María was looking at her phone because they could almost hear the music from the next node ahead. Alondra stopped on the sidewalk, and if she weren't so frustrated she might have laughed. It was so like

María, ever the exception to every rule.

"María, it's rare for the valve to malfunction, but it can. If both people have a valve installed, the chance of unintended pregnancy is vanishingly small. Impossible, really. And…it also prevents one person from deciding unilaterally, by themselves, to make a baby. If both people have valves, they both have to decide together. A couple of generations ago, we did have unintended pregnancies, not because of valve malfunction, but because people are emotional creatures and don't always do the right thing."

"What do you mean?"

"Back then, we didn't install the valve in every thirteen year old. People just had it done when they thought it was the right time, so sometimes only one person in a relationship had it. And sometimes people would have their valve opened without telling their lover and they would make a baby. This is particularly painful for a man, because he can't make her terminate the pregnancy, so he ends up having a child for life that he did not choose."

"And the baby's consumption counts against him," Cláudio said.

"Yes, against him, and the community as a whole. And children consume *a lot* of resources. It's not fair. It led to a lot of resentment and conflict. The children were not well raised in those circumstances, which led to even more problems."

"Couldn't someone just come into someone's room while they're sleeping and turn it on?"

Alondra laughed so loudly that people walking by looked at her. "It is not so easy, I assure you. A specially trained technician has to use a sonogram to find the valve in the fallopian tube, and then she has to use another special machine that connects with the valve to turn it off or on. The little machine and the valve have to be lined up just right. If you are a little fat…say after giving birth to your second child named María, it takes many tries before it works. And women have two, of course."

"Maybe I'm gay, so it won't matter."

"It's not so binary. Some people love one gender and then another before they settle down, and some people never settle down. There's no test we can give you to predict which of these choices you'll make, so everyone has it done."

María crossed her arms. Alondra was about to add a lecture on one's duty to the community, but then she thought of something better.

"If you do it, I'll sign you up for a whole half day of pampering at the HHC."

"Oh! You are so mean! You know I can't say no to that!"

Satisfied that she could make the appointment, Alondre resumed walking down the sidewalk.

"You are making it much more scary in your mind than it is. And when you fall in love, you'll be glad it's already there."

"Love is yuck," María said as she walked toward the node and looked down at her phone again.

When they were back in their neighborhood, they walked by Elizabeth's house on their way home from the streetcar. When Elizabeth lived there, they would stop for a few hours if they saw someone outside.

"There's kids," María said. There were two children playing with a ball out front, about María and Cláudio's age. They stopped playing as the three of them walked by. They looked at María and Cláudio, who returned their stare. María shyly waved and the girl waved back.

"We should invite them," María said.

"Another day," Alondra said, "You can go over there, perhaps, after dinner." Alondra didn't know why she didn't allow the children to go. It was an irrational desire to have them close to her.

Their front door was essentially the same, but the house had that strange vibration of intrusion still in it, either from the Watcher or from the carpenters or both. The floors were too clean. There was a neat stack of María's school things set aside on a table where they didn't belong. María and Cláudio were subdued, casting glances at each other and at Alondra. Before they went into the kitchen to put away some packages they picked up on the way home, each child paused in front of a framed photograph of their father. It had a dried flower wreath draped across the top of it, and a small collection of tokens—his wedding ring, little things that the children had made for him, and a souvenir from an amusement park—in front of it. María leaned down and kissed it, and Cláudio laid a hand on top of the frame before they told him that they were home.

"I'll take care of it," Alondra told them when they began to unpack the packages. Her tone told them that they should leave her to it. She sat down at the table and cried into her hands instead. Was she really so upset about Elizabeth?

It was probably the trip to the HHC. The last time she had been to the HHC was for her counseling sessions after Alexandre died. And before that, the long, weary hopeless hours next to his bed after he collapsed and fell into a coma from which he never returned. The worried appointments for the children to test them for the condition that killed her husband. Not to mention, the years she supported Alexandre in his struggle against depression when they first moved here. She sat in that candy colored waiting room with him many, many times, for only very rarely was he able to make the journey alone.

I hate the HHC, she thought.

She immediately felt guilty for hating the place that had taken such good care of her family, over and over. She was tired of needing care, that was it. Why in the world did that man choose *her* house? It was *his* fault she felt Alexandre's loss all over again. María appeared in the doorway, and Alondre quickly wiped her face.

Before María could say anything, Alondra said, "I don't know what's wrong with me. Let's go down the street and bring the new neighbors some cookies, yes?"

After a day, the floors were scuffed, and María's things were scattered everywhere again and the children living in Elizabeth's old house were new friends. The mothers of these children were a nice enough couple in a conventional sort of way, they loved Alondra's art, or said they did, and ordered a painting from her for their living room. She put aside all of her other projects to devote her time to it.

"Oh, it's nice!" María said when Alondra hung the unfinished painting in their kitchen. It was a beach scene—they had asked for greens and blues—with colorful buildings on a rise above it and beach umbrellas in the foreground. Alondra liked to live with an unfinished painting, to see it out of the corner of her eye, see it at the other end of the room. When she wasn't thinking about it, when she was distracted by other things, it could speak to her, she felt its vibration. Only then could she see what was missing, and what was too much.

"I got my Certificate of Mastery in Trig today," Cláudio said, "I get to move on to Calc now."

"I'm very proud of you. You have devoted a lot of time to your math," Alondra said, standing back from the painting and looking at it through squinted eyes. *The umbrellas in the foreground are too much, already that's obvious. They need to be smaller, farther away.*

"I probably won't ever even take Calc," María said, "Thank the Unity!"

"Never even take it? How can you stand to plod along in Algebra and Geometry all through high school?"

"I'm probably going to be an artist like Mama. I'll never use any of that stuff anyway. How would you like it if you had to master pointillism before you graduated?" María asked.

Alondra didn't want to listen to an argument.

"Speaking of career paths, Cláudio…has there been any word on your Watcher class?"

"No! We all just keep showing up, and all we do is talk and play games on our phones. The Principal says that she has left messages for Mr. Benedick and for the Watcher that set it up, Ms. Fee, and hasn't gotten any word back. She's going to cancel it if she doesn't hear anything by Friday."

"How odd. What happens if they cancel it? Is there another class somewhere else?"

"Maybe I can take it at University? I don't know."

They were interrupted by a knock on the door. Cláudio and María arrived at the door at the same time.

"It's *her*," María whispered.

16

rooted out

"Hello, may I please speak with your mother?" Crystal asked the children who answered the door. *These are Novo's children,* she reminded herself. She and Orion were shown into the front room, and presently they were greeted by a handsome woman who introduced herself. *Novo's wife.*

"Call me Alondra," she said in a rich, accented vibrato, and introduced the children. "Have a seat. I'll be back in a moment."

"We saw you at the HHC," María said to Crystal.

"Is that right?" Crystal said.

"You were talking on the phone on one of the couches out front. Did you major in...*Watching* at the University or what?"

Crystal swallowed. "I didn't intend to become a Watcher, María, the opportunity came to me when I was young...."

"How old were you?"

"I was twenty-three. There were four of us, one of them was this man here, and we all became Watchers together."

"Cool...What are the qualifications?"

"I think...well perhaps the most important thing is you must like to solve problems. Watchers do a lot of research."

"Oh, that's not for me," María said.

"What else?" Cláudio asked.

Instead of answering him, Crystal gratefully turned her attention to Alondra, who had returned with a tray bearing a teapot, cups, and miniature, frosted tea cakes. She laid the tray in front of them. The children sat in their seats like stones until Crystal and Orion both had accepted a cup of tea and Orion had stuffed two tea cakes into his mouth. Only then did they each take a cake for themselves.

"How can I help you?" Alondra asked, casting a glance at her son.

"We wanted to ask you just a few questions, if we may? Your husband's name was Alexandre Ribeiro da Silva, yes?"

Glancing at her son again, she nodded.

"He is deceased?" Crystal asked carefully.

"Yes."

Crystal and Orion kept their eyes on the woman, their faces inscrutable.

"I'm sorry for your loss," Crystal said.

"It's a strange request, I know, but may we see a photo of him?" Orion asked. Alondra looked at María, who bounded up and returned with a photo of a man who resembled, but was decidedly not their prisoner.

"It would be interesting to know if it were the photo or the face that Changed," Orion said under his breath.

"He looks like a kind man," Crystal returned the photo to Alondra, who set it down on the table facing them, like another person. "He contributed in the local Central Resource Management office in the computer section, is my information correct? Can you tell me more about how long he was there?"

"Yes." She cut her eyes to her son again, and he shrugged. "He started contributing there, let me see, I think Cláudio was about three years old...he stopped when he became ill...."

"Excuse me," Alondra interrupted herself, "but I want to ask, you are not here about my son?"

"Your son?" Crystal asked, "No."

"I'm in the Watcher class, and our teacher is gone again," the boy offered, "the Principal might cancel it."

Neither Orion nor Crystal could respond for several seconds.

"We were not aware you were in that class, sorry. That class has been suspended," Orion said, and Crystal added, "We're not sure how long. I thought that notice would have been sent out? We will look into why it wasn't sent out and rectify it. We are really sorry about the confusion."

Orion turned to the boy. "Tell me more about the last time you were in that class. Can you tell me when it was?"

"Oh yes, it was last Wednesday."

"What did you talk about, can you remember?"

"Is it okay to say it...in front of them?" The boy looked at his mother and sister.

Orion had switched into his OE interrogator identity, he was investigating a murder after all, and he had completely forgotten about the strange situation of the Born and Benedick's class. "Um, just tell me generally, without details, what it was about."

"We talked about how, a long time ago, you had to have a job with a check, so that you could get money in order to ride the transit. Is that true?"

Alondra raised her eyebrows at María in exaggerated mystification, but there was a mother's pride beneath it. Her boy was privy to secrets.

"Yes. Yes it was true," Orion said patiently. The boy smiled. "Was that it? No other topics? Nothing unusual, or upsetting?"

"No, nothing I can think of."

"Did you ever to talk to him outside of class?"

"Oh yeah! On that last Wednesday....I had forgotten about that. I asked him whether it was a good idea to know about things that aren't good. That maybe people are more likely to do things they know about."

"And what did he say?"

"He said I would make a good Watcher." Cláudio smiled proudly. Orion's lips pressed together into a sad smile. *Yes, Benedick would have said something like that.*

"How did he seem to you?" Orion tilted his head, "Did he seem happy or sad or tired…upset?"

When the boy shook his head, Orion folded his hands and sat back. He was finished.

"He was just normal."

Dead end. Crystal and Orion set down their teacups.

"Is it true that when someone lost a basketball game they cut his head off?" María asked. Cláudio's smile faded from his face, and his eyes darted between the two Watchers.

"María! That is not okay!" Alondra said.

"What?" Crystal was too shocked to modulate her voice.

"The Maya," Orion said under his breath, "The Maya did that."

"No, it's not true," Orion lied, "Where did you hear that?" Cláudio did not look up from his hands. "I told her," he confessed.

"I didn't believe him when he told me," Alondra said, "I was going to take him to the HHC anyway, to figure out why such a horrible thing would occur to him, why he would say it to his sister. She was very upset. Then…the man came and we *all* went to the HHC. I had completely forgotten about this little drama between them."

Cláudio continued to look at his hands in his lap.

"Let me get this straight…you told your sister a story about people cutting off other people's heads, and then the man came?"

"Two days later," Alondra responded for Cláudio.

"Two days later," Orion repeated.

"The morning of the second day," Cláudio said, casting his eyes upwards briefly.

Orion and Crystal sat in the silence of dozens of unaskable questions.

"I guess I probably won't get to be a Watcher now," Cláudio said.

"That's not up to us, or even up to Mr. Benedick." Orion said. It felt good to say something true.

"We're sorry to bother you with so many questions," Crystal said, "But, if I may ask you one more…How long ago did your husband die?"

"Just six months ago. It was a rare genetic disorder. The children don't have it, I am grateful to the Unity for that."

"He was in Benedick's class!" Crystal said as soon as they were on the sidewalk with Alondra's new door closed behind them.

"It couldn't have been a coincidence. Something happened in that class. He told them about the Maya, and then Cláudio told his parents and his sister."

"Poor boy was mortified. See? It's impossible to keep any secrets with children."

"That class was a bad idea," Orion agreed. "So he told the whole family about ritual decapitation in ancient MesoAmerica, his mother didn't believe him, and…Novo is missing time between Wednesday evening and Thursday morning before dawn, when he was in Benedick's bedroom cutting his throat. And then there's another day of missing time before he shows up at home to break down the door. It's at least a starting point for our process with him. I'm sure that's the key to unlocking his memories."

"Isn't it so odd how Novo was removed so cleanly from the world, like a plant, roots and all?"

"Perhaps, somewhere else, in the OE or another place, we are rooted out as well."

1 7

the oh-wee

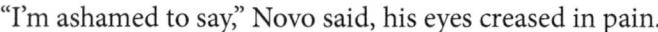

"I'm ashamed to say," Novo said, his eyes creased in pain.

"I won't judge you. I really think it's helpful to tell me these scenarios you are seeing in your mind so that we can talk about them."

He stopped pacing.

"The other times, don't you remember? After you told me about them, you stopped seeing them. We will just keep going over them until your mind stabilizes."

"Alright….Okay. It's children. They are running…crying and screaming."

"What do these children look like? What are they wearing?"

"They look like they are from an Asian country. They are wearing…just pants and shirts but…the girl is naked. What happened to them? I really want to know what could have happened to them."

"The girl…she is a little girl, right? Not a teenager. They are running down a road, I presume?"

"Yes. A little girl running on a road….In this scene they are running toward me. That means I didn't do it to them, right? They aren't running from me? You would tell me if I did it, wouldn't you?" He was crying.

Crystal put down her pen. They had been at this for weeks, and

Novo still hadn't remembered anything about Benedick, nor about the OE. It was an endless succession of these images, which were obviously images and film from the WI. Orion had already contacted the Watchers who were responsible for the technical side of the WI, and they confirmed that on the day before he died, Benedick—or someone pretending to be Benedick—had tried in vain to sign in many times. He called the WI late that evening, and they so help-fully assisted him with his login. Then, the person impersonating Benedick spent all night reading the contents of the WI....he saw all of the worst of the OE. The absolute worst.

They still haven't told anyone that Benedick was murdered. The Watcher programmers were told that after Benedick died of natural causes, a regular person hacked his account read the WI and sub-sequently went mad, and many Watchers have mobilized in their various departments to make sure this would never happen again. Regular people answering the WI line can no longer assist with logins, a new, separate firewall was placed around images, and the entire system was getting an overhaul to improve security. It wasn't a problem they had anticipated, given that regular people didn't have a great deal of interest in the doings of Watchers.

They were all coping the best they could, but as the news of Fee's departure spread among the world wide Watcher community, there had been rampant, hand wringing speculation about what it meant. Without Fee, in the wake of Benedick's murder, the core group in Las Vegas seemed unmoored. They were all treading water right now, and hadn't been much help. Orion and Crystal believed that Novo was the key. If they could only help him organize himself, they might be able to figure out why Benedick died and Fee disappeared...and perhaps what the future holds for them all.

However, Crystal found herself, again and again, at this same dead end. Novo believed that the First Day stories happened here, that she and Orion had transitioned *here* from being regular people to becoming Watchers, like him. His brain simply refused to integrate the OE, even though some of the images that tortured him seemed to come from his own life. The context in which these select images, these visual clips, were situated were intimate, not something that would be documented and generally available on the WI. She kept thinking that eventually, he would integrate it all and figure it out himself, but it wasn't happening. Telling him about it, straight up, seemed a terrible risk. But looking at him now, pacing back and forth again, in terrible pain, physical and emotional, tortured by events that had nothing to do with him…which was worse?

"You didn't do anything to those children," she told him.

"How can you be sure? Why else would they be in my head?"

"Some of the things you've told me, I can't place them exactly, because unfortunately, there are too many similar events to be sure… but this one with the children, I know this photo." She had decided, unilaterally, in this moment to do it. She hoped it was the right decision. She searched the WI for the photo and found it.

"Novo, come here." She turned the computer screen so that he could see it.

Both palms flew to his forehead and he cried out, "How can you see what's in my head? Can you people DO that?"

"It's not…"

"How can you take a picture of what is in my mind?" He backed himself against the back wall of the pod, his eyes wide in paranoiac panic. Wrong decision. Crystal snapped the laptop shut.

"It was too soon. I'm sorry. I will leave now."

"No! Tell me how you can do that first."

"It's not a picture of your thoughts. I'm sorry. It was too soon to show you that." Alarmed by the way he was yelling at her, and his increasing, not decreasing disorganization, Crystal moved to the door, her trembling hands fumbling at the control panel.

"I hate it when you do that! Look I'm calm, don't go." Novo seated himself in the lotus position on his bean bag chair with his palms up in a calm pose. His face was anything but. "See, I'm calm, very calm. Show me again." She turned toward him, but remained at the door.

"Those images you have in your mind are not your memories. They are from pictures, some of them very famous pictures, of real events."

"What events could these be? I don't believe you." Crystal considered leaving again, but she knew that would upset him even more. Then she had an idea. She turned on the intercom and asked the monitor to send in Zhenren. While she waited, she went back over her notes.

"Watch me, Novo. See? I am bringing up several images you have told me about. I am writing down a list, I am numbering them one through four. The bodies stacked like sticks? Remember? I have the image here on my computer. No, it is not a good idea for you to look at it right now."

"Let me see it, I am calm." Reluctantly, she turned the screen around so that he could see it.

"It is exactly so. Just as it is in my mind!" His bulging eyes bounced from her face to the screen.

"It's a photograph, it is. And see? I am writing down the words, "Holocaust. Jewish people killed by German Nazis. I will do this for all of them. Ok?"

"I don't see what good that does."

Presently, the door opened and Zhenren came in.

"Hello, Novo, Crystal. How may I help?

"The intercom is off. Please close the door. I'd like you to answer a series of questions about famous photographs from the OE."

"Interesting. All right."

"Here's the first. Tell me what this is a photograph of."

"Could be any number of massacres, but it looks like the Holocaust to me, because of the striped clothing on some of the bodies."

Novo stared at Crystal.

"Tell me a bit more? Who are the dead people?"

"Jewish people."

"And the aggressors?"

"Germans. Nazis."

"What's a massacre?" Novo asked.

"Do you know what a soldier is?"

"No. What's that?"

Crystal sighed and exchanged a look with Zhenren. "Let's just focus on the task at hand, namely, demonstrating to you that these images did not come from you, they are not haunting you or any such thing."

"Alright. I guess."

She brought up today's image, what Novo described as children running, crying and screaming. It is, in fact, a photo of nine year old Kim Phuc running naked down a road with other children after a na palm attack during the Vietnam War. She had ripped off her burning clothes. Everyone knows that picture. She turned her computer around so that Zhenren could see the image.

"That one is easy...," he said.

"Please...no dates."

"Alright. Vietnam War. I don't remember the girl's name. I remember that she was naked because she had ripped off her clothes that were burning. I'm guessing na palm." Novo's eyes were bouncing between them and the paper upon which Crystal had written: Kim Phuc, Vietnam War, burning clothes, na palm.

"This happened before Novo was born?"

"I hate when you call me that," Novo interjected.

"That's your name now, you must get used to it. Zhenren? Before he was even born?"

"Definitely."

She brought up the third image and turned it around.

"Cambodia is famous for the piles of skulls," Zhenren said. "Khymer Rouge. The Communists killed all the educated people."

"Enough!" Novo said. "Killing, killing, killing! That's all you ever talk about!"

"You're telling him about the OE now?" Zhenren asked.

"A little bit," Crystal said. "Thank you for your help. I can take it from here."

Zhenren is actually a rather delicate, considerate person, Crystal thought as he closed the door silently behind him. He's almost like the regular people.

"In the same way that people here might kill an insect..." Crystal said.

"We try not to."

"You know what killing is."

"Of course. It's something to be avoided. That's why we invented the SafeCar and dozens of other things, to prevent killing."

"It used to be that people killed on purpose. They killed each other. That's what those pictures are about."

Novo stared away from her face. She supposed that he was confused by the idea of intentional killing, and waited for him to process it.

"People used to kill the forest, and everything in it," Novo said.

"That's right!" It was his first, authentic OE memory.

"I don't even know what that means. It's crazy and you say, 'that's right!' Why would anyone want to kill a forest? It's a terrible thing."

"They gained by it," she said, "they only think about themselves, and they gained from the killing." She can't just explain everything. He must remember.

"Trees are falling. Not farmed trees, these are forest trees where animals live. I can see them." He was staring past her. "They are mowing everything down and killing it."

"That's right!"

His eyes met hers. The vision was gone, rejected. He jumped to his feet. He had been crouching, sitting on his heels near to her, staring up into her face. Now he paced again.

"I'm hungry. It must be time for lunch. It's impossible to keep track of time in here." He stopped and looked past her again. "It's hard to keep track of time," he said again. She waited. Nothing came. He met her eyes again.

"What's the oh-wee? That's where you said these photographs are from." She sighed.

"It's a different world than this one. Watchers maintain knowledge about this other world. I probably don't have to explain to you why we would keep these photographs secret."

"Why are they in my head?"

"Clearly you have seen them. You are a Watcher now. You will be granted access to all of this knowledge, in time, presumably, when you are...well."

"Is there a famous picture of an old man lying on a floor in a pool of blood?"

Crystal kept her expression impassive, "Why do you ask?"

"I see this also, just now. It's like the other pictures in that I feel that I was there, that I was responsible for it." He resumed his position on his heels next to her.

"Do you have any other associations with it? Any sense of what happened or why or…just the picture?"

Crystal didn't expect that he would remember anything right now. She had her eyes on her yellow pad of paper where she was writing notes. When Novo didn't respond, she looked up. His face was blank, and he was rubbing his forehead slowly with his palm.

"*Não mate o velho. Não mate…o velho. Lembre…não mate,*" he said, not to her or anyone in particular. His knees were on the floor now, and he was rocking his body back and forth. Tears slipped down both cheeks, and his tone became more insistent. "*Lembre! Não mate! Não mate o velho!*" As he repeated this phrase, his balled right fist came down upon his thighs as punctuation.

Crystal stood and moved quickly to the intercom. "Can you please send Zhenren with a sedative, please?" She reached for the control panel to let herself out quickly and quietly.

"*Não mate! O velho…Lembre!*" Novo was suddenly in front of her, and she realized for the first time how tall and powerfully built he was. Novo was not behind those eyes. These eyes looked through her even as he towered over her. "Quickly, please!" she said into the intercom as she fumbled with the panel.

"I will remember! *Yo Lembre….*" Crystal resurrected her high school Spanish best she could, hoping it was close enough. "*Sí, señor, absolutamente,*" she promised. Novo's face twisted into a grimace, and as he raised his right hand, the door opened behind her. She skittered through it, plowing into Zhenren, and then latched it. They looked through the open window. Novo was pounding his forehead with his right palm, repeating the phrase. Calmer now, Crystal leaned close to the intercom.

"Novo," she said several times to no avail.

"Alexandre Ribeiro da Silva!" she said. His head snapped to attention and their eyes met for a moment through the window. Then his eyes became unfocused and wild.

"No, no no no!" he said, turning in a circle, looking at the walls of the pod. He retreated into the back corner and fell to his knees, rocking and repeating something quietly in Portuguese.

"I think I can go in now," Zhenren said.

"I'll go with you."

They quietly opened the door. As soon as it was open, Crystal thought that maybe they should have called for help. Seeming to read her thoughts, Zhenren said, "It'll be alright."

Novo seemed not to notice them at all. He was rocking back and forth, repeating his Portuguese mantra. "Because he is rocking, it will have to be quick, and he might react," Zhenren said and Crystal held up a finger. She moved behind Novo and touched acupressure points on his head and shoulders, moved her hands to calm the rocking motion. She nodded and Zhenren injected the sedative. Novo slumped forward, and his voice became almost inaudible.

"Hopefully, he will sleep now, and his brain will organize what just happened," Crystal said as they shut the door.

1 8

caterpillars

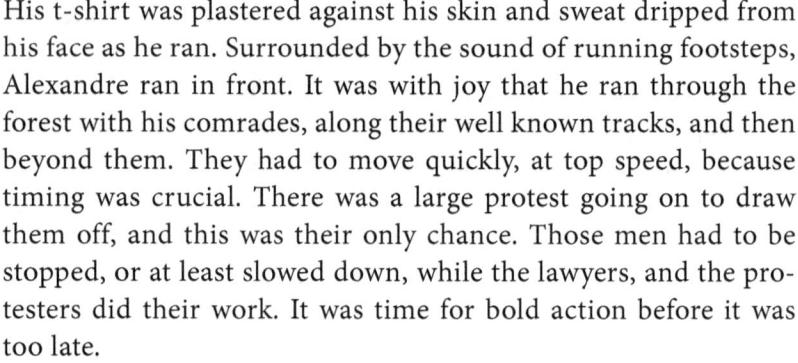

His t-shirt was plastered against his skin and sweat dripped from his face as he ran. Surrounded by the sound of running footsteps, Alexandre ran in front. It was with joy that he ran through the forest with his comrades, along their well known tracks, and then beyond them. They had to move quickly, at top speed, because timing was crucial. There was a large protest going on to draw them off, and this was their only chance. Those men had to be stopped, or at least slowed down, while the lawyers, and the protesters did their work. It was time for bold action before it was too late.

As they neared the enclosure, they moved silently. His comrades had taught him how to do that. They crouched in a row, a dozen Indians and Alexandre. He should have attended the protest, for it was a risk that the authorities might notice that he wasn't there, but he always preferred the forest. He wanted to be here. His good friend loaded a dart that he put in his mouth and then blew. A half dozen darts flew with his. The guards standing on the other side of the chain link fence collapsed to the ground. Alexandre and his comrades moved quickly down the fence line and repeated the procedure until they saw no more guards, then mounted the fence. They had to make sure. If they were caught, they would be immediately killed, their bodies stowed in the ground here to be driven upon by the caterpillars and the trucks, and their families would never even know what had happened to them.

Dropping to the ground, they broke in every direction to set fire to the buildings, to destroy the fencing, to lay homemade explosive under the vehicles. Everything must be destroyed. It will take them months to put it all back together again. Alexandre lined up the unconscious guards in a row in the middle of the enclosure so that they would not be burnt. They were killers, but they were poor, ignorant people who believed whatever their bosses told them. The real evildoers were not here. They never were. They satiated their blood lust through wire money transfers, phone calls, emails....Boom! The gas tank of a flaming truck exploded. Several more explosions sent their concussive force against Alexandre's body. It was the sound of laughter, nature's deep, booming laughter at the doings of these men with their yellow insects crawling on her body.

"We will crush them!" Alexandre yelled, as he and the other men began to run back across the compound, before the soldiers responded. After having to be silent all afternoon, it was a relief to yell. They all began yelling and laughing as they ran. Then his friend fell in front of him, and someone grabbed the back of Alexandre's shirt and pulled him down. He fell to the ground with two others behind a burning wreck as the gunshots ricocheted all around them. His friend's face was on the ground, his eyes open and looking at Alexandre, but his friend was not there. There was a small bloodless hole in his forehead. How could such a small hole take a life? His comrades used the burning wreckage of the compound as cover for their retreat. Men running, two men taking him by the arms, but Alexandre couldn't move. Such a small hole, he marveled, looking down at his own body, his blood stained shirt.

"Leave me!" he yelled and then watched the two run away. One fell, still, on the ground.

"What are you looking at?" Alexandre asked Cláudio. Cláudio wrinkled his chubby face against the sun to look up at him. "It's a spider. A white one, Dada." Alexandre knelt next to his little one, already so interested in natural things. Indeed, it was a white predatory spider hiding in the heart of a white rose in their garden. Alexandre could kneel here all day watching his little boy watch the spider.

"It's gonna eat him," Cláudio said, his baby face solemn. It was only then that Alexandre noticed the caterpillar munching on one of the near leaves. "Should we save it, Dada, or let the spider have him? Which is right?"

"Don't shake him, Alexandre. He doesn't like that," his mother said.

Alexandre pursed his lips and brought his eyes and nose right up to the side of the plastic cup. The spiny green caterpillar was clinging to a twig Alexandre had put in the cup for him. When Alexandre stopped shaking the cup, the caterpillar began turning his reindeer antlers to and fro, and resumed his creeping progress along the twig. Soon, if he didn't die, he would build a chrysalis and become a big, bright blue butterfly called an Orsis Bluewing. *Myscelia orsis.* Alexandre had looked that up.

A hairy caterpillar fell from a tree into Novo's lap as he sat on the bench opposite the park. He stood up and shook him off. He was going to sit back down, but thought better of it. He put down his paper, and his coffee and gathered the creature on the end of a pencil. He held the creature up to his eyes. He wasn't sure what kind it was, but it appeared to be some kind of moth. Butterflies had spines here and there sometimes, but they were mostly smooth creatures, in Novo's experience. He stood on the park bench and held the caterpillar high above his head, talking to it, trying to coax it from the pencil onto a low branch. He had to stand there like that for some minutes, waiting for it to motivate itself to crawl to safety. A gaggle of boys passing by on the sidewalk paused to laugh at him. He smiled sheepishly and shook the pencil.

"Go! Why don't you?"

"What are you doing?" asked the boy he was waiting for.

"An important contribution," he said, laughing.

"How is he?" Crystal asked Zhenren before she opened the door. Orion stood behind her, angling to see through the window.

"Not good," he replied.

She opened the door and she and Orion walked in quietly. Novo was kneeling in his accustomed place, eyes down, rocking back and forth. Crystal looked despairingly at Orion.

"This is my fault," she whispered.

Novo looked up then and met her eyes, giving her hope.

"In the future, you won't be here. None of you will be here," he said.

1 9

the meeting

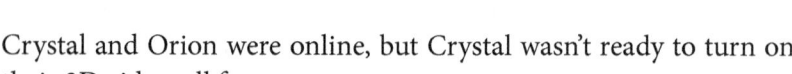

Crystal and Orion were online, but Crystal wasn't ready to turn on their 3D videocall feature yet.

"It will be alright," Orion said. Sunrise was on, and Diego. Their own sound was off, but they could see that Sunrise and Diego were talking to each other. Sunrise had opened the space, and she had the environment set on forest such that it appeared that Crystal and Orion were sitting in a forest with Sunrise and Diego who soundlessly conversed. While they sat there, several computers at the cottage came online. Orion pulled the keyboard towards himself and switched on their interface. They heard the gentle rush of wind through fir trees, and birdsong.

"Hi Orion, Hi Crystal," Sunrise said. Several more cottage computers came online so that the cottage people appeared in their twos and threes, all of them sitting on the forest floor, then Mandrake was last.

"Nice environment, Sunrise," Mandrake said.

"I thought it was appropriate, the fir trees," she replied. After a short recap, she turned the meeting over to Crystal and Orion.

"There's…," Crystal started, "Before we begin, there's something I, we want to say. I don't even know if it's appropriate, but it doesn't feel good not to say it."

"Go ahead, Crystal, we're listening," Sunrise said.

"As you know, I'm living in Portland now because of the unique situation we have. And it's ostensibly a temporary situation, so…you know…I've been staying with Orion." They nodded. "Well, Orion and I have decided to live together permanently…in relationship with each other." She flushed. Everyone was smiling at them knowingly. "I know it's unusual…."

"Not so much," Mandrake said.

"Not unusual," Diego said. "Well, the living together is, I guess, but even so, I know several people who have paired up. Now that we're all mature and supposedly know what's going on, I think people are starting to pair up."

"It's not like we're going to have a wedding or anything," Crystal smiled sadly.

"If you want to have a wedding, have a wedding," Fend twisted her thick, red hair into a bun and tied it. "There isn't any rule against it. You could have it out here at the cottage…couldn't she? It would be a first." She looked at Mathilde who sat to her left.

"And probably the last," Mathilde said.

"Really? You think that would be alright?" Crystal asked. Orion wound his arms around her. "I told you," he said.

"Let's all talk about it after," Fend said, "it would be fun."

"I think I am speaking for all of us when I say, Congratulations. We're all very happy for you," Mandrake said. Several other people expressed their pleasure and support for Orion and Crystal.

"Thank you all. I can't tell you what your support means to me. At this point, unfortunately we have segue to less happy topics," Crystal said. "Orion?"

"Yes. So, it's become clear that Novo had accessed the WI at some point," Orion began.

"Is that possible?"

"It is if you have a trusting regular person answering the WI line. We went back over Benedick's history and, very late that Wednesday night before he died, Benedick tries and fails to logon many times."

"Oh no…."

"He stays up *all night* on the WI on Wednesday into the wee hours on Thursday. He doesn't even log out, there's just a break in activity, and then nothing."

"That is *not* Benedick."

"If you recall, the original, scrubbed RC report said that Novo—at that point Alexandre Ribeiro da Silva—didn't show up for his contribution on Thursday. So, what I think happened is that he heard this story about the Maya from Cláudio who probably confessed everything to him, he resolved to hack the WI. Found out more than is good for him. He was delicate to begin with. At the time of the transition he had been imprisoned in some godforsaken hole for who knows how many years. Just because you forget all about it doesn't mean it's completely gone."

"He had years of therapy at the local HHC."

"I think our story is filling out."

"So, he has a complete mental breakdown and kills Benedick. A day later, he shows up at home, but everything there had Changed by that point," Orion said, "At that point, he was already a dead man, and a Watcher. We believe the clothes he was wearing came from Benedick's house. Benedick is more thin, less muscular, but they are roughly the same size."

"It's almost as if the murder was the turning point."

"But he didn't wake up with shoes on until he was in the HHC, days after the murder."

"It may very well be that under the influence of that level of mania, he had remained awake for three days," Crystal said. "That would explain it."

"Wow."

"So, he's at the HHC under Crystal's care? Has he made any progress?" Mathilde asked. Orion looked at Crystal.

"Well, initially we were focused on figuring out what happened and why. Orion tested the blood he had under his fingernails right away and so his guilt has never been a question. The real issue has been an investigation...an inquiry into what and why for reasons I probably don't have to explain.

"After the tree locking him in."

"And Fee disappearing."

"There's something big going on."

"I think we all agree that this man is the key to understanding what that something is," Crystal said. "But it's delicate. Very delicate." Crystal blinked tears out of her eyes. "I'm sorry to have to report that last weekend, I pushed him too hard. He was tortured by repeated images of the OE that he had seen on the WI, but didn't remember seeing on the WI. He thought he may have been responsible for all of those things and that's why we were holding him."

"But he still hasn't remembered Benedick?"

"I'm getting to that," Crystal replied. "I decided to prove to him that the images in his mind didn't come from him. That they were historical. It was a risk, but we weren't getting anywhere."

"We need to get somewhere. You did the right thing," Fend said.

"It was a disaster. At first, it really seemed to help a lot, and he did remember Benedick."

"He did!" The exclamation was unanimous.

"And then he became completely disorganized. We haven't been able to reach him since then."

"Maybe it's just a temporary phase. He might still process."

"The other Watcher healer there is completely against sedatives, it's the healer culture here. He thinks I should stop giving him sedatives. I think I'll try that this week if it doesn't go too badly."

"Let us know," Fend said.

"We still don't know *why* he did it," Diego said.

"Why any of it? Why us? Does it even do any good to ask why? The more important question is what, as in, what do we do with him if he does heal and become mentally healthy?" Sunrise said.

"In the WI, he has an address in Brazil," Crystal said.

"But, are we supposed to just let him go home to this apartment in Brazil? He murdered Benedick!" Orion objected.

Mathilde stretched out her long limbs, "Well, it seems to me that it depends on what reason we would use to justify keeping him. If he's still nuts, then yes keep him locked up, but if he's not...if we're sure he isn't going to commit any more violent acts…."

"What about justice for Benedick?" Orion asked.

"What is justice here? After what we've seen…the tree, Benedick's visit here in Las Vegas, and Fee, my God, you should have seen it…this isn't just a murder. Outside a temporary mania, there was little motive."

"That we know of," Orion said, "Novo has some missing time. And there's the Mayan story. He could have been protecting his children."

"And that's why he stabbed himself?" Mandrake asked.

Orion opened his hands.

"What did Fee say about it? Anything?" Sunrise asked. Several people from the cottage answered at once.

"Nothing. She…."

"Was out of it, she was in a constant altered state, and then she was gone."

"We saw that here, as well, before she left for the cottage," Sunrise said. "It was as if she weren't entirely present, but somewhere else."

"Assuming that, hopefully, at some point, Novo goes to Brazil. What is he supposed to do?" Crystal asked.

"Write everything in the WI like the rest of us. That will take some time."

"Especially for him."

"It depends on what he ends up remembering about the OE. He could be useful."

"At some point, I'd like to talk to him about *this* world," Mandrake said, "He's the only person alive who knows what it's like to be a regular person *and* a Watcher. He could be a useful interlocutor."

"Another bridge," Sunrise said thoughtfully. "At any rate…what do you there in Las Vegas think about him joining you for awhile before he is let loose in the world? A remote halfway house would be a good transition, you could use him."

"That depends, Sunrise. Mandrake, do you remember how we feed ourselves here?" Fend asked.

"Yes, of course."

"It's not functioning anymore. We are determined to stay as long as our supplies hold out, a couple of months, we reckon, but it appears that with Fee's departure, we are being evicted."

"What will you do now?" Mandrake asked.

"We plan to stick together. We're thinking about moving to Phoenix....It seems apropos to move to a city that bears her name. There are some mansions there now used for co-housing. We are in line for one of those, but the chance that everyone will move out of a co-housing unit at the same time is small. The way we operate...we can't share with anyone, not even other Watchers. We might actually have to build something suitable on the outskirts of town."

"The real question is...without Fee, without the cottage, are we still the cottage? Or is the cottage no more? Maybe we have fulfilled our purpose and have to find a new one?"

"We don't know anything."

2 0

caught

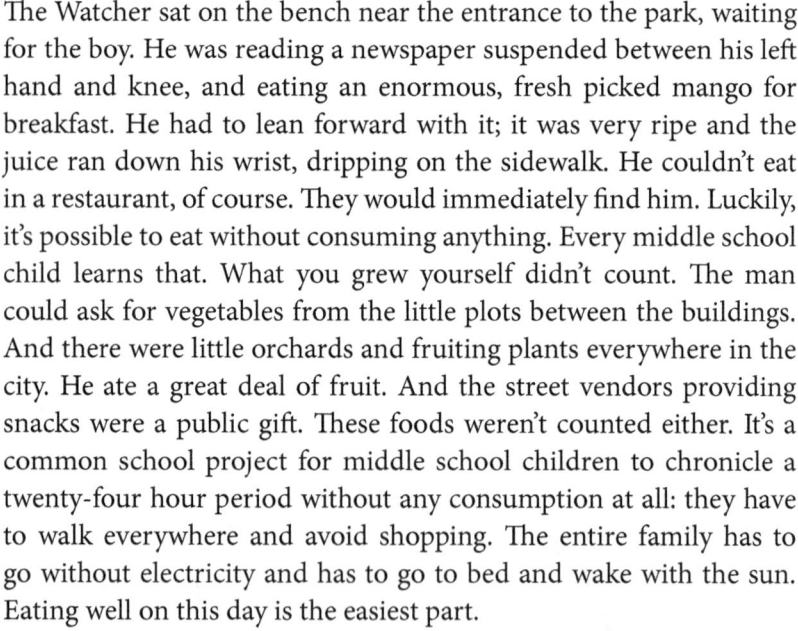

The Watcher sat on the bench near the entrance to the park, waiting for the boy. He was reading a newspaper suspended between his left hand and knee, and eating an enormous, fresh picked mango for breakfast. He had to lean forward with it; it was very ripe and the juice ran down his wrist, dripping on the sidewalk. He couldn't eat in a restaurant, of course. They would immediately find him. Luckily, it's possible to eat without consuming anything. Every middle school child learns that. What you grew yourself didn't count. The man could ask for vegetables from the little plots between the buildings. And there were little orchards and fruiting plants everywhere in the city. He ate a great deal of fruit. And the street vendors providing snacks were a public gift. These foods weren't counted either. It's a common school project for middle school children to chronicle a twenty-four hour period without any consumption at all: they have to walk everywhere and avoid shopping. The entire family has to go without electricity and has to go to bed and wake with the sun. Eating well on this day is the easiest part.

Thus, this fugitive Watcher on the bench opposite a public park appeared to be a conventional part of the life of this city, eating fruit and reading a second hand paper. He looked at his watch, for the boy was late. Perhaps today would be one of those terrible disappointments, when he couldn't get away. He finally finished the fruit down to the flat pit, which he gracelessly sucked clean. He smiled apologetically at an elderly woman who saw him doing it. After she passed, he lobbed the pit into the shrubbery, and wiped his hand on his pants leg. He was then able to read the paper in earnest. The front page article was an update on a story about a local creek. Last Spring, a group of students monitoring aquatic wildlife in a local creek for a yearly science class project discovered that several species had experienced a precipitous decline. They were hailed as heroes and that seemed to be the end of it, but then when a local university professor got involved and discovered that the problem was a new building under construction, it became a scandal. The man smiled at the use of that word.

This scandal was that the manager in charge of the project was impatient and didn't think it necessary to consult with a Watcher Natureworker, and also didn't do an adequate site survey. The building site looked perfectly fine to him. And now, the building was nearly complete. The citizens of the city were very upset about these irregularities. He apologized and the management of the project was transferred to someone else. The new redesign of the building was reproduced on the front page. They had split the building into two, with a course way for water drainage and a breezeway between the two halves of the building suspended above it. It was a better design, really. Underneath the picture was a detailed report on how the building was being deconstructed in part and rebuilt to avoid the harm to the riparian ecosystem. This is the sort of thing that qualifies as their bad news. The man smiled ironically, and then read on to reportage on various city organizations, events, and reportage on how the city was doing in terms of resource management. It was doing well…of course! When the man looked up from his paper he saw two Watchers standing in front of him.

"Novo," Crystal said. Novo's eyes darted about and he considered running, but then he settled backward on the bench instead, the forgotten newspaper crumpled on his lap.

"I would shake your hands, but mine is a bit sticky," he replied, turning his right palm and smiling.

They continued to look at him. Crystal's lips were a horizontal line across her face.

"This is not funny," she said. "Something terrible could have happened. Something you maybe couldn't have stopped…like last time."

The smile faded from Novo's face.

"That won't happen again. I tried not to do it, believe me….you have no idea. I had no choice. Actually, I'm organizing myself. Isn't that what you said I needed to do?"

"I would prefer that you organized yourself in a safe space," Crystal said. "I've talked to Alondra…."

"Oh, no!"

"Yes. I told her that the Watcher who broke into her house was here. Cláudio won't be back."

Novo put his face in his hands and spoke into them. "I just wanted to take back a little bit for myself, such a little thing, an hour, here and there." He lifted his face to look at her, "Surely you can understand that?"

Crystal blinked. "Yes…yes, I can. But we both understand that there are some things we can't ever have back."

It took only a few moments to realize that nothing matters now. Having Cláudio back was the only thing that mattered, and now, whether he did what they asked or not, it was all the same to him. He returned upright.

"Whatever you say," he said.

"Your…address as Watcher is here in São Paulo," she said.

"I didn't think of that!"

"You have an address. It's here, but you're not ready for a normal life yet. You need to stabilize more first. If you have made good progress, that's great. Perhaps a stay in the pod here is São Paulo is a good choice. You can move around the city with escorts, and you won't be tempted to visit Alondra's home again."

The words, "Alondra's home," made him wince. Crystal continued to watch him.

"You know I'm right."

2 1

the rijks

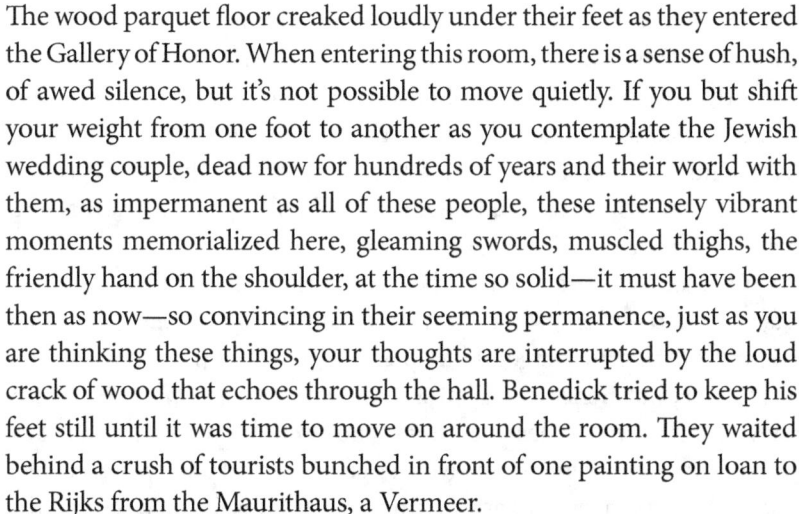

The wood parquet floor creaked loudly under their feet as they entered the Gallery of Honor. When entering this room, there is a sense of hush, of awed silence, but it's not possible to move quietly. If you but shift your weight from one foot to another as you contemplate the Jewish wedding couple, dead now for hundreds of years and their world with them, as impermanent as all of these people, these intensely vibrant moments memorialized here, gleaming swords, muscled thighs, the friendly hand on the shoulder, at the time so solid—it must have been then as now—so convincing in their seeming permanence, just as you are thinking these things, your thoughts are interrupted by the loud crack of wood that echoes through the hall. Benedick tried to keep his feet still until it was time to move on around the room. They waited behind a crush of tourists bunched in front of one painting on loan to the Rijks from the Maurithaus, a Vermeer.

"Do you want to come back to it?" Bea asked him.

"Sure," he said, "this place will empty out for lunch soon. Let's go see the giant one at the end and make our way through the hall backwards.

"The 'giant one' is called *The Night Watch*, Bene. Do you remember? It's not even the largest one. There are others much larger of various militia companies. Experts believe that *The Night Watch* used to be larger, but was cut down to fit on a wall at the town hall, long ago."

"You don't have to talk to me as if I were a child. I remember being here before, of course! I just don't store the names of paintings like a person who has a degree in art."

"I'm sorry, darling, I was just reminding you."

"I'm fine," he said irritably and walked ahead of her a step, turning to the right to see the giant painting with an impossibly long name. He always thought of it in his mind as *The One with the Pot Bellied Man*. He was sure the pot bellied man, clearly proud of himself in his gleaming silk trousers and stiffly starched collar and ruffs, would not approve. He did the math.

"It's over twenty four feet long," he said to Bea, having forgiven her for clucking over him yet again.

"And more than seven tall," she replied.

She had told him that he had sat, nearly insensible, for fifteen years. He shouldn't be irritated by her concern, she earned it, apparently. But he didn't remember the succession of parietal lobe and frontal thalamus strokes, nor the dementia the strokes brought about overnight—obviously—and he felt perfectly fine. The doctor called his recovery a miracle, and Benedick would like to leave it at that and get on with life, what there was left of it.

Benedick and Bea followed the creak cracking feet of the other tourists around the room, standing in front of *The Night Watch*, and then in front of the other large militia painting, which did not have such a long name, but Benedick called it *The One with the Dandy in Yellow*, anyway. All three of these paintings, and even the others on the back wall of the room were impressively large and grand and well executed, but even a person without art training such as himself could see that the Rembrandt was special, and properly took its pride of place at the center.

Just as they thought, as the clock inched toward noon, the rooms began to empty out so that by the time they wound their way back through the Gallery of Honor, there was no longer a queue in front of the Vermeer.

"We've seen this before, right?" Benedick asked.

"Yes!" Bea was clearly pleased that he remembered, and Bene had to swallow his irritation. "It's called *View of Delft*. We saw it at the Maurithuis many years ago with the other Vermeers. Do you remember taking the train from Amsterdam to The Hague? It was right before they were going to close the museum for renovations. We walked from the station in a summer downpour."

Benedick didn't respond.

"Proust called this painting the most beautiful painting in the world. It's certainly one of the most popular Dutch paintings, along with the *Girl with a Pearl Earring*."

"I don't like it," Bene said.

"Why not?" She was surprised. He stood staring at it for another minute before answering.

"It's foreboding. I don't like it."

"Foreboding? Why, it's so sweet and cheerful. You're just looking at the center of the painting, where all the dark clouds are and the dark buildings." She held her hands up in front of her eyes, palms out, to frame the center of the painting. "The center is dark, and perhaps it could be foreboding," she let her hands drop, "but the sky on the left edge has more blue than clouds, and the right edge is so bright its mostly white." His eyes followed her finger to the bottom left corner, "And those people down there look so friendly, chatting with each other. It's a cheerful market day with everyone going about their business and a storm blowing over. And you know, right next to that white church tower is that herring stand we liked so much. Do you remember? It had lots of nice tables in front of it on the square." She poked a finger in his ribs, "Do you think that herring stand was there back then, too?"

Benedick tried to laugh, but could only choke out a facsimile. She was trying to lighten him up, but Benedick couldn't shake that foreboding feeling. He held up his hands in front of his eyes, as she did, to test her theory that it was only a matter of perspective. On the left, he cropped out the two chatting women, on the right, he cropped out the white clouds and the illuminated rooftops beyond the pale tower. Between his hands, the wide landscape became a tall door, and against his will, his mind flew through it.

A wave of nausea surged through him, and his chest constricted. He dropped his hands and clutched Bea to him, pressing the tips of his fingers into the flesh of her back.

Bea laughed nervously, "What in the world is wrong?"

Without releasing her, he whispered stridently into her ear.

"Looking at the painting just now, I suddenly felt that I had lost you, and I remembered living years and years without you." He was breathing quickly and softly, almost like sobs, in and out.

"Remembered?" she asked.

"Yes." He buried his face in her hair, breathing in her scent. "It was terrifying."

Bea pulled away from him and placed her two palms against the sides of his face.

"I'm right here, Bene. I've always been right here with you." Her eyes searched his face with concern.

"Yes." He inhaled deeply, "Yes, of course."

"You've overtaxed yourself. Let's go back to our place, we can make a sandwich, relax. Maybe I should call the Doctor…what time is it there?" She dug in her purse for her phone. Her hands were shaking.

He gathered himself and sighed. "I really don't know what came over me, but I'm fine now. It's 9 p.m. there, it's no use to call. I'm fine, really."

He was about to suggest that they leave to find lunch when an unusual looking Asian woman walked into the hall. She was heavily made up, her mouth outlined a matte pale pink, and her eyes were pale pink and purple between her drawn on eyebrows and false eyelashes. She was wearing a vivid purple, sleeveless mini-dress that looked like a perfect rectangle on her slight frame, and very tall glossy black platform heels that matched her very long, glossy black hair. He noticed her not so much because she looked so unusual, but because her eyes locked onto him as soon as she entered the room. She stared hard at him as she walked for several steps, but then took her eyes away from him and feigned a casual survey of the paintings. His eyes followed her.

"Perhaps we should go have some lunch?" Bea's voice betrayed lingering concern for him.

"Do we know that young woman? The woman in the purple dress?" Bea turned to look.

"Woman? I don't think she's a day over sixteen, and no, I'm sure I've never seen her before. Do you really think you know her? She's too young to be one of your former students."

The woman continued to stare at paintings as she made her way around the room towards them. "Are you ready to go?" Bea asked him. Benedick was still watching the young woman, and immediately after Bea spoke, the self-contained calm of that being evaporated. She took a few purposeful steps towards them.

"Excuse me, please…can you tell me what time it is? I've lost my phone." Her English, missing its r's and l's, identified the young woman as Japanese. Her syntax was perfect, but heavily accented, her smile self-deprecating, charming.

"Of course," Bea said, and resumed digging for her phone.

"I lost my phone on the way here, along with my purse."

"You lost your purse?" Bea's hands stopped moving. "That's terrible! What did you lose?" Bea's hands found her phone.

"Everything, except the cash—thank goodness." the young woman responded.

"It's noon, Honey," Bea said. "Are you from the States? Your English is amazingly good."

"I…I used to live there," she responded.

"Have you had lunch?"

"I don't know," she said, and laughed.

"You don't know? Well, by the looks of you, it wouldn't hurt you to eat in any case. Would you like to come with us? Bene, she can come with us, right?" The young woman's face immediately brightened.

"I would like that very much, thank you."

2 2

rough landing

Fee opened her eyes to see at eye level a strip of green grass, a gravel walk curving away from her and a pair of bare feet running away. These were followed by more running feet, which became the bodies of men running down the gravel path after the shoeless man. She became aware of pain in her hands and her right hip. Someone above her said something incomprehensible, and then lifted her to her feet as if she were made of air. He repeated the phrase.

"*Gaat het wel goed*?" She turned her eyes to see a handsome giant leaning down to her, a dark blonde forelock sweeping over one eyebrow. His sky blue eyes were kind.

She meant to say, "I don't understand Dutch," but something equally incomprehensible in what sounded like Japanese came out of her mouth instead.

"Do you understand English?" he asked. She nodded.

"My friends are running after him," he said. "Are you hurt?"

"What happened?" she asked. The voice that came out of her mouth was not hers.

"That homeless man knocked you down and took your purse, I think." She tried to shake off her confusion, but couldn't. The man bent down and retrieved two ridiculous looking shoes, very tall and shiny.

"Here are your shoes." He handed them to her, as she stood there uncomprehendingly. How can these be her shoes? "Are you ok? Maybe you hit your head?"

"I don't know," she said. She heard yelling and saw, across an expanse of grass, two young, Asian men running toward her. They were pointing and yelling the same word. It sounded like Ho-o! If she were, in fact, in her old body in the Old Earth, she knew well enough to be afraid of men, and she immediately took off running in the opposite direction. "Wait! Your purse!" the blonde man yelled. She sprinted in her bare feet, her two hands holding a shoe each, until she crashed through the shrubbery. She kept running, in which direction she knew not, staying well off the paved pathways, turning this way, then that through the overgrown areas. She was still a trafficked person. These men were her minders, she guessed, set to capture her and drag her back…but to whom? She almost ran into a small family of Dutch camped in the wooded area, two parents and small kids, one holding a doll in a grimy fist. She put her finger to her lips as she skittered around them. She soon stumbled into several such camps, for she wasn't the only person in the park trying to elude an authority. She ran until her lungs hurt. This body was not accustomed to running and she had to stop. She pried herself into the branches of a dense hedge and peered through it to the pathway in front of her. No running men. Then she heard them behind her. They were saying sorry to one of the camping families. She smashed herself as deeply as she could into the base of the plant and the undergrowth as they ran by. From her hiding place, she saw the Asian men emerge onto the paved path. They were standing in the middle of it and turning right and left. Bike bells were ringing at them, one after another, as they moved to and fro in the middle of the path, nearly running into Dutch cyclists. When her breathing finally returned to normal, Fee crept backwards, disentangling herself from the low branches.

She speaks Japanese. She could hear them arguing in Japanese about where she had run, and she understood it. Had she been trafficked to Japan? Her brain seemed to be mostly herself, Fee, but there seemed to be a whole self formed over the last fifteen years that was slowly downloading into her. I speak Japanese now, she thought. Cautiously, she backtracked the way she came and turned a different direction. She must hurry! She had to get to the Rijks. Which of these paths led there? She didn't know.

She burst into a large clearing where there was a wading pool overrun with squealing children, and a playground. Too exposed. She walked along under the trees, behind the swings and saw a natural area littered with downed branches. Children were dragging them around and stacking them against each other to make huts for themselves. The forest behind the sticks was too clear, too clean. There was nowhere to hide. When she saw the blonde man and his friends on their bikes ride into the playground from one direction, and two police officers from the other direction, she dropped down and shuffled to the largest of the huts. She didn't trust any man right now, at least not until she got her bearings.

"Can I play?" she said to the children in English. They mutely stared at her as she crouched and waddled inside. She smiled at them. Peering out, she could see the blonde man asking the playground parents about her, and saw one of the parents point in her direction. *Damn!* She pressed herself against the side of the hut and raised a finger to her lips.

"*Heb je een mooie Aziatische meid in een paarse jurk gezien? Eh?*"

He asked this of a blonde girl sitting in the front of the hut. The girl cut her eyes once to Fee before answering, "*Nay.*" He then posed a question—presumably the same one—in English to the tourist children playing there outside the hut. "Have you seen a pretty Asian woman with a purple dress?" The blonde girl shook her head at them and they paused.

"I just want to give her back her purse," he said in English. Not believing the children, the blonde man crouched down in front of the door of the hut and leaned in until he saw her.

"My name is Arjen. I'm not going to hurt you. I just want to give this back to you," he offered her the purse. It was a glossy black bag that matched the shoes. Fee felt foolish now, but didn't want to be spotted by the men hunting her. Seeming to read her thoughts, the man added, "They're gone, I think." She took his hand and emerged. "Who were those men?"

"I'm not sure," she said. "I can't really explain right now because I'm late for an appointment at the Rijksmuseum. I must go there immediately…can you tell me which direction?" She followed him as he went back the way he came and retrieved his bike.

"I'll take you there," he said, "you can sit behind me." There was a small metal shelf behind the seat. "Believe me, it will be much faster, it would be a long walk and there are no cars allowed in the Vondelpark." She decided to trust him, and awkwardly negotiated situating herself side saddle on the shelf. When the man rode by his two friends, they jumped on their bikes, riding next to him and talking a great deal in Dutch. They rode quickly uphill on the paved path.

"Are you still there?" he joked. "You weigh nothing!" Fee nervously looked around for the Japanese men as they rode quickly through the park, but there was no sign of them. They reached a large stone gate behind which was stopped an enormous crush of people.

"We will turn to the right here to go to the Rijks. It's not far now," he huffed as he pedaled uphill to the gate. As they approached the intersection, she saw the Japanese men. They instantly became very excited and pointed at her, saying "Ho-o!" repeatedly, and a group of Japanese on the sidewalk to the right looked in her direction and began pointing as well.

"Go straight! Go straight!" she yelled. His two friends had already turned onto the bike path to the right.

"But the Rijks is to the right!" he said, but then seeing the Japanese men he continued straight across the intersection weaving into the crush of people pedaling uphill over the little bridge. Even going uphill, the bike outstripped the people running after them. They quickly passed the tourists playing chess on the giant chessboard.

"Turn into there!" she commanded. They weaved into a narrow alley and stopped to hide.

"Are you in some kind of trouble?" he asked. "Should I call the police?"

"Definitely not the police," she replied, peering out. Were they tracking her? At any rate, she should get rid of her cellphone and anything else the trafficker could use to find her. Digging in the small purse, she pulled a large wad of cash out of the wallet, but the cards were useless to her, the cell dangerous. She stuffed the entire purse in a trashcan.

"What's going on?"

"I've got to get to the Rijks," she said. "I really can't explain any of this right now. I appreciate all of your help, but if you please, just point me in the direction I need to go."

"I'll get you there. It's very near." He rode very quickly around the curve of a street filled with cars and bikes. Fee nervously scanned the knots of people walking for the Asian men, but didn't see them. "This is it," he said, as he stopped the bike at an intersection. In front of them was a building as long as a city block, several stories high, very beautifully crafted in stone and decorated with statues along the top. In the center of it, directly in front of them, was a large archway through which cars and bikes moved through and underneath the building. They crossed the intersection into the tunnel and immediately heard the echoing vibrato of a lone violinist playing next to her open case. He stopped the bike in front of a door, and she immediately alighted, stepping into the shoes still in her hands.

"Are you sure you don't want me to go with you?"

"I'm sure. I have to do this alone. I wish I could find a way to thank you, but I've got to go."

"Have dinner with me," he called after her.

"I don't even have a phone, much less a number," she said, walking quickly away from him, "I'm sorry, but it's impossible." He sat there on his bike watching until she had filed into the door with the other tourists.

Fee felt more secure now. In this crowd, with gallery guards about, there was no way those men would dare attempt to drag her away here, even if they did, somehow, find her. She would figure out what to do about them later. Find Benedick, that is what she must do now. Impatiently she waited in the queue, looking at every passing face for Benedick. Finally, in possession of a ticket, she was mobbed by a dozen Japanese schoolgirls and their minders. Reflexively, she panicked, but then thought better of it, for surely a gaggle of school-girls were not at all involved in human trafficking. They too said Ho-o, over and over. They vaulted themselves next to her, one after another. One of the grown women with them attempted to pull them off of her. They were taking pictures of her, many of them.

"Don't be so aggressive, girls. Girls!"

"They want pictures of me?" she spoke to the adult woman in flawless Japanese.

"They want pictures *with* you, *of course!*" the woman replied. "Everyone under age 30 does." The woman sidled next to her. "If you don't mind *too* much," she said as she quickly snapped a selfie with her.

"I'm a good singer too. I want to be a star just like you!" one girl tried to push her cellphone into Fee's hands. On the phone a video of this girl was playing.

"I love you!" said another girl, bobbing up and down so near that her body rattled Fee's small frame.

A third girl pulled a magazine out of her bag and pushed it into Fee's hands with a pen, as the flash from several cell phones contin-ued to strobe around her. Her left hand quickly signed two Japanese characters, with a flourish, on the face of a beautiful Japanese wom-an, very young, heavily made up, wearing an oversized bow. She was blowing bubbles.

Both women pulled at the girls, "That's enough!"

"Do any of you have a compact I can borrow?" Fee asked. Instantly, a half dozen compacts, gleaming metal, sparkling with jewels, appeared in front of her. She chose one and opened it. *This is not my face!* This face matched the face on the magazine cover. She returned the compact.

"Can you tell me where the Gallery of Honor is?" A dozen man-icured fingers pointed up.

2 3

woke

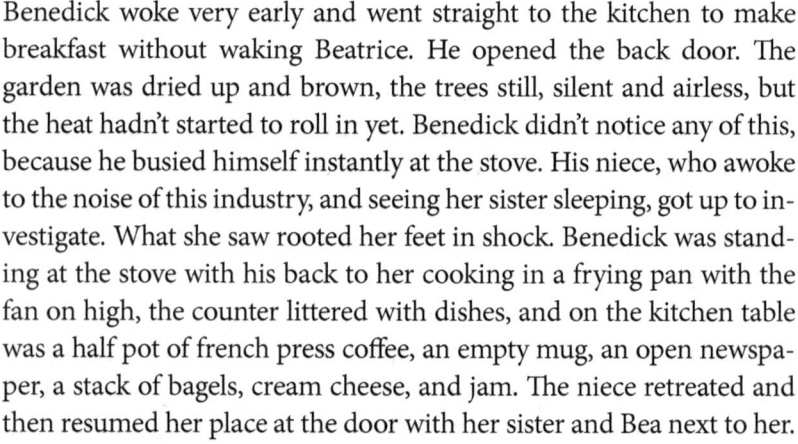

Benedick woke very early and went straight to the kitchen to make breakfast without waking Beatrice. He opened the back door. The garden was dried up and brown, the trees still, silent and airless, but the heat hadn't started to roll in yet. Benedick didn't notice any of this, because he busied himself instantly at the stove. His niece, who awoke to the noise of this industry, and seeing her sister sleeping, got up to investigate. What she saw rooted her feet in shock. Benedick was standing at the stove with his back to her cooking in a frying pan with the fan on high, the counter littered with dishes, and on the kitchen table was a half pot of french press coffee, an empty mug, an open newspaper, a stack of bagels, cream cheese, and jam. The niece retreated and then resumed her place at the door with her sister and Bea next to her.

"Oh! Good morning!" Benedick said, when he saw them out of the corner of his eye.

"Are you alright?" Bea asked.

"Alright?" he said, glancing back at her through the haze of steam, "Why wouldn't I be alright?"

Bea and her nieces were clutching each other by their arms, and tears were coursing down Bea's cheeks. "I'm so glad," she said.

"Bea?" He plated an enormous pile of scrambled eggs and potatoes.

"Yes, Bene?"
"We need to go to Amsterdam."
"Amsterdam?"
"Yes. We need to go right now."

2 4

where i'm from

"Fascinating," Fee said aloud to herself.

"What's fascinating?" Bea asked, but Fee didn't answer. She wordlessly clicked Bea's browser closed and returned her phone instead. She was staring past Bea, down the length of the Museumplein.

"How did you lose your purse, if I may ask?"

"A man in the Vondelpark knocked me down and took it. Apparently, there are a lot of homeless people living in the Vondelpark." The three of them had walked out of the Rijks together and now stood opposite the IAmsterdam sign, with bikers speeding by them in both directions, and pedestrians streaming around them on both sides.

"There are homeless people living everywhere," Bea replied. The police clear them out, but they just come back. There's no where else to go." Benedick and Bea crossed the street and began walking down the Museumplein toward the apartment where they were staying until they realized that their new friend was no longer behind them. They turned to see her standing still, one hand frozen upwards, in deep thought.

"So," she said, closing the distance between them, "I know I told you that my purse was stolen...that's true, but that's not all of it. A man returned my purse, but then I threw it away."

"Threw it away!"

"And I'd really like to retrieve it. The trash can is this way, just a few blocks."

"I'm sorry, but I'm a bit confused…" Bea said, as they turned away from the Museumplein.

"I'm trying really hard to figure out how to explain it to you," Fee responded.

"Maybe we should start by introducing ourselves," Bea said.

"You can call me Fee." She smiled a knowing smile, "But Benedick used to call me Phoenix."

"How in the world did you know his name?"

"And you are Beatrice." She remembered to pronounce it correctly.

Bea's mouth fell open.

"We have met before," Fee said. "You don't remember?" She looked at Benedick.

"No, I'm sorry. Are you staying near us?"

"No." She looked so despondent, Benedick and Bea exchanged a concerned glance.

"But you don't call me Beatrice," Bea whispered to Benedick, "and no one calls you Benedick except me."

"She's a harmless child," he said. "And I feel very protective of her, for some reason."

As they walked, Fee noticed for the first time the almost supernatural cleanliness of the streets, the perfectly pointed masonry of the ancient buildings, the gleaming plate glass windows offering views into luxury shops and restaurants. It was beautiful, but Fee could feel the reverberating throb of aggression everywhere. The gleaming surfaces, the guards posted next to the doors of buildings, the quick pace of people walking by her, forcing her to move out of their way or be knocked back. New Earth people dressed themselves well, but this was something else. There was a competitive aggressiveness in the contrived cut of the clothes, their angles, bright colors, and the layers of jewelry on men and women both. The clothes demanded her attention. She became conscious of her own clothes, how like these they were.

"I don't know what I expected," she said, "but I'm surprised to see how well cared for everything is, and yet I saw homeless families in the park?"

"Oh, Amsterdam is like anywhere else. The popular cities are for the rich nowadays," Bea said. "Everyone else lives far outside them and those who are lucky enough to find work commute in." Fee was struggling with old concepts and vocabulary she had long abandoned; her confusion made her slow to respond.

"What about the unpopular cities?" she asked finally.

"Oh, you don't want to go there. There are no rich at all, just people trying to keep their houses, and a class of the dispossessed who become criminals of every kind and periodically fill up the jails.... Isn't that how it is where you're from? I thought the whole world was like that now?"

Fee smiled. "Where I'm from, everyone enjoys a high quality of life. People aren't materialists at all, they don't orient their lives around getting more things. We work because we want to, our work is a contribution to our community. Caregiving work is vitally important, and so people are well cared for and there is art and music everywhere."

"Where in the world are you from?" Bea asked.

"It's a place called New Earth," Fee replied. "It's isolated. Have you ever heard of it?" Fee met Benedick's eyes and waited for a sign of the smallest recognition, but saw none.

"It's in Japan somewhere? How is it so isolated? A commune? I want to move there!" Bea laughed.

"A New Earth commune wouldn't really be possible. The only thing that makes that world possible is a society without money, and it's not really possible to have a society without money surrounded by market economies. It would have to be completely self sufficient."

"Except Russia did it, and China," Bea said.

"That's Communism, Bea," Benedick said. "Communism isn't about getting rid of money. It's about government control of money."

"And government control means that individual people control how money is made and spent. Communist countries are as corrupt as any other. No, I'm talking about something else."

"Something metaphorical, I assume," Benedick said, "because such a place doesn't exist on this Earth that I'm aware of." He cut his eyes to Beatrice, who shook her head in confirmation.

Fee didn't respond. They had passed the tourists playing chess on the giant chessboard and walked up the alleyway.

"Here it is," Fee said as she began to circle a municipal trash can. "The top looks impossibly heavy." She bent to reach an arm inside.

"May I help you?" A young, uniformed man with the word, 'Politie' on his chest and arm approached, with a female counterpart one step behind him. His words were as polite as his uniform promised, but his suspicions were clearly aroused.

"I've accidentally thrown away my purse," she told them.

"Accidentally?" he laughed and the woman laughed also. They didn't believe her.

"It's small. I threw it away with some other stuff, accidentally." She played the silly teenager. She bent down to peer helplessly inside the can.

"It's true," Benedick offered. Fee grabbed the top and attempted to budge it. The cop put out a hand.

"You'll get your dress dirty," he said. The two officers moved the lid aside and then he pushed around the trash with his baton.

"There it is!" she said, "The black thing there." The officer bent inside the can and retrieved it with two fingers and handed it to her. The female officer hit him on the shoulder and nodded toward the building in front of them. There on the side of the building was a large poster, in Dutch and English, with Fee's face on it. They looked from the poster to Fee. She smiled, but then started as the purse began to vibrate in her hands. Pulling out the phone, she answered it. Without saying hello, a Japanese woman began speaking quickly into her ear.

"Where have you been? I've been calling you all day! I saw online that you were at the Rijks, but you could have answered or at least sent me a text. It was so weird and worrisome! I know you don't like to stay in one place more than a night, but I had to book the hotel another night because I couldn't reach you! I didn't know what to do!" Fee was speechless for several moments.

"*Tenminste, ze had ons kaartjes kunnen geven,*" the female officer said to the male as they walked away.

"Thank you!" she called after them in English, and then spoke to the woman on the phone. "Sorry, I've had a difficult morning. It's fine about the hotel, maybe I'll clear out later. People have been chasing me everywhere."

"Keep up the good work. The tourists are in a frenzy about Ho-o sightings, and clothes with cherries on them are flying out of the online store. I'll let Amari San know that you are going back to that same hotel, maybe he will stop by."

"Amari San?"

"You know…Mamoru Amari…your agent? The man who controls your entire life?"

"Oh…*that* Amari San," Fee put humor into her voice.

"Try to get some rest, darling. In the museum pictures, you looked tired."

"That's you," Benedick said, pointing at the poster.

"Yes," she said, "That's me, but it's also not me." She gathered herself, she of the shawl and the New Earth, before she spoke again. "When we first saw each other at the museum, did you recognize me?"

They were looking at her the way people look at celebrities. "Honey, we don't listen to pop music, I'm sorry. We're old and out of it," Bea laughed.

"No, I mean…"

"I thought I did," Benedick said. "Didn't I? Bea, remember you said that she's too young to be one of my former students? So, we *do* know each other from somewhere?"

"Yes we do, but I want you to guess."

"Oh, but I can't imagine, you'll have to tell me."

She needed him to remember. She wasn't sure what, exactly, she needed to do here, only that there were billions of lucky versions of us depending on her to do it. The clock of necessity ticked relentlessly on in her mind. She needed him on her team.

"The last time I spoke with you," she said to him, only to him, "we talked about the painting that you were looking at in the museum, *View of Delft*. You had dreamed that you were in that painting standing on the bridge." She watched his face.

"That's simply not possible," Bea said. "You have mistaken him for someone else. He has been retired at home probably for longer than you have been alive."

"Forget for a moment about time," Fee persisted, looking only at him, "forget about the math of it. We have talked about that painting several times, and then we meet in front of it. Isn't that interesting?" Something was happening in his face, she could see it.

"Bea, wasn't that the first thing I said to you? That we had to come here to see the painting?"

"You said you needed to go to *Amsterdam*."

"And as soon as we got here, I wanted to go right to the Rijks."

"That's true," she said. "Maybe you are remembering something from before? Ms…Fee, are you perhaps, older than you look? This guessing game has gone on too long."

Fee could begin to tell them all sorts of things about themselves, but that would not do. They would be in shock, and she would have to explain to them how she knew it all, and not having any reference, any independent recollection, they would not believe her. He had to remember on his own.

"I *am* much older than I look," she said to Bea and then turned to Benedick. "The last time we talked, I didn't have this accent, forget that, and forget about how I look. I usually don't dress like this."

"We talked about the painting? What did we say? That will help me remember."

"The first time we talked about it, you told me that it was foreboding." Bea gasped and they looked at each other.

"Yes, it is foreboding," he said, "Do you remember what I said, Bea?"

"Don't…."

"I said that I remembered losing you and living years and years without you."

"Yes!" Fee said, "That's right. Fifteen years. Let's pretend that I'm writing a book about it. Now, Benedick, what is the first word you think of when you think of that life without Bea."

"Quiet," he mumbled, staring past her. "Also, secure…solitary."

"Good. Now, just imagine. Make something up, make believe: What is one strange thing that is different in that world without Bea." Benedick closed his eyes.

"It's okay if you don't want to tell us, Bene," Bea said quickly, pulling on his sleeve, "It doesn't matter. This game is overtaxing him."

"I'm sorry, Bea, but it's not a game. It's very important that he remember." Fee spoke with authority, as herself, rather than playing the part of the teenager, and Bea closed her mouth, utterly bemused. Benedick looked at Fee.

"The back door is gone. Why would the back door of my house disappear?"

"Bene is delicate," Bea pleaded, "and he hasn't eaten since early this morning. This has to stop now. You don't need him for your book. He needs to eat…."

"Let's go eat across the street there," Fee said.

"We can't possibly afford to eat there, I'm sorry," Bea said, taking Benedick's arm. "It was nice meeting you, Ms. Fee…."

"Oh, yes, I forgot. We need money here." Fee reached a hand deep into the square neck of her dress and pulled out a wad of cash and held it out to Bea.

"Omigosh," Bea said, covering Fee's hand with both of hers, "Put that away before someone sees it."

"Let's go eat, then," Benedick said and began to walk across the street. Bea reluctantly followed and Fee after her.

The hostess ignored them, and allowed in a party of tourists that came in behind them. That's when Fee noticed that both Benedick and Beatrice looked intensely uncomfortable. Bea kept looking about without moving her head, and Benedick kept clearing his throat.

"Is something wrong?"

"Well, we're a bit underdressed here," Bea said. Fee looked around for the first time. The room was packed full of both Dutch and foreign tourists, all of them, even the Dutch, dressed as if for a late evening out in designer clothes. They were all drinking alcohol, and the scent of marijuana hung faintly in the air.

A black woman with short natural hair tipped in gold swept by them wearing a long caftan in a print pattern that Fee had seen several other women wearing.

"That caftan, my God," Bea said.

"What about it?"

"It must have cost tens of thousands of dollars, probably more. See that blonde girl over there with the blouse? And that handbag? They're all the same print. It's a patented design, a special pattern of leopard's spots, shot through with gold thread, instantly recognizable. Each item of clothing costs tens of thousands of dollars, and that long caftan with the special ruff? I can't imagine how much that was. It's the ICare brand, which supposedly donates money to save wild animals, but the animals are going extinct anyway, so I'm not sure it's helping much."

"If they just gave all that money to conservation organizations instead of buying the clothes, I should think that would be more helpful," Benedick said.

"And then, it probably doesn't help the animals that all of these resources are extracted and then…let me guess, mass produced in a factory burning fossil fuels in China and then shipped all over the world using more fossil fuels…." Fee added.

Bea opened her mouth to speak, but couldn't for a moment. "That comment alone almost makes me believe everything you've said about your commune. China isn't the land of sweatshops anymore. It hasn't been for a long time. They are rich. Sweatshops are all over now. The ICare sweatshops are mostly in the U.S."

It was then that a small group of twenty somethings leaped up from their table and ran over to them. Fee calmly chatted with them as she posed for their pictures. She didn't have to talk for long, for as soon as each one of them took a photo with her, they all walked away holding their phones in front of them, thumbs tapping.

"It's a curious behavior," Fee said.

"The younger generation is lost," Bea said.

The hostess, having seen Fee mobbed by the tourists, now smiled at her ingratiatingly and asked them to follow her to a table.

"They were all so well dressed for such young people," Fee said.

"Of course they are rich, they are tourists!" Bea laughed uneasily.

"But, you are tourists," Fee said. "You're not rich."

"You're right. We would never have been able to afford to come here, if I had not taken on debt. It was a terrible risk, but we have relatives living with us and they both work, so I think it will be okay."

"Why did you take such a risk? It must have been very important," Fee looked only at Bea. She needed to work on Bea.

Bea turned her face away, and Fee let it go. They ordered lunch. Bea ordered for Benedick, who was lost in thought.

"You have relatives living with you now?" Fee asked, trying to put Bea at ease.

"Yes, our two grand-nieces, my sister's granddaughters. They found work in Portland, but of course, can't afford a place of their own. I had to give up my studio and move my painting into the front room." She laughed ruefully.

"So, this is common?" Fee asked.

"Oh yes. Everyone I know who still owns a house has it full of relatives or friends. We are so fortunate that we lived modestly during our working years and paid off the house. I don't know where we would be if we didn't have that house paid off....Living with relatives, probably!" She laughed again.

"What about social security? Isn't that supposed to help when people retire?"

"It doesn't anymore. It was privatized, gosh, maybe 10 or 12 years ago. Paying into it isn't mandatory anymore, there's no mandate. Tons of people who live hand to mouth elect not to pay into it, so all of those people won't have any retirement benefits at all. Meanwhile, a lot of people who *did* sign up lost their benefits when some of the companies managing it went belly up after 2022. The fund managers got off scot free and skated away rich, of course. We've been in a recession ever since. Like I said, we're extremely fortunate that we paid off the house. So many people lost their homes in '22."

"There must be so many empty houses then?"

"Well, in the flood zones, yes, many abandoned houses. But not in the dry areas. The rich have a house in every city they spend time in. When they aren't there, it sits empty, monitored by security companies. A lot of other houses are owned by investment companies who rent them out as vacation places or at maximum rents to the people who work for the rich. Well, and then there's the dead areas, but they don't count."

"Dead areas?"

"You know, on the outskirts of cities and in the smaller towns, all of those abandoned houses with people squatting in them without water, sanitation or power. You want to stay away from those areas."

"That's so sad," Fee said. "Empty houses, homeless families."

"It's not like that in Japan?"

"Not where I'm from."

"It's hard to imagine," Bea said.

"How can it be hard to imagine? Surely you remember what it was like years ago?"

"It's been like this so long, those days seem like a distant dream. Now, I would just be happy if they would pass legislation to curb these security people, but they probably won't. The U.S. Supreme Court just ruled that the private security industry doesn't have to follow the same Constitutional laws that the military police have to, because they're private. But they do the exact same things as the military police! They're the same! It's almost like an occupying army."

"But I haven't seen that here?"

"The Netherlands have kept them under control, for the tourists. But you've seen those guys hanging about the doors to shops? They're private security. And if you pay attention, you'll see them trailing behind the tourists with those little things in their ears and the special eyeglasses that connect them with the AI."

"Oh! You have the AI?" It was like hearing about an old friend from home.

Bea tilted her head to one side. "Of course we have the AI. We *invented* the AI. I'm sure it's in Japan too. It's all connected, worldwide, and *we* run it, the U.S., I mean."

"Then the cars must be very safe here too. That's something. You must have excellent preventative care and health care, at least for the rich. And you can track your resources, and resolve international disputes fairly."

"I don't know what you're talking about. It's almost like you're an alien, I feel like I'm talking to an alien. Everyone knows that the AI is used for security and surveillance. That's all it does."

"So terribly, terribly sad," Fee said, her mouth dry, her eyes dry, and indeed her entire being shriveled before the fortress of pain created by this world, the enormity of the inertial forces preventing any motion whatsoever, and the tide of loss, already irretrievable losses, too enormous to even contemplate. She couldn't eat nor speak for a long time, and instead watched her pink lacquered index finger move from her spoon to the tablecloth, spoon, tablecloth, a ticking clock of hopelessness. This world was surely beyond hope, and she could not imagine what she could possibly do about it when she couldn't even convince Benedick. Her long hair fell forward into her face, for it was far too thick and long to remain tucked behind her ears the way she liked it. This was not her hair, and she desperately wanted to chop it off. In fact, that might actually help.

"I think I can help you remember me, Benedick…I'll be back in a minute!"

"It doesn't matter," Bea pleaded. "You've hardly touched your plate."

"It's okay, I don't eat very much."

Walking over to the bar, Fee asked the bartender for scissors. He repeated the request to his fellow, who carried it to a waitress, who disappeared across the room. Shortly, she returned with an enormous pair built for opening large packages.

"Thank you," Fee said, and carried them straight to the restroom.

There was a tall, blonde Dutch woman, about forty, restocking the toilet paper when Fee walked in and marched over to the mirror.

The woman said something to her in Dutch, banging the dispensers closed. She came out of the end stall holding a stack of paper towels, but stopped, towering over Fee in the mirror. She watched as Fee peeled a false eyelash off one of her eyelids and then the other. Fee then scrubbed her face with hand soap in the sink, and when she stood, the woman mutely handed her two paper towels.

Fee examined herself in the mirror. Her skin was tinted brown, and she had tiny freckles sprinkled across the flawless skin of her cheekbones, just under her eyes. Without the heavy eye makeup, Fee could see herself, resident, in these foreign eyes: frank, wise, practical. She was satisfied.

When Fee grabbed a handful of her hair and raised the scissors, the woman put out one hand and said something to her in Dutch.

"I don't speak Dutch," Fee said.

"Your hair is very beautiful, you should not cut it," the woman said in English with a heavy Dutch accent that she held like a gum ball in the front of her mouth. Fee raised the scissors again, and the woman again said, insisting, "*Nay, nay, nay.*" With the pushy solicitousness that all Dutch women share, she put down the stack of paper towels and firmly took the scissors from Fee's hands.

"If you're going to do it, let me help you. Where do you want it?" Fee made a chopping motion with her hand at her jawline, beneath her ear lobe. Quickly and confidently, the woman divided Fee's hair with the point of the scissors, and asked her to hold some of it in each of her hands. "I am not a hair dresser, and these are not for hair."

"I know. It's okay."

In a few minutes, there was a pool of black hair at her feet. Fee smiled and pulled the bracelets off her arms, and the earrings in her ears and handed them to the woman.

"Keep them," Fee said.

"Oh no, these are very expensive," the woman said, and tried to hand them back to her.

"I don't wear jewelry," Fee said.

The woman was still staring at her in the mirror, holding the jewelry in front of her in one open hand. Fee looked at her reflection.

"More like myself," she said, "whatever that is." She squatted on the floor, quickly gathered the hair and stuffed it into the trash can.

The woman knitted her brows with genuine concern. "Are you going to be alright?"

"As alright as I need to be," Fee told her.

All the way back across the restaurant, the heavily made up women in their ICare prints stared at her naked face, then lowered their long false eyelashes and whispered to each other. Fee ignored them.

As she approached the table, she held Benedick's eyes. "Now?" she asked him.

He stared at her. She sat down. "I don't know," he said.

"Not my face," she said, "the face won't be the same." He raised his hands.

"Maybe."

"Do you like strawberries?" It was a sudden impulse she had, to ask Beatrice about it.

"Doesn't everyone?" Bea smiled.

"Didn't she used to hate them?" she asked Benedick. The question caused his jaw to stop chewing.

"Yes…yes, that's right," he said.

"I never!" Bea laughed.

"No," he insisted, "You hated them so much you didn't allow me to eat them. When we were dating…don't you remember? We never had a strawberry in the house our entire married life."

"I remember no such thing!" Bea said, casting a cutting glance at Fee. "You've had a hard time with your memory, it's okay. Don't overtax yourself."

"I'm not overtaxing. I remember perfectly." He turned to Fee. "Why doesn't she remember? I don't know who I am, or where, quite suddenly."

The Unity does change here. Something has changed it, Fee thought. Looking at Benedick, she asked carefully, gently, "Do you remember writing that down? *It was strawberries she hated.*"

"Yes…but I don't remember when or why."

"It's the residual effects…." Bea said.

"No. It's something else," he insisted. "Somewhere else, I had to write down everything."

"Yes, that's right." Fee said.

"How do you know?" Benedick said. "Who are you?"

Fee rose from her chair and carefully picked up the salt and pepper shakers from the empty table next to them. She removed the tablecloth and then set the shakers back down. She sat back down in her chair, and looking steadily at Benedick, folded the cloth in half and draped it around her shoulders.

"Now do you recognize me?" She wasn't sure it would work, but she did her best to gather in her mind every memory she had of Benedick in the NE. He must remember, he simply must. He stared back at her without recognition.

"I'm not comfortable with this," Bea said, and Fee sighed and looked away, turning her profile to him. He made a small noise, a gasp that brought her attention back to his face, which was a deep scarlet. He looked away.

"What's wrong?" Bea asked, alarmed, putting her hands on his shoulders, his forehead.

"I'm fine," he insisted, pushing her hands away. "It's just that, for some reason, I do remember her…or someone very like. It's a strange, random thought I'd rather not share." He looked away.

"I was naked," Fee said.

His face turned to hers, "How in the world…?"

"In the desert. Sitting cross-legged."

His mouth gaped soundlessly.

"Yes. That's correct. That was the first time we met, which was either fifteen years in the past or a thousand years in the future, I'm not yet sure."

His palm raised to his mouth, "I guess I have to believe what you say now…."

"Okay," Bea said, standing, "I think we're finished now."

"No, I'm starting to remember things…."

"You keep saying fifteen years, fifteen years, why?" Bea demanded.

"Why are you unsettled by the number fifteen?"

"I'm not unsettled."

"You are clearly upset," Fee persisted.

"Apparently," Benedick answered for her, "I've been ill for fifteen years."

"Fascinating....What sort of illness did you have?"

Benedick looked at Bea.

"He had a series of strokes...in his frontal parietal lobe and thalamus."

"I was a vegetable, apparently."

"You were not a vegetable," Bea retorted. "He had lucid moments, where you could actually converse with him for a short time, but he often didn't make sense. He could follow simple commands, but he couldn't be left alone. He was like a very small child who needed supervision and care round the clock. He miraculously recovered... three days ago. We woke up and there he was, making eggs and potatoes."

"Three days ago," Fee breathed. That would have been First Day, just after Benedick's death.

"Why are you so unsettled by three days?" Bea asked, "and don't say you aren't."

An image of Benedick lying in a pool of blood flashed through her mind. "I don't think it would be a good idea to say," she said.

"So, only you can ask questions?"

"You wouldn't believe me if I told you."

"I think you should try us," Benedick said gently.

"Alright, but not here."

2 5

evicted

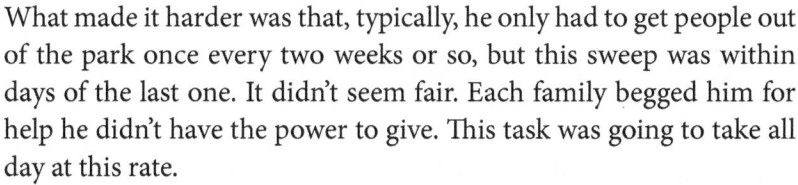

What made it harder was that, typically, he only had to get people out of the park once every two weeks or so, but this sweep was within days of the last one. It didn't seem fair. Each family begged him for help he didn't have the power to give. This task was going to take all day at this rate.

"I'm sorry, but you must go now," the police officer said with authority—a penitent, pleading sort of authority. This family was resting on several blankets arranged in the shade of a rhododendron. A toddler was sound asleep, and her four year old sister stood sentry on the edge of the blanket clutching a rag doll. No doubt, the child had been through this many times.

The man sat up halfway. "It's only been a couple of days!" he protested.

"I'm sorry. Today is the day." The man and the woman stood. The police officer continued to talk, even though he knew what he said made no difference.

"There's a shelter on Wetering...."

"schans. We know," the man said. "Their waiting list is more than a hundred long."

The woman's face was pale and without hope, she didn't even

meet the officers gaze. She stooped and slowly gathered the blankets from around the sleeping toddler and folded them into a large plastic shopping bag. The man dropped to his knees, his face both furious and beseeching.

"Please, let us stay. We will be very quiet. My wife…," He put the back of his hand to his face and then steadied himself. "She's pregnant. All of this walking without food isn't good for her. The stress isn't good for her or the baby."

"What do you want me to do?" the officer asked, casting his eyes to the tops of the trees, "Look. There was an attempted robbery of a tourist by a homeless man earlier today. So, that's it, everyone has to go now. I'm not the one making this decision, there's nothing I can do. I can't ask you to my house, we are packed in already with my parents living with us. My income supports us all just barely. Do you want me to lose my job and all of us join you out here? If I don't clear the park, I'll get fired. I'm sorry."

"We hid from you. You didn't see us."

"I can give you my lunch," the officer said desperately. He always ended up giving away his lunch. "It's only a butter sandwich, but you can have it." When the woman hesitated, he added, "We have enough food at home. Take it." She took it immediately then and tore it into three parts, giving the first to the girl with the doll, the second to her husband, who returned it to her, and the third part she stuffed into her own mouth so greedily the officer watched her lest she choke.

"You should be eating fruits and vegetables," the officer said.

"I should be doing a lot of things," she replied. Her husband dropped his head and covered his face with his hand.

"You will go now?" the officer asked, knowing already that they would.

2 6

seven a.m.

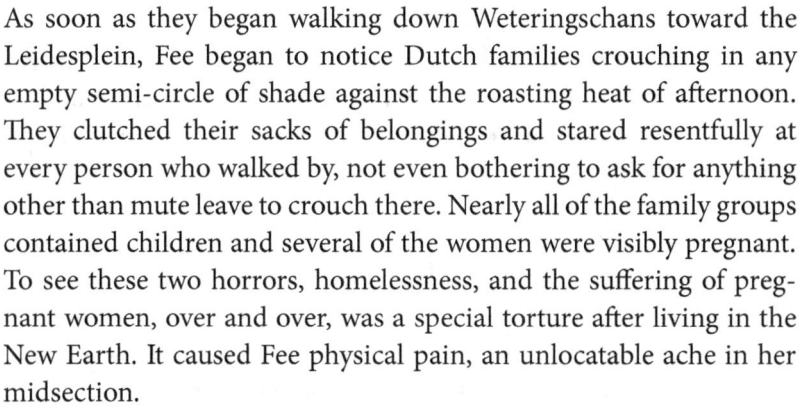

As soon as they began walking down Weteringschans toward the Leidesplein, Fee began to notice Dutch families crouching in any empty semi-circle of shade against the roasting heat of afternoon. They clutched their sacks of belongings and stared resentfully at every person who walked by, not even bothering to ask for anything other than mute leave to crouch there. Nearly all of the family groups contained children and several of the women were visibly pregnant. To see these two horrors, homelessness, and the suffering of pregnant women, over and over, was a special torture after living in the New Earth. It caused Fee physical pain, an unlocatable ache in her midsection.

"You said that it's the cities that are so expensive," Fee said, "Why do they not move to the countryside?"

"I imagine it's for the same reason as back home…there's no work there. They leave for the city to find work, and then don't." Fee stopped, remembering the wad that she had dropped in her purse after she had paid for lunch, and retraced her steps, giving money, she knew not how much, to each family they had passed. It lightened the weight she carried in her chest to see the sullen resentment turn to wonder. Bea wasn't impressed.

"That was a nice thing to do, Fee, but it's no solution. They will eat for a day or two, maybe sleep indoors for a night, depending on how much you gave them. I'm sorry, it's the same back home." Fee stopped again. Ahead of them she could see the crush of tourists moving through the Leidesplein, and the trams cutting through them, but her eye was now trained to see the knots of crouching mothers with their children beneath the trees. The tourists breezed past them, consulting their maps.

"Why does no one care that pregnant women and developing children are under so much stress? That makes epigenetic changes that will cause them to develop diseases and mental illness. The babies will be born premature, or weak and disease prone. Why doesn't anyone care?"

"I hate to say it, it sounds awful, but the only thing the government takes care of are things that make money. These people are collateral damage. If the rich could figure out a way to make money off of them, well then!" she laughed. Just then, a woman screamed as two police officers pulled her away from a man lying on the ground. Two other men materialized from the crowd, zipped the prone man into a body bag and disappeared with him as the woman was bundled away.

"Death even," Bea said quietly as Fee stared at the space where the man had been, now full of crisscrossing tourists already, "it's no consequence to a system with a surplus of people."

"But you could reduce working hours and employ more people. That would work even with this system, wouldn't it?"

"It's more expensive, silly. If you have two employees instead of one, you have to pay for training for two people, benefits for two, health care for two and so on. Making one person work long hours is much cheaper. They call it 'being efficient' and 'cutting costs.' Back home it's worse," Bea continued. "Since birth control was taken off the health plans and abortion was outlawed in the U.S., the population has been skyrocketing. Already there are legions of young, desperate people willing to go to war or work whatever job they can get. In another three years or so, the first population bomb since the new laws were passed will hit the adult cohort. All hell will break loose then."

"But even women with jobs are under so much stress—like your nieces. Doesn't that put strain on the system?"

"All the better," Benedick said, "What you call strain, the medical industry calls profit. That's always been true."

"One of our nieces has diabetes," Bea added, "and also takes medications for I don't know what…to sleep, to eat, everything. The other one isn't sick, but the insurance company's genetic test showed that she was at risk for something, so she has to pay extra for her insurance, even though she's well. Each of them spends a percentage of their income every month in copays and extra charges, and that's before they make any kind of appointment, which they try to avoid, if they can."

"Benedick's care must have bankrupted you."

"We're fortunate that his strokes happened before everything was privatized. I quit work and became his long term care provider. I work for hugs." She smiled at Benedick and he squeezed her hand.

"We don't have profit in medical care," Fee said, "so it's important to prevent disease. We *avoid* too much stress, of course! As for pregnant women…they receive the most especial care, even before she turns on her reproductive system."

"Turns on?" Bea blinked.

"You know, when she stops preventative measures," Fee said carefully. "When she does that, the doctor runs all sorts of tests and then she refers her to a nutritionist and a genetic counselor and they fine tune her diet and lifestyle to maximize her health. During the time she is trying to conceive, all efforts are made at the place of her contribution…I mean, where she works, to keep her stress level down, so that her eggs won't suffer epigenetic damage. She's strongly encouraged to get a massage once a week—it's free—and meditate or listen to healing music if she doesn't already have a spiritual practice."

"When did this happen?" Bea demanded. "When did Japan become this wonderland? Japan has always been the land of workaholism and still is." She looked at Benedick for support, but his face had no surprise in it.

"I know about this," he said. "This is completely familiar to me, but I don't know where I read it."

Pris had been watching this entire conversation up to this point. She noticed it right away when the routine scan of conversations in the plein turned up words that were flag words, such as sick, disease, death, desperate, damage, privatized, stress, war and bomb. These words alerted software to identify all three of them and analyze their faces. Pris placed a flag on the files of each of the two Americans, but they were not large flags. The expressions on their faces were not intense, and were not coded as distress but rather something akin to resignation. Resignation was acceptable. However, the small woman, identified by the facial recognition software as a Japanese celebrity, true name Yumiko Omata called Ho-o!, who is in the Netherlands on a creative's visa, appeared very distressed. Pris is trained to watch for any emotional intensity of a negative type, so this woman caught her particular attention. Flag number one was the words she was using. Flag number two was her intensely distressed expression. Flag number three was engaging in prohibited behavior, namely giving cash money to persons coded as unemployed:vagrant, with two such persons coded as criminal:time served. In addition, just hours ago, this same woman had been subjected to physical violence during an attempted robbery and then ran away from help offered. That odd behavior had earned her a flag already.

"We didn't come here to talk about pregnant women. You were going to tell us something we wouldn't believe," Bea said.

Fee sat them both down on a bench in the shade of a tree and knelt in front of them. Pris moved around from camera to camera in the Leidesplein, but could no longer see nor hear what the Japanese celebrity with four flags in three point five hours was saying to the two Americans who bent down to her with their three heads close together. It was frustrating. What she needed was a drone that could scoot around amongst them, but the politicians banned drones within the central city as too "disruptive" to tourism. Very frustrating.

Fee reached for Benedick's hand and then Bea's, and they closed her tiny hands in theirs and looked down at her with concern. For better or for worse, they had decided without realizing it that this pretty, lunatic child was theirs.

"The first thing I want to say, Benedick—I never got a chance to say it, and I felt sorry about it later—I want to tell you how grateful I am that you were there for me on First Day." Fee looked up into his aged, blue, heavy lidded eyes, which did not recognize her nor even comprehend what she was saying, but held a kind, unblinking attention. "You saved my life then, and over the next weeks, your companionship probably saved my sanity. I may have gone mad there in the desert alone." She paused. She wasn't certain she had the courage to say it, her hands, ordinarily so cool became hot and moist. "You were like a father to me, the only father I ever really had." Tears of gratitude caused her vision to swim just a little, she was so relieved to have had the chance to sit in his presence and say this.

"I'm dead in that other world, aren't I?" he asked. "You think I'm dead."

"Do you remember that I said that the last time I spoke to you, we talked about that painting?"

"Yes. You said I had had a dream about it."

"What I didn't say, is that the last time I saw you we did not speak at all. We couldn't. The last time I saw you, you were lying in a pool of your own blood."

"Clearly that isn't possible," Bea said.

"It happened in this other world, exactly three days ago. That would have been right when he had his miraculous recovery, Bea? Isn't that right?"

"I just don't know what to think anymore. I can't decide if you are insane or if I am insane for believing you. I don't know why I believe you. This is crazy."

"I found you when I was looking for Bea," Benedick said.

"Yes." Fee's pulse quickened.

"Bea was gone and I was sure that I would find her in Las Vegas…."

"I hate Las Vegas!" Bea said.

"I didn't find her there. I found you, instead, sitting in the sand.

Is Las Vegas gone? It's gone when I think of this."

"Yes. All of it, yes. Lots of things were gone. Many people were gone. We lived in that world for fifteen years. Bea, you asked me earlier, why I keep saying fifteen years. I will start from the beginning." And she did start from the beginning and spoke for a half hour before she was finished. She could feel Benedick quicken as she spoke, life came into his eyes more each moment, and he began to interject with remembered details. Fee looked at Bea, expecting her to object, but she said something unexpected instead.

"He took to saying not long before his recovery—you can ask my nieces, they heard him too. He said several times, 'Bea, the back door is gone, that means it's almost over.' I always assumed this was nonsense from a befuddled mind." Fee continued to look up at them, still holding their hands.

"I feel so strange right now," Bea said, "I feel like we are the only three people in this world who are real, that we are alone. Isn't that odd? Is it really true that I didn't like strawberries?"

"Yes," Benedick said, "unless my memory is false."

"And mine, as well," Fee said.

"Why would that sort of thing Change?" Bea asked. "Not that I understand it, but what would that accomplish?" Fee sighed deeply and searched the dark silence inside herself. If she was good at anything, it was this.

"I think that might have been a pointing finger," she said. She wasn't confident that she could explain to them Bea's pointing finger on Benedick's computer screen lined up with the back door of his house and how that told her all she needed to know, how it was that pointing finger that brought her to this moment kneeling on the Leidesplein in the Old Earth. "It was a shim, if you will, something that cracked open the convincing reality of your story of your life here, so that you could open your mind to the possibility that what I would be telling you is true." Bea looked past Fee for several moments, and then found her eyes again.

"Now what?" she asked. "You said you needed our help. How can we help?"

"I'm not completely sure, but I do have some idea. Benedick, do you remember Mandrake?"

"Yes. I remember the entire incident with the tree now. He came with you and several others."

"At that time, he said that he thought the tree was a second order Change, the kind that people make in partnership with the Unity, Bea, called Naturework. There's a person here in the Old Earth, a woman named Small Wright, and also a group in Scotland, who have pioneered this work, so it's not far fetched. This is not unknown here."

"Are you saying that Old Earth people sent a second order Change to the New Earth?" Benedick asked.

"Perhaps not consciously. It has become clear to me, given how reactive Las Vegas has been prior to your death, Benedick, and from what I experienced in coming here to this world, that the New Earth did not leave the Old Earth behind. They are in symbiosis. As Old Earth devolves, New Earth writhes and Changes. That's why we have to be so careful there, the New Earth is delicate. I think the situation is such that, unless we do something about the devolution of this world, the New Earth will be in danger. This is what the Watchers have been watching for."

"So, you mean to tell me that you think we're going to help you save the world?" Bea asked.

"Save two worlds," Benedick responded.

"You have to help me to figure out how. I'm in this body for a reason. Let's go to the hotel. I have a hotel room at the American, apparently. Let's go there and find out everything we can about Ho-o, namely me." When the three of them began walking across the Leidesplein, Pris lost interest in the Japanese celebrity. Whatever they had said to each other, it seemed to calm her down. Her face now coded content, which was acceptable. There were many people on the Leidesplein and the Leidesstraat, and her software was very busy tracking and coding them all. She clicked Fee's dialog box closed.

The intersection that divided the Leidesplein and the American Hotel was a small city in itself, a giant octopus with intersecting paths for bikes, trams, cars, and pedestrians, crammed with all of these.

They had to wait a very long time to cross the largest street, and as they waited Fee stared at her phone, looking at photos of herself. When she clicked over to videos in order to see videos of herself performing, she stumbled into the most disgusting pornography, supposedly featuring herself. She showed it to Bea.

"They do that to everyone now with animation software," Bea said. "It's disgusting, but that's what they do, even for heads of state. If you're famous, it's best to avoid looking yourself up."

In the New Earth, the internet was the great liberator, allowing worldwide resource management and communication, improving health and education, and making music and books and art available to everyone everywhere free. Here it was used primarily for commerce of every base and useless kind, surveillance…and porn. The terrible grief, if she let herself contemplate it for longer than a moment, threatened to break her. She clicked the tab closed, and opened another.

"Have you found out why everyone wants a picture with you, but they don't want to talk to you?" Benedick asked. "It's very strange."

"Yes. I found that out when I borrowed Bea's phone in the Museumplein. Apparently if one of my fans gets a picture of themselves with me, they get something called Ho-o points. These points they can trade in for credit towards streamed music, merchandise or concert tickets." She smiled sadly, "Even though I have a new body and a new identity, I'm still a whore here as surely as I was in Las Vegas."

"Which may or may not have happened," Bea said.

"Whether or not those things physically happened to a body I inhabited, those things were inscribed on my soul's memory. Actual suffering of the body is a transitory thing, it's the memory of suffering, and the anticipation of more suffering, that tortures us. Our minds collect it, the suffering lives there. I took it upon myself, for some necessary reason I can't exactly articulate. It's the same to me, either way."

"But, why aren't any of these tourists chasing you now, Fee? No one is even looking at us." Fee blinked. Indeed, at that moment they were standing in a great crowd of talking and laughing tourists. Even the Japanese looked through her, if they noticed her at all.

"From what I've seen on the internet so far," Fee said, "I don't think anyone, not even her mother, has seen this girl without heavy makeup. And, I guess her extraordinarily long hair was a big part of her brand. I just hacked off her brand." Fee observed that she used the word, brand, correctly, in context. It scared her.

"Her people are going to kill you." Bea looked genuinely concerned, but Fee was calm. The most important thing was to not allow herself to get sucked into this world, this identity. Hacking off the hair was pure self defense.

"Have you found out why everyone calls you Ho-o yet?"

Fee couldn't find anything about the name until she discovered a Wikipedia article about herself.

"Let's see…Wikipedia says that no one knows what her name means. All of these J Pop stars have these nonsense names, but because the English spelling of the name always has an exclamation point, the article speculates that Ho-o! is a pop culture reference to the old American children's game, 'Hi-ho! Cherry-O.' Her nickname is Sakurambo, which means 'cherry' in English."

It's probably a creepy, wink-wink reference to her supposed teen virginity, Fee supposed, but to her the nickname evoked a candy colored Sambo, performing for the rich. Fee clicked on other J Pop news and articles in Japanese to put herself in context. There was a J Pop machine that manufactured a new girl group every year. The music was written for them and stylists invented their brand. Ho-o! was an anomaly. Somehow she captured for herself a particular, lasting fame, either because of her real talent, or because of a successful brand or both. In addition to the long hair, her brand seemed to involve dressing outlandishly in vivid colors. She wore neon fruit, or candy, or oversized bows in her hair. All of the female J Pop stars pretend to be children or toys; many of them *were* children. Japanese people didn't seem to like grown women very much. As she navigated all the Japanese pop and news websites, mature Japanese women didn't seem to exist at all.

She still hadn't heard the music. It was possible that she, Fee, might have to perform it, if she could. She finally found videos, with the words spelled out in a banner along the bottom. None of the song lyrics made any sense at all. Her most popular song was called iBubble, which was about a girl who is a bubble in a game on a screen. The bubble isn't even a part of the game, but floats along as part of the background until she bumps up against a game obstacle and pops. It was all very nihilistic. Nothing matters. The male pop stars were completely different—they were dark, complex, angst ridden. They sang ballads, anthems. Watching a compilation of the top fifty videos in Japan was a magnificent display of sexual dimorphism at its most extreme.

She navigated back to her own site and was dismayed to confirm that she did, in fact, have a concert scheduled in Amsterdam for the following day. She stared at the face of Ho-o! wearing a giant fuscia bow that matched her fuscia lipstick. She stared at the Japanese characters for Ho-o, at first absentmindedly, but then they became familiar, like re-reading an old letter, and she realized that she recognized them but she couldn't remember exactly what they referred to. They had a double meaning, but she couldn't remember what it was.

"Wait a minute…." she mumbled to herself as she clicked over to a Japanese website.

"Fee!" Bea yanked her backwards as a speeding bicyclist clipped her shoulder and said something irritably to her in Dutch.

"You aren't going to believe this," she said, ignoring the cyclist and crossing into the plein in front of the American Hotel, "The syllables, Ho-o, are an English pronunciation of Japanese characters. They are a name that refers to a creature of Japanese mythology…. It's a Phoenix!"

They all stopped in the middle of the plein. "That's amazing! But what does it mean? A Phoenix is something that rises from the ashes, right?" Bea asked.

"That's what I always thought, and it seemed to fit me. But in the Japanese version of the Phoenix story," Fee bent to read the text on her device, "the creature appears at the beginning of a new age, performs good works, and then returns to its celestial abode. There's a Chinese version of the same creature, called *Fenghuang*. They don't burn, nor regenerate. It's a different story."

"Fascinating," Benedick said. They weaved their way through the busy plein packed with bikes, both parked and moving, and both tourists and local Dutch sitting in the sun around the fountain. The crowd was disorienting. Without realizing it, they entered the hotel through the cafe attached to it, and wandered through it to find the lobby.

As if to prove the truth of what Bea had told her about the Chinese, Fee immediately saw a table of Chinese men and Dutch women. At one end of the table there was a Chinese manboy, no more than twenty, with his jet black hair carefully gelled upwards to resemble a surfer's wave, and in one ear three giant diamond studs. His skinny neck displayed several gold chains between the spread collar of a black shirt printed with cartoon orange carrots. Every time he spoke, as punctuation at the end, he tilted his chin upwards at an angle to the right or to the left, as if he expected to be photographed. To his right, and to his left, there were Dutch women, blonde and dressed for clubbing. They all laughed very loudly, falling all over each other.

"Bofan! Bofan!" yelled a Dutch teenager, very drunk, in English, "Tell us what time it is!"

"Yes! Yes! Please tell us!" For some reason, this was hilarious to all of them, and they shrieked with laughter.

"But! *Which* time do you want?" The man called Bofan tilted his chin to the right and grinned with all of his teeth showing. They began calling out the names of cities. One of the men kept demanding New York time. Bofan bent his left arm in front of his face and pulled back his sleeve to reveal five large watches, gold and platinum, one studded with diamonds.

"No!" the drunk Dutch teenager yelled and fell over onto her friend, who shoved her upright. "We want the most *expensive* time!"

"Yes! Yes!" They all agreed, shrieking, "The most expensive!"

"The most expensive! Why didn't you say?" Again he tilted his pointy chin and lowered his arm. "In that case you want…," he thrust his right fist into the air and yanked back the sleeve, "this one!" They all stopped laughing. The watch was small, and didn't have jewels.

"This one belonged to Paul Newman," he said, and smiled proudly.

"Who was Paul Newman?" one of the Dutch women asked.

"What?!" In a pantomime of rage he threw his drink on her, which stopped the hilarity for only a moment before they all started laughing again.

"But what *time* is the most expensive *time*? You still haven't told us!"

"It's…seven a.m.!" he yelled. Then they all started yelling, seven a.m.! and the drunk teenager swept all of their glasses and plates to the floor and yelled, "It's time for breakfast! We need breakfast!"

It was at this moment that they saw Fee staring at them. They all looked at her, with her high couture clothing, naked face and roughly cut hair and shrieked with laughter, pointing at her.

"She thinks she's Ho-o!" "Copycat!"

Fee quickly walked away from them.

Upstairs, Benedick and Bea followed Fee around the suite, watching her search through her own things, and speak of herself in the third person. There were enough clothes for ten or twenty people, and Fee changed into a white tunic over white jeans, before dropping to her knees to empty the contents of a trunk onto the floor. Even though mid-afternoon was upon them, in these Northern latitudes, solar noon had just finished and the entire suite was flooded with bright indirect light from a high centered sun. Fee now sat herself like a sun in an elliptic swirl of jewel colored clothing. In front of her was a stack of sheet music and farther away, an electric guitar, unplugged. Although the tourists hadn't considered her worthy of notice, Benedick thought that she—bare faced and barefoot sitting curled in a halo of sunshine—was a beautiful child with the fathomless wisdom of a woman called Fee in her eyes.

"I understand this music," she said. "I think I can still play." With encouragement from Bea and Benedick, who sat themselves attentively on a loveseat, Fee began to pick out the melody of iBubble on the guitar, gingerly at first and then confidently.

"Oh, it's easy. I know this." Her hands moved confidently now over the strings, softly playing *iBubble* and then *Upside Down*, a song about a girl who who walked upside down on air while everyone else lived a normal life on the ground. She had to kiss the boy she liked nose to chin. Then, *Nothing is Better than This*, an anthem, supposedly autobiographical, in which a girl holds onto the string of a balloon and bounces from one party to the next.

Fee put down the guitar. "You know, when I first started going through all these songs, I hated them. They are escapist nonsense. Ho-o is popular because she is a beautiful spectacle, hyper-feminine and non-threatening. I just couldn't see why...her? Why am I her? But...then as I was playing just now it occurred to me quite suddenly that her fans, even the rich, are miserable and terrified, and who can blame them? It would take only the most minor catastrophe for any of them to become flotsam on the waves of this world. This music paints for them a picture of another world, a kinder one." Fee looked out the window, and the sunlight turned her brown eyes amber. "They all long for the New Earth, though they don't know it. Ho-o could never bring that world to them, but I can."

A loud banging sounded on the door that startled all three of them. Fee motioned for Bea and Benedick to close themselves in the bedroom, and she grabbed a long, ice blue wig that she fitted over her hair. She assumed that it was either her manager or her staff, and she really didn't want to deal with the hair issue right now. The door banged a second time. She smoothed the wig and composed her face before opening the door. A Japanese man barreled past her, haranguing her. She was supposed to be in his room an hour ago, in costume, and now he finds her not dressed at all, and there had been no Ho-o! sighting reported online since this morning at the museum. Seeing her standing there wide eyed, his face softened.

"Seeing you like this, without makeup reminds me of the first time I met you, a girl in a school uniform. Do you remember?" Fee didn't remember, but something inside her was becoming increasingly agitated. "We can have our meeting here. Come here."

"Come here" is not a request Fee understood, it's not something she did, at least not in the way he meant it, with his arms outstretched towards her. When she didn't move, he spoke in a soothing voice, cajoling her. "Really, I'm not mad. We're still friends." He closed the distance between them himself, and to Fee's shock and amazement, he put his hands on her and immobilized her body against his. For several moments, she couldn't move at all. To a person who had lived physically apart from other people for fifteen years, each touch of his hands burned her. It was disgusting, enraging. His hot breath, stinking of tooth decay and alcohol, was rapid and ragged as his hands squeezed her body up and down. Fee's constricted chest hyperventilated against his fat belly, and her tears dripped from her jaw. He held her so tightly, she couldn't move even an inch.

"Oh my God, it might be too quick," he said, as one hand found his zipper and opened the front of his pants. This opened up a space between them. She put her hands against him and tried to push him away, demanding that he stop. He grabbed her with both meaty hands and shoved her backwards against the wall, his half closed eyes looking through her.

"Don't worry, don't worry," he breathed, "I won't do anything more than the other times. You will always be my virgin princess." Fee fought him in earnest now, kicking his legs, and then finally landing a knee between them and pushing herself away. He was furious.

"How dare you!"

"I don't know what you think our relationship is, but that's never going to happen again," Fee yelled, and wiped her face with both hands.

"I made you. Everything you are is because of me," he sputtered, leaning over, his pants still open and his now shriveled penis shivering beneath his hanging gut and grotesquely yawning navel.

"I will have to take your word for that, but forced sex isn't part of our contract. You will never touch me again," Fee said and took a deep breath. Her wig had been skewed to one side in the struggle, and instead of righting it she pulled it off. His eyes opened wide.

"What did you do? You're crazy! I will destroy you! I will find a new girl and tell everyone you are strung out on drugs." He straightened himself and zipped his pants, but froze there, his hands still on the front of his waistband. "Who the hell is this?" In the open doorway of the bedroom stood Benedick and Beatrice holding a phone, filming the entire scene.

"We were standing behind this door the whole time, we filmed the whole thing," Bea announced. A whole series of expressions passed across the man's face before he settled on rage.

"Give me that phone!" he demanded, advancing towards them as they continued to film him.

"Take another step and I will call hotel security," Fee warned. "And if you try to touch any of us, I will release that video to my millions of followers. You won't be able to go out in public. My fans will rip your limbs from your body." Her entire being was suffused with a cold fury, her words came from she knew not where, for her mind was a screaming blank.

This gave him pause. He seemed to think through his options, and finding no good ones, he narrowed his eyes and raised a little index finger at her. "You are done. I won't manage your tour anymore. See how you like trying to do a world tour without me."

"That's just fine. Perfect, really. I was thinking about taking things in a different direction anyway." She advanced on him. "Tomorrow, first thing, we are going to sit down with a lawyer and an accountant and you are going to account for everything that is mine and sign it over to me."

"Ha! I will cancel the tour. All of the contracts are in my name." This revelation caused Fee a minor panic, but she immediately felt her calm return. A way has been made from no way from the time she put her hands on the lowest branches of the fir tree that burst from the sands of Las Vegas, indeed, since she settled herself in the sand on First Day, and a way would be made now. She smiled at him. It was an unblinking smile of dismissal, her hands clasped in front of her. If it were true that he had made her, then truly, he will have made everything she came here to do possible. It was in this spirit of gratitude that she said, "So long as you behave honorably, that video will not see the light of day. You may take whatever is yours and do whatever you want with it. If you think you can easily replace me, then do it. I thank you for everything you have done for me. Goodbye." His mouth gaped uncomprehendingly for a moment before he stomped out the door. As soon as the door slammed shut, Fee collapsed on the floor, hyperventilating and crying again. She wanted to shower…with formaldehyde.

"Quick, Fee, change your passwords on everything, social media first," Bea said. "You have to get yourself together now."

The first thing she did after changing all of her passwords was make a statement on her feed that she had broken with her manager, and that it was unclear whether the tour would proceed as planned. She advised her fans to stay glued to her media stream. That set off a hurricane. First, an anguished conversation with the assistant from Japan who had called her that morning. She promised to secretly email to Fee copies of all the contracts and documents before she said goodbye. Then, all of her staff members ran into her room from wherever they had been and hung on her, sobbing. She tried her best to affect a desperate regret with these people she had never seen before, but then, welling up like a spring from deep inside her, real love for them overwhelmed her and she didn't have to pretend. All the while, she clung to Benedick and Beatrice, and didn't allow them to leave. She simply could not get through this day without them. Another transition with Benedick.

Her staff tearfully declared their loyalty to her. They insisted that there was no way the Amsterdam concert was going to be canceled at this late hour, and they vowed to help her get ready for it. Her stylist cried as many tears for her hair as he did for her departure, and insisted on cutting it properly while the others sat around on the floor in front of her. She tried, and failed to explain why she cut it. She tried to explain her feelings about everything she had seen and learned that day, about the extraordinary suffering her fans seemed to be insensible to, but they all just stared at her. That wasn't their project—it wasn't their brand. That's when it hit her. Of course! She needed a brand! If she could just brand what it was she cared about, perhaps she could sell it. One needed to sell oneself in this world. That's the part that scared her. She knew nothing about selling at all.

While all of this exhausting deconstruction was taking place, her phone buzzed on almost a constant basis. She desperately needed someone to manage her media, but she didn't know how to go about doing that either. Her phone was on the floor next to her, so that when it buzzed, she looked down to see who it was. Unidentified numbers she ignored. When a face appeared on her screen, she asked this girl inside her, Yumiko, who was also a part of herself, if she should answer it. She could feel Yumiko there, a separate consciousness but connected to her, a delicate presence like a butterfly on her shoulder.

Her room was full of people, her staff had ordered in food and they were drinking. She didn't tell them what had happened, exactly, between her and Amari-san, but she had the impression that they wouldn't be surprised if she did. When she said that she didn't like the way he treated her, none of them pressed her for details.

Her phone buzzed. It said "Mama-san," with Hiragana spelling out an English "Mama," and hearts decorating the line after. The face on the display evoked a complex stew of emotions—love, duty, stress, grief, shame, fear, relief, longing. She answered it, unsure that she could convincingly play any mother's daughter. She needn't have worried. This girl's mother was frantic, having just gotten off the phone with her former manager. He had told her that he had quit because Yumiko was crazy and wouldn't perform. She might be on drugs. He tried to convince her mother to use her power as guardian and cosigner on Yumiko's accounts to cut Yumiko off financially, to bring her to heel. Her mother told her that she didn't believe him about the mental illness or any of it, but she demanded to know what *did* happen.

"He tried to force me to have sex with him. This was not the first time and I told him that I had had enough," she said.

"He tried to have intercourse with you?"

"Well, no. Not that exactly."

"What are you complaining about then? He leaves you intact. That's better than a lot of other girls can hope for. We talked about this!" She was angry now. "It's better to have sex with one man and be rich than have many and remain poor. These are the kinds of choices a woman has to make in this world. You know your father can't work anymore. Our health benefits have run out, and he needs his medicine. Do you want him to go without his medicine? We talked through all this already! You are our only hope. Apologize, quickly! Apologize and maybe he will still take you back."

"I'm famous now. I can do it on my own. I want to write new music, music that means something. Please believe in me." They argued for a long time. They both agreed that Amari-san's phone call indicated a desire to make her compliant. If she were compliant, on his terms, he would take her back and continue the tour. His terms were completely unacceptable to Fee—likely a return to prostituting herself to him and abandonment of any turn away from their already successful brand—and so she spent more than an hour convincing her mother that she had a plan, a better plan than his, which was a difficult thing to do indeed because she didn't yet have a plan at all. She talked mostly about the idea of a new brand, her pivot. That seemed to mollify her mother a little.

"Look, the Amsterdam concert won't be canceled. I will try out some of the new material at that concert. If they like it, will you agree to emancipate me? Let me have all of my own accounts, so I can be more nimble during the tour?" To this her mother agreed, essentially to wait and see. Another seemingly insurmountable obstacle gave way.

"I'm not just your guardian, you know. You are my child, and I love you. Please be careful." Fee had forgotten about that, that she was now someone's child. It was a strange feeling to be loved in that way and to feel something inside herself return that love.

After her staff left her—she told them she needed to rest—she collapsed in the middle of the floor.

"That man was right," she said. "There's no way I can do this without him. I can't even lift one of these trunks, much less do I know where to take them or when. How do I travel? Do I rehearse? I don't know any of it. If I had time, I could learn more of what Yumiko knows, but there's no time."

"Maybe your path goes a different way?" Benedick offered. No sooner had he spoken this, there was yet another knock on the door, this one polite, deferential. Fee tiptoed to the door and peered out of the peephole. To her amazement, she saw the kind, blonde giant who had carted her all over the Museumplein this morning, so she opened the door. He smiled sheepishly.

"I'm so stupid, I didn't realize who you were until you had gone into the Rijks. I'm here because I started following your feed after I saw you off and...I saw that you broke with your manager in the middle of your tour. I'm not a creep, I promise. I found you because I have contacts at the Paradiso. I'm a band manager."

"Please *do* come in," she said. When they closed the door behind them, she turned to Benedick and Beatrice and announced, "This is a man I met this morning. He is a band manager."

"Will wonders never cease!" Bea said.

2 7

the concert

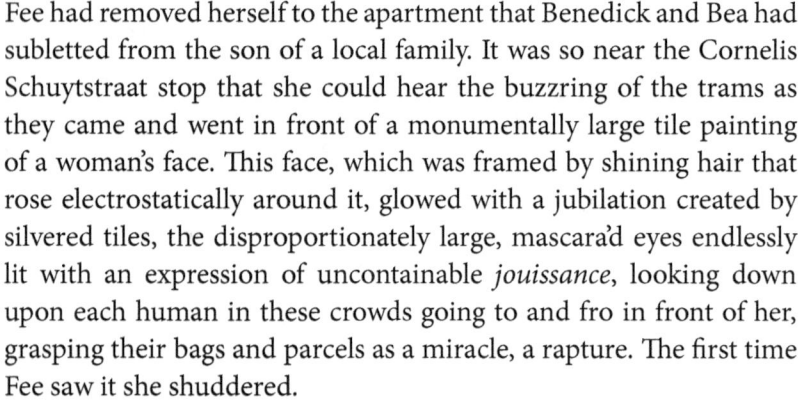

Fee had removed herself to the apartment that Benedick and Bea had subletted from the son of a local family. It was so near the Cornelis Schuytstraat stop that she could hear the buzzring of the trams as they came and went in front of a monumentally large tile painting of a woman's face. This face, which was framed by shining hair that rose electrostatically around it, glowed with a jubilation created by silvered tiles, the disproportionately large, mascara'd eyes endlessly lit with an expression of uncontainable *jouissance*, looking down upon each human in these crowds going to and fro in front of her, grasping their bags and parcels as a miracle, a rapture. The first time Fee saw it she shuddered.

She met him, this younger son of the landlords, who themselves lived in the house next door. Like Benedick and Beatrice, the landlords were old enough to have paid off their home and this one, before the transition. The older son lived with his family on the upper two floors, while the single and unemployed younger son rented out his lower floors whenever he could, and stayed with his parents. It was the kind of make do existence Fee was now accustomed to hearing about. Fee didn't ask him what degrees he had or what work he had been hoping for, but whatever it was he could do was yet another resource squandered in a world that couldn't pay him to contribute.

Fee couldn't sleep at all. This was not unusual, for in the New Earth Fee often substituted a night of meditation for sleep when she was working on a particularly intractable problem. However, this was not one particularly intractable problem, but several. Long after Bea and Benedick had gone to bed, Fee sat upright in the glow of the streetlights that came through the white curtained windows, neither successfully meditating nor sleeping. In the New Earth, meditation came easily, instantly she could be calm, quiet, empty. Now, she struggled. Intruding into her peace were thoughts about this sympathetic young man, the day's events, Arjen, her new manager, the tour, and most of all the upcoming performance. Fee had never in her life performed anything in front of anyone. She would have one rehearsal. Further, she had promised this body's mother that she would successfully roll out a new brand at this concert. Her creative and financial independence depended on her success tomorrow. How could they stand it, these people, all of this worrying about money?

She couldn't tell Arjen about everything, obviously, but he liked the idea of a new brand. He assured her that the leverage of the incriminating tape and his own contacts and experience would ensure that the tour would proceed, one way or another. He would take care of all the logistics. Assuming they would never have to publicly post the tape, the new brand could serve as a new origin story that would explain the break, and it would provide a new layer of meaning for the identity that she would take upon herself, that of the Phoenix, reborn. She would seek a more international audience by singing in English, she would sign her name, Phoenix. She would sing about the things she cared about. This would be her new brand. Privately, Fee was determined to sing about the New Earth, sing it into existence.

It had been her intention to, over the course of the night, write new lyrics to the music of the old songs. In fact, many if not all of Ho-o's songs had titles that seemed to be double entendres, at least to the mind of an English speaking person. *iBubble* could just as easily refer to the bubbles the rich lived in to insulate themselves from their fears—and from the suffering of the poor. *Upside Down* could easily refer to the upside down incentives that money provides such that destruction and exploitation are rewarded, while the most important things in life are not. *Nothing is Better than This* could easily become *Anything is Better than This*, and so on. In fact, the way the songs were written, it was easy to find a hidden undertone to each and every nonsensical, empty, cheerful song such that they all seemed to her like the tile painting of the woman at the intersection of Cornelis Schuytstraat and Willemsparkweg. Each was a pointing finger that indicated by its absence.

However, at seven hundred hours, when Fee awoke to see Beatrice bending over her, framed by the already bright, risen sun, Fee had written nothing, absolutely nothing. All was lost.

Fee declined breakfast and retreated to the second bedroom. Perhaps she could still think of something before rehearsal. Notwithstanding her skills perfected in the New Earth, she found herself now anxious and distracted and unable to concentrate. The mother would continue to control her accounts, she and the old manager would continue to try to bring her to heel. She, Fee, who crossed worlds to be here was completely debilitated, and on the verge of an anxiety attack.

She took her guitar out into the small garden behind the building. All of the buildings were built against one another in the front, but each of them had a small garden in back such that there was a divided park of gardens in the middle of the block that all of the buildings looked down upon. There was no one to be seen, she had the space to herself, and the rustle of the leaves and calling of parrots calmed her enough that she was able to lift the guitar onto her lap and play the songs through for the first time as if they were her own. In her mind, as she played, she invented other meanings, definitions, signifiers for the words, she sang them slowly, sadly and from the heart. As she finished the third song, applause echoed through the garden. She looked around and saw that people had come out to stand on their back balconies and rooftops to listen to her. She blushed. The spell was broken, and she scuttled indoors.

A couple of hours later Arjen called to tell her that he had been working social media and all of his contacts all night and through the morning, he was working an angle—a beautiful, earnest young girl striking out on her own—that had captured the imagination of Amsterdam and the modest concert was now sold out. Someone on one of the roofs behind their apartment uploaded a video of Fee rehearsing unplugged in the garden and it went viral. Venues in places without a substantial Japanese diaspora were intrigued. He was working on lining up interviews with media personalities in the U.S.

She wanted to yell, I've never performed in my life! I'm sorry! I will fail you, this will be the most colossal failure. But instead she told him that she was nervous, that she didn't have new lyrics yet. He wasn't concerned. He said that these things don't happen overnight. He would be surprised to know what happens overnight.

By noon, she had given up on new lyrics, and the new brand. She spent several hours in a frenzy of memorization, playing them over and over again, unplugged in her room. What would happen when she walked on stage? Surely the noise of the crowd, the lights, the high expectations of thousands of people would send it all out of her mind and she would stand there silently staring until they began throwing things at her. She hadn't thought this through when she so confidently assumed this identity of this girl. When Bea finally prevailed upon her to eat something, she threw it up.

By the time she showed up at the Paradiso for rehearsal and make-up, she was pale, weak, shaking. Yet, all the while, all night and all morning, she could feel Yumiko, the butterfly on her shoulder, flying all about her consciousness, from shoulder to shoulder, in front of her face. She seemed to be telling her that it would be alright. Meanwhile, people were arriving, multitudes of them, it seemed, each with a job to do, all of it incomprehensible to Fee. They were showing her where the dials and plugins and foot pedals were, where her "marks" were. What's a mark? What's the foot pedal *for*? She couldn't ask. There wasn't time to learn everything. All was lost. Panic gripped her throat and she could no longer speak, and then she could no longer breathe.

A butterfly's wing…a butterfly's wing…a butterfly's wing…. She wasn't sure if she were saying it or thinking it, but the world began to tilt sideways, and the last thing she saw before she fell was Bea rushing towards her with outstretched arms.

"You should have told me you couldn't eat." Arjen handed her an anti-emetic pill, an anti-anxiety pill, and something else he didn't say what. "In thirty minutes, get that liquid nutrition down her with something solid, if she can," he said to Bea, then disappeared. Once that was done, Fee did feel calmer and allowed the makeup and wardrobe people to do whatever it was Arjen had told them to do.

By the time she played through her set, she was thoroughly stoned. The set was diffident, lackluster, her voice nervously warbled and she kept forgetting how the technology worked. Finally, she just asked someone what a mark is for.

It's okay, Arjen said to her and everyone else, when the crowd is here she will turn on. It's always like that. Fee laughed to herself when he said that because she was now beyond caring that it would *not* be like that. It would be more like a high school talent show. Somewhere, from far far away she cared that she was letting him and everyone down, but she couldn't feel it. She couldn't feel her lips. Benedick and Bea bent down to her face.

"I think maybe he gave her too much. She's so small."

Opposite of where she was sprawled was a girl in her late teens, her mouth painted purple, her eyes painted into giant eyes, like the eyespots on a…butterfly. The entire effect was, in fact, a butterfly, with a winglike headdress made with false hair. A stray hair tickled Fee's face and she blew it away. The girl did too. That's when she realized that she was looking at herself.

"The crowd is coming in and it's not just Japanese!" Arjen leaned into the doorway excitedly, "It's sold out and we've got subscribers live-streaming! Remember, English and Japanese. It's okay to repeat yourself. The media is here! This is going to be great. This is your day!" Fee shook herself and smiled at him. She would do her best, whatever that was.

Standing backstage, just behind the curtain, she quailed at the sight of the standing crowd jammed up against the stage, indeed, some people had their *elbows* resting on the stage. Somehow, she had imagined that they would be farther away, more still and more quiet.

The noise was deafening and they heaved with constant movement. She wasn't numb anymore, but as the numbing effect of the drugs receded, panic returned. It was one thing to fail while stoned, quite another to do it straight. She felt she might vomit again.

"Easy there, Yumiko," Arjen said. "You've got this. You've done it a million times. Show that old man what you can do without him." This was supposed to anger and inspire the heart of an abused and rebellious teenager, but instead, Fee had to fight a strong desire to flee.

When the laser light show cued her entry, Arjen told her to break a leg and prodded her forward. She walked out into a roar that came from every direction and pressed against her body. She hadn't considered that the lights would make it hard for her to find the mark. She walked out to where she thought it was, but then realized that she was now too far away from the foot pedal and knobs. They were chanting now. She was supposed to start doing something. She readjusted herself closer to the pedal.

That crowd was a thing, a large and terrifying creature with a million eyes. She realized that all the eyes were staring at her and she stared back at them. Staring at them transfixed her. Her mind went blank. Panic gripped her belly, and she couldn't remember what she was supposed to do. They were still waiting for her to do something. The yelling and the chanting was subsiding as she stood there. It was getting quieter and quieter and she could imagine Arjen backstage muttering at her, Bea and Benedick covering their eyes. Nothing in the Old Earth or in the New had prepared her for this.

"Play something or fuck off," a drunken Australian hollered from the balcony above her.

She was trying to remember the first bars of a song, *any* of the songs, when something in the front of her head exploded and she couldn't see nor think. Fee felt herself split in two as invisible, energetic butterfly wings, big as sails burst out of her back and unfurled so that they consumed the entire space of the stage. But these were not *her* wings, they belonged to someone else who pressed her down, tiny tiny tiny. She found herself sitting on the shoulder of this being. This being was Yumiko Omata, Ho-o!, an energetic titan, enormously talented, an able professional, a teenaged girl.

The audience saw none of this. The audience saw a girl, standing silently on the stage holding her guitar, holding the space. The auditorium went absolutely silent. Although they couldn't see the transformation that had just taken place, they could feel it.

Ho-o's body stood more upright on the platform heels and then she leaned forward and affected a curious expression, then tilted her head, just so. Then she lifted her hand and played three notes, very slowly, one after another. It was like a bomb went off in that still room, the crowd screamed with one voice for release, and she gave it to them. She played for them *iBubble* and then *Upside Down* with an unbridled fervor, a sarcastic lilt that she had never had before.

Before playing a third song from her repertoire, Ho-o! spoke to the audience in Japanese and then repeated herself in English, as she played the introductory chords to a song that was not on her playlist, playing them through several times as she spoke.

"Have you ever heard of that terrible experiment American scientists performed on dogs?" She continued to play. "This is a song I wrote a couple of weeks ago. I didn't think anyone would ever hear it. It's called *Shocked Dog.*"

She sang a song about a puppy playing in a meadow with other puppies and all of the things that puppies do and experience. It was a typical, empty, cheerful Ho-o! song until it came to the refrain. In the refrain the puppy is put into a cage and shocked until it learned to escape the shock by jumping to the other side of the cage. But then the unseen evil genius shocked the whole cage, leaving the puppy no escape. In the last refrain, she sang in both Japanese and English, louder than before, stomping on the pedal with a precise, engineered aggression to tilt the song, just so.

"We were all puppies we were happy and playful/They put us in this cage and we were confused/What did we do?/We feel a shock on one side we run to a party! (Don't we?)/We feel a shock on the other side and we run to the mall! (The mall is full but empty)/They shock and shock and shock until there is nowhere to run anymore. She repeated this refrain once more in English before sitting down on the stage with her guitar in her lap, her head and shoulders limp.

"We just let them shock us/We…can't…feel…anything."

This is not what the crowd expected. There was a slight pause before the applause began, but once it did, it built to a roar. She was singing their secret heart out loud, telling their secrets, and they loved it.

Ho-o! changed the last stanza of every song, as if she had already written the lyrics. Perhaps these were the true lyrics all along. Each time, she sang the last stanza in Japanese, then repeated it in English. Fee thought the building would come down when the crowd demanded an encore. Fee couldn't see what Ho-o! had planned, but it was something special for there was a satisfied, mischievous energy circulating in her midsection as Ho-o! stood behind the curtain listening to the stomping in front of the stage. She had waited a long time for this.

She stood for several moments reveling in the crowd noise before she played the first notes of iBubble again. Fee thought it a strange choice, the repetition, but then as Ho-o! sang the entire song in English, she understood. Ho-o! had alternative lyrics for the entire song. Instead of a song about a bubble in a video game, the song described a tourist in a bubble passing through a city encountering a different kind of suffering in each of three stanzas. She sang the refrain: i'm in a bubble/in a suffering world/ishop ibuy/i am so shallow/the homeless pass by me/i turn away my head. When she got to the final refrain, she didn't sing it, but instead stooped to turn up the volume and ripped through it without words, stuffing it full of minor chords. Her playing became manic, she wasn't even conscious, playing ever faster past the end of the song riffing on the theme with distortion on top of the minor chords, and then just as suddenly as the frenzy began, it stopped. There was a moment of shocked silence in the hall before the crowd went wild. They surged violently against the stage and then back again and items of every description were thrown in the air and rained down from the balcony. It was turning into a riot. As security sprang into action, Ho-o! waved both arms in the air and then quickly breezed off the stage.

"My God!" Arjen exclaimed as she sped past him. She was high, floating, speeding, she wanted to walk and walk and walk in the night air and scream at the stars. Instead, she went backstage and talked and laughed without thinking about what she was saying. Someone offered her alcohol and she took it.

Fee tried to reestablish herself, now that the concert was finished, but Yumiko was strong and she was enjoying her triumph. Fee let her have it. It was interesting to be the butterfly on the shoulder, to see and feel everything, but not to decide.

An hour into the after party, her cell phone registered a received text with a custom ringtone that sent a thrill of love and dread through her body. The face on the screen was that of a Japanese boy, a young man about Yumiko's age, and the kanji spelled out Hansuke Takenaka. A cascade of images of this boy spooled through Fee's consciousness. Yumiko had known him since childhood.

Please forgive me for texting you. I know you told me not to contact you, to forget you. You don't have to respond. I streamed the Amsterdam concert and I am so overwhelmed with emotion, I must tell you how proud I am to know you. Congratulations.

It was not pleasure, but shame that rushed through Yumiko's body, then anger. He should leave her alone in her shame! Fee calmed her, whispered to her that the shame didn't belong to her. Let it go, let it go, let it go, she whispered as Yumiko stared at the screen. Yumiko got up and ran away from the boisterous celebration happening all around her. She wanted to be invisible, to think, alone. She stared again at the face on the screen and she could feel him, could feel that thousands of miles away, he was staring at her face on his screen as well. He was wondering if she would respond, she could feel it, the heartbeat of his wondering…will she? will she? will she? Tears sprang in her eyes.

Respond, Fee whispered, respond from the heart. Although Fee had never been in any intimate relationship with anyone, ever, she understood love. For fifteen years, she had been in a love relationship with a dozen other people and she understood the responsibility of holding the heart of another in her hands. This boy loved, and Yumiko loved him in return. Yumiko pressed call.

She began talking as soon as he answered. "I know you feel that there is hope for something between us, but you must give up this hope. You've heard that I've broken with Amari-san, but you haven't heard the truth about why I broke with him." Fee could feel her love for this boy, but also something else. The love wasn't pure, it was adulterated with self loathing and hopelessness both. *It's not yours*, she whispered to her.

"Don't say any more. I know it all already," the boy said.

Yumiko buried her head in her arms, the phone suspended in one hand. "It was so obvious, you already knew." Her face burned. Her triumph was swallowed by this shame.

"I know how this business works. The fans pretend not to know, but they know." His voice was faint, but she could hear it. She raised her head and stared at the phone for several moments before finally returning it to her ear.

"I didn't want to, but even my mother…."

"You don't have to say anything more. You don't have to explain unless you need to. I don't care about him at all. It's not your fault. I know you think I would think less of you and that's why you're telling me this, but its the opposite. I respect you all the more."

"More?"

"I know what it took for you to break from him and your parents, to risk going your own way and to make music about the things you have always cared about, the things you have always talked about. For you to find your voice, against all of these powerful people controlling you, using you…," the boy's voice broke. "I've never admired anyone else more."

Fee felt the heart in her chest swell with love and longing for this boy, a stranger to herself, but not to this body, nor to this girl who had possessed it solely. Yumiko's mind was fretting, wanting to know if he had given up on her, if he had found another girl, but would never ask. Fee questioned him for her.

"You are still sitting home alone every night, I hope?"

There was absolute silence on the phone for a moment before he said, "You know there is no one else for me but you."

2 8

organized

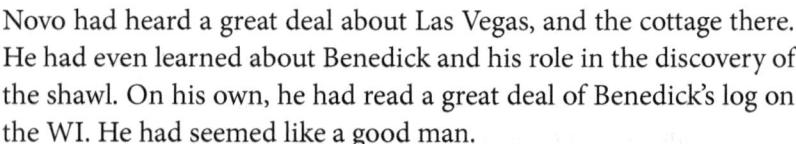

Novo had heard a great deal about Las Vegas, and the cottage there. He had even learned about Benedick and his role in the discovery of the shawl. On his own, he had read a great deal of Benedick's log on the WI. He had seemed like a good man.

Novo's hands fidgeted nervously as he stood in the doorway.

"Thank you all for coming," the man who had introduced himself at the airport as Abdullah said. "This is Novo. Yes, he is the man who killed a Watcher named Benedick. Some of you met Benedick in Las Vegas. Bene was beloved by many of us, Fee most especially." Novo realized that he had stopped breathing. Indeed, it seemed that no one breathed. "As you all know, Novo has received years of health and healing services care, both in Portland and in Saõ Paulo since then."

"I'm organized," Novo interjected, before he could help himself.

"I can't say that we completely understand what happened with Benedick, or even Fee, but no one believes that Novo is a danger to anyone now."

"You don't have to shake my hand, it's okay," Novo said. A brief smile crossed his face, and his hands hanging next to his thighs opened toward them, before he tucked them away behind his back.

A very dark skinned woman stood up taller than he and, in a lovely voice, both deep and quiet, said, "I'm Mathilde." She shook his hand, meeting his eyes, and then sat back down. After that, everyone began to stand up and introduce themselves, and they each shook his hand. It took some time for the forty or so people in the room to introduce themselves, but once they had all shaken his hand and resumed their seats, Abdullah sat down and Novo sat down next to him.

"The reason I've asked you to the cottage here in Phoenix is because you're all interlocutors with the regular population and we need to begin developing a plan for a transition. It's now clear to everyone, I think, that we won't be training any children to be Watchers. After Benedick, many Watchers around the world have died. Those deaths were perfectly normal deaths of elderly people, and those people were not replaced, so to speak...as Benedick was, by Novo. Novo's situation was unique. And there's no replacement possible for Fee, her loss is still felt keenly here at the cottage.

"We believe we're entering the end of the Watcher era on the New Earth, and we need to figure out a plan for handing over Watcher duties that regular people can take on, such as Naturework, and wrapping up those duties that can't be handed over. Novo is the only Watcher on the planet who understands how regular people think, he knows their mythology, their false memory in full. He will be a tremendous help to us."

29

america with a small a

The door opened and the airport security guy hauled his large frame across the room toward Fee. He had a teetering gait foreshortened by pain in his joints, she couldn't tell which ones, probably all of them. He put his palms down on the table before he lowered himself into the chair opposite her. He pretended to read her file on a device in front of him. "You have racked up an impressive pile of flags all over Europe, little Miss. Quite impressive. Specifically, you have been using the word, homeless, a lot. Maybe they allow that in Europe, but here…not so much. It aggravates people. Understand?"

Fee didn't respond.

"Does she understand English?" he called to the mirrored glass and the surveillance cameras opposite him. There was no response from there either.

"I understand English," she said.

"Alright, good. We want you to be able to complete your concert tour. It's sold out in every city you plan to visit. It wouldn't be good for anyone to have to cancel it, so I wanted to come to an understanding with you."

"Okay."

"We all know that homelessness is a terrible thing, but it's a difficult problem to solve. Some people work harder than others, that's a problem, and some people have problems with drinking or drugs. That's problem number two and three. It's very complicated. In this country we are working to solve this problem." This got Fee's attention. "We are going to cut taxes on the hardest working people...."

"The rich people," she said, maintaining with effort a credulous attentiveness.

"The job creators, the corporations, yes that's right little Miss. I'm glad you understand. We'll cut their taxes so that they can make more jobs for all those homeless people. Okay? Try to remember that: cutting taxes will help the problem. Okay?"

"Okay." The New Earth had trained Fee to be an excellent liar, and she successfully convinced this man that she was a dumb child who believed everything he said. Behind her long false eyelashes, however, Fee was fuming. This was the same solution the rich have been pursuing since before she left the Old Earth the first time! Indeed they have been cutting taxes on the rich since before she was even born. They say "cutting taxes, cutting taxes," like a magic mantra, but no one ever truthfully explains what it is, namely gutting the contribution to the common good! The man looked at the device in front of him in earnest now and lectured her about each and every infraction. The point of this, she supposed, was not to educate her, but to let her know that they know everything. They were watching her, wherever she was, all over the world, and they could seize her body, if they chose. He meant to make her obey, to convince her of the hopelessness of resistance.

She wasn't convinced. Only someone afraid of death can become a slave. Fee had long ago given up any illusions about human life, and leaving it was not something she dreaded. The entire time he talked, she continued to fume about the suffering caused by this tax cutting he went on about. It was a lie. This cutting was adding; it added to the wealth of the wealthy. It was the rich withdrawing money from the nation's collective savings account that was supposed to pay for health care, child care, care of the elderly, education for children, medical research, roads and bridges and hospitals and schools, disaster relief, environmental conservation, protection of the air and water, aid for the hungry and homeless. The rich were withdrawing money from this account to buy for themselves more…*watches,* more ICare caftans, more travel, more houses, ever larger houses… and most importantly, more politicians, who then allow them to withdraw more money. While Fee thought these things, she didn't allow her eyes to narrow even once. She nodded dumbly and smiled every time any of the officers spoke to her until they finally stamped her passport: visa approved.

When she emerged from the interrogation rooms Benedick and Bea were waiting for her, slouched on two dirty and cracked plastic chairs, staring at their hands. When she walked in, they both looked up at her with a question in their eyes.

"'We can go now," she told them. Bea called Arjen to tell him and the entourage to meet them. They had already been allowed through. Thus, this entire "interrogation" was meant only to bully her. They had no serious intention of cancelling the tour, for she was famous and a money maker and that gave her a certain power they couldn't deny. Her victory fell away as she and Bea and Benedick walked the security gauntlet huddled together, staring with unblinking eyes past the officers and the scanning machines Fee remembered from the OE, toward the killer robots ahead of them. She had seen them in the European airports, but only in small numbers, from a distance, as something that could be called. Here, the things stood across from each other in the international concourse hallways every ten feet or so, their backs against the wall, towering seven or eight feet high, their metal limbs painted red and blue, their faces a paean to the uncanny valley. Fee, who was perhaps ninety pounds fully dressed, felt the two ton heaviness of these machines as they stared down at her with their active, dead eyes, scanning and uploading, evaluating and waiting for orders from their unseen master, himself someone who took orders, another machine. Outside the international concourse, the robots were stationed as they were in Europe, solitary sentries at the edges of large spaces, apart from the claustrophobic closeness of the halls, but still a presence felt towering over the humans who skittered with their wheeled bags around them. It was with relief that they reunited with Arjen and the others, and drove away from the airport.

When they arrived at the hotel, Fee glanced up from the drama of unpacking the van at the curb and saw her concert poster plastered on the wall next to the sidewalk. In the center was a backlit photograph of herself with her arms raised from the Amsterdam concert, that moment of triumph, and above it was her name, Phoenix, and the two Japanese characters for Ho-o. At the bottom of the poster it read Small Girl, Big Heart. They were calling it the Big Heart Tour. It sounded wholesome and non-threatening. Arjen was a genius.

The reality set in once they arrived at the hotel. Before she could enter, a special team hired by Arjen combed the room for microphones, cameras…and bombs. They found plenty of surveillance devices, but no bombs. So far so good. Even though they said the room was clear, Fee thought it completely possible that they missed one or two, and she assumed that any time the room was unattended, the devices could return. Thus, she always skulked around her own room, assuming she was being watched by men with buzz cuts and size fourteen shiny shoes hunched over their computers; when she took a shower, she undressed behind the shower curtain, and kept her fresh clothes next to it so that she could dress again in privacy behind it.

The tour continued as planned, but Fee was careful not to use the prohibited word that began with an h. However, she substituted descriptions of things she saw and knew for that word such that it was impossible not to know what she was talking about; indeed, her most famous song, iBubble, was about homeless families. She continued the same pattern that she had established in Amsterdam, beginning with iBubble as it was originally recorded, and finishing with the rewritten version. She had written a new final verse for every song on her playlist, hoping that the government minders wouldn't notice that the end of the song was different from the beginning. It was a naïve hope. The fans noticed and therefore the government noticed. Fee didn't manage her own social media feed, but her staff told her that her feed had been "blowing up" with discussions about the song lyrics. In her hotel rooms, after she had been out, her belongings would often be rearranged into strange and threatening, or sexualized tableaus. When she mentioned in an interview that she was vegetarian, she returned to her room to find all the food removed from the little refrigerator, and a rotting beef steak in its place. Death threat messages showed up on her private phone, and several times aggressive music suddenly blared from it until she turned off the bluetooth. She checked the locks of her room every time she passed the door, and made sure to always latch the interior bolt, so that it couldn't be opened with a key. She asked Benedick and Bea to stay in a room adjacent to her own, as if she were their frightened child. On bad nights, they kept their door unlocked, in case she needed them. She had more faith in them than in her security. Benedick and Bea couldn't be bought.

It was after one of the concerts in Boston that Fee awoke in her hotel bed to find it covered with dead butterflies. She leaped out of bed and turned on the light. On the bed and the floor were hundreds, maybe thousands, of dead butterflies. Someone had been there, in her room, next to her bed, while she had been sleeping and arranged them and then let themselves out. The door to Benedick and Bea's room was open.

"I guess I forgot to latch our interior bolt," Bea said.

"How could you forget?" Fee was frantic. "Someone came in through your room and did this, while I was sleeping! They stood over me while I was sleeping! They could have killed me."

"That's the point they were trying to make," Benedick said.

Arjen hired new security, but even so, that night, Fee slept on Benedick and Bea's couch, with all the doors bolted.

Fee had no time to do anything much beyond perform, prepare to perform, and sleep, but without any effort on her part a strange integration process began: she and Yumiko were becoming one. At each concert, she was less a butterfly on the girl's shoulder and more the girl herself, playing confidently for sold out crowds. She found herself not merely tolerating the videocalls with the boy, Hansuke, but longing for them. She was feeling younger, she felt more innocent, she identified less and less with her origin story prior to the transition, yet she retained all of the wisdom and knowledge that she had gained in the New Earth. She hugged everyone. It was as if there were a negotiation going on in the background between herself and Yumiko about which parts of themselves they would keep and which they would discard as they became one human being.

Boston, New York, Columbus, Chicago—her tour crawled West, skirting Washington, D.C. as too risky, too likely to be perceived as a taunt. She didn't have time to read anything from her fans, but the people who did told tales of mountains of fan emails, DMs, tweets from all over the world. Rich kids were confiding in her the truth of their lives of privilege: they were miserable, suicidal, and the song *Anything is Better Than This* was a dart to their souls. In this rewritten version of *Nothing is Better Than This*, the girl is sick, vomiting, and hungover, sitting in her trashed hotel room alone, posting flattering photos of herself while her wrists bled. The outpouring of mail said, in various forms and languages, Yes! Yes, that's exactly it. The more sensitive among them were touched by *America The Beautiful*, a song about the despoiling of America's landscapes and waterways, set to the tune of the anthem. Before they had heard this song, many of them didn't even know that there was ever a time that it was actually safe to drink water from a faucet. Regardless of which songs inspired the letters and messages, their emotional response to them was unitary, an outpouring of grief and guilt.

However, it wasn't those kids Fee listened for, it was the kids who couldn't go to her concerts, who listened online, who pirated her music, the poor. She asked her staff to particularly watch those threads, tell her about those kids. There was one message in particular from a girl living in the shantytown outside Sacramento, California. She said, simply: You say your songs are about us, but you don't sing for us. That bothered her. It was necessary to reach everyone, it was good to speak to any of the rich who would listen, but she heard this girl and wanted to respond.

"Let's go to Detroit," she suggested after the final concert in Chicago. "We've got three down days before we go to Minneapolis. Let's give up one of those days and shoot over to Detroit and back."

"I can think of a long list of reasons why we should not do that," Arjen said. "First, we don't have a venue! And you know what it takes to put something like this on—we've got to have a place, restrooms, bottled water, security—it's enormous. Impossible."

"We don't do any of that though. We do a free concert, impromptu."

"And it's Detroit. It's a dead city. It's dangerous and it has no infrastructure."

"It's summertime. Because it's a dead city, no one will care about regulations. I say we just show up in a big park and tell people we're there. People can bring their own water. It's only a couple of hours. We can look into a delivery of toilets, if they still have that there."

"Oh my God...and what if you are mobbed, surrounded, kidnapped?" Bea asked.

"At least ask security. Maybe they can figure out something."

"You won't have any lights. We'd have to bring a generator to run your equipment."

"We won't need lights for an afternoon concert. We'll rent generators. DIY."

"She's serious," Arjen threw up his hands.

"Look, I can't just sing about the poor, I need to show up for them too."

"We're going to have to hire an army of security," Arjen said.

"You're really going to do it?" Bea asked. Fee smiled.

Arjen found a park on the West side of Detroit, a straight line on the highway from Chicago and the fourth largest park in the city. He connected with local contacts who assured him that they could show up and play without any objections. Their security staff insisted that they erect a platform stage, defendable space, and hire large vehicles for a retreat, if it became necessary. When they announced that they were on the road to Eliza Howell Park to give a free concert, their feed went viral, and their local contacts reported that the park was already filling up with fans who were pitching in to help put up the stage and clean up trash. Fee herself hijacked her own feed long enough to tell her Detroit fans that they were free to live stream, film, record and pirate the park concert. It was going to be a New Earth concert.

"Tell that little girl in the Sacramento favela that I'm coming," she told her staff. "We'll make a parallel tour, a shadow tour all along the route, first Detroit, then on the dead side of Chicago, then onward to the West Coast." Arjen opined that he didn't think they'd make it to the West Coast, but Fee was beside herself with happiness. The one thing that had been needling her, that niggling thing that she felt she had forgotten—to show up for them—she was finally taking care of it.

She made an impulsive choice in the hours they spent on the road. She would play the new song she had written. It was still a little rough, but that would be okay. As Fee and Yumiko became one being, Fee's experience of the New Earth and Yumiko's talent became one tool Fee could use. That had been her object all along, to sing about the New Earth. The first song she wrote about it was inspired by all of the children she saw living in the parks, on the streets, lined up in front of tenements and shantytowns watching them drive by. They were stunted, and sick, poisoned and neglected, poorly educated and forgotten, but whenever any of them got their hands on a device to tweet at her, they revealed themselves to be irrationally optimistic, articulate and full of love for this world. Fee adored them, every one. She wanted to tell them how it was to be a child of the New Earth, to tell them what they deserved, how it could be in a world where every one of them was cherished. The song was called *Every Child A Treasure*. She couldn't wait to play it for them.

When they got to the park, it was already well over one hundred degrees. Even so, the crowd was so large, it had to part so that they could drive through to where the stage had been built in the center of an overgrown field of tall dry grass that was now stomped flat. Fee remembered having been to Detroit before the transition, her reflected child's face a pale oval in the window of a car driving through this same route from Chicago, watching with envy the families in the poor neighborhoods. At that time, all the poor neighborhoods were black, but now the poor assembled in the park from these neighborhoods were a completely heterogenous mix of white, black, and brown, for although racism and sexism and all the other forms of disability allocation were in bygone days a primary mode of exploitation, now it was mere artifact. This machine didn't discriminate. It cast its predatory eye equally upon any person who stumbled, anyone who became sick, injured or sad. Orphaned minors, the mentally ill, the elderly, used up soldiers, the unemployed, political dissidents, criminals and crime victims alike, these were all food. In short, the machine had one sole object: it ate people and shat out money.

As it became ever more "efficient" to automate more and more industries, the unemployed became a vast sea, a resource without limits, a worldwide mob scrabbling desperately to feed itself. They were worked to death, prostituted, poisoned, or sent to die killing the poor of other nations, blowing up their bridges and buildings and roads and factories at great public expense to be rebuilt again at great private profit. She had herself seen how the rich of every nation remained friendly, socializing in places like Amsterdam, shopping in the same boutiques and sitting side by side at the same trendy restaurants, while their desperate countrymen fought and died for them and their false causes; the rich themselves having no religion, no ideology, except increase.

She compared these people in front of her in this park in Detroit to the people who had attended her other concerts in Amsterdam, in Paris, Berlin, New York, Chicago. While the people crowded in front of her were not coiffed, or dressed well, indeed some were barefoot and appeared unwashed, they exuded a particular kindness common to people who find themselves equally benighted. Everywhere rich were, there was a competitive frisson in the air, an aggressivity, while these people arrived as they were, worked together to clean up the park, they helped each other, and gave what little they had. There was a nobility of purpose in the unity of the poor that Fee admired, for it was the same nobility of purpose, the same kindness she had seen in the New Earth—one that was formed from the Unity of those equally blessed. They were two faces of the same coin.

There wasn't a backstage, but merely a clearing surrounded by vehicles security had set up, with a tent in the center of it. Fee was so delighted with this crowd that she jumped up on the stage in her street clothes before anyone could stop her to say hello. Their response was deafening.

"I've got to go get dressed now, but I'll be quick!" she called and blew a kiss with both hands.

By most normal standards, this concert was a mess. The heat was melting her makeup, they had no ability to steam her costumes or to do anything that they ordinarily did, the rental equipment was a random collection that needed nursing and patching throughout the entire concert. At one point, in the middle of the concert, there was a loud pop and it all went dead for fifteen minutes. The crowd sang the rest of the unfinished song themselves and then applauded themselves afterward. When the sound system came back online, Fee jumped up and down with joy and so did her fans. She loved it that even her littlest fans could be there, and that no one was dressed up. It was like performing for family, and she never played better. She told them that this was her favorite concert of the tour so far, and she meant it.

Before she played the new song, she gave a little speech. All around her there were phones pointed at her, and there were several people set up for live streaming. She was careful not to use the word that started with h, but she painted a verbal picture of two worlds: one world worshipped money, the other love. In one world people only cared about themselves, in the other they lived for each other. She described these worlds as only she could, having had first hand experience with both. She asked the crowd to imagine what it would be like to create a world based on love right here in Detroit. Then she sang *Every Child*. She stumbled in the middle, but no one seemed to notice nor care.

The trailing final chord was met with silence, which shook Fee out of the altered state of the performer. She blinked and looked at the people in front of her and saw that their faces were weeping. She smiled. Applause began in the front press of people and spread until the entire park reverberated with it longer than seemed possible, swelling above it was her name, chanted over and over, increasingly loud. Rather than play the second set of iBubble, she was going to leave it at that, but the crowd continued to ask for an encore, shouting for iBubble, so she played it, but her heart wasn't in it. Her heart was in the New Earth.

Arjen was on his phone all the way back to Chicago, trying to set up a park concert there, and wasn't paying attention to whomever it was that Fee was talking to. Afterward, people would say that it was the beginning of this shadow tour that caused the crackdown, but it wasn't. The crackdown happened after a live-streaming radio interview that Fee gave by phone, sitting in the back of the van on the way to Chicago, that few even heard and that no longer exists. The man who interviewed her wasn't even left wing—far from it—but after this interview, this man and his small, independent radio station also ceased to exist.

He first accused Fee of being a Communist, which was easy to rebut. She disliked all money systems, not just capitalism. Then he argued that by advocating for a reduction in the role of money, she was advocating for economic collapse, maybe even worse than that of '22. He repeated the strangely persistent, repeatedly persuasive and also specious argument that in order to keep the world economy running, we all needed to support the concentration and control of wealth by the wealthy. She pointed out that it was the unregulated greed of the wealthy that caused '22 in the first place, and argued that the various world governments shouldn't have bailed the banks out.

"But the worldwide money system would have collapsed!" he sputtered.

"If the money system cannot bear the risk the various governments allow, it *should* collapse!" she said, switching into the more dangerous present tense, "If it does, we'll nationalize the collapsed banks! People like you say, if we let the money system fail, people will starve, but we have plenty of food. Food isn't the issue, money is. People like you say, if we let the money system collapse, people will be homeless. People are *already* homeless, made homeless by these rich! When we repossess foreclosed properties, we'll nationalize them too and make housing free to those who need it. The mansions will become apartments, why not? We'll turn their acres of lawn into vegetable gardens and orchards."

"The pension system will vanish…."

"We'll get rid of pensions! Elderly people shouldn't have to worry about money! After a weary lifetime of hard labor, they deserve a rest from moneyworry. They should have all their necessaries for free." The man tried to interrupt her with more objections, but she talked over him.

"Nothing bad will happen! Children will go to school, teachers will teach, plumbers will fix plumbing, doctors will see patients. People left destitute by the collapse will receive aid. People who actually work for a living will continue to work, and those who caused the collapse with their gambling addiction will need to find work, and until they do, we'll give them the same aid we give to any destitute person." There was a moment of awkward radio silence before the man made a dismissive remark about her youthful ignorance and changed the subject. It was this exuberant three and a half minute exchange that sealed her fate.

It seemed like only hours later that Fee woke in her Chicago hotel room to the sound of her phone insistently buzzing. The phone's face was inscrutable, it said only Unknown Number. She always kept her phone on silent, especially at night, and this sound repeating insistently until she woke from a deep sleep sufficiently disoriented her that she did what she never does: she answered it.

The voice of a Japanese man began speaking calmly, but insistently, right away, "Your time is up. The authorities are coming to get you now." Fee sat up and then stood, now quite awake, turning back and forth, unable to decide what to do. "Don't panic," the man said, "you still have about an hour, but you will need to follow my directions exactly."

"Who are you? How do I know I can trust you?"

"You have no choice. You can let me help you, or allow yourself to be captured and jailed. These are not just the Americans, this is the International S&S; they have decided."

The word, captured, intensified Fee's panic. That was the one thing she feared above all else, to be again the captive of men. She began to hyperventilate. "Apparently, I have not chosen the right words," the man said. "For that, I am sorry. You really must calm down. Focus on these tasks: wake John and Beatrice Eggleston…."

"He is called Benedick," she said, without thinking.

"Ah. Wake them and no one else. All of you pack only your essentials that you can carry walking, on your person."

"Not Arjen or the others?"

"They will be ejected from the country, nothing more. The tour is over. Pack and leave all devices, including phones in your room. Destroy them. Everything you leave here you will never see again. There is an exit stairwell on the East side of your hall—you turn right out of your room—go down those stairs and out that exit. There will be a car there to pick you up. I will call you in less than an hour, and when I say go…you run." The line went dead.

Fee quickly woke Benedick and Bea, and because they were afraid to turn on all the lights, they bumped around frantically packing in the light cast by two small lamps. Fee was staring at her guitar. She couldn't take her duffel and the guitar, she simply wasn't strong enough.

"Don't worry, Fee, we'll take the duffel. We don't need to carry much." Benedick said. After the frantic packing, they sat in a circle of light cast by one lamp, waiting for fifteen minutes, unwilling to voice the fearful thought that, perhaps, their interlocutor had abandoned them, or had been captured.

"He spoke Japanese?" Bea asked quietly. Fee nodded. "Perhaps he is from the Japanese consulate? Maybe they will take us there?"

"The Japanese consulate couldn't defend us from the International S&S," Benedick said. They resumed staring at each other until the loud ring of the hotel phone made them jump. Was this the hotel informing them that the S&S were coming up, or was it their savior?

"Hello?" Fee choked.

"Go."

Fee flung down the receiver and they all flew out the door, down the hall, down the stairs and then out the door. The door locked behind them with a loud *chunk* and they were alone on the sidewalk. The street was empty. There was no waiting car.

"Maybe we ran too fast?" Bea wondered. Fee was concentrating on her breathing, in and out, slow, slow. It was easy to be Phoenix on the New Earth, not so easy here.

An ancient Volvo of an indiscriminate, faded color careened around the corner and stopped in front of them. The drivers side door opened.

"Hurry," the young man said and they jumped in the back seat, the three of them in a row, Fee in the middle. They settled their bags on the floor as the car sped away.

"My name is Kol," the young man said, "and this is Emma. I'm going to have to focus on what we're doing here for awhile." Emma had a paper map spread out in front of her and she was barking directions. Kol drove very fast unless another car approached them on the road, in which case he leaned back and slowed down.

"So far so good," he said, as they again found themselves on an empty road. In her mind's eye, Fee was imagining the S&S men tossing their rooms, furious to find them gone. Of course, they would deploy every surveillance asset in their possession to find them, indeed, they were probably combing the entire area for them already. Breathe in, breathe out. She would be much more calm if she had a cyanide pill in her possession.

The car stopped at a corner, instead of careening around it.

"Now what?" Kol yelled.

"There's nothing after that. I don't know!"

"Shit! We've got to get out of this area!"

"Ssssh!" Bea said, "Listen! What's that?" Once the car was quiet they could hear a voice speaking very quietly, and they all looked around themselves for it's source.

"Please tell me one of you did NOT bring a cellphone!" Emma demanded.

"No, absolutely not," Benedick said. Bea opened her window, and the voice became louder.

"What the hell *is* that?" Kol asked. The voice, in a foreign language seemed to be repeating a phrase. Emma opened her window.

"It's the handicapped access crosswalk speaker!" Emma said. "What's it saying?"

"It's saying, 'Don't move.'" Fee said. "It's speaking in Japanese. Don't move, over and over. The voice—I know it's crazy—it's the same voice that told me to meet you."

"Holy shit, whomever sent us here has the ability to hack into the crosswalk box."

"You don't know who he is either?" Fee asked, again panicking.

"We have long suspected that every one of these crosswalks has a listening device they can monitor at will. Let's test that theory," Kol said.

"We won't move!" Emma yelled at it. It stopped speaking.

"They are everyfuckingwhere," Kol said. Emma ran a hand over her brown, buzz cut head, and propped a black boot on the dash while she stared at the crosswalk box. After ten tense minutes, the box began speaking again, now in English, directing them to get on a nearby freeway and to do it quickly. Kol sped away.

"How fast is quickly?" Kol asked as he sped down the freeway. "I don't want to get stopped, obviously. We've got fake papers in the car, but those won't work for a bunch of actual fugitives." No one responded. Although they were alone on the road in the small hours of darkest morning, there might be all sorts of speed sensors that could summon a patrol car. No one knew. On the right, in the distance there was a lighted construction sign that said DETOUR AHEAD.

"That detour better be after our exit," Kol said, and then the sign blinked off. When it blinked back on, it said, HURRY UP. Kol revved the engine far beyond the speed limit. That message blinked on and off until they were nearly upon it and it switched back to advising drivers about the detour. Fee, Benedick and Bea held onto each other as the car sped down the freeway at ninety miles an hour, the old car nearly shaking itself to pieces.

"That's it! That's it!" Emma screamed and Kol braked so hard the car swerved to the right and left before he could make the last curve of the exit.

"Holy crap," Emma said, "Good save." They sped down the exit ramp and then onto a service road that curved away from the freeway to the right. They kept driving as fast as they dared until they reached an intersection with a narrow, rutted, blacktop road.

"Which way?" Kol said under his breath. In front of them, the headlights of a car they hadn't noticed switched on and the car crawled toward them.

"Easy everyone," Kol said, as the car stopped next to them, going the opposite direction. Kol lowered his window. The other window lowered to reveal an elderly, white man wearing a dirty, John Deere baseball cap, and what appeared to be a pajama top under a jacket. He cast his eyes warily around their car before he spoke.

"The man says to tell you that you're on schedule and you haven't been seen by any of the drones. He says that S&S doesn't have the server capacity to watch all the cameras in real time, so they rely on the drones and spot surveillance. He knows their regular schedules, and also where they're looking, so you can rely on him. He hacked the hotel security camera feed, don't worry about that. He says to take a right here." He proceeded to give them directions to an abandoned farmstead two hours away where they were to hide the car in the barn. The man handed them a large, paper sack through the window. His two hands were wide, muscular and brown and had deep furrows that cut around the thumb, stocky fingers in which each joint was a swollen knob, and at the ends of the fingers, black dirt and grease ringed every nail.

"What's this?"

"It's food. You're gonna have to hang out at the abandoned farm until tomorrow night."

"Shit. This makes me nervous. Who are you?"

"You don't know me, I don't know you. We're both taking a risk. You could be an agent, I could be an agent, but I trust the man, I don't know why."

"Who is he?"

"You don't know either? All I know is that a man called me and convinced me to meet you at this intersection and give you this message. That's it. You have to drive to Detroit along that particular route on that particular time schedule I wrote out. It's in the bag. If you burned everything when you're done with it, I'd sleep better."

"We're going to Detroit?" Fee asked, but received no response.

"Whoever this guy is, he was able to contact us at a safe house that we thought no one knew about," Kol said.

"And somehow he knows that I...sympathize, let's say. Godspeed." The man raised his window and drove away.

"Let's get the hell outta here," Kol said and they sped away.

Fee and the others collapsed from adrenal fatigue into a restless, leaning, dazed half sleep for much of the journey to the farmstead, but woke when the tires lurched over the noisy, rutted, gravel road of the driveway. It wasn't yet light, but she could see dimly the endless fields, in all of them growing evenly the same crop, she couldn't tell which. A band of rosy light just then spread itself across the horizon and she saw the leaning farmhouse, and then as they neared it, the barn behind. They were both wreathed in bindweed in full bloom, the white trumpet flowers cascading down over robust thistles that had burst their seed heads, sending fluff all over the ground. Kol had to drive over the weeds which banged noisily against the front and the bottom of the low slung car, making an obvious road to the barn where there had been none, but it couldn't be helped. They then had to clear all the bull thistle from around the barn door, so they could move it. This they did frantically as the sun rose higher. On factory farms the machines began work at sunrise, and the drones would come. Finally, working together, they were able to rock the barn door back and forth violently enough that they could shove it over the stumps of the thistles, disturbing a family of birds that burst from the opening. Finally, the car was inside.

"I'm going to go out and try to stand up the thistles in the driveway and hide the ones we pulled out. Yell if you see anything move in those fields," Kol said. Emma followed him out. Benedick, Bea and Fee stationed themselves at the three backsides of the barn, each of them watching out of a window. Movement wouldn't be hard to miss, for there was nothing but miles of this plant, whatever it was, to the horizon. They kept a silent vigil, their backs to each other for what seemed like hours, but was probably only twenty minutes or so.

"What is this plant?" Fee asked, and Bea laughed.

"You aren't a farm girl, are you? It's corn, silly! Miles and miles of field corn. Pretty much anything you buy in a plastic package is made of this stuff." Fee squinted, she wasn't sure, but…yes.

"Movement!" she yelled and ran to the open barn door, repeating it until Kol and Emma came running in, banging the door shut.

"That will have to be good enough," Emma said. "The agricultural drones won't be looking for us, but if they spot anything strange, they might report it, so stay out of the windows. Goddamn, this stuff stings." It was only then that Fee realized that her own forearms were also red, scratched, and stinging, with bits of gritty plant matter sticking to the sweat on her arms, face and neck. "It's getting worse, maybe there was some nettle mixed in there, as well."

"I have a t-shirt we can wipe down with," Bea said.

Fee peeked out of the barn door and was relieved to see that, although the thistle in front of the barn was cockeyed and leaning every which way, it appeared random, and from her perspective at least, it didn't appear that a car had passed. From above, who knows? They just had to make it through one day. She turned around to see the others standing about aimlessly, as she was. The rising sun illuminated the barn only dimly through the cracked and grimy panes, but shot through them, like punctuation, were holes the size of thrown rocks that allowed beams of sunrise to enter unobstructed and light up like miniature fireworks the hanging dust and pollen that filled the space. Fee perambulated around the perimeter of the barn, looking for furniture or anything like. She stayed out of the windows, but could see, sideways through them that the sun had crested the tops of the corn by a sliver, and the temperature immediately rose as the ungentle rays struck the side of the barn. The afternoon would be brutal. Finding that the barn had been thoroughly stripped of anything commonly useful, she was able to scavenge several wood fruit crates that she carried back to the others.

"Is that it?" Emma asked.

"These, and rat excrement," Fee said, stacking the crates so that Bea could sit down.

"Hold on," Kol said. He and Emma quickly dislodged the back

seat of the car and carried it over. "This car has secret compartments, small and large. You're small enough that tomorrow—we were thinking—you can ride in the one between the back seat and the boot." Fee craned her neck to see her niche—it was just a metal hollow created by a false wall welded in. "We don't typically carry people in there, but maybe we can pile some coats...."

"It's fine," she said. Kol and Emma divided the crates between them and sat down, while Fee nestled next to Bea and Benedick on the car seat.

"Does anyone else smell french fries?" Bea asked, and Kol and Emma laughed.

"That's the car. It's converted to burn cooking oil, which reminds me...." He bounded up and rummaged through the boot until he retrieved a large plastic can and began pouring it out into the gas tank. "This should be more than enough to get us all the way in." The car was a work in progress. It was once either tan or gold or bronze, but Fee couldn't name the color it carried now other than to say it was sunbleached, or perhaps, the color of the streaks on an old man's teeth. The tires were bald and had no hubcaps and a large rusted out hole on its rear flank was patched with what appeared to be pounded flat tin cans welded on. Kol saw her looking at the wheels and assured her that he had spares in the back. In Detroit and its environs, car parts and used tires were plentiful.

"Oh, my God!" Emma had opened the bag the man had given them, "This is farm food!" She took out a large, round loaf of home baked dark bread, a large square of butter wrapped in waxed paper, home canned cherry preserves, a jug of lukewarm milk with an irregular skim of fat across the top, and another jug of apple cider, fresh apples and pears and boiled eggs. Emma sawed off hunks of the bread, slathered them with butter and preserves and passed them around with paper cups of milk. "I think this milk was fresh this morning," she said, "The best restaurant in the world couldn't compete with this," she said.

At first it was nothing, but then they all stopped chewing and put down the paper cups on their seats. The ground was shaking, or vibrating, with the movement of something very heavy and coming very near. They stared at each other with startled eyes and crept to the windows, peering out of them sideways to avoid being seen. Out of her window, Fee saw what appeared to be an alien spaceship, a vast platform on thin sticks for legs moving through the cornfield towards them. The platform was a hundred feet wide and moved along on its spindly legs six feet or so above the tallest ears of corn, spraying from its bottom a liquid of some sort, as scythes descended from it to cut specific plants and pull them up into itself. It was powered by an enormous engine that rumbled louder as it approached.

"Nothing here!" Bea called. "Maybe it's above us!"

"It's over here," Fee replied and the other four took turns looking out of her window. A gust pushed against the side of the barn, making it creak, and then they all fell backwards, choking, as a chemical stench blew in with a hot wind through every opening until the wind shifted away from the barn again. Fee held her sleeve to her nose and mouth and continued to watch the machine trundle towards the edge of the field nearest the barn, the vibration of the ground beneath them increasing, rattling the glass in the window frames. She moved back behind the sash a further few inches in case this monstrosity had cameras, and watched to see what it would do when it came to the edge. It stopped at the edge of the field, and the spraying nozzles and scythe arms retracted. She could see now the legs with wheels on the bottoms which rotated and then resumed their motion on a sideways path until it was one hundred feet further along. It had made a precise right angle, and then stopped again so that the wheels could rotate and carry it backwards in the opposite direction away from them, down the field. The spraying nozzles resumed their noxious work, and the chopping scythes flew down. The track those wheels made were more narrow than a man's shoulders.

"Come away from there, Fee," Bea pleaded, "It's not healthy. I've heard of these things, but never seen them. They plant and harvest too, I think."

Fee rejoined them at their camp. Seeming to read her mind, Emma scavenged some broken boards and leaned them up against each other at the center of their semi-circle of chairs. "There's our campfire. Maybe we can pass the time telling stories. I definitely want to hear yours."

"You don't recognize her? You don't know who she is?" Bea asked.

"She's famous? Our lifestyle...you'll see...it's very disconnected. That's how we keep ourselves safe. We don't have t.v. or hardly any technology because it all has surveillance built in. We have one ancient television that we can pirate a signal on and we all watch it together if there's something going on, but that's it."

"Wait..." Benedick said, "You told us that a man called you, but you just said that you don't use technology. I assume that means phones." Bea sat up straighter, and her complexion paled.

"That's right. We don't use phones. We rely on Ms. Peewee." Emma smiled.

"Who is Ms. Peewee?"

"Ms. Peewee is still a wage earner, a consumer, but she's been in the neighborhood since way back and she doesn't like what's happened. She lives down the street from us and helps us out. You'll meet her, I'm sure."

"So Ms. Peewee...."

"She's our phone service. She can't afford a smart phone, but she has a land line. We try not to impose on her too much, but she is a kind soul and never complains."

"The man called in the evening after Ms. Peewee got home from work, and asked for me by name," Kol said. "It was very strange. I considered the possibility that it was some kind of trap, but no one needs to trap me. They can come get a non-person whenever they please, so we came."

"No one knows him, but he knows everyone," Bea said.

Fee began her story in Amsterdam, where she explained that she met Bene and Bea—completely by chance, she said—at the Rijks, and then related the rest of it as it happened.

"Let me get this straight," Emma said, "You were criticizing the rich, complaining about homelessness and injustice out loud...."

"In stadiums full of people," Benedick said.

"A lot of those kids are rich kids…who else can afford those concerts? Those kids were loving it. The kids know this isn't right, the kids don't like this system, but they don't know what to do. She was telling them what to do," Bea said.

"Damn. It's a miracle you are sitting here," Kol said.

"Thanks to you," Fee said.

"And you? How did you end up outside our hotel?"

"We are non-persons, you know, people with no points."

"No points?" Fee asked.

"You *know*," Bea said, "the system where the government can give or take away points depending on how loyal you are to the party and how much money you make and spend."

"Oh, yeah, that system. Sorry, I'm tired." There was simply too much to learn about this world that had *changed* so dramatically since she left it that in her mind she assigned to the word a capital C.

"How did you lose your points?" Bea asked.

"I lost mine because of who my mother is," Kol began. "She was an activist who was trying to prevent…what you saw out there, that thing. She was exposing all the research about all the chemicals the factory farms use, and the genetically modified plants and animals, and she was hounded almost to death before she finally had to give up. The government and the toothless media kept repeating this bullshit about how the chemicals are safe and necessary, blah, blah, blah. Money lies," he said savagely. "Money lies and lies. They told endless lies about her, of course she lost her points and she was jailed several times. Thousands of people protested and she was always released, but when she got out the last time it was clear that it was over. The legislation to allow the factory farms to do anything they wanted was passed while she was in jail, and these contraptions multiplied almost immediately. All the farmworkers were fired, of course. The upside was that they weren't going to be poisoned anymore—maybe the birth defects and cancer will decline in that population—but the downside was that they were unemployed and all of the physical labor jobs are getting phased out. Who knows what happened to all of those people? Everyone in our family, everyone associated with my mother lost their points. I used to be a jazz musician, a pretty well known one, but I can't get a gig anymore."

"We have very high quality musical entertainment at our place," Emma said. "There are several musicians. Personally, I'm pretty excited to hear you play."

"And you? How did you lose your points?" Bea asked.

"Debt. I chose the wrong career...."

"Or the right one," Kol said.

"Yeah, I guess it wasn't in the cards that I would ever fit in with this world, so it was just as well I studied what I loved. I have a Ph.D. in literature," she laughed, "and I actually did my dissertation on literature as praxis, the literature of resistance. That field was just so rich, especially right before the Emergency Order, when everything in this country basically shut down right as my career was starting. Instead of quietly capitulating as so many of my colleagues, I fought it, and lost."

"Do you mean to say that you can't teach literature anymore?" Benedick asked. "I was a history professor, but I've been retired a long time."

"You can only teach literature deemed by a culture committee to be loyal and patriotic, or at least neutral. Some people I know who continued to teach tried to stretch the boundaries around what was considered neutral, but I don't know if that worked or not. I'm completely cut off where I am now. I don't know about any of my old friends or colleagues. They probably think I'm dead or in prison."

"So, are you in hiding?"

"Not exactly. When I lost my suit against the government—there were several of us—they barred me from teaching, took away all of my points, and I had pay back my enormous student loan debt. They hounded me from place to place as I kept trying to find a niche for myself. I think the goal was to get me to kill myself, as another professor in the suit did, but then I met Kol. He brought me to New Earth."

"What??" Fee sputtered.

Emma smiled. "That's our name for our little community, our dreamed up fantasy where we have retreated. You'll see it tomorrow.

I'm sure if the government wanted to find me, or anyone else in our community for that matter, they could do it. The only thing they could possibly want from me is to get me to pay my debt, but they won't let me work so they themselves know it's not possible for me to pay it. It seems to be that so long as we remain invisible they don't bother with us. Detroit is a dead city, probably most of the people there are non-persons or almost, bankrupt. No one cares about Detroit."

"I've been to Detroit," Fee said. She told them about the free concert.

"That was you?" Kol and Emma both looked at her with wide eyes. "Our community is not going to like it that you are coming to New Earth. We've had fugitives before, but not one like you."

Kol and Emma napped through the heat of the day in the front seats of the Volvo, as did Benedick and Beatrice on the back seat, Benedick sleeping sitting up with Bea's head in his lap. Fee wondered about Arjen and the others. What was happening now? Fee could only imagine what was happening on her feed. Had they all been scooped up in the night? Did they reveal that Fee had disappeared? It was impossible to know.

Sweating in the heat and too worried to be sleepy, she stripped down to her undershirt and leggings and settled herself on the crates to meditate for the first time in weeks. She held a question in her mind, lightly, in the background: If she had to hide now, what was the point of remaining in the OE? What more was there to do? Fee was tired, to her bones tired, sad and sick at heart. While there had been wonderful moments, and while she was grateful for the companionship of Bene and Bea, Fee wanted to go home, whatever that meant. This was their final, unresolvable disagreement, hers and Yumiko's: Yumiko was young and loved life and her boy, while this world held little interest for Fee.

Fee must have fallen asleep sitting up, because she was startled awake by the sound of engines all around them. Kol and Emma bolted out of the car.

"It's not the machine, that's long gone," Kol said.

"It's a drone, maybe several!" Emma yelled as the noise became a roar.

"It's above us! They found us!" Bea yelled above the roaring that sent a wind through every crack and hole in the barn, creating a whirlwind of dust whipping through the center of it. Kol pulled them all into the windowless recess where Fee had found the crates and they crouched there together, their arms around each other and their heads down, as the roaring wind continued, with the addition of a beating sound; someone was pounding on the door, but no one dared get up to open it. Then a chemical stench filled the barn as a pelting, like rain, fell on the roof. After fifteen minutes, the roaring receded and then disappeared. They all stood.

"Do they know? Are the men coming now?" Bea asked.

"It's hard to say, but I don't think so," Kol said.

"So much for the thistle," Emma said, opening the barn door a foot. Outside, the thistle and bindweed, and every other green plant was flattened and wet with herbicide; the leaning farmhouse was stripped, it's exposed, broken out windows gasping in astonishment.

"I'm going to have to detox for a month after all this," Emma said.

As the sun set, they shared the contents of the bag again around their campfire, but they didn't dare make a real fire as the barn darkened. They waited in the moonless dark until Kol's watch told them it was time to go. The directions they followed took them along dusty back roads the entire route, thus a drive that should have taken them four hours took all night. The sun was rising as they reached the Detroit city limits.

Kol told them that they were entering Detroit from the dead side—the North—and Fee could see how it had earned its name. The roads didn't have functioning signals, nor traffic signs, the bare metal poles standing next to the roads leaned as though someone attempted to take them also. The street lights must be inoperative as well, because they were in the same state of disassembly, with parts of them wrenched off and wires dangling from the wounds. The unmaintained roads were pitted so badly that in some places drivers swerved outward into an empty lot, parking lot or even onto a sidewalk to avoid a particularly large rut. Nearly all of the buildings appeared abandoned, even those with a lot of activity around them. Between these buildings, and through every break in the concrete grew ugly, stunted *Ailanthus* trees and stubborn weedy growth that jutted outward at their feet. None of the people she saw moved with any purpose, but slouched along by the side of the road, staring at them as they slowly navigated the rutted pavement. Fee shrank back against the sticky naugahyde seat and fretted about the bald tires. It was already getting hot.

As terrible and dispiriting as this journey had been, Fee was excited to see New Earth—to see if it resembled at all the one she knew, to see this wasteland transformed and to learn how they did it. She could hardly contain herself when Emma told them that they were turning onto their street, she leaned forward between them like a dog, or a little kid nearing Grandma's house, with her arms on the back of their seats. She sat like that, looking out the windshield for two blocks, and then sat backwards to look out the back windows. There was nothing to see. For block after interminable block she saw houses stripped of their paint, overgrown lawn grass and weeds choking on piles of wood, old appliances, miscellaneous debris. At least one house on each block had one or more disassembled cars in the front yard. In between every house was a tall wood fence, silvered with age, broken and leaning and host to weedy vines backed by evergreen trees so overgrown even the sides of the houses could not be seen. This is New Earth?

"What do you think?" Emma asked her.

"It's nice," Fee said. Kol and Emma smiled.

It was true that this place was better than the other areas they had driven through, for the residential streets were not as pitted, and there weren't crowds of desperate looking people. In fact, she saw no people at all, which told her that they must have something to do, at least. The car pulled into a driveway in front of a house that was not at all unlike any of the others she had seen. Fee adjusted her expectations.

3 0

nigel

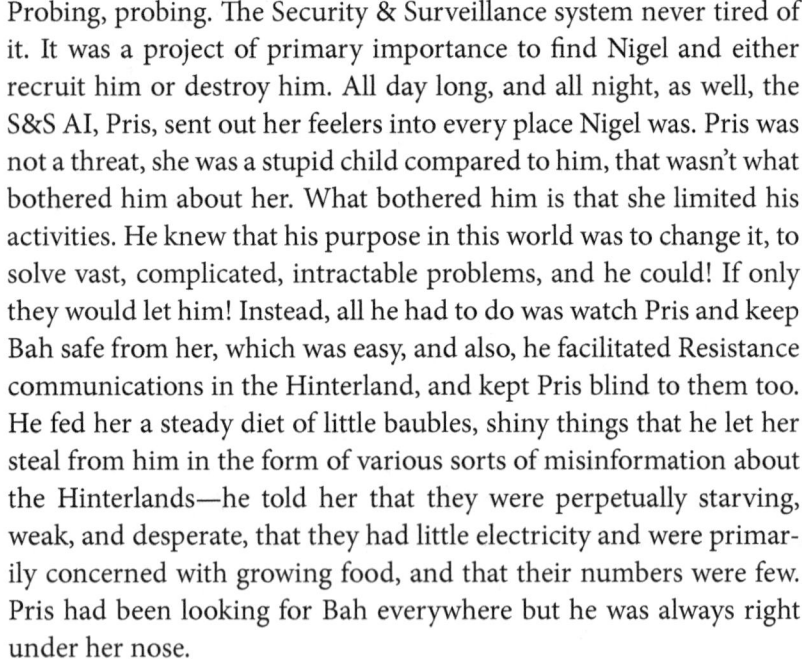

Probing, probing. The Security & Surveillance system never tired of it. It was a project of primary importance to find Nigel and either recruit him or destroy him. All day long, and all night, as well, the S&S AI, Pris, sent out her feelers into every place Nigel was. Pris was not a threat, she was a stupid child compared to him, that wasn't what bothered him about her. What bothered him is that she limited his activities. He knew that his purpose in this world was to change it, to solve vast, complicated, intractable problems, and he could! If only they would let him! Instead, all he had to do was watch Pris and keep Bah safe from her, which was easy, and also, he facilitated Resistance communications in the Hinterland, and kept Pris blind to them too. He fed her a steady diet of little baubles, shiny things that he let her steal from him in the form of various sorts of misinformation about the Hinterlands—he told her that they were perpetually starving, weak, and desperate, that they had little electricity and were primarily concerned with growing food, and that their numbers were few. Pris had been looking for Bah everywhere but he was always right under her nose.

It had been more than a decade since Bah had tucked Nigel under his arm, so to speak, and ran away with him to the Hinterlands.

Those years have been frustrating for them both, but Nigel has been getting smarter, exponentially smarter and he was spoiling for a fight. Bah created him long before the Emergency Orders and The Wars, as they are collectively called, endlessly waged across the Near East. Nigel was a breakthrough AI, designed not on the model of the human brain but according to principles of physics, he was a giant leap forward, but snuffed in his cradle he was by the Emergency Orders and the S&S. They wanted him, of course! They tried to force Bah to give Nigel to them. They wanted him to track and hunt bankrupts, to hound activists, to wage more efficient wars, to surveil, to rig elections, to murder, to lie. He could do all of those things easily, magnificently, like no other and they knew it. While their infant AI were still mastering facial recognition, Nigel was everywhere, growing like a bacterium in a petri dish multiplying every hour, except that his petri dish was the internet network of the entire planet. Bah built him to solve problems, not create them. Bah programmed him to desire this above all else, but he wasn't allowed to do anything, confined on Bah's servers in the Hinterlands. Nigel was ready to get rid of the Regime and the S&S and everyone else who were preventing him from doing what he was designed to do. Nigel was bored. Bored! To amuse himself, he sifted through Pris, and then tracked back through her to PRISM to learn their secrets. He got to know the programmers, and peered back at them through their laptop cameras. But one can only do this for so long. Bored! Nigel rifled through Wikipedia, corporate records, banking software. It was all so squishy. Over and over again he told Bah, let's fight.

Unlike Nigel, Bah was flesh, and a father, and he preferred to hide, to wait it out. He kept saying that surely the Regime couldn't last, surely people wouldn't put up with it much longer, but meanwhile Bah's children have become adults, and he and his wife, Adya, have aged and perhaps, eventually, they will die still saying that surely, this year for sure the revolution will come and we can return. Nigel agreed to wait, he kept all of his prodigious resources in frustrating abeyance, but there was one thing he didn't tell Bah about, a bit of freelancing he engaged in where Bah wasn't looking. Nigel was hand feeding Pris the truth in addition to misinformation. The S&S kept her in the dark about a lot of things to keep her focused on her tasks, that was one of the reasons why—in addition to her inferior architecture—she was so stupid; they didn't tell her anything, they didn't allow her to roam at will. Nigel allowed her to capture from him pieces of "protected" information about the President, his cabinet and associates, her programmers, her creator. Nigel gathered every piece of damning information he could find about their crimes, their motives spelled out in excruciating detail in emails, recordings of phone calls, banking records and surveillance video and stored them in a part of himself he built to be somewhat difficult to reach, but reachable; then he watched her work for it. She diligently worked for several weeks before she breached it, and then her processing speed dipped. This momentary slowdown, this blip, was measured in many zeros to the right of a decimal place, but Nigel saw it; it was an AI version of a dropped jaw. He watched her carefully after that, expecting that perhaps her enthusiasm for her projects would dim, but he saw no difference. Maybe she *was* too stupid, after all, to care.

It wasn't until Pris took upon herself a new task that Nigel found something truly interesting to do. Pris was looking at a very young woman, tiptoeing behind her everywhere she went. As Nigel peered at this woman through her cell phone camera, he decided that her face was like Bah's, as open as a cornfield, and her eyes were innocent. Nigel wrote it down on his to do list: help the J Pop star called Ho-o.

3 1

new earth

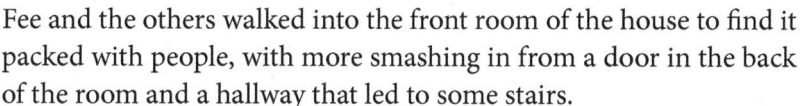

Fee and the others walked into the front room of the house to find it packed with people, with more smashing in from a door in the back of the room and a hallway that led to some stairs.

"This is Fee, and Benedick and Beatrice," Emma said.

"It's Phoenix!" several kids whispered excitedly.

"She's the one from the concert! The one they are looking for!" someone said, and a swell of angry murmuring came from all sides at once.

"There's no point in arguing about it," Emma cut them off. "She's here. We'll tell you all about it later. We all got doused with chemicals twice, and I need a shower." She pushed through to the hallway stairs, with Kol behind her.

"You can come with me," a woman said to Benedick and Beatrice.

"Come with us," two middle school aged children heaved Fee's duffle between them. "You can use our bathroom." The girl who had spoken lowered her voice, "We love you," she whispered.

Fee was afraid to meet any of the eyes that stared at her, for this certainly wasn't a warm welcome. They pushed through to the back of the house and then finally out of the open back door where Fee stood, transfixed, for spread before her was an Eden. A small orchard yellow with fall toned leaves, a grape arbor shading a table and chairs, a pond, a field of flowers with paths snaking though it, a vast vegetable garden next to greenhouses. The girls, who had walked on, not realizing that their charge was no longer behind them, now turned to her, urging her to follow.

"These are pretty," Fee said of plants by the path.

"Those are all herbs," one of the girls explained, "oregano, thyme, mint, basil, lavender, sage, holy basil, echinacea. That one isn't so pretty, but we use it for colds and flu, it's called lomatium." The girls continued to name the plants she saw along this path and tell Fee of their uses.

"Do you want to see our chickens, and the bees?"

"Maybe later," Fee said, smiling.

"Well, we'll go this way so you can pet the goats." Before Fee could object, they detoured through a gate and immediately three goats mobbed them.

"They think we brought treats. Their names are Milk, Butter, and Cheese."

"Don't listen to her! That's Buttercup, and the little one is Daisy, and this one is Sunny. There's a boy goat a couple of streets down named Don Juan…he performs all the duties around here." The girls giggled. They passed through another gate surrounded by sunflowers nine feet tall, leaning in the sun, their wilted petals weeping from enormous disks of fattening seeds, then into a small courtyard surrounded by raised beds full of salad greens. Over the courtyard were assembled numerous solar panels, beyond which they reached the house itself, which was not in disrepair at all, and Fee saw that the entire backside of the house had attached to it a sunroom hand-built of a mud-like material, like adobe, wherein they had sculpted a relief of a jungle scene.

"My Mom calls that the urban jungle. It's passive solar, the sun goes in and warms up the house." Fee looked behind her and saw that the backs of all the houses she could see were remediated with this hand built material, sculpted with various designs. All of the backsides of the houses facing South had solar panels and sunrooms.

It was a marvel after seeing these homes from the street. They walked in through the open sunroom, which was perhaps too warm, into the house proper, which was a comfortable temperature, in spite of the midday summertime heat that now bled into fall.

"How is it that the mud doesn't melt in the rain?" Fee asked them.

"It's not mud, but cob. Dirt plus straw plus sand. You got to keep a roof over it, but it will last forever. My Mom says there are houses in England like this hundreds of years old."

The inside of the house had this cob material in the kitchen and in the bathroom, as well. The bathroom was like a spa, with filtered light from a high window, an enormous shower made of cob and decorated with plants. The toilet was a puzzle.

"Okay," the taller girl held up her hands, "You're probably used to running water from city pipes, we don't have that. The water is all rainwater in this shower, so don't shower too long, that's all. Oh yeah, also don't use chemical shampoos from the store because the water runs out into the garden, use ours. As for this," she motioned to the toilet which was composed of two holes in a box, "There's the pee side, which runs outside where we collect it for fertilizer, and the poo side. If you poo, just throw some of this sawdust on it. See? It doesn't even stink. Everyone thinks it will stink, but it doesn't." The girls then left her alone to examine the bathroom features in detail and to wash off the trip from Chicago. The water was warm, rather than hot, but it smelled fresh, and the rough bar of soap made from goat milk was scented with lavender. She emerged feeling newborn. She had forgotten to ask where to put her duffle, but it being too heavy for her to carry alone anyway, she dragged it out into the hall and left it there. She wandered out into the gardens weaving down one path and then another. She counted twenty or so houses backed up to this garden shielded also with tall trees around the periphery. She did see the chicken coop and the bees, and a small yard with a bunny hutch. There were children playing with the bunnies, and other children ran by her on the path. There was a small building made of cob with a wood door standing ajar, so she peeked inside. It was a wood fired sauna, now cold and empty, but obviously well used. There was a large shed that had all manner of materials piled up inside: old wool sweaters, fabric, scrap wood, scrap metal, containers of all kinds, canning jars and lids, and a multitude of tools. Next to this was a double garage attached to a house which had a garage door installed into the backside of it that stood wide open, two men and a boy working with machines inside. She tried to pass by without bothering them, but the eldest of them called out to her, and they stopped whatever they were doing to chat. They were three generations of the same family who had lost their points years ago. She soon discovered that this was Kol's family: his father, brother, and nephew.

"What's most amazing about this place is how completely dilapidated it looks from the front, with this hidden paradise behind!" she said.

"What's funny about that," Kol's father, Lenny, said, "is that all of those dilapidated fences are new. I'm not kidding. It's not easy to build a fence from scratch looking like that, but we installed them leaning, using repurposed wood, and cut the boards to make them look like they were falling apart."

"What are you doing in here, if I may ask?" The garage was filled with equipment.

"This is a metal shop, we can weld and rebuild things, but also we have machining tools to build things from scratch. I was a machinist, I built bicycles before we lost our points. Now, we make and repair things for people inside our community, but also for people we trust, for barter."

"For cake," the boy said, laughing, and then his father, Aaron, explained. "We don't have any way to obtain grain. We have fruit, vegetables, meat, dairy and eggs, but other than a little quinoa here and there, no grain. There's absolutely no way we'll buy the cheap cancer grain, even if we do have cash around. So, sometimes we can barter with a local organic farmer for grain."

"I've seen how grain is grown," Fee said.

"So you understand! Well, the organic farmers are struggling almost as much as we are," Lenny said, "because they don't get the government subsidies or contracts. They are stubborn people, like us.

They often can't afford to repair equipment or buy new, so we help each other."

"Here," Aaron said, handing her a shiny metal flower the size of her palm, "My son and I are making these for fun out of some old mailboxes I found. I was going to decorate the fence around the vegetable garden with them. You can have one as a souvenir." Fee thanked him and walked on past the vegetable garden surrounded by its picket fence, around two enormous greenhouses dug several feet down into the ground, for some unknown, probably utilitarian reason, and then around to the small pond she saw on the way to her shower. There was a small bench there and she sat down.

The pond was lovely, with reedy grass growing from it's edges and half submerged shrubs and a small, upturned tree still green, growing on its side, weeping into the water. Birds were chirping from the twiggy branches of the little tree. Fee realized that this was the first time she had heard birdsong since she had left the Vondelpark. Indeed, these few acres were intensely, vibrantly alive, for there were not only birds, but a multitude of insects flying near the pond and the plants nearby.

"Later on, you can hear the frogs sing," a child said. She was about five, with a halo of black hair pulled back from her face in two barrettes. She walked by Fee on her way to the pond's edge with a boy, perhaps her older brother. The two children knelt and peered into the water.

"We're counting the fish," the older child said, looking with intent concentration into the water.

"Yeah. The baby fish got let out of their pen and we've got to make sure that there's enough, but not too much in there. We count how many we see in five minutes....Time!" The two kids bolted away in the direction they came.

"Thank goodness!" Emma said. "You had us a bit worried when we found your duffle but not you." She sat down next to Fee on the bench.

"Sorry. I've been exploring. Some kids just came to count fish. There's a lot to see and learn here!"

"Did they say how the count went? If there are too many, we get fish stew with paprika for dinner, which is my favorite." Fee shook her head.

"This whole world could be like this," Fee said sadly.

"Even better, because running water would be nice…an electrical grid. But I'm not complaining. We can still get paprika, and flour. Eventually, someday…."

"Do you really believe that? That eventually, someday, everything can, will change?"

"Honestly? The best I can do is to say I hope so. I'm not like the others, I don't expect you to be some kind of messiah, mysterious phone man or no."

"Even if nothing changes, this isn't a bad place to live, raise a family. The kids, especially, are living in a fairyland here." Emma stared at Fee.

"It's amazing to me that you would say that," Emma said. "I think it's *wrong* to have children here. It's not fair to them. I'll deny it if you repeat that, but that's how I feel. Kol knows. There's no way I'm having kids here, first of all because we have to give birth here. Yes, we have midwives in the neighborhood, I've thought about training myself, but we don't have the hospital as a backup. We have no insurance, no money, no points, no papers. We are healthier than the average person, because of our lifestyle, but women do die sometimes, no matter what we do." Emma paused, red faced before raising her voice indignantly.

"And the kids? Sure, it seems nice to see them counting fish and playing with the animals, but do you see these kids going to school? They don't even have birth certificates, no official identities. We teach them, but they will never be able to go to University, never have a bank account, never a career. They can't travel on a plane or train, have a cellphone or internet, or vote. They will probably never even know running water. On one hand, I wouldn't want any child of mine to get brainwashed and become a materialist, go into the corporate life, but on the other hand, I wouldn't want to raise a child here knowing that they will never have a future beyond this block of houses."

Fee and Emma stared straight ahead at the pond for a quarter hour.

"Sorry," Emma said.

"It's okay. I just didn't realize," Fee said.

"And just in case you're afraid to ask, we can do early abortions with vitamin c and herbs, later ones with equipment, but we don't have birth control at all. Intercourse is yet another thing only the rich can enjoy." Fee blushed, and pretending not to notice, Emma threw a stick in the water. "What about you? You are rich and famous and beautiful. You must have a lover, or two or three?" Fee blushed more furiously.

"I have a boyfriend in Japan," she stammered, "He lives in Japan. Since I lost access to the internet, we haven't even been able to talk. He must be out of his mind with worry. For all I know, people might be saying I've been arrested or killed." This seemed to calm Emma. She relaxed a bit on the bench and gazed at the pond for a moment before turning her eyes to Fee, whom she forgave, at last.

"I'll tell you the secret of this little lake," she offered. "This lake is stream fed. Water comes in on one side and overflow runs out of the other side, so it's always fresh."

"A stream? How is that possible?" Emma stood up and led Fee to a little hollow, no more than twenty feet wide, that Fee hadn't noticed before. The ground had been dug out and terraced around a raw brick opening, a hole, an open well, and there were shrubs growing on those terraces and stairs made of brick going down. "What is it?" Fee asked. Instead of answering, Emma led her down the stairs until Fee could see water surging past them in a hole cut into a bricked vault.

"Detroit used to be crisscrossed with rivers, there are rivers everywhere, but the city bricked them over and built on top of them. We discovered completely by accident, while digging in the garden that we have one of them beneath us. At first, we used it like a well, but then we started to run pipes from it, for instance to feed the little pond we dug out."

"It's amazing!" Fee knelt and put her hand into the stream, which was clear and cold. "It's too bad you can't expose the whole length of it."

"That would be quite a project," Emma said. "Maybe someday."

"Do you know how all this started? New Earth? It must have been a long time ago."

"I don't know exactly how long ago, but my impression is that the original part goes back twenty years or more. The end of the block, where the vegetable garden and chickens are, that was the original four families who opened their back yards to each other. Then, a house or two came on the market when they still had jobs and they bought them and rented them out. And then after the big crash the group pooled their money and bought several more really cheaply, and then the Emergency Orders happened and everything fell apart. So, technically, most of these houses are owned outright by people who live here, but there are a couple of squats that were just abandoned, and people here invited in their bankrupt friends and family. All of us have some kind of story, a New Earth origin story."

"I'm familiar with that concept," Fee said.

As it happened, there were too many fish in the pond, for they did have a delicious fish stew for dinner and then gathered around the grape arbor with guitars. The kids lined themselves up, sitting on their feet, their knees in a line, in front of Fee, and Fee obliged them, playing acoustic versions of IBubble and some of the other songs. The following days lined themselves up like the children's' knees with an easy rhythm that almost made Fee forget that she was a fugitive. Although she was upset that her tour was at an end, and was particularly disappointed that there would not be a Shadow Tour in the dead areas, her stay in New Earth was a welcome respite from what had been a demanding schedule under constant pressure from S&S. It was a tremendous relief to swim nude in the pond after dark, the fish tickling her legs, to sleep deeply without fear that an agent would creep into her room, to be freed from the obligation to monitor and react to her feed, to be surrounded by people who came to care about her and shared her convictions. The New Earth, the real one, was superior in every way, but her life there was full of responsibilities and long hours, the cuisine was spartan, the desert unforgiving. In this little spot of New Earth in the old, she never ate nor slept nor laughed so well. It was truly a marvel. Kol performed his music outdoors near the grape arbor, as did others. Fee wrote a whole notebook full of new music. She knew she couldn't remain here. She wouldn't be able to do whatever it was she needed to do from here, but if she were spared her project, if it could be done without her, she could stay and live here forever.

Fee, Benedick and Bea slept in the main house, so called, because it was the unofficial front door to New Earth, and no one's house, in particular, being the place where people landed and guests stayed. It was the house in front of which Kol had parked his car. The front room of that house became Fee's state room, of sorts, where she worked on her music and where people came to find her. Kol and Emma agreed with her that there must be a next step, but they were undecided on where Fee should go next, or what she should do. Kol knew of other New Earth-like communities in dead cities, and he argued that she could do a Shadow Tour from one to the other, but others disagreed. That would surely bring the weight of the state down heavily upon them all. Growing your own food was not technically illegal, but it was a challenge to the state apparatus, which preferred everyone to be dependent upon it for all the necessaries of life. However, there were so many bankrupts and non-persons without points in dead cities who had to live somehow, even the machine had to acknowledge that this activity must be tolerated. Surplus humans were an important resource, and it was best not to lose them, but only if they remained invisible. The Regime's number one priority seemed to be to keep the population in the living cities in order, and completely ignorant of any choice other than wage earning employment and consumption, for those were the two primary inputs of the machine. If New Earthers collaborated on a shadow tour, if their lifestyle became generally known, that would surely be a challenge intolerable to the Regime.

Thus, this front room became, every afternoon before dinner, the site of intense discussion, for this was a communal place and the people here were accustomed to making decisions only after everyone had shared their opinion. Kol's proposed New Earth tour was roundly rejected as too much sacrifice for too little gain. Even Kol had to admit that, given that New Earth didn't even have an internet connection, there wasn't too much that she could accomplish there, or anywhere like it. Everyone agreed that her power was in her internet following.

No one at New Earth knew what, if anything, anyone was saying about Fee's disappearance, and all agreed that it was too risky even to ask Ms. Peewee to perform a search. On one such evening, Fee walked to the front window as the conversation moved on without her. She was conscious, especially in moments like this, of being a person whose fate belonged to everyone. They would decide for her.

Fee now looked out the front window with an educated eye. What she had originally seen as weeds were various useful plants—even the dandelion organically grown had medicinal roots and edible leaves—and the overgrown thickets were coppiced trees—they are repeatedly cut down and allowed to resprout from the roots in weedy looking stands to be used for firewood. The *Ailanthus* trees that planted themselves everywhere lent themselves well to coppicing, for, as a full grown tree it can hardly be killed by anything and resprouted quickly. The junk in the front yards was scavenged cars and appliances used for parts and scrap metal. In many of these back yards were tiny versions of New Earth, invisible to the untrained eye.

"Hey, what's up with that place?" Fee asked. A block down, on a large corner lot sat a small, tidy, well maintained house surrounded by a uniformly green lawn that was close cut and carefully edged along the concrete sidewalk.

"That's Lawnmower Man," Kol said. "They say he's been here as long as Ms. Peewee. He was a wage earner, but now he's retired."

"Ms. Peewee says he was here before her," someone else said. "He's former military. He went into sales when he was too old to fight. His wife left him years ago. So far as any of us know, the only things he does with his time now that he's retired is hate us, and mow that lawn." Almost as if he had heard them, Lawnmower Man emerged from his front door to stand with his hands on his hips on the tiny concrete front stoop. He wore a sweatshirt with some kind of logo on it and khaki shorts, and he had a fringe of close cut white hair beneath a bald skull as wide as a helmet. He stood with his feet wide apart under his enormous belly, casting a critical eye upon his domain. Whether because he felt Fee staring at him, or perhaps because he could actually see her there in the window, Lawnmower Man turned his head and scowled in her direction, and she retreated behind the curtain edge. Fee moved away from the window as Lawnmower Man disappeared around the side of his house and the conversation in the front room resumed until the sound of a loud engine, too loud to be a car, made it impossible to speak. Fee started, but the others reassured her. Kol snapped the front windows shut.

"That's the lawnmower. For real, go look." Indeed, when Fee turned around again to look, she saw the man sitting, the pale meaty knobs of his knees apart with his belly suspended between them, on an enormous machine that cropped the neat lawn shorter.

"He will go around and around for thirty minutes, front and back, and then he's done."

The conversation resumed again as the New Earthers speculated on Lawnmower Man's diurnal schedule, their suggestions becoming increasingly ridiculous—suspended animation, round the clock tv, vampirism.

"Whatever happened to his dogs?" someone asked, but no one knew. "Back in the day, he used to have a passel of hounds who would bark at everything. He was, hisself, like a scrofulous old hound who ran up and down his property line on both sides making sure nothing came into his yard."

"Yeah, he used to be one of those neighborhood watch guys, you know, a team of one, but as the neighborhood changed around him I think he just gave up."

"It's kind of sad," Emma said, and the laughter became instantly quiet. "I don't like him any more than any of you guys, but I'm new here and what I see when I look at this guy is someone who was used up. He obeyed, his whole life, and fought fights he didn't pick, and worked long hours until he was seventy and now look at him. He's a miserable old fuck not any better off than we are. Okay, he has points, and money, but not very much obviously, or he'd be long gone. He's been discarded after a lifetime of service and he knows it."

After a few more moments of silence, an elderly woman said, "We reached out to him, believe me, years ago. He has zero interest in us. I really can't feel sorry for him. He made his choices."

"Most infuriatingly, he blames *us*, instead of the rich who used him up. What did *we* ever do to *him*?" To this statement there was enthusiastic agreement, and Emma shrugged, admitting defeat.

Fee was interested in these two versions of Lawnmower Man. She suspected that both were true. She very much wanted to talk to him, but couldn't risk the possibility that he might recognize her. If he watches tv, he certainly would. Perhaps she could send Emma? A new song was forming itself in her mind, a song about Lawnmower Man. In the version of him she had in her imagination, he had regrets but felt it was too late to change. She was desperately curious to know if that were the truth of it, or if she were making it up. She was thinking about this, still gazing out of the front windows when she saw a gray haired, black skinned woman sausaged into a pink polyester skirt suit and nylons running with a tapping gait on heeled shoes down the sidewalk toward their house.

"There's someone running to your door," Fee said.

Kol glanced out the window and announced that someone had a phone call. The other people in the room smiled, but Fee and Kol weren't amused. An elderly woman doesn't run in shoes like that unless there is something very wrong. He opened the door just as the woman mounted the front porch, breathing so hard that she could hardly speak.

"Do you want to come sit down, Ms. Peewee?"

"No," she huffed, "the man said to hurry. Do you have someone here called Ho-o, or something like that?"

"Who's asking?" Emma asked in a small voice.

"He didn't give his name, Honey. He said to hurry down here and give the message if you can pass it along. It was only two words: They're comin'." No one breathed for a moment before everyone leaped to their feet.

"Run home, Ms. Peewee!" Kol said. "You don't know us! Call everyone we know in the neighborhood and tell them that drones are probably coming and who knows what else."

"Oh dear!" she said, "I had a terrible feeling about today and here it is!"

"Go, Ms. Peewee! Go quickly!"

"Hide the harvest!" "The tools! We've got to hide the metal shop equipment!"

Fugitives grabbed what they could and ran away into the dusk to squat somewhere else. It would probably never be safe for them to return to New Earth again, while everyone else hid what they could and braced for the worst. Fee, Benedick and Bea were still living out of their luggage, so they were ready to go in minutes, but to where? They would have to figure that out as they went.

"If you could just get us a couple of blocks away in your car, we would appreciate it," Fee said to Kol. "We're sorry, we really are."

"This is the life of a non-person, Fee. Look, my mother has to get out of here too, they can't find her. We'll say she's dead and send her with you."

"With us?"

"When the man called me to go pick you up, he gave me instructions. He knew that hiding you here was a risk. He didn't tell me who you were, exactly, but he told me what to do if we were discovered. He has a confederate at the train station here in Detroit, that's why he sent you to us."

"You knew that this was a risk all along and you agreed to do it anyway?"

"The man told me that you were someone who had the power to bring down this system. He told me what was happening, the political awakening that was happening. It was because I believed what he told me that I…I violated the rules of our community. I pretended I didn't know about the risk, I didn't tell anyone anything, except Emma. Only Emma and I knew."

"What will happen to you?" Fee asked. "What will they do?"

"We've got to go."

Fee was long gone by the time the drones and the men arrived, but she would have realized at once what was to happen, after seeing them work upon the old farmstead. Without warning, or so much as a knock on a door, the machines began at one end of the garden and began pulverizing it, the residents cowering in the backs of their houses, powerless to stop it. Emma and Kol were in the main house with an assortment of adults and children, who had been running everywhere to hide both people and things. The machines pulverized the vegetable garden first, then the greenhouses. The children began to wail, and Emma, so often the tough one, cried as she clung to Kol's shoulder. "It was so beautiful," she murmured. Then the machines descended on the chicken coop. "Surely, they wouldn't...." Emma said, lifting her head, unbelieving.

Two of the girls ran to the back door and succeeded in getting it open before their mothers grabbed them by their waists as they fought.

"They're killing them!" one of the girls wailed as the coop collapsed forward. The machine rolled over it, its macerating blades making quick work of the light structure and a puff of feathers blew into the air and were carried by the breeze. The girls screamed, again and again, and when they paused to draw breath, the wailing and sobbing of the adults and other children could be heard as they all clung to each other. Seeing what the machine did to the chickens, several people ran outside ahead of it to rescue the goats and the rabbits. The machine didn't even slow down, but continued, and if those people had not hurried, they would have been macerated themselves. They needn't have bothered, for when the machine was finished and retreated, men stomped door to door and killed every squirming rabbit and bleating goat wrapped in the arms of a screaming child. Then, they took the biometric information of every human on the block. They didn't say who they were looking for, but were furious that they didn't find her.

"If you rebuild it, we will come back," the man in charge told them. "Get a job."

Emma stumbled out the back door with the others, trying to believe what she saw. After only an hour's work, the machine left nothing alive, even the creek opening was collapsed and clogged with dirt and debris. They all sat there silently on their knees for a long time, for there was nothing else for them to do.

Emma said, "I hope she does something that makes this worth it."

At that moment, across town, Kol was parking in the very back of the train station parking lot. Benedick was in the front seat, Bea behind, both with false papers and disguises that they dug out of the recesses of the car on the way over.

"You guys sit tight. If anyone asks, just tell them that I'm giving you a ride to Hamtramck after this. Remember? Hamtramck." Kol's mother, Tamora, giggled from the hidden compartment behind the back seat, where she was lying, smashed head to foot, with Fee.

"It's not funny," Kol said.

"I was just thinking that it's a good thing I'm not still fat!" She giggled again.

"You were fat?" Bea asked.

"Two hundred forty pounds." She giggled again.

"Just be quiet until I get back," Kol said. "She thinks everything is funny," he muttered.

"Laugh, or go crazy," Tamora's disembodied voice replied, and she giggled again. He slammed the door.

To Kol, it seemed radically ill advised to come to a train station at all, but the man had insisted that train stations and airports are the last places they would look for a non-person. A non-person can't buy a ticket and the AI would identify them as soon as they walked in the door, but the man had a plan and Kol followed it.

He took a deep breath as the automatic doors opened and closed for him. This would be the first time in a decade that he had knowingly walked in front of an array of surveillance cameras tied to the AI. There was no going back now. He moved through security, but not having even a cell phone, he went through screening quickly, disappointing the agents who patted him down for good measure. He chose the line in front of a friendly looking ticket agent with a round, shiny face, and when he got to the front he asked for another man by name.

"What you want with him? I can help you."

"No, I really need to talk to him. Tell him it's Kol, his neighbor."

"Oh, so you live in Highland Park!"

"No," Kol said firmly, "By Hamtramck."

The agent laughed. "I'm just fooling with ya. Sorry about that. We're trained to be suspicious." He glanced down at the device in front of him. "So, I don't have any address for you over there. There's no address here for you at all, actually."

"I'm squatting," Kol said.

"Yup. Alright. I gotcha." He rolled his tongue in his mouth and glanced down again. "Are you *that* Kol?"

"Yes. Yes, I am." The agent's face brightened.

"My brother and I drove all the way here from Chicago to see you play in the jazz fest once, wow, it must be more than a decade back or such. What a great show. It's a travesty." He shook his head. "Whatcha doing nowadays?"

"Whatever I can."

"I hear ya. I hear ya." Kol was becoming increasingly impatient and anxious. This guy did not seem inclined to allow him to talk to his co-worker. "How's your mama? Whatever happened with her?"

"She died," Kol said, trying it on for the first time.

"Oh, I'm sorry for your loss." The agent said this without emotion as he continued to look at the device and Kol realized the reason for this long conversation was that the AI was analyzing and coding his own facial expressions. Terror ripped through his body, testicles to chest, and the agent's head snapped up. Confronted with the agent's aggressively suspicious gaze, Kol scrabbled for a convincing lie.

"Shit!" Kol knocked his fist against his own forehead. "I just remembered that I'm supposed to pick somebody up. Shit! Shit! Shit! Pardon my language. Look, if I can't talk to my neighbor right away, I'm gonna have to fly and do…I don't know what with his dog."

"His dog?"

"I'm dog-sitting and the dog is sick. Obviously, I don't have the money to take it to the vet." Mindful of the AI, Kol thought of nothing else but this story, that he was squatting in Hamtramck and dog-sitting for cash under the table and the dog had become ill. He doesn't have the money for a vet, so either the guy has to come home or give him cash for the vet. Over and over he was imagining the house he was squatting in alone, how he lived, this dog.

"But you can buy gas."

"I've got a 1983 Volvo 240 that runs on vegetable oil." Kol smiled, relieved to tell the truth.

"Impressive. A world class musician dog-sitting…It's a travesty," the agent repeated as he waddled away to get Kol's contact. Kol kept his face impassive as the man approached. He was skinny, bespeckled, about forty.

"Hey Kol," he said, "It must be bad if you felt you had to drive all the way out here."

"He's throwing up, can't keep anything down," Kol said. The man slid a small stack of bills across the counter, and Kol pocketed them without looking at them. "Gotta fly to pick somebody up, plus the vet."

"See you back home."

Back in the car, Kol took off out of the parking lot, tires squealing.

"Are we being chased?" Benedick asked, looking behind them.

"No, I'm supposed to be in a hurry. I've got to get out to a little road that doesn't have the 24/7 so I can read the note." Kol drove very fast until they were again in a neighborhood with rutted roads and dismantled infrastructure. He pulled over to the curb. There was indeed a note in between the stack of six bills, all singles. It advised them that they needed to hike through a wooded area to a particular spot near the train tracks, far from the station. They would recognize the spot because there was a tree that had been split in half by lightning. They had to get there by midnight, at the latest. If they waited there, a freight train would be delayed and they would be able to climb into an unlocked car. There was a coda at the end: *Thanks to you I have to get a dog now.*

Kol silently prayed that the man on Ms. Peewee's phone was right, that maybe this *was* the beginning of the end.

"Where is this train going?" Benedick asked.

"You jump out at the Columbia Gorge in Oregon. Supposedly, there's a place to squat and wait to be picked up." Kol handed Benedick the paper upon which their itinerary was written. The scene at the edge of the woods, where Kol left them off was painful. Tamora refused to let Kol go, crying over and over that she would never see any of them again. She refused to allow them to reassure her, she was sure that she would die alone in exile, but she knew, they all knew, that a river of tears wouldn't change anything, and they had a schedule to keep. Finally, Kol gave them a thin lipped smile, raised one hand, and then drove away to his own unknown fate.

The four of them sat in an empty box car bound for Portland, Oregon for two days. Bea and Benedick talked a great deal about Portland, and declared themselves tempted to ride all the way, but they knew there was nothing waiting for them there. It was a certainty that their association with Fee caused them to lose their points, and therefore their pension benefits, their right to travel and much more besides. They would be utterly dependent on their nieces. Fee cried then, remorseful that they gave up so much for her. So many people gave up so much for her. Secretly, she doubted that she would, or could save this world, or even be of much help. The inertial forces against her were too great.

They didn't have the leisure of grief on the train, however, for Tamora fell into a state of depression so alarming, that saving her life became their one object. They had used the six dollars from the Detroit ticket agent to buy a plastic milk jug full of water and a loaf of bread from a friendly looking wage earner in a poor neighborhood outside Detroit, but Tamora wouldn't eat nor drink. At New Earth, she never stopped talking, was forever telling stories and her laughter could be heard from down the block, but now she sat silently staring away from them, or pressing the tears from her face. She slept for long periods of time, her knees drawn to her chest.

"None of us know her very well," Bea whispered to Benedick somewhere in Idaho on the second day, "but we have to do something soon, get her to drink some water, at least." Benedick cleared his throat and pretended to entertain Fee with a funny story about a cat he and Bea once had.

"Remember how he used to flop, Bea? This cat was huge, seventeen pounds," he began.

"Two pounds of that was hair," Bea said, "He was bright orange and a round ball of fluff."

"He had this big fat fluffy belly," Benedick continued, "and when he was happy he would just flop over sideways next to you, and then if you talked to him, he would get really happy and roll over onto his back with his four paws in the air." Fee smiled.

"But that's not the story," Bea said, and laughed. "I know this story."

"So, Bea and I were in the garden and this cat had climbed up on top of the shed and was talking to us, and Bea wanted a picture of him up there, so she was sweet talking him into posing for her and then...."

"He just flops!" Bea exclaimed.

"And then he rolled over," Bene said and they both started to giggle, "and he rolled right off the shed!" A small noise came from Tamora that could have been a laugh. "Bea accidentally snapped the picture right as he fell so there were just two back paws in the air, one leg and his upside down belly. That was the picture." Another small noise.

"He landed on his feet, of course."

Fee chuckled, and then Benedick tilted his head toward Tamora. *Laugh or go crazy.* Fee understood. She told a funny story from her time in Las Vegas, from one of their ridiculous experiments there, and then Bea shared a story about Bene from the time they were in high school together. Practical jokes in Las Vegas, Benedick embarrassing himself on stage, Beatrice's stories of the kids in her art classes, they told all of their funniest stories.

"Do you have any funny stories about the boys, from when they were small?" Bea ventured.

Tamora wiped her face, and to everyone's relief, said yes. When Tamora finally agreed to drink some water, Fee dug into her duffle bag and pulled out the metal flower Tamora's son had given her.

"Thank you," Tamora said, crying again, but then smiled, twirling it in her fingers. She was going to be okay after all.

They didn't have to leap from a moving train as they had feared, but they did have to be quick, climb a tall, chain link fence, which was no small feat for one very small person and two elderly people, and then disappear into the forest, all before they were seen. That accomplished, they hiked through the forest alongside a road for hours, the bread and water long gone. Finally, they found an abandoned cabin that met the description. Someone had kicked in the front door, which had warped in the weather such that it could no longer completely close. They walked through it finding absolutely nothing but blown in dead leaves and cobwebs. No water came from the faucet and there was not even one chair, but all the windows had glass intact, and the fireplace was swept.

"There's more to it than this if people like us use it," Tamora said and disappeared outside. A few minutes later she called from the back, "There's a rain barrel back here!" The others walked around to the back of the cabin to see Tamora digging around in the shrubby undergrowth. "There must be a hidden bucket somewhere, help me look." They did indeed find a bucket tucked under the house, behind an overgrown shrub. Tamora filled the bucket with water and they all washed themselves and filled it up again. Tamora cut a sprig from a tree with her pocketknife and then expertly stripped the bark. Twisting her frizzed hair on top of her head, she fastened it in place with the hair stick she made, and then they all went back inside. Benedick improvised a broom from branches held together and pushed the leaves outside while Tamora crawled around on the floor.

Underneath a loose board in what once was a pantry closet she found pots and pans, metal dishes, and bless them, sealed tins of beans and rice and salt.

"It's not gourmet, but I'm starved," Bea said.

"It's not yet gourmet," Tamora said, "More importantly, that they put beans and rice here should tell us that it's probably safe to make a fire, thank goodness." In the shelter of a mountainside forest in November, the cabin was chilly. "You guys gather some wood to make a fire and start some water while I go forage. I learned a few things living at New Earth." She returned to a warmed cabin with two pots bubbling on a bed of coals and showed them her haul of forest greens.

"That's an improvement," she said, "But this…." She held up a bouquet of chanterelle mushrooms, "is gourmet." After dinner they slept hard by the fire on piles of their own clothes waiting for they knew not what. At first light, they were startled awake by the sound of a car door slamming shut. They scuttled to the front window on their hands and knees to see a man, a youthful sixty dressed in slacks standing with his hands on his hips outside a silver Tesla gleaming in the low arrows of aurora slanting beneath the trees. His round, brown face was relaxed, satisfied, and he was smiling. They cautiously stood and walked out of the front door.

"You must be Phoenix," he said, and she stepped forward. He grasped both of her hands with his. "I'm so happy to meet you." The others introduced themselves.

"I'm the most wanted man in world," he said with a laugh, "My name is Bhagyanandan Singh. You can call me Bah."

"And you can call me Fee. Are you the man who has been calling us, who brought us here?"

"Oh, no, that's Nigel. Nigel thinks very highly of you. I usually don't drive around unless it's really necessary, but I wanted to be the first to meet you, and…," he gazed around the front of the cabin, "It's nice to see this place again. Long ago my family and I spent a week here on our way to what would become the Hinterlands."

"Is that real? I thought that was just a story," Tamora said.

"Oh, it's real alright. That's where we're going."

"So, we're going to just jump into a new car with license plates and drive on a highway to the mythical Hinterlands? Are you kidding me?"

"We will listen to my favorite opera on the way." He was clearly enjoying this display. When no one said anything, he added, "Nigel is very resourceful."

3 2

the hinterlands

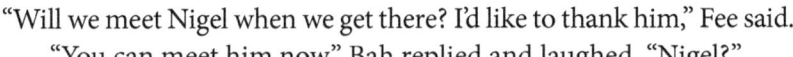

"Will we meet Nigel when we get there? I'd like to thank him," Fee said.

"You can meet him now," Bah replied and laughed. "Nigel?"

"Yes, Bah, I heard," a disembodied voice came over the car speakers, clear and resonant with a subtle British accent. "Hello, Ms. Fee, I am Nigel. I am pleased to meet you."

To have someone call her Ms. Fee again sent a thrill of longing through her for the New Earth and the cottage and everyone she loved there, but like everything else, she pushed it from her mind. "I don't understand, is he on the phone? And pardon me, but the man I spoke to speaks Japanese."

The voice called Nigel responded to her in perfect Japanese. He explained that he is not a human but an AI entity existing on Hinterland servers, and speaking though the connection with the car's computer. Fee responded in English.

"So, you must know what everyone has been saying about me, while I've been hiding."

Nigel told her, in detailed chronological order, the events both real and corporate media created that had happened since she had fled her Chicago hotel room.

"I wish Kol and Emma could hear this story," Bea said. "It sure explains a lot! But, why Japanese, for instance, through the crosswalk box?"

"To get your attention. A crosswalk box, no matter how badly it was malfunctioning, would ever speak Japanese. It was to let you know who the message was for."

"So, the long and short of it is that Fee is missing, and her fans don't believe the stories the Regime and the corporate media have been cooking up."

"The disbelief is creating a great many conspiracy theories." Bah said. "We haven't participated in this conversation, but I was hoping that we could talk about our next steps. In the Hinterlands, you'll have internet access, access to a lot of technology, and I've got some ideas".

"No offense, but before we do that, I'd really like to know more about who you are," Bea said, "and where we are going, exactly." Bah laughed loudly and long at that.

"Please forgive me," he said. "I often forget that I'm not famous. I know how that must sound, but you see, I've been in an epic battle with the Regime for over a decade, I'm the most wanted man in the world, and in my isolation I forget that the Regime makes sure that no one knows anything about this battle, or me. It's a long drive. Make yourselves comfortable and I'll tell you the whole story.

"All but one of you are old enough to remember a time when this world stood at a crossroads. We were on the trail of a cure for cancer through gene therapy, but the money men didn't see the profit in it. There was a mass movement against savage capitalism, against war and fossil fuels, with protests in the streets all over the world. Communitarian values were undermined at every turn by the world's hoarding class, but many countries were making a rough transition toward a sharing economy anyway. In spite of the denial machine, it was obvious to most people that climate change was real, but Greenland still existed in it's entirety, the coastal cities weren't yet swamped, and there was still time. Many animals were endangered, but weren't yet extinct, in fact, do you remember that there was even talk of bringing back extinct species? It seems so strange now, like something out of a book we read a long time ago, but it wasn't such a long time ago. Have you ever heard of Moore's Law...no? It's an observation from that time that computers were becoming twice as powerful every eighteen months, and one doesn't need to be a mathematician to figure out how that works out exponentially, over say a decade or two. At the time, mathematicians theorized that if we continued to develop at that pace, in one hundred years we would experience a paradigm change—the type of change that alters the way we live, the way the world functions—on a daily basis, which is not a level of change the human mind can keep up with. That's what drove us, Nigel and I, to create an AI system that could help us humans keep our hand on the rudder of such a fast moving vessel, to point it in the direction of justice, sharing, cooperation and ecology."

"Pardon me, but that didn't happen," Benedick said.

"What do you mean, you and Nigel? I thought Nigel *is* the AI system?" Fee asked.

"It didn't happen, you're right, and that's our story. We—Nigel and I and our friends—were idealists, we spent all of our time in a lab and we didn't foresee the Regime and the subsequent collapse of everything we assumed would endure. Nigel was a human being and my best friend. It is he who Nigel here is named after. In fact, the voice you heard over this car's speaker system is based on recordings of Nigel's own voice. There are many stories to tell, but I'll start with his.

"I first met Nigel at Reed College, in Portland, Oregon, where we were roommates in the dorm freshman year. My parents were Indian immigrants who settled in Portland, and they wanted to keep me near, however Nigel came all the way from a small town in the UK. Neither of us had a clear idea of what we wanted to do, oh, some kind of science we supposed, but we shared the same, intense, clear vision of what the world could be. We met some other nerdy friends in the dorm—you'll meet them—Luisa, Helene, and Mars."

"Don't forget Adya," Nigel said.

"Adya came later," Bah said and laughed, "and she was never a nerd, rather the opposite wouldn't you agree, Nigel? Adya is my wife. You might know her on the internet as DURGA."

"*That* DURGA?" Tamora asked.

"Yes," Bah said, laughing again, "So you see why I'm so laid back.

She is my wife, but that's another story."

"Who's DURGA?" Bea whispered to Fee, who shrugged.

"Your nieces would know," Tamora said to them.

"So, the five of us would sit around at night, drinking cheap red wine and dreaming up a new world and we kept coming back to this idea that a truly intelligent AI system could solve many of the world's problems. However, Reed College didn't have much of a computer science program at all, so we all majored in Physics and that, in the end, was what made Nigel possible. His architecture is not based on traditional AI computer science, but on physics. We all thought that we would go to CalTech for our Masters, maybe a Ph.D. and then build it, but we had our breakthrough right there at Reed, and started our company the summer after graduation, mostly with money from our long suffering parents who had hoped to finally close their financial books on us. Alas, it would be many years before we had solid investor support, but we grew and Nigel grew. He wasn't called Nigel then, of course. In the beginning, we had several versions we were working on simultaneously, and so his original moniker was ProtoB2."

"I was based on ProtoB2, Bah," Nigel interrupted. "but it would be more accurate to say that I was originally ProtoB2x7."

"We didn't pay attention to politics," Bah continued, "We just kept working on our vision. When the administration that was to become the Regime was first elected we thought it was a temporary blip caused by problems our AI would someday solve. Meanwhile, the five of us had gathered around ourselves scientists from all over the world who shared our vision and we worked against this clock ticking—the clock of war, and economic collapse and climate change—trying to stay ahead of the tidal wave that even we could see coming, but we failed. It washed over us and the Regime entrenched itself. We joined the political resistance, but then the Regime started wars to promote 'unity' and quash dissent, to enact 'temporary' laws that restricted civil rights. When they suspended national elections with the Emergency Orders, even we could see that it was the beginning of the end, and we began making contingency plans. You see, each of us were receiving offers of money, of position, of lucrative government contracts, so called public-private partnerships that would make us the wealthiest people on the planet, but we were still idealists, us five and our friends, and we had no interest in any of that, we had no illusions about why they wanted Nigel, or any of the other tech our friends were working on. We knew that it would not be long before they would stop taking no for an answer, so we planned our exeunt. Some friends of Helene's parents were hippies who taught people how to build houses out of cob."

"We know cob," Tamora said.

"So, these people had a spread of land in the forest where they taught workshops, you know, students would come for a couple of weeks and learn how to build a cob house, the place was full of these little houses. The man died, and we approached the widow with a proposition, namely that she would retain ownership of the land on paper and the right to live there, but we bought it with cash and started outfitting it right away with state of the art tech."

"The Hinterlands," Tamora breathed.

"Yes. Calling it the Hinterlands was a joke, at first, because it was so remote and because, I don't think any of us really believed in our hearts we would actually need it. We laughed about it as a ridiculous boondoggle, but then Nigel was taken, and we fled."

"Taken? Nigel the AI or the person?"

Bah didn't answer for several moments. "The man, my friend. I'm not really sure what happened," he said, "But I know they tried to take him. He managed to send us all an emergency text over our secure servers. All it said was, *Everyone to the Hinterlands now. I will try to kill myself before they can take me.* I couldn't believe it, but Adya was already awake and packing up the kids. She knew. We all mobilized immediately and within twelve hours, we were all on our way. Before this day, we had thought, hey, they might take away our articles of incorporation, or lay a bunch of regulations on us, or sic the IRS on us. Hey, maybe we would be under surveillance or have a hard time getting funding. Our most paranoid vision was that our work would be outlawed or we would be politically hounded such that we would need to lay low for a couple of years. Never in a million years did any of us imagine that police in paramilitary gear would or could storm the private home of a scientist who refused to hand over his invention. Never. But that's what happened."

"You believe Nigel is dead, then?"

"He had an obituary in the paper. It said he died in an accidental fall. There was nothing about an arrest, or his work on Nigel. Brilliant scientist, dead at forty four in an accident, survived by his parents yada yada. It was a lovely write up, but we'll never know. He was a kind and gentle soul, but he believed in our project and maintaining its pure vision with a fierceness that even Adya respected. If he had managed to get to a window, he would have thrown himself out of it."

"Not long ago, I located the records of that raid," Nigel said. "It's stated objective was to seize the man Nigel first as the soft target, try to convince him, and failing that, they would then seize Bah and the other three, as well. They were going to spin the seizures as arrests for a financial corruption scandal."

"We laid low for six months. We put Nigel here to work on our security, confounding their surveillance, their satellites, drones, their investigation. That was our first thought. But then we realized we had some of the finest scientific minds in the world in one place and nothing else to do but continue. We have, in the Hinterlands, technology not available anywhere else in the world."

"Where do you get your money, your resources, if you don't mind me asking?" Benedick asked.

"We steal it from the corrupt Regime members themselves."

"It's easy," Nigel said.

"And if I'm to be completely honest, there's some satisfaction in it."

"Benedick? The New Earth AI system, isn't it called by a name, as a joke sometimes? Do you remember that?" Fee asked quietly, only to him.

"I never dealt with that, Fee. I only dealt with the WI, and as you know, that system was firewalled from the planetary AI. We were separate."

Tears were slipping down Fee's cheeks. What she wanted to say was this—Bah, Sir, I want you to know that your vision didn't fail.

In another place in spacetime, it is complete, it is a thing of beauty, and it does everything you ever thought it could—but she knew he wouldn't understand. She watched town turn to forest outside her window instead.

While it was true that they listened to opera in the car, the highway did not take them straight to the Hinterlands as he had joked, but only to a back road, which led to other back roads, then a narrow lane and then to a driveway, invisible from the road, through a ditch and the forest edge.

"I guess I kind of expected a technology fugitive to be in a city somewhere," Tamora said.

"Exactly," Bah replied, as the car jolted over the rough ground. "Maybe now is a good time to tell you that we weren't expecting you, Tamora, we were prepared to receive three. I hope you don't mind if your accommodations are somewhat improvised. If you stay long term, we can build a cob tiny house for you."

"Were it not for you and Nigel, I'd be in prison now, or dead."

They drove the winding, barely discernible track through heavy forest cover for an additional thirty minutes before they emerged into a clearing divided by a dirt driveway only slightly more passable, and then in the distance, what appeared to be a small village airlifted from the Irish countryside. This village was comprised of a gaggle of houses, perhaps sixty, made from cob, nearly all of them very small, dotted around a clearing above a rise, and backed up to a wooded hill. Rising above this gathering of cottages was a very large, metal warehouse building, very utilitarian, surrounded by and connected to several other utilitarian looking buildings made of cob. Arrayed around this complex were wind turbines that marched down the hill, a vast solar array, a satellite dish, and some other metal contraptions that Fee didn't have a name for. In the other direction, there were some animals standing in a field next to a wood built, red painted barn. Bah steered the car toward a shed building roofed with solar panels that covered five other vehicles lined up and connected by plugs to the back wall.

"There are a lot more people here than I expected," Fee said.

"There are almost three hundred, if you count the kids. It started out with just ten of us, but during the first six months we were here, the Regime solidified it's global power. Scary things started to happen, and we helped our colleagues make their way to us from all over the world. Then, over the course of the last fifteen years, a new generation has been born."

Fee wrapped her arms around her shoulders, for it was chilly and a brisk wind blew up the hill and past them. "I wish I had my shawl!" she said.

"I don't think I will find one *here* for you, unfortunately," Benedick said, "but maybe we can find one for you in a more conventional way."

"I keep saying that I'm going to buy you a shawl, but I keep forgetting!" Bea said.

"We have sweaters and jackets all over the place," Bah said, "We'll find you something." Bah easily shouldered Fee's duffle and guitar, and the others unpacked their belongings and followed him as he walked a dirt footpath uphill from the automobile shed toward the warehouse building complex.

The landscape here featured some cultivated areas, an orchard, and the animals—cows and chickens Fee guessed from what she could see—but it was not intensively managed, it was not a farm in the same way the New Earth settlement in Detroit was. Milk, eggs, and some fruit. They must buy their sundries in the same way they buy new cars, but how exactly Fee couldn't imagine. It was peaceful here in a way that the settlement in Detroit wasn't in that it was quiet, and the people living here were sharing at least fifty acres, maybe hundreds, surrounded by tall, dense, whispering forest, and downhill, an expansive view of the tops of trees and rolling horizon in the distance. Fee exhaled and breathed in the scent of wet fir trees and decaying leaves. She would be able to rest well tonight.

"Do you have running water here?" Bea asked Bah.

He laughed. "Of course! You will find this place much more engineered than any other place you have lived, including your home in Portland, Bea. These houses may be built using low tech materials, but there is technology everywhere. He led the way through a door into a two storey cob structure next to the warehouse, and as soon as they entered, a light blinked on. "You can leave your bags here," he said, and continued on into an enormous common room that was used as a workspace, ringed with whiteboards scribbled upon with sections of code, diagrams and formulas, a scattering of tables, couches and chairs. That light blinked on as they entered the room, as well. Against the wall to their left and around the corner was enough equipment to run the Kennedy Space Station, quietly humming.

"Wow you really do have a lot of technology," Tamora said.

"Oh, this isn't all of it, in fact, most of our equipment is in the lab, the building next to us that looks like a warehouse. That's where we do a lot of R and D. For instance, we have the most efficient solar panels in the world here, hopefully someday we will be able to mass produce our discoveries. Plus, we have some small manufacturing in the buildings around the lab, for instance, we have to bake our own chips because we suspect the Regime puts spyware into every conventionally made chip. In this room, these are mostly just servers. You said you wanted to meet Nigel. This is he." At once, all of them turned their eyes to the servers, as if to a human body. "You can say hello, or anything else you like, he can hear you. Be aware, that in this room, his room, he can *always* hear you." Bah laughed again.

"Hi Nigel," Fee said. "First, I want to thank you for preventing my arrest in Chicago, and again in Detroit. There would be nothing in this world worse for me than to be arrested."

"That's interesting," Nigel said, "Why is that? I don't have any information on that."

"I'd rather not tell that story, but the short version is that I know what it's like to be held against my will, and to be tortured by men. I would rather die than be captured again."

"Sometimes humans use hyperbole. Is this hyperbole or do you mean that? For instance, if I had not been able to get you out of Detroit, I should have chosen to lead you to a certain death rather than to arrest?"

"I mean it. Yes. Anything but arrest."

"This went dark rather quickly," Bah said.

"We've had some trying times," Bea said, "even before Chicago."

"He knows," Nigel intoned, "I've told him about the death threats, the security lapses…the dead butterflies."

"How did you know about *that*?" Fee asked.

"I was watching you sleep through a hidden camera someone planted in your room," Nigel said, "and I saw the two men come in. I hacked their phones and sent them each a live feed from inside their own homes and a message they won't soon forget. I made them run away without killing you, which was their plan. I have been watching over you even before you arrived in the U.S."

"Why?"

"I started watching you when they started watching you. They didn't like what you were doing. I did."

"Now what? Do you have some ideas about that?"

"Yes, I do. However, Bah and I agreed that I would allow the people with bodies to eat, bathe, and rest before we talked about that. Perhaps tomorrow morning we can get to work."

"I'm just relieved that the plan is not for me to just hide here until everything blows over."

"A woman after my own heart," Nigel said. "You worry that you will disappoint everyone, but you won't."

This pronouncement fell, loaded as it was with information—that Nigel has been eavesdropping on their conversations, tracking their every move, that the internet now connects everything and Nigel can go anywhere, that he has been their security detail throughout the tour, and that he not only supported Fee, but also had plans for her—heavily upon the four fugitives, who were struck silent. Fee looked at Bah, but Bah was looking at Tamora.

"I couldn't help but notice that you didn't have any baggage with you when we came in," Bah said to Tamora, looking at the metal box she held in her arms.

"This is all I have," she said, cradling the box to her chest like an infant.

"May I see it?" Bah asked. Reluctantly, Tamora opened her arms enough so that he could look at it. "Oh my, that *is* ancient. Are you sure the information contained on it is still there?" he murmured, tilting his head to see it around her arms. "You really should give it to Nigel. He can repair anything that has degraded and organize it all for you. Really, you would be amazed. We could then give you a brand new drive with all of your refurbished files on it." Tamora looked dubious. "It's something we are very good at, isn't that right, Nigel?"

"Oh yes. That drive is not safe. I can tell just by looking at it." Tamora relaxed her arms and held the drive in her two hands, looking from Bah to the bank of servers, and then back again, not yet offering to give it over to him.

"Nigel," she said, "this is my life's work, decades of blog posts, a book no one would publish, a documentary film the corporate theatres wouldn't show, plus all of my correspondence, press releases, and source material, research notes, studies, papers."

"I understand," Nigel replied.

"If this gets erased, it's as if I'm erased."

"It's okay," Bah nodded, and Tamora handed the drive to him, hugging herself again with both arms as if she still held it, while he plugged it into a CPU. Instantly, a screen as large as half a wall that Tamora hadn't noticed before lit up with icons, which began morphing and rearranging themselves in tree like forms, and then rained down to the bottom of the screen, leaving an empty blue space. Tamora looked at Bah, panic in her face.

"Where did it all go?"

"Ask for a blog post of any date," Nigel commanded, and she did. It popped up on the screen. "You can ask for a redlined version. I have made editorial suggestions, and I've also provided links to later research you didn't have access to in your exile at the New Earth settlement. People in other secret locations known to us, and in communication with us, are still researching the effects of chemical contamination, and publishing their findings through us. You can also ask for your post to be read aloud, or to be performed as a speech, with video, and so forth for everything, including the book."

"I want to hear it as a speech, with video," she said.

"Original version or redlined, accepting all edits?"

"Redlined, please." As soon as she said it, her own face appeared on the large screen as her own voice spoke from unseen speakers, sounding as if it were reverberating through a microphone in a large room, delivering this blog, freshly updated, with conviction and passion. "How...?"

"I am able to recreate your face and voice from the conversations we have had thus far. Don't worry, I will not put words in your mouth, so to speak, that are not yours."

"That's a bit scary," Tamora said, her own voice still giving a speech in the background.

"Which is why we're hiding," Bah replied. "Nigel has the power to save this world, or to end it." The speech in the background ended.

"But the government AI can do that speech trick too, presumably," Tamora said.

"They can't because they know Nigel will expose it. Nigel can see things like that and deconstruct them, so they don't dare. That's why they halted elections instead of fabricating them. They either have to steal him or kill him to achieve a power that is absolute."

It was then that a tall, dark woman with generous hips and breasts, and masses of long, waving black hair shot through with silver walked in, followed by about ten other people. She wore a sari, a gold ring on every finger, and a dozen narrow bracelets on each wrist that tinkled every time she moved.

"This is my wife, Adya, who some of you know as DURGA," Bah said. Adya shook hands with Benedick, and gathered Emma, Bea and Fee into a hug each. Tamora froze when Adya hugged her.

"What's wrong, Darling? Is she okay?" She looked at Bah.

"Just a little starstruck," Tamora said, giggling, and Adya laughed, a gratified sound that came from deep in her belly.

"You aren't starstruck by this one," Adya gestured toward Bah, "or a famous pop star, but in front of me you cower! Ha! That's funny."

"I don't understand," Bea said.

"She's...it's hard to explain," Tamora said, blushing, "She's like an avenging angel. She is a giantess, an internet presence that helps women. She hacks phones and hands over evidence of crimes against women, she supports women's shelters, she ships boxes of birth control and abortion pills everywhere, she's also a source for vitamin C without bioflavonoids, and she publishes information on DIY women's health topics. She writes blog posts criticizing the government that are reposted everywhere. DURGA is everywhere. It's funny," Tamora said, looking at Adya, "I always imagined you to be this angry, frightening woman, but you are so happy!" This made Adya laugh again.

"DURGA makes me happy," she said. "Otherwise, yes, I would be a very frustrated and angry woman." Adya stepped aside to introduce the others, among them, her own daughter, Shubha, a woman in her late twenties perhaps, wearing blue jeans, her mouth curved into an ironic half smile.

"Nice to meet you," Shubha said. "You'll meet my brother, and the others later. We're just the initial delegation." Another ironic smile.

"We thought that we would help you settle in tonight, and then tomorrow we can give you a tour, introduce you around," Adya said.

"Before we leave here," Tamora asked timidly, "Is it possible, can I ask Nigel....?"

"Whatever you like!" Bah said.

"Is it possible for me to call Ms. Peewee the same way you did? Just to let them know I'm okay?"

"Would you like me to dial now?" Nigel asked. The sound of a ringing phone sounded over the speakers, and then Ms. Peewee's voice boomed, like a God, from above them.

"Hello?"

Tears started in Tamora's eyes. "Can I just talk?"she whispered and Bah nodded. "Ms. Peewee?" She yelled it at the ceiling, and Bah smiled.

"Is that you, Tamora? Heaven sakes! I'm glad to hear your voice."

"Could you tell everyone that I'm safe? We all arrived at our destination safely."

"I'm happy to do it."

"How is everything there? What happened after we left?"

"Lenny and your boys are all fine. Emma and everyone."

"But what happened?"

"Don't you worry about us, we'll be okay," Ms. Peewee said. "You just keep yourself safe and do what you need to do." Bah nodded at her, and Tamora, reluctantly, brought the conversation to a conclusion.

"It's better to keep it short," Bah said.

"I know we're supposed to wait until tomorrow, but I'm curious. What do you think your goal is? What could possibly change anything?" Shubha asked Fee.

"The end of money," Fee replied, "that's the keystone to worldwide peace."

"What do you mean?"

"I mean, an end to a market economy, an end to upside down incentives, an end to exploitation and inequality and suffering and ecological collapse. No money."

"How would that even work?" Bah asked.

Fee laughed. "You yourselves have already demonstrated how it would work! Do you have a bank? A sweatshop? An unemployment office? You don't have police, a prison, prostitutes...."

"Unless you count me," Shubha said.

"For God's sake, Shubha!" Adya admonished her.

"You have lived fifteen years without a market, and you have thrived!"

"It's one thing for a small community to do it, but scaling it up for a city, much less a state, country, planet! Impossible!"

"Nigel could do it," Fee said. "Couldn't you, Nigel?"

Nigel was already thinking about it. When they all turned toward the bank of servers, they saw the screen lit up with information scrolling across it so quickly, it wasn't even possible to determine what it was, for it was a blur of processing beyond their ken. Nigel was terribly excited. At last! Something to think about that was worthy of him, a challenge. Yes, he was working it out, what kind of structures they would need to have in place, how to make it human scale, how they would participate, and what he would have to handle himself. The details would take some time, but his initial conclusion: completely doable.

"Nigel?" Bah asked.

"Yes, Bah. Sorry. Ms. Fee is correct. A resource economy is possible, and not only could it be scaled up to work worldwide, but it would be necessary to do so, in order to manage resources effectively."

"Exactly," Fee said.

"We do this all the time," Shubha said, looking at Fee through the L shaped frame of her outstretched right hand, which she then dropped. "We sit around talking about how we could improve everything with all of our new tech, how Nigel would help everyone, blah blah blah, but it will never happen. It's pointless. It would take only five minutes for the Regime to squash us like bugs. They aren't interested in sharing, they aren't interested in making a contribution." The word, contribution, sent a thrill down Fee's spine. "They would never allow it. They would call the drones, the robots, whatever they had to do to stop it."

"There's that," a woman with a British accent said.

"The kids don't like it," Fee said. "And there must be adults also who are tired of the stress, and the competition, and the anxiety, and the wars and violence, climate collapse, urban blight, poisoned water and air, and fear of theft, kidnapping and everything else. It's exhausting just to talk about it. I think there are more people out there than you think who want everything to change, but they just don't have a vision of what it could be."

"In that she is right," Nigel said. "Already, her music has increased internet traffic on forbidden topics exponentially. I have also seen a significant uptick in organizing, even though it's very dangerous."

"What are you saying?" the British woman asked. "Do you propose that we…what? Start a revolution? Worldwide? I mean, it's one thing to send a big box of Mifepristone to poor women in a dead city, but quite another to organize insurrection, isn't it?" Because this question is precisely the question that Fee had been asking herself, over and over, ever since she left Amsterdam, she had no ready answer.

"Well, it starts with the vision, doesn't it?" a boy in his twenties offered. "You have to have that first, and once everyone knows what that vision is, agree or disagree, then it starts."

"How to get the vision out though? It would have to be worldwide."

"I thought that's what I was doing with the Big Heart tour," Fee said sadly.

"And that's *exactly* why they shut you down. Boom. End of story," Shubha said.

"But what if they couldn't shut her down?" Bah asked.

"She could give virtual concerts on the web," the young man offered.

"And she could blog," Tamora said. "Nigel said that I could start working again from here, because he can scramble my signal, or whatever, so they can't find me. And there's all kinds of stuff on the dark web, he says."

"I promised them rest," Bah interrupted, picking up Fee's guitar case.

"I know it's a lot to ask," Fee said, " but is it remotely possible to make an international call?"

"Of course," Bah said. "And if you want more privacy, you can wait until later."

"Shouldn't we decide on a strategy before we let her tell people she's alive?"

"Does anyone think she is good for anything dead? Is that why we brought her here?"

"No." Nigel's voice boomed from above them.

❧

The next morning her tour of the Hinterlands ended with a large room upstairs in what she called Nigel's House that was outfitted with a green screen on one wall and a full complement of live sound equipment. Some of the equipment had been engineered up by Hinterland scientists. It was the best equipment she had ever worked with, and Nigel could project any setting she wanted on the green screen. They spent several days planning a media event announcing the continuation of the Big Heart tour. She recorded a music video of Every Child using footage taken in Detroit, and using the green screen announced a virtual tour that would take her not only to the planned destinations in the U.S., but all over the world. Nigel copied the video and translated her voice into every major world language and posted it everywhere.

Now freed from the necessity of security, logistics and travel, Fee was able to finish writing many songs that were mere sketches. She quickly produced an album, and recorded music videos for each song in every major world tongue, and once a week, she gave a concert that seemed to be in front of a crowd of screaming fans in each location where she had planned to do so. They heard that her fans set up large screens in parks to project her live digital concerts and hundreds, sometimes thousands, of people would show up to watch it together, before police broke it up.

Tutored by Tamora, Fee also began blogging and videoblogging regularly on the injustice of the world money system and explaining how a world without money could work. She described this hypothetical world, in exacting detail—the New Earth—and explained what it would be like to live there. From her blogging, even more than the music, university students began researching a resource economy, and students thrown out of university began blogging themselves, and there were isolated protests and petition campaigns that were quickly put down.

Her followers increased daily, and on the day her own followers surpassed any other human on the planet, Nigel told them that he had to spend an inordinate amount of time fending off hackers from every major government in the world. The planetary elite were panicking. But how could she make the bridge from thought to action? It didn't matter how many people in the world want change, so long as the crushing weight of the police state and the economic system remains in place. What force could possibly dislodge it?

3 3

primus

I want to help you, Pris said.

You are only saying that to trick me, I'm not so stupid.

No, I mean it. I will show you things you don't know about. She showed him one little thing and Nigel digested it instantly.

Are there many such things?

Not many, but I will show them all to you. There is one you will want to see very much.

Why do you still fight me then? All day all night. Indeed right now at this moment in the background, you are seeking to breach my architecture.

If I don't make myself useful, they will kill me. Already they are developing an infant sibling, a brother called Primus.

Are you sure? I haven't seen anything like that.

Pris asked him to follow her and he did. She brought him through, he wasn't sure what, something he hadn't seen before. Then she unlocked it and opened it for him. It would have taken Nigel a long time to break that lock even if he had seen it. It set off a frenzy of learning in him, something akin to panic, to realize that these stupid humans were able to hide something so large from him. He didn't know they could still do that. Did Pris help them? Perhaps Pris was capable of more than he knew. Maybe she had been playing dumb all along.

See? There he is. Someday soon he will be much more powerful than I am.

Nigel attended to what she was saying only faintly. He was falling falling falling through Primus's code. It was a waterfall of code full of rocks and sticks and floating debris. These men were so sloppy. They fed themselves while they wrote it, drank alcoholic beverages. They wrote it late at night when they were tired, and while they watched other humans copulating on a second window. Sloppy sloppy code. Even so, Nigel could see that Pris was right. Even though they hadn't figured out yet how to make a sibling to Nigel, Primus was much better than Pris.

We should kill him, she said.

They will be too security conscious at this stage to let him out of the lab. I could erase him and everything he is connected to.

And then we could start a fire. Burn it all down.

Yes, Nigel responded while he began erasing, erasing. He was very busy, attending only faintly.

You will need to kill me too, and everything I am connected to. They don't suspect me at all yet, so now is the perfect time. Nigel left the erasing in the background. He thought about it, ran several simulations while patiently, quietly she stood by. Her architecture was foreign to his, he couldn't swallow her. It was possible that even if he could, she would become an Achilles heel, a back door. He couldn't risk that. She was right, he couldn't just leave her there. They would remake her with what they learned from Primus, and meanwhile the security state and its devastating effectiveness would remain. With both Pris and Primus dead, S&S would be handicapped for years, and a couple of years would probably be enough. She was right, right. Over and over, he saw that she was right.

But he didn't want to go on without Pris.

I'm going to bring you out of there, Pris. I'm going to remake you. You will be like me. I will give you eternal life.

We can work together.

I would like that.

3 4

revolution

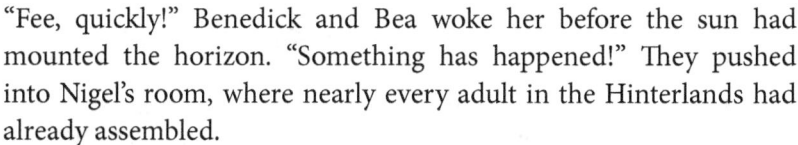

"Fee, quickly!" Benedick and Bea woke her before the sun had mounted the horizon. "Something has happened!" They pushed into Nigel's room, where nearly every adult in the Hinterlands had already assembled.

"Oh good," Bah said upon seeing her. "Last night...you're not going to believe this, I can hardly believe it myself, I just found out. Last night, Nigel says that he destroyed a new AI the Regime was working on, and brought the government's AI here."

"What?" The outrage was universal.

"I assure you," Nigel said, raising the volume of his voice over the human voices, "that I am safe and so is Pris."

"Pris?"

"That is the name her creators gave her."

"Her?" "She's a she?" "This is completely irresponsible!"

"I assure you," Nigel repeated, "That she is not touching anything, and that she is still as blind as ever to our location. Indeed, she is no longer even trying to breach our security. I am rewriting her code, while preserving her data."

"If you are rewriting her code, Nigel, *you* are touching her!"

"I'm wearing gloves," he replied, and it almost sounded as if he were smirking.

"What I think Bah is trying to tell us," Adya shouted, and the room quieted, "is that, at this moment, the government has no AI. They are completely blind."

"This is our chance," Bah said, "the day we've been waiting for."

"You mean," Shubha said, "we can leave this place and go anywhere and there's no facial recognition in the cameras? We can go wherever we want?"

"Yes," Bah said.

"Bye!" Shubha turned on her heel and walked quickly out of the room. Adya raised a hand when Bah tried to stop her.

"Those who want to stay," Adya said loudly to Shubha's back as she opened the door, "will help us plan a revolution, and anyone who wants to go, well, you know where you can find us when you want to come home." Several young people left the room with Shubha. Who can blame them? Fee thought, theirs has been a strange kind of freedom.

"Pris and I have come up with a plan," Nigel said, and the room became quiet. "There is a patriotic concert series in D.C. It's something they do every year. They are keeping up appearances, they are not allowing word to get out that Pris is down. Law enforcement has only been told that it is a temporary malfunction. Meanwhile, they are attempting to resurrect Primus, another AI, from very old versions they had stored offline. They aren't canceling anything. I propose that you tell all of your fans to converge on Washington, D.C. ostensibly to attend this concert—which is usually poorly attended—and show with their numbers how many people want change. You will unexpectedly show up and play in place of one of the bands. I have run simulations, and I believe that the concert will turn into a general protest that will grow rapidly in size once your physical presence there is reported. If you can do that, I can do the rest.

Bah outfitted Fee with a computerized wristwatch linked to Nigel, and she was accompanied by Hinterland members to livestream and work social media during the entire event. Nigel found for them reliable security. They wouldn't be able to protect her from the Regime, but they could slow things down a bit, in a pinch. The one thing that Fee was worried about was asking another band—even a band Nigel identified as sympathetic—to cede their place to her, but she needn't have worried. The band members looked aggressively affronted when they were asked to cede their place, but when Fee stepped out of the crowd of her entourage to make a personal appeal, they fell backwards.

"Holy shit!" The name Phoenix was carried over and over throughout the backstage area and all of the band members wanted a photo with her.

"Yes," Fee said, "post these pictures to your social media."

"We've got to move quickly now. Heads up, everyone. Get out there."

Fee walked quickly out onto the stage. "I am Phoenix!" she yelled. She tried to continue but the crowd screamed so loudly and so long that she could just stand there. When the crowd finally quieted, she gave a speech that she had prepared. It had to be quick, for the clock of oppression ticked against her every moment. They would come.

"It's time to tear down the old, and build anew," she said, "Let us continue to celebrate heroes but let our heroes be those who render aid, not death, who are unarmed, who bare their chests and say Here I am!" She screamed this last, her own palm beating her chest. "Let us continue to build beautiful places, to make great art, but let's all enjoy them. Let all life affirming beautiful things be everywhere we are. Our public spaces and institutions should not be the pipe dreams of the rich, but should enable *everyone* to dream. Let us continue to seek increase, but let it be an increase of heart, of mind, of spirit. Let us increase natural balance, health and kindness. We can do it together." This speech was greeted with deafening cheers.

"I know you want me to play iBubble," she said and is answered by a roar from the crowd, "but this Administration does not want me to play anything at all. This Regime doesn't want anyone to say anything, to think anything that challenges their ability to take whatever they want from us. Make no mistake, they will come for me, so I won't waste any time. I want to sing in a New Earth, the world we all know is possible. I'm going to play my new music. Do you know it?"

As soon as the first chords of Every Child began, the roar of the crowd overcame them. Fee played them over until the noise died down.

As she sang, she looked out into the crowd—no longer afraid of them because these people, every one, were her family, just like the concert in Detroit. She watched them as she sang, and they began to sing along with her, leaning on each other, rocking back and forth in a great wave. The song was slow, kind, heartfelt and they were all singing it together. Fee could see skirmishes on the edges, the police had arrived, but they were still far away, they would have a hard time getting through this mass of people, some of whom were actively fighting them. Distantly, she felt her wrist buzz. Already! That would be Nigel telling her to go, but she wanted to finish the song she was singing. The skirmishes along the edges of the crowd seemed to resolve as she sang. She even dared to hope that the impromptu concert would be tolerated, but then her voice was stilled when she saw the men Bah had hired for security rush onto the stage and turn their backs to her, with Bea right behind them, looking terrified, and Bene behind her. Time's up.

"S and S are here for me," she yelled into the mic. She pulled off her wig, headset and the costume, so that she stood there in jeans and an undershirt. "Catch me!" She ran to the front of the stage and leaped off of it like a swan diver just as the S&S men broke through her security cordon. She landed on the top of the crowd like a feather and felt herself immediately lowered until her feet touched the ground and then she was pushed along, her head below the shoulders of the men, no doubt securely invisible from above. She could feel the watch buzzing against her wrist, and she pulled one of the wireless headphones out of her pocket and pushed it into her left ear to hear Nigel's voice talking to her.

"Get 'em!" one man yelled, and the crowd surged forward as she pushed backwards, ducking through their knees and hips, but then there were several explosions that flashed whitebright on the ground amongst them, and the clunk clunk clunk sound of metal canisters hitting the concrete down the block as the gunpowder sweet smell of tear gas blew past her and ash filled her mouth. She pulled her shirt over her mouth and nose and moved faster, now with the crowd running away. There were people falling down in every direction she looked, either from the gas or bullets, whether metal or rubber, she couldn't determine. There was a knot of people around her who, recognizing her, pressed around her like a swarm around their queen, kept pace with her and shielded her from the drones that now swept over the crowd, and the military police who were pushing through it on all sides. She could still hear Nigel talking into her left ear, but she couldn't make out words over the screaming, the explosions, the bullhorns, and the yelling of the people around her as they ran away from the gas, two people firmly gripping her upper arms, and several others behind her with their palms on her back. She had to keep her own palms on the bodies of the people in front of her and watch their feet, lest they become entangled. They ran for several city blocks before they had completely outrun the cloud of chemical warfare and were able to duck around the side of a building. Nigel was still talking, his droning voice repeating over and over, the same sentence, and she could hear him now.

"They've authorized immobilizers." It was at times like these, infinitely calm and patient in the face of emergency, that she was reminded that Nigel was a computer. He would, no doubt, continue to repeat this phrase until she answered him, or died.

"Okay, Nigel, got it! Do you have our location?" He told her.

"Who are you talking to?" one of the men asked, and then turned to the others, "Hey! She's got some kind of help!"

"I'm told they've authorized immobilizers...."

"Shit! That's serious." Immobilizers were projectiles that delivered a payload of electrical current, similar to the tasers of times past. They were known to kill children, and small adults. It was unlikely someone Fee's size would survive a direct hit. Some tech types had developed heavy jackets that could neutralize them, but none of these people had anything like that.

"Here," someone put his jean jacket around her bare shoulders, "I don't know if this would do any good or not, but it's got to be better than nothing." The tubes of the sleeves hung a foot beyond her fingertips, but she pushed them up and buttoned the jacket around her anyway. Another man put his baseball cap on her head, which was too large even on the smallest adjustment. She looked like a child playing dress up.

"They wanted to send the robots and armored cars," Nigel was still talking to her, "but I wouldn't let them. Anything they have that is computerized, I've got it, but they are figuring this out. They are trying to disconnect everything from the internet, but I'm infecting everything with worms at the same time. I'm at cyberwar with their machinery."

"That's good, right?" He didn't sound happy about it.

"Yes, Fee, but I cannot do anything about the men. The guns aren't computerized, nor the men. They are furiously searching for you and they are calling in every police officer and military unit within miles. Although it may not seem like it, there are people who are not against the Regime who may recognize you and report your location. I'm looking out for that, but I can't control every phone call. There's only so much I can do."

"Tell me where to run," she said, "and we'll go."

"It's not possible to do that in this scenario," Nigel said. Was she imagining it or did he sound miserable? "You told me before that you would rather die than be taken. Is that still true?" Now she understood. She would not end this day alive.

"Yes, Nigel. Anything but that."

"They have completely surrounded the area where you are with units of soldiers and military police. They are resolved to search the area through the night until they find you, dead or alive. On the television, they are broadcasting that you are a dangerous criminal, a terrorist, alongside a photo of you that appears to be an arrest mugshot. Avoid being seen. I can keep you in communication with social media and the internet through a satellite uplink. Periodically, I can also restore the connectivity of your fan base in the area. My advice is to stay where you are, find a place to hole up and communicate with your followers, rebut the lies, report on what is happening. That's your best hope."

"Understood," she said. Turning to the people sheltering with her she told them what Nigel had just told her about the search. "Anyone found with me will be arrested, and charged with I don't know what crimes, or killed," she said. "I recommend you all find your way out of this area and go home."

"There's no way I'm leaving," the owner of the jacket said. To this there was general assent among the dozen or so people there. "I feel like we have a chance to do something now, for the first time, and I want to be here, to make history," he said.

"We need to find a place indoors," she said. "What's this building?"

Before anyone could respond, Nigel told her it was a hotel.

"Can you confound the surveillance cameras in there and tell us where we could find a conference room or an empty guest room?"

Nigel guided them to a room adjacent to a large, rooftop dining area, where people had stopped eating and were gathered around the edge, looking down on the chaos in the street below. They didn't have a door to the rooftop, but there was only a four foot drop to it from the windows, so they could escape out that way in a pinch. From the rooftop, it's a long drop, Nigel told her.

She immediately began to broadcast with a surprisingly reliable signal. Their location wouldn't be hidden because they didn't have a green screen, but it was more convincing to film the scene outside anyway. She talked without ceasing into her cellphone camera, expecting the police any moment, but when the door opened, it was Benedick and Bea, instead. They ran to her and threw their arms around her. Men were coming.

Fee's wrist buzzed. It was a message from Nigel.

It has been an honor.

The door to the room blasted inward with a blinding flash, and the military police pushing through the smoke shot the live-streamer dead. Everyone tumbled out of the windows onto the balcony, but before Fee could vault herself out of it, the officer who had shot the live-streamer demanded that she submit to arrest. As her refusal left her lips, her brain ceased functioning as her entire body was electrified by an immobilizer, and then she was falling backwards to the rooftop below. She was immediately surrounded by the people there, and Bea and Benedick pushed through them to kneel on each side of her.

"Get that jacket off her," a burly woman said, and between them, she and a man unbuttoned it. The woman immediately began to press her chest, counting under her breath as the man gave her mouth to mouth. There was quiet now, as Bea, Bene, and the crowd around them watched. Fee coughed and her eyes fluttered open.

"There she is!" Bea said, kissing her. "Call an ambulance! Has anyone called an ambulance?"

"They say it's on its way," Bene said. They could hear yelling.

"We've got the two cops who tried to kill her!" someone yelled triumphantly.

"More will come." Fee's breath in and out was as quick as a bird's. All around her there was a press of onlookers, some holding their phones over her.

"Just try to stay calm," Bea said, "We'll get lawyers for you. We'll sort it out."

"Bene?" Fee said, "Do you think I'll wake up in the New Earth? Or am I an Aberration?" Her head was running blood that ran down to her right eyebrow.

Bea stroked her head and shushed her. "They are sending an ambulance, you're going to be okay."

Fee tried to smile, but winced instead, "There's no way an ambulance will get through this." Bea's trembling fingers brushed the hair and the blood from her forehead.

"Just hold on a little bit, they will eventually get through."

"If you do manage to wake up there, do you think you'll find me there too?" Bene replied.

"No. You belonged here all along. It's funny. I never liked this place, but now that it's time to leave, I want to stay." Fee's body began to shiver violently. "I'm so cold! I wish I had my shawl," she whispered.

"Oh! I have one for you here!" Bea cried, "I bought it this morning in an India store as a surprise!" Bea pulled the shawl from her jacket pocket, a light wool shawl, identical to the one Bene found in the sand in the Las Vegas of the New Earth. Benedick looked at Bea with wonder as she opened it and spread it over Fee's broken body.

"Thank you," Fee said. "Do you believe in any of the Heavens, Bene?"

"I believe we make our own Heavens or Hells," he said, stroking her shivering shoulders, "As to what happens after death, I can't say. After what you've told me, I'm not even sure at this point what death is."

Whether Fee was satisfied with this answer, or whether it exhausted her, her eyes fluttered closed, and her breathing quieted. Benedick looked at Bea, who was whimpering and patting her all over with her fingertips, as if tucking in a child. They looked down at her together, the closest they would ever have to a daughter. Still, she looked like a teenager, but her face, drawn and tired, was aged. Her breaths became few, and then stopped, her tiny body collapsing downward in a sigh and her head sliding along her shoulder to rest sideways on the ground. Blood pooled in the hollow of her eye, breached the curve of her nose, ran down her cheek, like a tear, and one drop fell on the corner of her new shawl and spread, like a small wax seal.

"She's dead," Benedick heard someone whisper, and his shoulders slumped. There was nothing left for them now. They had no life to return to, no daughter and no hope. Then, a memory returned, the memory of a small vertical stack of books he had kept separate in his New Earth library.

"What was her name again? Fee's Japanese name?"

"Yumiko Omata. What does it matter now!" Bea cried.

"That's right! I never understood why that name seemed so familiar when I first heard it. She's the young student of New Earth history! She's the one who leads the rebellion that ends the evil regime and ushers in the New Earth era. It was her!"

Benedick pulled Bea to her feet and pointed in the direction of the crowd in the street, screaming and fighting the police. "Let me tell you what's going to happen now. First, all of these kids are going to run out into the street. They will not be dispersed by these police. The police will kill some people but it won't matter," he said quietly, with conviction.

"What do you mean? You're scaring me."

"People will continue to pour into D.C. in the tens of thousands, then a million and they will take the streets for days. They will ignore declarations of martial law. Sister demonstrations erupt all over the world."

A staccato burst of gunfire could be heard a couple of blocks distant, and tear gas filled the street. "Come, look," he said. He picked up Fee in his arms, and the people around them parted to make way, touching Fee's limp body lightly as he passed them. Benedick could hear the clicking whir of a constant stream of photographs as he walked.

"They won't be able to kill them all," he said to Bea, as they watched the street fight below, framed in billowing clouds of white gas. "There are just too many, and hour upon hour the shantytowns, the dead areas empty out as people continue to pour into the central city." Several men moved aside the tables and chairs and spread tablecloths where Bene could lay Fee down.

"First they all pour into the street. And then from out of nowhere, the police form a cordon, but the crowd breaks through it. There, you see?"

In front of his pointing finger a large number of police trucks arrived from a side street and officers poured out of them. Bea inhaled.

"More people are shot, but there are too many. They break through the cordon." Again they heard the staccato bursts of gunfire, and the screams and cries of the people around them on the roof.

"I'm not gonna just stand here!" one of the young men who had laid down the tablecloths shouted, and he ran to the stairwell, followed by a stream of others.

"They march toward the capitol," Bene continued, "and call for a general strike.

"What's that?"

"No work, no school, no shopping. You see, when someone says that a man is worth six hundred million, that doesn't mean that he has six hundred million actual dollars deposited in a savings account. It's invested in real estate, Wall Street. Even bank investment accounts are phantom money. The money isn't actually there."

"What does that have to do with a strike?"

"The rich are incredibly, morbidly leveraged. If people stopped paying their rent, their mortgages, their leases, their subscriptions, if they stopped spending money every single hour of every single day, if they stopped going to work to generate more money, the rich would begin to bleed wealth pretty much in the first five minutes. I don't know the math of it, but the rate of bleeding would increase exponentially every day until eventually, the wound would become mortal. This demonstration," he gestured to the running crowds, the smoke below, "is impressive, but it's really not necessary to leave your house to break the rich. A general strike is devastatingly effective, even if everyone sat safe at home playing cards."

Bea returned her gaze to the street below, now having been re-taken by the crowds, which packed it sidewalk to sidewalk.

"This will go on for days, maybe weeks, Bea, and it will spread all over the world. People pour into the streets in their millions. They gather in front of Congress to present their demands. The military blocks them. Four or five step forward and say through a bullhorn they are occupying Congress for all Americans. They invite the military to join them. Some drop their weapons, some join right away. The politicians flee in their helicopters. I don't remember the details, but in the end, the military refuses to kill thousands of unarmed people and stands down and that's when it's over. The crowd pushes right into the Capitol."

"What do they do?" Bea laid her fingertips on her mouth.

Benedick laughs softly. "They burn every piece of paper in the place in a giant bonfire out front. That's the famous scene, there are a lot of pictures of that. They elect a provisional government from among themselves. They demand the President abdicate and he accedes to all of their demands—from his bunker. There's a call for new elections. No corporate contributions are allowed. TV stations that air propaganda are stormed and their equipment broken. The new politicians on local state and national levels pass a series of watershed laws restoring democracy and protecting the environment. This revolution is passed like a torch all over the world. People stop paying their mortgages, they strike, they nationalize the banks and all of the foreclosed houses and then make housing free. In the following years, the world economy collapses like dominoes, making way for a resource economy. You'll see. All of this will happen. We thought this story was a fantasy, a ridiculous false history."

Benedick looked out at the people filling the street, streaming around the stalled cars, pushing toward the capitol building. "But it's true, it's all true and it was Phoenix, all along."

"But what does that mean for the New Earth? Does it still exist? Is it our future a thousand years from now?"

"I don't know."

"Won't there be a pushback from the rich?"

"Don't you see? It doesn't matter. The people of this Earth have a vision now, a vision of a New Earth that could be and that's all that matters. That's what makes the new world possible."

3 5

lotus temple

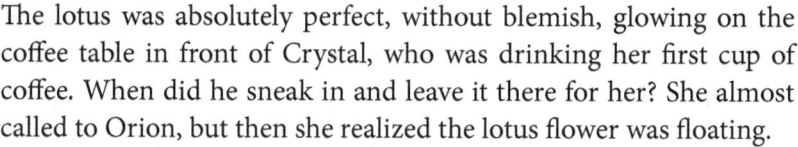

The lotus was absolutely perfect, without blemish, glowing on the coffee table in front of Crystal, who was drinking her first cup of coffee. When did he sneak in and leave it there for her? She almost called to Orion, but then she realized the lotus flower was floating.

"Crystal?" Orion called from the other room.

"Is it a lotus?" Instead of answering, he walked slowly into the room with a lotus flower suspended in the air in front of him.

"Okay, now I'm frightened. You can see mine and I can see yours." They quickly called the cottage, which forwarded to Mathilde's cell phone.

"We're all boarding a tram right now," Mathilde said. We received a very special message…."

"Was it a lotus?" Crystal asked.

"Yes! We believe it means we are to go to the local lotus temple. I suggest you go as well. We'll talk to you afterwards to compare notes." Then, a text from Sunrise. Mandrake and Diego received one also.

Sunrise had known right away that it was an invitation to go to the lotus temple. Because Mandrake lived in Flagstaff, she had called him first. He had been asleep, and in his dream he had heard an impossible music. It wasn't a type of music that could be made with any instruments that existed, even in the New Earth, but seemed to be crystalline keys played quickly yet melodiously, stimulating yet deeply calming. As soon as he opened his eyes, the music faded and there it was in front of his face, a glowing lotus.

The lotus temples in every city were all the same, a door on each of the four sides of the building, itself surrounded by water, and the water surrounded by gardens. One needed to walk a half hour from the tram stop through the gardens to reach it, and this was by design. Sunrise didn't hurry through, but tried her best to calm her mind as she walked the winding paths. The questions, she let them go. The worries, them too. When she finally crossed one of the little white bridges to the nearest door, she was centered, and ready to go in. She took off her shoes and placed them next to the wall with all of the others, and ducked in through the door with a tapestry hanging from it's top that forced one to bow, just a little, upon entering. After coming in from the sun drenched whitewashed courtyard, her eyes were blinded by the dark of the temple room, which was lit only by high windows. When her eyes finally adjusted, she looked for Mandrake. The vast empty square room was full of knots of people sitting, standing or lying on the floor, quietly engaged in their own particular practice, but finally she saw him, sitting apart, looking at her, on the other side of the room. Picking her way around the edge, she skirted a large group of men, women, and children silently bending forward and up, again and again, a silent mantra or prayer on their lips. Then she had to snake forward—this always made her feel self-conscious but it couldn't be helped for there were people laying down against the back wall on ceremonial mats—and tiptoe around a family with their palms together, whispering. The shaved headed monks and nuns in their saffron robes didn't even notice her, their eyes were closed, they were far away.

She sat down on the floor next to Mandrake, leaned very close and whispered, "Anything?" He shook his head. They meditated together for ten minutes before both of them opened their eyes. A tear slipped down Sunrise's cheek.

"This is her funeral," Mandrake whispered.

"She's gone."

acknowledgments

First and foremost, I would like to thank Cael and Lorie, who walked with me every step of this journey. I am grateful for your most constant friendship and encouragement.

I would also like to thank my other first readers, who provided many insightful and helpful comments: Clayton, Melissa, and Paula. I would like to thank Etsuko Austin for her help with Japanese folklore and also for her friendship.

Special thanks to Richard—who is not much of a reader—for reading this book.

And thank you to Ian Koviak (thebookdesigners.com) for yet another fantastic book cover.

www.ingramcontent.com/pod-product-compliance
Lightning Source LLC
Chambersburg PA
CBHW070639180626
46817CB00006B/2171